# THE RELUCTANT FUGITIVE

MICHAEL TEFFT

# DEDICATION

*Dedicated to my wife Colleen, the Joan to my Malcolm, for her love and support*

# CHAPTER ONE

"*B*loody Hell," Malcolm Robertson muttered as he struggled to fix his tie. "Do we really have to do this?"

"The stag party is a time-honoured tradition, going back to fourth century BC Sparta. Do you really want to disregard over two thousand years of tradition?" Charles Saxon said. "Here, let me adjust your tie. I swear, how did you ever dress yourself in civilian life?" He untied Malcolm's tie and retied it.

"Joan usually took care of it for me," Malcolm said.

"I can't, for the life of me, understand how a man with your mechanical aptitude can't tie a simple necktie," Saxon quipped. "There, a perfect four-in-hand knot. It's pains me to say it, but you look very dapper."

"Thank you, Charles. I don't know what I would do without you."

"Tomorrow, you'll be Joan's problem."

Malcolm looked at himself in the mirror and agreed with Saxon's assessment. After returning from his mission to Mars, he, Joan, and Saxon left the secret base on Boreray Island and returned to Joan's father's estate in Kent to prepare for the wedding delayed by their recruitment into the Royal Space Service. The past three weeks had been a whirlwind of activity as they tried to pull together the wedding before Malcolm's and Joan's leave expired and they would have to return to Boreray. After the wedding, Saxon would part ways with Malcolm and Joan, opting to rejoin the British Secret Service instead of his most recent assignment to the Royal Space Service.

"It's hard to believe after all of this time that we're actually going to be married." Malcolm thought of their first meeting four years ago in St. Petersburg, Russia. On that first day, he found her strikingly beautiful. He chuckled to himself. He remembered the moment when he found out she was a spy; she had a derringer pointed at him ready to kill him and he hit her with an empty chamber pot. Despite the inauspicious start of their relationship, Malcolm couldn't believe that after four years, he was about to marry her. "God forbid that anything should prevent our wedding this time. I pity the person who tries to interfere."

"Any last-minute doubts?"

"None whatsoever," Malcolm said. "I want to make up for all the time our careers have kept us separated and I can't wait to build a new life together." He sighed. "I suppose we should get this over. The sooner it's done, the sooner we can finally be married."

They left Malcolm's room and descended to the foyer, where the chauffeur was standing at attention. Joan de St. Leger, Malcolm's fiancé, dressed in a forest green jacket and long black skirt and her auburn hair pulled up and held in place underneath a fascinator, waited with her father Richard, her uncle Arthur, and Malcolm's father George. Joan forced her father to invite his brother despite their long estrangement. "My, the two of you look quite dashing," Joan said. "You two look ready for quite the night on the town. Have a good time…just not too good of a time."

Malcolm took her hand and gave it a chaste kiss. "I wouldn't dream of it. If it were up to me, I wouldn't even go."

"Fortunately, it's not up to you," Saxon said. "I would be derelict in my duties as Best Man if I did not celebrate your last night of freedom. Are we ready?" Joan's father and uncle nodded, and the men left the house to the waiting limousine.

The men were silent during the five-minute drive to Wealden Hall.

As they stopped in front of the pub, Malcolm marvelled at the timber frames intermingled with its brick walls. Graceful half arch timbers broke up the vertical and horizontal structural timbers, providing a sharp contrast to the brick walls. They entered the pub, opening the heavy oak door. The pub was busy on a Friday night as its patrons sought to escape the worries of the work week. Saxon led the party through the main hall and into the private room he had booked for the party.

When Malcolm entered the room, a cheer rose. He was astonished to find many of his former crews from both the airship *Daedalus* and his current command, the spaceship *Icarus*; Lt. Douglas Brown, gunnery officer on the *Daedalus*, Lt. Leslie Blackburn, navigator on the *Icarus*, and Lt. Commander Thomas Jennings, Chief Engineer of the *Daedalus*. Malcolm was most surprised to see Ernest Rutherford, the Nobel Prize winning professor and Peter O'Hallarhan, the chief engineer of the *Icarus*, with whom he butted heads frequently. He turned to Saxon. "How did you arrange this?"

"It was no mean feat," said Saxon. "Trying to procure leave for everyone was a logistical nightmare, but I leaned on Admiral Beatty to arrange it. I played on his guilt for disrupting your original wedding date. As I understand it, Captain Bromley of the *Daedalus* was apoplectic when he was forced to give leave to several of his bridge officers."

"Thank you, Charles." Malcolm made his way around the room, shaking hands with the party. "Ernest," Malcolm said as he reached the professor. "I had no idea you were coming!"

"It seems your bride to be and your best man conspired behind your back. They invited Mary, Eileen, and I to the wedding and your best man twisted my arm to join your stag party."

"I'm sure he didn't have to twist it too hard," Malcolm said with a laugh.

"No, it was a rather simple task. Congratulations, Malcolm."

"Thank you, Ernest." Malcolm lowered his voice. "I'm surprised that you didn't leave once you saw O'Hallarhan."

"Yes, I'm as surprised as you to see him here. He has been much more...humble, for lack of a better word. Is that your doing?"

"Not that I know. I think he's had to do some soul searching since our last mission. Speaking of which, I should talk to him."

"Better you than me," Ernest said.

"Peter, I didn't think I would see you here," Malcolm said as he approached O'Hallarhan. The young officer wore an ill-fitting suit, but Malcolm saw O'Hallarhan now had a prosthetic arm with a hand covered in a black glove after losing his arm on their mission to Mars. Malcolm held his hand out.

"I hope you don't mind, sir. When I heard about your stag party, I asked Commander Saxon if I could join." O'Hallarhan reached out and shook Malcolm's hand with his prosthetic hand.

"Not at all, but perhaps you could use a little less pressure on my hand."

"I'm sorry, sir. I'm still getting the hang of this new arm." Malcolm withdrew his hand, still aching from the crushing pressure of the handshake.

"Did you build this? It's quite impressive."

"Yes, sir. I started work right after we returned. I'm still on recuperative leave, but I hope to return to the Service. The Admiralty has assured me that there will be a place for me as long as I can meet the physical requirements for the Service."

"Please, call me Malcolm. I'm not your commanding officer tonight."

"Very well, sir... I mean, Malcolm. Can I buy you a proper drink of whiskey or do you intend to drink that awful concoction you call whisky?"

"Those are fighting words, Peter," Malcolm said, and O'Hallarhan laughed. "I will take you up on your offer and struggle to choke down your swill."

O'Hallarhan left for the bar and Saxon came over. "I hope you don't mind, Malcolm, but O'Hallarhan begged to join when he got wind of the party. He was very insistent, and I found myself unable to say no."

"That's fine, Charles. Is it me, or does he seem to be a changed man?"

"Losing one's arm will do that to a person."

"True." At that moment, O'Hallarhan returned with two generous glasses of whiskey. "I think this is well aged, as the barkeep had to blow dust off the bottle. I guess there's not much of a call for Irish whiskey in Kent. Slainté," he said, raising his glass.

"Slainté," Malcolm and Saxon said, each raising their glasses. Malcolm would never admit it to O'Hallarhan, but the whiskey was not too bad. "Thank you, Peter," Malcolm said. "If you don't mind, I should make the rounds."

Malcolm made his way first to Lt. Commander Thomas Jennings, his Chief Engineer aboard the *Daedalus,* and spent a few minutes talking to Joan's uncle when Saxon cleared his throat. "Perhaps we should get this party started," Saxon said, using his command voice. "Everyone, please take your seat."

Everyone made their way to the long table in the centre of the room. Malcolm sat at the head of the table with Saxon on his right and his father on the left. His father seemed unusually quiet. Malcolm leaned over and asked, "What's wrong, Da?"

"Nothing," his father said. Malcolm gave his father a probing look before his father said, "I feel like a right git among these officers and gentleman."

"Nonsense, Da. Most of the people here come from backgrounds no loftier than ours. Dr Rutherford," he said as he pointed to the Nobel winning professor, "grew up on a sheep ranch in New Zealand. Peter O'Hallarhan was the son of a lighthouse keeper."

"What about Charles Saxon?"

"You have me there. Charles isn't a self made man like you or I, but I can tell you, social status means nothing to him."

Saxon stood and cleared his throat. "We gather here today to mourn the loss of our friend, Malcolm Robertson, from the brotherhood of bachelors as he leaves to join the flock of married sheep. May God have mercy on his soul!" Saxon raised his drink. "To Malcolm!"

"To Malcolm," the room echoed.

Dinner was served and, to Malcolm's surprise, the server placed a traditional Scottish dinner of haggis, neeps, and tatties before him. He turned to Saxon with a quizzical look.

"I thought that the condemned should enjoy his last meal as a free man. It took some doing, but I secured haggis for you and your father and the few men who could stomach it; the rest of us are eating a proper dinner of roast beef. It was no mean feat trying to get haggis in Kent."

"Thank you, Charles," Malcolm said as he dug into the food. "What do you think of the haggis, Da?" Malcolm said, turning to his father.

"Your mum's is much better, but it's not bad and the English cooks did a decent job."

"After living on fish for the last year, I can't tell you how much I'm enjoying this."

Malcolm finished the whiskey that O'Hallarhan had bought and ordered proper drams of Auchentosan, the whisky made near his hometown, for himself and his father, because one should only eat haggis with proper whisky. Malcolm hadn't realised just how much he missed the traditional food of his youth. In the last few years, he had either eaten in the posh restaurants that Joan preferred or endured the food of the Service. As Malcolm finished his dinner, it was all he could do to not lick the plate clean.

After the servers removed the plates, they poured the after-dinner drinks: more whisky for Malcolm and his father; port for the rest of the party. Saxon clinked a knife on his glass. "Gentleman, may I have your attention?" When the room quieted, Saxon continued. "We're here to celebrate Malcolm Francis Robertson on his last night as a bachelor. In keeping with time-honoured tradition, I open the floor to anyone who wishes to share any stories about our guest of honour, the more embarrassing, the better."

Ernest Rutherford rose. "The first time I met Malcolm, I tried to take a swing at him. I'm sure he's elicited that response from all of you at some point," which brought a laugh from the party.

"Here, here," said O'Hallarhan.

Rutherford's face darkened, but he continued. "After our initial meeting, I got to know Malcolm better, and I still wanted to take a swing at him." When the laughter quieted, Rutherford continued. "In all seriousness, I count myself fortunate to call Malcolm a friend. As an engineer, Malcolm has a penchant for solving problems, which will hold him in good stead in married life. As one of the few married men here, let me give you some advice. Joan will always be right, especially when she isn't. To Malcolm and Joan," he said, raising his glass.

O'Hallarhan rose next. "Like Professor Rutherford, the first time I met Malcolm, he threw me in the brig." After a brief silence, he continued. "And he was right to do so. He and I have butted heads through most of the time that we've known each other, but it pains me to say, he was often right. I have little to add, but to give an old Irish blessing: May you be poor in misfortune, rich in blessings, slow to make enemies, quick to make friends. But rich or poor, quick or slow, may you know nothing but happiness from this day forward. Slainté!"

After Lieutenant Brown, Lieutenant Blackburn, and Lieutenant Commander Jennings gave their tributes to Malcolm, Saxon rose. "I don't know who it is you are all praising. I've worked closely with Malcolm for nearly four years and I can corroborate everything everyone said. He's obstinate and has a unique talent for getting under a person's skin. Not long after he met Joan, she pointed a derringer at him and he disarmed her by hitting her with a bedpan. I kid you not." After the laughter died away, Saxon continued. "All kidding aside, I've seen Malcolm's and Joan's relationship grow since that inauspicious beginning. They've had their fair share of arguments, which I've somehow always ended up mediating. But one thing I don't doubt is Malcolm's and Joan's love for one another. They share a unique bond and I wish them the best as they start this journey together. And may I add, my happiness at not having to be the one to look after Malcolm. To my best friend, Malcolm, and to Joan!," he said, raising his glass. The party toasted Malcolm. "Does the condemned have any last words before he receives his sentence?"

Malcolm rose. "Let me begin by saying with friends like this, who needs enemies?" which elicited laughter from the group. "In all seriousness, thank you all for coming. It's no secret that Charles had to almost drag me to this party, but I'm glad that he wouldn't let me out if it. It's great to meet with friends old and new. When I first became captain of the *Daedalus,* I never thought it would lead to this. I still don't know what I did to deserve Joan, but I'm thankful every day that she wants to spend the rest of her life with me. I'm happy that after many fits and starts, we will start our life together. And thank you for my send off." Malcolm raised his glass to the party and returned to his seat.

The party continued for another hour as Malcolm chatted with each of the guests before he realised he needed to make a trip to the privy after several whiskies. He left for the privy and when he returned; he was surprised to find the party was gone. Malcolm left the room and went to the bar. "Do you know what happened to the party in the back room?"

"When you left, they all snuck out in a hurry," the barkeep said. *I should have known better*, he thought, suddenly remembering the time-honoured tradition of leaving the perspective groom to find his way back. Malcolm sighed. "Is the bill settled?"

"Aye," the barkeep said. "May I offer my congratulations on your upcoming nuptials?"

"Thank you and thank you for hosting the party. I hope we were not too much of a bother."

"Not at all. A fine group of gentlemen you were."

"Thank you, again. Good night." Malcolm turned and left the pub, stopping to get his bearings. He pulled out his Granda's watch, calculating the time it would take him to walk back to the manor house. A voice from the shadows stopped him cold. "I understand congratulations are in order, Malcolm."

The hair on the back of Malcolm's neck rose as he turned to see Mattias Frietag, his former friend and agent of the German government. Although silhouetted in the darkness, Malcolm could still see the eye patch, a souvenir Frietag received when he tried to kill Malcolm with a gun that Malcolm had sabotaged.

"What in the bloody hell are you doing here?"

"I'm disappointed that you didn't send me an invitation to your wedding," Frietag said as he stepped out of the shadows, pointing a pistol at Malcolm. "After all, if it hadn't been for me, you two might never had fallen in love."

"You tried to kill both of us, so that may have had something to do with your lack of invitation. Are you here to kill me?"

"No, I have a much better idea. You are going to tell me where you've been for the last year and about that miraculous new ship of yours."

"What makes you think I'm going to tell you anything?"

"My associates can be, shall I say, very convincing." He nodded and two men came up behind Malcolm and grabbed his arms. Realising he had no chance of escape, Malcolm yanked on the watch chain connected to his Granda's watch while pretending to break free. When it was free, he discreetly dropped the watch before things went dark from a blow to his head.

# CHAPTER TWO

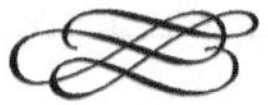

Saxon knocked on the door of Malcolm's room. "Malcolm, it's time for the wedding breakfast. Are you ready?" He waited for several moments and, receiving no answer, he knocked again. "Stop playing about Malcolm. Do you want to make your bride angry on her wedding day?" After several more moments, he opened the door and stepped inside. Malcolm was nowhere to be found, and he noticed that Malcolm's bed was undisturbed. Scowling, he searched the upstairs and found a footman. "Excuse me, have you seen Mr Robertson this morning?"

"No, sir, I haven't. Do you want me to find him?"

"Please. I'll continue looking myself."

The footman hurried away, and Saxon continued his search. When he couldn't find Malcolm on the second floor, he went down the grand staircase and continued his search. He went room by room, searching for Malcolm, to no avail. He asked the servants who were preparing the wedding breakfast in the Great Hall and no one had seen Malcolm this morning. As Saxon was leaving the library, the footman met him. "Sir, I haven't found Mr Robertson. I asked the doorman if he remembered Mr Robertson returning last night and he said that he had not seen Mr Robertson return."

"I see. Thank you," Saxon said. *What the devil is Malcolm playing at?* he thought. Saxon felt a pang of regret for leaving Malcolm to walk home from the pub. *Could something have happened to him on the way back?* The thought concerned Saxon, and he pulled the cord to ring a butler. When the butler arrived, Saxon asked him to have the chauffeur bring the car around and drive him back to the pub. In minutes, Saxon was in the car. "Please drive slowly," he asked. Saxon watched every second of the short drive to the pub, looking for any trace of Malcolm. When he arrived at the pub, it had not opened for the day. He searched around the pub and found Malcolm's watch lying on the ground. His heart sank, knowing how much that watch mattered to Malcolm. He pocketed the watch and once inside the car, instructed the driver to hurry back to the manor.

He raced upstairs to Joan's room and knocked on the door. "Joan, it's Charles. I need to speak to you. It's urgent."

The door opened, and he saw Joan dressed in an extravagant robe with her auburn hair pinned up. "Charles, what is so urgent that you interrupt a bride getting ready for her wedding?"

"It's Malcolm. May I come in?"

"Now, what has he done?" She said as she step aside to let Charles into the room.

Saxon entered and paced several times before Joan interrupted him. "Good Lord, Charles, you'll wear a hole in the carpet. What's wrong?"

Saxon took a deep breath, forcing himself to say the words. "Malcolm never came home last night from the party."

"What do you mean, he never came home?"

"When he left the room, we slipped out and left him at the pub. I went to get him this morning, and he wasn't in his room and never slept in his bed. I asked a footman to search, and he didn't find him either. The doorman said that he never returned last night."

"He didn't return? Where is he?"

"I don't know."

"You don't think he had second thoughts?" she said, struggling not to cry.

"You know that's not the case. Malcolm has been looking forward to this day for over a year. I fear that there might be a more sinister reason for his disappearance. I went back to the pub, and I found this lying on the ground near the pub," he said as he pulled out Malcolm's watch and handed it to Joan.

"That's Malcolm's watch! He goes nowhere without it!"

"I know. That's what concerns me and why I think that wherever he is, he didn't go willingly."

Joan collapsed in a heap on a fainting coach as she struggled not to cry. "Damn it all to hell! Why did this have to happen today of all days? Are we never to get married?" She covered her face, as she could no longer contain her tears.

Saxon felt like he had stabbed her in the heart with a dagger. He sat on the coach next to her and put his arm around her. "I don't know." He pulled her close and let her sob as he, too, struggled to keep the tears at bay.

When she collected herself, she pulled herself away and wiped the tears away from her face. "What should I do?"

"The first thing I intend to do is question the barkeep at the pub to see if he can shed any light on what happened to Malcolm after we left. I'm sorry, Joan. I never should have left Malcolm at the pub by himself. We meant it in good fun and now I fear I've done him great harm. This is all my fault."

"Thank you, Charles." She sighed. "I suppose I have to break the news to my father that the wedding is once again off. When I'm done with that, I will go with you to the pub to question the barkeep."

"Is there anything I can do?"

"No, I'll go see my father and let him take care of letting everyone know." She looked at Malcolm's watch. "Let's meet in the foyer at noon. The inn should be open by then, and we can talk to the barkeep."

Charles nodded and left Joan. He went to the library, trying to distract himself with a book and failing utterly. His thoughts dwelt on what could have happened to Malcolm when Joan's father entered. "What is going on? Where is Malcolm?"

"I don't know, sir," Saxon said as he rose. "He never returned from the party last night. I went to the pub this morning and found his watch lying on the ground. He goes nowhere without it; I fear that something sinister has befallen my friend."

"It better have or believe me, something sinister will befall him if I find he ran off and left Joan," Joan's father said as he stormed out of the room.

Saxon tried to concentrate on a book, but found it a useless exercise. He alternatively paced the library or settled in a chair. Neither activity could assuage the growing unease he felt. After what seemed like an eternity, he went to the foyer and found Joan, now dressed in a plain dress, but with her hair and makeup prepared for the wedding that wouldn't happen.

"The car is waiting," she said as she swept out of the front door.

Saxon hurried to join Joan. They got into the car and, as it sped to the pub, Saxon couldn't help but notice that it would have been a beautiful day for a wedding. The sun shone brightly in a bright blue sky, a rarity in the English spring. The car had barely come to a stop before Joan bolted out of the car and went into the pub.

The pub was nearly empty, except for a few older gentlemen already nursing their pints. She hurried to the barkeep, who said, "I'm sorry, miss, I can't serve you unless you're here to eat."

"I'm not here to drink," Joan said. "Were you the barkeep last night?"

"Aye."

"Did you see what happened to the guest of honour of last night's party?"

"He went to the privy and when he found out the party had left without him, he asked where they went and whether someone had paid the bill. He left, and that's the last I saw of him."

"Did you see anything out of the ordinary last night? Anyone who looked like they didn't belong?" Saxon asked. He had to tread carefully if they hoped to get any information from the barkeep. With Joan's emotional state, he thought it best if he took the lead.

"Now that you mention it, there were a couple of gentlemen

dressed in suits. I asked them if they were part of your party, but they said no. One of them wore an eye patch and had a glove on one hand. He left after a bit and the other two sat over there in the corner, nursing a pint all night. When your friend left, they followed him."

"An eye patch and a gloved hand, you say?" Saxon asked. His hands clenched into fists and his heart sank as he knew who abducted Malcolm.

"Aye. I remember it because that's not something you see every day."

Before Joan could say anything else, Saxon pulled a five-pound note from his pocket. "Thank you. You've been most helpful. I hope this covers any troubles." He grabbed Joan's elbow and led her out of the pub. When they got back into the car, he said, "I didn't want to have this discussion in front of the barkeep. You know what this means, don't you?"

"Yes. Matthias Frietag abducted Malcolm," she said, her voice seething with anger. "But to what end? And where did they take him?"

"I don't know, but I intend to find out," Saxon said.

# CHAPTER THREE

Malcolm awoke to a splitting headache and darkness. He opened his eyes, but couldn't see anything. When he tried to gather his thoughts, his mind felt like mush. He wanted to rub his head when he realised his hands were bound behind his back. As he gradually got his bearings, the memory of the previous night came flooding back. *Bloody hell, I should have killed Frietag when I had the chance.* He took several deep breaths to gather his scrambled thoughts. As he listened, he was sure he heard the low thrum of an airship engine. *I wonder how long I've been out?* He realised he was sitting in a chair. His legs were also bound, and a gag covered his mouth.

Malcolm took stock of his situation; bound and gagged on an airship going God knows where. He decided his best course of action would be to pretend to still be unconscious to gather more information. He sat still and strained to listen; catching snippets of conversation in German, but couldn't make out any words other than *Deutschland* and *Sachsen*. Then, he remembered Saxon telling him that his family was originally from Saxony or *Sachsen* in German.

That effort proved too much for Malcolm, and despite his best efforts, he drifted in and out of consciousness. Malcolm wasn't sure how long he had been there before someone pulled the gag from his mouth.

"Drink, it's water," a voice said. Someone forced a glass to his lips and as soon as Malcolm drank, he immediately tasted something odd about the water and spit it out before swallowing. A hand grabbed Malcolm's head and holding his nose tight, pouring the water into Malcolm's mouth. He tried not to swallow, but eventually had to swallow in order to catch a breath. He heard a laugh and footsteps receding in the distance. After a while, Malcolm could no longer fight whatever was in the water and lost conscious once again.

Upon regaining consciousness, he found himself still blindfolded, with his arms crossed and restrained. They had also shackled his feet. Malcolm heard Frietag say, "Ah, our guest is conscious. I was afraid we might have sedated you too much. We're nearly at your new home, Malcolm."

Malcolm struggled to focus, still groggy from the aftereffects of whatever drug they had put in his water. "And where would that be?" he struggled to say.

"A special place for troubled cases like you. You'll see soon enough. Unless you wish to speed up the process and tell me everything I want to know now."

"So if I tell you what you want to know, you'll just let me go?"

"Oh, no. I have a special fate planned for you. But if you choose to cooperate, I promise your end will be much less painful."

"If you think I'll cooperate with you, you're sadly mistaken."

"Yes," Frietag said. "I would expect nothing less from you, Malcolm. My associates will have fun with you. There hasn't been a man they haven't been able to break."

"So you say. If they are as competent an agent as you, I don't think I have much to worry about." Malcolm's head suddenly whipped to the side as Frietag's metal hand struck Malcolm. Malcolm's head exploded in pain, but he lost consciousness before he could process it.

When he awoke, he found himself strapped to a hard bed. He was no longer blindfolded, but he had a gag in his mouth. The room was dark, and it took several moments for his eyes to grow accustomed to the darkness. The only light in the room came from under the door. Malcolm couldn't make out much in the darkness, but the room seemed tiny. He listened intently for any clues to tell him where he might be. He could hear faint moaning and occasional footsteps outside of the room, but nothing that helped him. With his head still pounding from both the original and Frietag's blow to his head, he thought it best to allow himself to drift off to sleep.

Bright light filled the room and Malcolm jolted awake as he felt the gag removed from his mouth. As his vision cleared, he saw Frietag standing with someone who looked familiar, but whom Malcolm couldn't place.

"Good morning, Malcolm," Frietag said. "Do you remember my associate, Captain Ernst Toht of Imperial Naval Intelligence? No?"

"You may not remember me, but I most definitely remember you," Toht said. He was a bald man with rat-like eyes hidden behind wire-rimmed spectacles. "You most rudely interrupted my conversation with Mycroft Holmes."

"Conversation? You had him strapped down to a table and were jolting him with electricity!"

"Yes, unfortunately, Mycroft was not a conversationalist; I simply attempted to loosen his tongue."

"You may as well hook me up, as I won't tell you anything!" Malcolm said.

"We shall see," Toht said. Malcolm did not like the smile on Toot's face; he looked far too eager to begin his interrogation.

"Where am I?" Malcolm asked.

"You are a patient at the Colditz Asylum," Frietag said. "A very troubling case, which required the best minds to cure you."

"Cure me? There's nothing wrong with me!" Malcolm spat.

"As you can see, the patient is quite belligerent." Frietag turned to Toht. "I believe you have something to calm him down?"

Toht turned to a nearby table and picked up a syringe and a small bottle. He expertly drew the contents of the bottle into the barrel of the syringe and squirt a little out to remove any air. "We'll start with a small dose; I would hate to have him pass out before our conversation." He nodded and two orderlies came over to Malcolm and held him down. Malcolm struggled against the vice like grip of the orderlies to no avail. Toth pushed the syringe into Malcolm's arm. Malcolm immediately felt the sting of the needle and a slight burning in his arm as the unknown fluid entered his bloodstream. Within a short time, Malcolm felt the drug take effect as his whole body relaxed and went limp. He felt very drowsy, but couldn't quite drift off to sleep.

"Very good," Toht said. "Can you hear me, Malcolm?"

"Yes," Malcolm muttered.

"Good. We're going to have a conversation and you're going to answer my questions."

"No," Malcolm said. His mind was foggy. Trying to keep a thought in his head was like trying to pull a spoon out of thick oatmeal.

"That's not a very auspicious way to begin your treatment, but I wouldn't expect anything less. Now, tell me, where have you been for the last year?"

"Here and there."

"Can you be more specific?"

"No," Malcolm said. He was finding it harder and harder to keep his thoughts straight.

"You left your position at the Peninsular and Oriental Steam Navigation Company. What did you do after that?"

"This and that," Malcolm said. He blinked several times as he felt the room fade away.

"You gave him too much, Toht! He's losing consciousness!"

"Patience, Herr Frietag," Toht said. "This is our first session. It may take some time to find the right dose that will make him pliable, but not lose consciousness."

As Malcolm fell asleep, he heard Toht say, "What fun will it be if he gives us all the answers right away?"

# CHAPTER FOUR

*J*oan and Saxon got into the limousine and said to the driver, "Take us to Clare House." Saxon looked at Joan quizzically and she said, "I arranged for our former employer to stay with a family friend who has a room suitable for him. I hope we can catch him before he leaves for the church."

They sat silently as the car wound its way through the country lanes. Joan forced down her heartbreak and disappointment. She concentrated on Malcolm's pocket watch, wishing it had some magic to return him. Squeezing it until her knuckles turned white, she only stopped when the car pulled up the driveway in front of the Regency house. She scarcely noted the four pairs of Tuscan columns holding up a balcony running along the front of the house under a domed roof. The car had barely stopped when Joan leapt from the car before the startled chauffeur could open her door. She rushed to the front door and knocked before Saxon could catch up with her. By the time Saxon reached her, she was already waiting inside the lobby of the house. Ahead, a large circular stairway lead to the upper floors and two wings on either side.

Joan paced nervously in the lobby until Mycroft Holmes arrived some minutes later. "Joan, what are you doing here? Shouldn't you be getting ready for your wedding?" he asked when he caught sight of her.

"We need to talk somewhere, privately," she said.

"Now?"

"Yes. It concerns my prior employment with you."

"Ah," Mycroft said. "Follow me. My room is conducive to private conversation." He turned and led Joan and Saxon up the stairs to a windowless room on the second floor, lit by electric lights. On a secretary's desk, Saxon noted a large contraption. Mycroft went to it and fiddled with the dials. "Now our conversation will be private. What is so urgent that you come here mere hours before your wedding?"

"It's Malcolm. He's missing, and we think Matthias Frietag abducted him."

"Let's not jump to conclusions. Tell me everything, from the beginning."

Saxon recounted leaving Malcolm at the pub and after finding he never returned home, returning to the pub to find Malcolm's watch and the description from the barkeep of the gentlemen that appeared to be waiting for Malcolm, including a man with an eye patch and a gloved hand.

Mycroft sat in thought for a moment before saying, "Yes, that's a logical conclusion. If Frietag has Malcolm, we need to return to London immediately. The resources of my department are at your full disposal. I will pay my respects to my guest and will prepare to leave." He pulled his pocket watch from his vest to check the time. "Mercifully, I believe we can't take a train to London. However, my driver won't arrive until tomorrow."

"I'm sure that I can have my father's driver take us to London," Joan offered.

"Very good," Mycroft said. "I'm sure that you need time to notify your guests and pack for a return to London. I shall be ready whenever you can slip away." He paused and put his hand on Joan's shoulder. "I'm so terribly sorry that this has happened and know that you have my full support."

"Thank you, Mycroft," Joan said, surprised by the gesture. "Come, Charles, we have a great deal to do."

After returning to her father's home, Joan wasted no time in finding her father. "I need your car to leave for London immediately."

"What do you mean, you're leaving for London now?"

"Father, I need to return to London to find Malcolm!"

"You mean he's run off to London? I'll go myself and drag that worthless Scotsman back here myself!"

"No, Father." Her father's insinuation that Malcolm abandoned her felt like a dagger to the heart. "We think he's been abducted and Mr Holmes has been kind enough to allow us to use all of his considerable resources to help us find him. We only need to borrow your car and driver to take us back to London."

"Can't you leave tomorrow? We have guests descending here at any moment, expecting a wedding that has no groom and, shortly, no bride!"

"Time is of the essence, Father. The sooner we get to London, the better our chances of finding him. Please, Father!" Joan pleaded. Her sadness and frustration spilled out in tears. "We need to go now!" With tears now streaming down her face, her father pulled her close and gave a hug.

"Are you sure?" He continued to hold her. It had been so long since her father had hugged her, she felt like a little girl. She nodded.

"Very well, you can take the car. But if I found out, he wasn't abducted and abandoned you."

"You'll have to stand in line to get your revenge," Joan said. They laughed and her father gave her one more squeeze. Joan wiped the tears from her face. "Thank you, Father." She turned and went to Saxon's room. "Father, reluctantly, gave us leave to take his car and driver to London. How soon can you be ready?"

"I'm nearly packed."

"I should be ready shortly. I had already packed for our honeymoon," she said before trailing off. She sniffed to hold back her tears and turned and said. "I'll meet you at the car in ten minutes."

"I'll be there," Saxon said.

Joan threw a few more items into her luggage before she called for the butler to take it down. She followed and went out to wait by the car. She looked at Malcolm's pocket watch frequently as she paced, wishing Saxon would hurry. What if her father's suspicions were correct? What if Malcolm had second thoughts and made his escape? She looked at the watch and shook her head. Malcolm would never leave the watch behind. Unless he wanted her to think something had happened. Saxon's arrival jolted her from her thoughts. The chauffeur loaded Saxon's bags into the limousine and they sped off to Clare House, where they picked up Mycroft. They sat in silence for the three-hour trip through the Kentish countryside to London. Again, Joan alternated between the thought that Frietag had abducted Malcolm and Malcolm had left her. The cobblestone and gravel roads jarred them constantly as they passed through the quaint villages and lush countryside of Kent. After a long time, the open fields gave way to town houses and factories, which gave way to the crowded streets of London. They stopped at Charing Cross and gathered their belongings before making their way through the station to an obscure kiosk far from the ordinary trains. Mycroft addressed the ticket agent, "I'm afraid that I left my tickets in my other suit, but there is an emergency at Uncle Edward's house that I must fix. I believe the hydrangeas in Hyde Park are excellent this year."

"I hear that the violets in Regent Park aren't to be missed," the ticket agent replied. He opened the gate and let the trio in; they quickly boarded the secret train that would take them to the underground entrance of the British Secret Service.

When they arrived, they went directly to the library, where four agents were waiting for them. Mycroft turned and said, "Before we left, I radioed our analysts to begin the search."

"Thank you, Mr Holmes," Joan said, quickly slipping back into her role as one of Mycroft's agents.

Saxon and Joan took seats near Mycroft's chair, but Mycroft remained standing. "What have you found?" he asked the other analysts.

"Nothing so far," one of the analysts said. "We are trying to get the records from every aerodrome from Kent to Dover, to London for any airplane or airship that has departed since last night, but we have received no news."

"Have we picked up any German radio transmissions?"

"We have detected no radio transmissions in the last twenty-four hours. We've contacted our associates in Germany to see what they've heard."

"You mean we have nothing?" Joan asked. She deflated at the news. She hoped for some indication that Malcolm had truly been abducted.

"As hard as it is, we must be patient," Mycroft said. Joan glared at him before he continued. "Let us lay out everything we know. Somehow, Matthias Frietag knew about Malcolm's stag party and planned his abduction accordingly. Given it's only been three weeks since you returned, how was he able to get that information?"

"I had to contact several people in the Admiralty to ensure leave for many of our guests. I'm sure it was fairly common knowledge at the Admiralty," Saxon offered.

"Very good. That means that Frietag had very little time to put together his abduction attempt. It's likely he overlooked an important detail that will give us a clue where he took Malcolm. If I'm not mistaken, I believe there is a small aerodrome near to your father's house?"

"Yes! We need to get back immediately!" Joan said.

She was about to leap from her chair when Mycroft put up a hand. "No need. I dispatched an agent there before we left for London. In fact, I'm expecting his report at any time. I suspect a private airship took Malcolm. It's also possible they took him by ship, but the trip to a port would increase the odds of discovery. If we can find the airship, we should be able to find Malcolm."

# CHAPTER FIVE

When Malcolm awoke, he couldn't tell if he'd been asleep for five hours or five days. The small strip of light below the door did little to illuminate the room. His head still throbbed and his mind still felt a little cloudy. He shook his head, trying to clear his mind, but it was still difficult to concentrate. With great effort, he took stock of his situation. He remained tied to the bed; unable to move. His mind was still cloudy from the effects of the drugs and he knew he needed something to focus his mind, so he wouldn't succumb to the German interrogation methods. He focused on his fight with Frietag on the *Daedalus*. After disarming Frietag, he realised his mistake as Frietag backed next to Joan. He watched in horror as Frietag used Joan's derringer, shooting her in the stomach before pushing her back at Malcolm to make his escape. Rage and horror welled up within him, feeling his heart ripped out again and the deep despair of thinking she had died. Thinking of Joan, he despaired that once again, their wedding had been disrupted, and the rage had turned into a furious fire in his heart, momentarily burning away the fog.

He tried to look around the dark room. It was a small cell with the bed taking most of the space. His captors dressed him in a long, dirty night shirt and he could just make out the leather straps that held him in place. He needed to find some means to escape from this place. He struggled to recall the location of Colditz Castle, finally remembering it was in southern Germany. To the south was Bohemia in Austria-Hungary and to the east was Poland, who had recently allied with Germany and Austria-Hungary. His only means of escape meant travelling hundreds of miles west to Switzerland.

But first he had to get out of this cell before he could consider anything else. He strained to lift his head up, but in the dark, he couldn't see much. His thoughts were scrambled; a thought would arrive, only to dissipate like early morning fog. Struggling to concentrate, he took stock of his situation. He was strapped to a bed. If he had any chance of escape, he would need sometime to cut the straps. As near as he can tell, the room had no furnishings save the bed. He realised he was lying on a bedpan, but he didn't relish the thought of having to use that as a weapon.

The thought made him remember the time he discovered Joan was in fact a member of the British Secret Service, intending to shoot him when Malcolm disarmed her by hitting her with an empty bed pan as he lay in the hospital. *Joan*, he thought. *What must she think? Does she think I stood her up at the altar?* He felt his blood boil that Frietag had prevented them from being married. He tried to use that anger to clear the fog in his head, but he found it a losing battle and drifted off to sleep.

Malcolm awoke to the sound of the door opening; the sudden onslaught of light blinded him. In his dazed state, he couldn't make out faces, but was sure by the silhouettes that Frietag and Toth had re-entered. Malcolm tried to remember his anger, and it helped clear his mind a small bit.

"Guter tag, Herr Robertson," Toth said. "How are you on this fine day?"

"I've been better," Malcolm said. "I'd be even better if you took off these straps."

"I don't think so, Herr Robertson. You might cause yourself injury."

*More likely I'd strangle you,* Malcolm thought.

"I'm guessing that you aren't here to discuss my well being. What do you want?"

"We want to you to answer our questions. Shall we continue from last time?"

Toth approached the bed with a syringe to inject Malcolm with more drugs. Toth lent a little too close as he tried to locate a vein. Malcolm raised his head enough from the bed to smack his head against Toth's without hurting himself, a talent he had picked up in his short time playing rugby at university. The syringe fell out of Toth's hands, struck the bed, and shattered before falling to the floor. Toth stumbled back a few steps, momentarily dazed. In that moment, Malcolm shifted his arm and found a piece of sharp glass cutting into the back of his arm.

Frietag stepped over and backhanded Malcolm across the face with his metal hand. Malcolm once again felt everything dim a little from the blow and when he gathered his wits, Frietag was standing over him, pinning him to the bed.

"That's not how you should treat your doctor, Malcolm. I have very little patience for your abuse of Major Toth."

Malcolm was begrudgingly glad that Frietag had hit him, because the pain in his jaw distracted from the pain of the shard of glass cutting into his arm.

"Now, Herr Frietag, please don't damage our patient. If he's not conscious, he won't be able to take part in our conversation." Toth went to the door and yelled something in German and within a short time, an orderly arrived with a new syringe and a vial. Toth prepared the syringe and as he approached, Frietag placed his metal hand over Malcolm's face and turned it to the side, pushing it into the bed. Malcolm felt the prick of the needle and the burning sensation as Toth injected the drug. When Toth removed the syringe, Frietag let go. Besides his sore jaw, the pain in his arm from the glass shard, Malcolm's neck now hurt from being wrenched to the side.

Malcolm felt his body relax, and he felt himself feeling drowsy again. He looked at Frietag and tried to focus his rage on Frietag.

"Now, Herr Robertson, my associate has questions for you," Toth said as he pulled up a chair and sat by the bed.

"Malcolm, let's start with what you've been doing since the mission to Russia, where you found the Martian ship."

"You mean when I beat your sorry ass?" Malcolm said.

Frietag raised his arm to backhand Malcolm again, but Toth interjected. "Herr Frietag, if you can't control your temper, I'm going to insist that you'll have to leave."

"He has a genuine talent for making people angry, Major Toth."

"I've been told that many times," Malcolm said.

Frietag's eyes darkened, but he turned away and took a step away as he took a deep breath to collect his thoughts.

"Again, tell us what you've been doing since the end of the Russian mission."

Malcolm's head was swimming; he was drowsy, and he felt relaxed, but he looked at Frietag and remembered the awful scene when Frietag shot Joan and he felt a small bit of clarity "I returned to England and they promoted and rewarded me for beating you."

Frietag's nostrils flared. Even in the half light of the room, Malcolm could tell he was angering Frietag, and he knew from experience that when angry, Frietag was prone to take rash actions.

"Never the less," Frietag said through gritted teeth, "I'd like to know why you left the Air Service two years later and what you were doing in Austria."

"That's easy. I left for an assignment in the Diplomatic Corps until you abducted me and I once again had to show what a pathetic agent you are."

"Herr Frietag," Toth warned, seeing Frietag tense and prepare to hit Malcolm. "Perhaps you should take a break and allow me to question the patient."

Frietag huffed and left the room, slamming the door of Malcolm's cell as he left.

Toth turned his attention to Malcolm. "Now we can have a

civilised conversation. My associate is young and his anger gets the better of him. But you and I are civilised men. We can have a conversation. Now to continue my associate's question, what were you doing in Austria?"

Malcolm looked at Toth and felt his anger dissipate now that Frietag had left. Malcolm struggled to remember the last time he saw Toth. He remembered finding Toth interrogating Mycroft in a castle in Königsberg. The rage he felt as watch Toth electrocute Mycroft Holmes to get him to talk. His desire to do the same thing to Toth and now, wishing that he had. He held onto that thought to hold off the seductive lure of relaxation.

"I was a member of the Diplomatic Corps. After I escaped from the clutches of your 'associate', I returned to England."

"There seems to be several months between the time you must have returned to England and when you joined Peninsular and Occidental. What were you doing?"

"I was travelling."

"Where?"

"I took an airship to the South Pacific, ending up in New Zealand before returning to England." Malcolm figured Toth knew as much and he wasn't giving up any secrets.

"What became of the Martians and the Martian ship you recovered from Russia?"

"I don't know. That information was above my rank."

"So you say. Yet, they recently promoted you to Commodore. Surely your new rank would give you access to such information."

"You have an unrealistic view of the powers of a Commodore."

Toth laughed and his high pitched cackled sent a shiver down Malcolm's spine. "So you say. I think I'm going to derive a great deal of pleasure in getting you to tell me your secrets."

Malcolm had a sinking feeling in the pit of his stomach. "I'm not sure why you don't think I'm not answering your questions."

"Yes, you are answering, but only giving very glib answers. I see my drugs will not be very effective to gain your compliance. I'll need to use enhanced methods. I'll leave you, Herr Robertson. There is no point in continuing this session." He went to the door and knocked to get an orderly's attention to let him out. As he left, he turned to Malcolm and said, "I can't wait for our next session."

As he left, Malcolm felt his blood run cold.

# CHAPTER SIX

"With all the resources of the Secret Service, why don't we have any information on what happened to Malcolm?" Joan said, pacing the floor of the meeting room. "It's been four days since Malcolm's abduction and we are no closer to knowing what happened to Malcolm than we were then." Where could Malcolm be? Was he alright? Frietag was dangerous when angered, and Malcolm knew how to anger him. The possibility of his death made her shudder. The frustration, worry, and anger welled up within her and she felt tears welling up in her eyes. She did her best to push her emotions aside and wiped her eyes before tears could fall. The four days since their planned wedding had felt like a month.

"Joan, you know Mycroft has every available agent scouring the country for any trace of what happened to Malcolm. Please, sit down, you're going to wear out the carpet. Let me get you some tea," Saxon said as he stood up from the table and went to the tea trolley.

"Do you have anything stronger than tea?" she asked, hoping for anything that might banish her dread.

"Unfortunately, no. However, I believe this tea has been here long enough that you could use it as tar," he offered as poured the tea into a cup and offered it to Joan.

She smiled a wan smile as she accepted the tea. She took a sip and said, "I believe you are correct." Although hideously bitter, the tea did help. After a moment, she said, "Thank you, Charles. I'm sorry I'm such a mess. I don't know what to do; I feel so useless."

"I know," he said. "We must be patient. Mycroft has made this the highest priority for the Secret Service. At first, I thought he was being uncharacteristically sympathetic, but I think there's more to it than that."

"What do mean?"

"We know Frietag knows about the mission to Russia and the recovery of the Martian ship. He's likely assumed that Malcolm knows what happened to the Martian ship and its technology. Given his role in the ship's construction that took us to Mars, Malcolm has a great deal of technical knowledge that the Germans want. I'm sure that Mycroft is concerned about the prospects of that knowledge falling into German hands. And we know from our past encounters, Frietag blames Malcolm for his failures. I think Frietag would do anything to extract that information from Malcolm."

"Do you think he can?" Joan asked.

"I don't know. We both know that Malcolm can be extremely obstinate, but everyone has a breaking point. If I know Malcolm, he's probably angered Frietag many times, hoping to get him to act rashly."

"He is rather good at angering people," Joan said with a small laugh. She remembered the fight she had with him when she found an engagement ring that he intended to give to her. Now, she would do anything to see his face again. She tried to swallow the feeling. "I worry about the lengths that Frietag will go to make Malcolm give them the information."

"Me too," Saxon said.

The door flew open, and Mycroft strode into the room. "At last, we have a glimmer of information. A private airship landed at the aerodrome in West Malling on the day of Malcolm's stag party. My agent reported that three men disembarked and hired a car; one of them wore an eye patch."

"That's definitely Frietag!" Joan said.

"I concur," Mycroft said. "Although there was no one at the aerodrome that evening, the airship was gone when staff reported the next morning."

"Do we have a description of the airship?" Saxon asked.

"Limited information. From the description, it was a small airship typically used to deliver post. The aerodrome staff believed it was a German design, particularly as they asked to replenish their hydrogen supply. As Charles knows, German airships still use hydrogen for buoyancy instead of helium."

"So we know that a German airship left West Malling. Do we know where it went?" Joan asked.

"The Royal Airship Station at Kingsnorth reported that an airship matching the description headed due east, but they stopped tracking somewhere over the North Sea. However, our friends in Belgium noted a German airship matching the description flying over Antwerp, heading for Germany."

"I could have guessed that much," Joan sneered. "But what was its final destination?"

"I'm afraid we don't have that information...yet," Mycroft said. "I have circulated the description to all of our German-based agents and considered likely landing sites based on the last known course." Mycroft went to the wall and pulled down a map of Northern Europe. He studied the map for a moment. "West Malling is here. If we draw a line due east that includes Antwerp and continue east, we can concentrate our search."

"Couldn't the airship have changed course? Flown north or south once it reached Germany?" Joan asked.

"It's possible, but I consider it unlikely," Mycroft said. "I believe that time was of the essence and they would take the most direct route. Unfortunately, that still leaves a rather large swath of Germany where they could have taken Malcolm. I have directed our agents to fan out here," he said, pointing to an area from Düsseldorf to Dresden. "My assumption is that they will take him to a rather remote facility where there will be few prying eyes."

Joan let out an exasperated sigh. "I know, Joan, this is not the news you want to hear, but be patient a little longer," Mycroft said. "I have every available agent working on finding Malcolm."

"I know," Joan said. She sighed. "It's much easier to accept the delay when you don't have a personal stake in the results."

"Is there anything we can do to assist?" Saxon offered.

"Not as such. Perhaps you can review our file on Frietag to see if it provides any clues. I have looked at it many times, but come up with nothing. If you'll excuse me, I'll return to my office. I will return the moment I have any additional information," Mycroft said as he swept out of the room as dramatically as he entered.

Joan picked up the file. "There isn't much information here," she said. She leafed through the file. His falsified birth certificate listed his birthplace as Alderney in the Channel Islands. His family moved to Northampton, London, and he attended Northampton Institute of Technology. After receiving his degree in engineering, he applied for the Royal Navy. He worked his way up to Assistant Chief Engineer on the *HMA Daedalus*. She remembered Frietag in his identity as Matthew Frye. His demeanour was kind and enthusiastic, a far cry from the man who shot her. She brushed that thought aside and read on. He left German intelligence after that and worked for the Austrian Emperor. After that, his whereabouts were unknown until he returned to Berlin for six months. She remembered the timing coincided with the maiden voyage of the spaceship *Icarus*. Did the Germans know about the ship? What else might they know?

Joan gasped with a realisation. "We have another problem. I think the Germans know about the *Icarus* And that means they might know about Peter O'Hallarhan's role in its construction. The Germans might also be after him."

# CHAPTER SEVEN

Malcolm found it impossible to keep track of time. Despite Toth's decision to stop using drugs as his means of interrogation, they kept Malcolm sedated most of the time, and he found it hard to stay awake. Although he didn't know how long it had been since the last interrogation session, it seemed like there was a delay. Given Toth's statement that he would try a new means of interrogation, Malcolm welcomed the delay.

In his moments of consciousness, he struggled to think of a means of escape. So far, his captors hadn't found the shard of glass he acquired during his last session. *A lot of bloody good it's done me,* he thought. They continued to strap him to the bed and Malcolm had no way to reach any of the straps with the shard of glass to cut the leather straps that bound him. Even if he could cut the straps, he wasn't sure he had the energy to affect an escape. He would cross that bridge after he solved the problem of getting loose.

He thought back to his time in the Air Service and even his short stint as an agent in the Secret Service and lectures on how to escape bounds. He realised the first step would be to loosen the bonds so that he had some kind of movement. Since the straps crossed his chest, he reasoned that if he could expand his chest, the next time they secured him, he might create slack in the restraints. He spent his time working on taking and holding big breaths. Because of the current tightness of his bonds, he couldn't hold a big breath, but he felt it was important to try.

His time to try his theory came soon enough. Two burly orderlies entered his room, released him, and hauled him out of his cell. Malcolm's legs were weak, and he found himself dragged down the hallway to a room where they stripped him of his dirty nightclothes and strapped him to a chair. Before they secured him, he took the biggest breath he could and, to his surprise, found it had the desired effect when he slowly expelled his breath; the restraints around his chest were much looser than they should have been. Before he could do anything, his mind went blank when one orderly poured an ice cold bucket of water over his head. He shuddered at the sudden shock, but before he could gather his wits, more icy water poured over his head. This continued for several minutes; by the time it stopped, Malcolm's teeth were chattering. He had never been so cold in all of his life. As he sat there cold and shivering convulsively, the orderlies left and Toth entered.

"Shall we continue our conversation or should I have the orderlies bring more water?" Toth said as he pulled a previously unseen chair next to Malcolm.

"Scottish winters are colder than this," Malcolm mumbled, his bravado undermined by the chattering of his teeth and his shivering. His body was numb from the cold and he felt like he wanted nothing more than to sleep. He once again tried to focus on his anger, but he found it hard to focus.

"Never the less, let us continue our conversation. We know that when my colleague Frietag served with you, your airship brought a Martian spaceship back from Russia. What happened to that spaceship?"

"I don't know. The Service whisked the ship away after we landed. That's the last I saw of it," Malcolm said. This was true; although pieces of that ship made up the *Icarus*, he didn't know what had happened to the ship itself.

"I see. Perhaps I should ask for the orderlies again."

"It's the truth," Malcolm said. "I have not laid eyes on the Martian ship since it left the airship."

"Yet, we spotted a ship of unknown design over Schloss Heiligenberg after you left Peninsular and Occidental. Do you know anything about that?"

"No."

"I don't think you're being truthful with me, Malcolm."

"I prefer to be addressed by my rank," Malcolm spat.

Toth sighed. "I'm disappointed in you, Commodore." Even in his state of confusion, Malcolm clearly heard the sarcasm in Toth's voice. "If you cooperate, I promise that your fate will be painless. I doubt you'll get a similar offer from Agent Frietag."

"If you think I'm going to cooperate with you, you can go to hell!"

Toth sighed as he rose from his chair. He knocked on the door of the room and the orderlies returned with more buckets of icy water. Each time they poured the water over his head, Malcolm had a harder time focusing, the water numbing not only his body, but his mind. He found it hard to give coherent answers and after several more rounds of questioning, Toth gave up and had the orderlies release Malcolm and return him to his cell. On the way back, Malcolm struggled to remember what it was he had wanted to do. As they reached his cell, he remembered something about taking a big breath. The orderlies pushed him onto his bed and as they tightened his restraints, Malcolm took the biggest breath he could. He struggled to hold it as his body shivered uncontrollably. He feigned unconsciousness, hoping the orderlies hadn't noticed. Struggling not to let his breath go, he released the breath in one great exhalation when he heard the door shut. Before he could find out if it worked, he drifted out of consciousness.

When Malcolm awoke, he realised someone had covered him in blankets. He was still cold to his core, but he was no longer shivering. The relative warmth felt so inviting that he wanted to fall back into its embrace. He tried moving his arms and found that he had had a measure of success; there was some play in the restraints and he could move his arms to a small degree. He felt under his mattress and found the shard of glass. He smiled and let himself fall asleep, knowing that he might still find a way out of this nightmare.

# CHAPTER EIGHT

When Joan realised O'Hallarhan might be the Germans' next target, she rushed to Mycroft's office, followed by Saxon.

A startled Mycroft looked up from his desk. "What is it?" he asked, exasperation in his voice.

"Excuse the interruption, Mr Holmes, but we think that Peter O'Hallarhan could be a target for the Germans." Joan said. "If they know about the *Icarus*, they may have deduced that he was its designer. Do you know where he is?"

"No," Mycroft said. "Explain why you think he's a target?"

Joan explained her deduction and watched as Mycroft considered her words. "It's a sound theory. I'll make some inquiries as to the whereabouts of our young engineer."

Within a few hours, Mycroft's agents learned that O'Hallarhan had told several of the guests at Malcolm's stag party he was leaving for his parent's home at the Wicklow Head Lighthouse on the east coast of Ireland the day after the wedding.

"This begs the question, why didn't Frietag grab O'Hallarhan at the stag party?" Mycroft asked.

"He was a last-minute addition to the party," Saxon offered.

"Unlike most of the other military attendees, he was already on leave. Frietag would not have known O'Hallarhan was coming. And even if he did, Malcolm's disappearance after the party could be a last-minute change of heart by the groom, but the disappearance of O'Hallarhan and Malcolm would raise suspicions. By going after O'Hallarhan at his home, Frietag can snatch him with relative ease."

"I agree with your line of reasoning, Mr Saxon," Mycroft said. "Please get to Ireland with all due haste to keep Mr O'Hallarhan safe."

Joan and Saxon spent the next two hours trying to secure airship passage to Ireland. Unfortunately, the quickest flight was not available until the next morning. Saxon turned to Joan and said, "We can't do anything else here for now. I think it will be best if we return to our flats and pack. I'll assume you're staying at The Savoy?"

"Yes."

"Very good. I'll arrive at the Savoy at 7:00 AM so we can catch our flight to Ireland. It will take us nearly all day to get to Dublin. We still need to hire a car to travel to the lighthouse, which will take another three hours to get there. I don't see us getting there until the day after tomorrow."

"What I wouldn't give to steal the *Icarus*. We could be there in minutes!" Joan said. "What if we don't get there in time? What if the Germans have already abducted O'Hallarhan?"

"We'll cross that bridge when we get to it. I hope the Germans haven't discovered his whereabouts. It's only been five days. It probably took O'Hallarhan at least a couple of days to book his travel and another to get to Ireland. He's barely had time to get there. I believe that we might have the jump on the Germans, but it is essential that we get there as quickly as possible. Come, let me escort you to The Savoy."

"Thank you, Charles, but I will walk by myself. I could use it to clear my head. I've been cooped up in this place for too long."

"Nonsense, Joan. It's getting late, I don't want to walking by yourself."

"Charles, are you seriously worried that I won't be able to handle myself?" Joan said, arching an eyebrow.

"No, I'm not worried about that. However, there's no guarantee that Frietag and his goons aren't looking for you."

"But I know nothing about the *Icarus* that would help the Germans at all," Joan retorted.

"That's true, but you would be a very useful pawn in securing Malcolm's cooperation. You know he would do almost anything to protect you."

"I...hadn't thought of that. You're right. Malcolm would do anything to spare me harm. I think we need to stick together until we find Malcolm."

"Then may I escort you to The Savoy?"

They left the Secret Service through the secret underground train to Charing Cross and exited on the Strand. Silently, they walked by the townhouses that lined the street; modern Edwardian buildings mixed with the Georgian townhouses. The lamplighters had just begun lighting the gaslights as dusk fell. The evening fog had rolled in from the Thames. When they reached Savoy Court, Saxon escorted Joan to the lobby of the Savoy.

"Thank you, Charles. That was totally unnecessary," Joan said. "I can take care of myself."

"I know that, but I would shirk my responsibility as Malcolm's Best Man if I let anything happen to his bride."

"We're not married," Joan said.

"Not yet," Saxon countered. "We will find him and you will be married."

Joan touched Saxon's arm. "Thank you, Charles."

They stood silently for several moments before Joan said, "I should let you go. We have a very early morning. Good night, Charles."

"Good night, Joan."

Joan entered the ornate lobby of The Savoy. As she crossed the checkerboard floor to take the lift to her room, she felt eyes following her movements. Her years spent in the Secret Service told her not to disregard this warning. As she neared the lift, she dropped her purse, appearing to fumble with the button to call the lift. As she bent down to retrieve her purse, she scanned the lobby and noticed two men seated in the corner, their faces blocked by the newspaper they read. At a cursory glance, they wore nondescript suits; something out of place for the opulence of The Savoy. As she stood up and turned to face the ascending room, she surreptitiously slid her hand into her purse and retrieved her derringer. It was only good for two shots, but that might be all she would need. As she waited for the lift to arrive, she moved to a mirror to the left of the lift doors. She pretended to check her hair as she saw the two men get up and move in her direction. They both wore fedoras that masked their faces in shadow.

The doors to the ascending room opened. Joan turned to the operator and said, "I'm sorry. I've decided to go to the dining room before returning to my room. Sorry to have bothered you." She turned around and walked towards the men before turning to The Grill. She noticed the telltale bulges of concealed guns under their suit jackets and went directly to the maitre'd. "Good evening. I've decided on an early dinner this evening. Is my usual booth empty?"

"I believe it is," the maitre'd said. "This way, madame," he said as he lead her to her private booth in the corner. Once settled, she saw the two men watching her before they too waited for the maitre'd to return to seat them.

"Excuse me," she said, catching the maitre'd before he left. "The two men waiting at your station. Are they guests? They look familiar to me, but I can't seem to place them."

The maitre'd turned to look at the men. "Yes, they were here for dinner last night. Do you wish for them to be seated with you?"

"No, I was just trying to place them, that's all. Thank you."

The waiter arrived, and Joan ordered vodka and perused the menu. As she scanned the menu, she watched the men who were assiduously avoiding looking at her as they sat at a table near the entrance. The waiter interrupted her surveillance when he arrived with her drink. She raised the drink to her lips and thought better of it. She opened her purse and fished out her compact to check her makeup. After opening the compact, she clicked the hidden latch to open a secret compartment. While appearing to check her makeup, she picked up a small vial containing a solution. Setting down her purse to block the view from the two men, she quickly poured a small amount of her drink on her bread plate and, while still pretending to fuss with her makeup, opened the vial and dropped three drops on the plate. She returned the vial to the compact, returned it to her purse. Looking down at the plate, she was relieved to see that it hadn't changed colour. She took a sip of her drink and was relieved that there was no bitter taste. After the strain of the last few days, she felt tempted to gulp it, but she would need to keep her whits about her. She surveyed the room, and the Grill was rather empty; it was early for the fashionable people to eat dinner. Although she had been a frequent guest at The Savoy, she didn't recognise the few diners seated. *No chance to join anyone to make my escape*, she thought.

As she pondered her next move, the waiter arrived with her dinner. She was still wary about eating in case someone had drugged it. Moving the salad around her plate, she considered her options. If she could make it to the lobby, she was certain she could slip away. She would need a diversion. She noticed a chair was slightly askew at a table nearby the two agents and smiled. When the waiter came over to check, Joan told him she felt queasy and would return to her room. She rose and moved towards the exit. As she reached the chair, she kicked it with her foot, making it look like she had tripped over the leg, and tumbled into the men's table, knocking its contents all over them. Her ruse had worked as the maitre'd rushed over to see if she was alright.

"Silly me," she said. "I wasn't paying attention and tripped over that chair. I'm frightfully sorry gentlemen. Please bring them new meals and put it on my bill. I should change." As she left, an army of waiters had arrived to help clean off the men and the mess that Joan had made. She slipped out of the Grill and quickly made her way to the stairs. She didn't particularly relish taking the stairs, but she didn't want to wait. As she started up the stairs, she shot a look back and sighed in relief there was no pursuit.

Quietly and quickly, she made her way up the stairs to her floor. She darted down the hall, making certain there was no one in the hall, and ducked into her room. After locking the door and pulling the chain shut, she moved the chair from the desk and wedged it under the doorknob. She left out a large breath, just now realising that she had been holding it since she left the stairs.

She pulled her trunk out from the wardrobe and laid it on the bed to inventory the contents; finding a few changes of clothes. Digging through the clothes, she found her Secret Service revolver, carefully loaded it, and attached the silencer. She hoped she would not have to use it here, but better to be prepared. She changed into her night-gown, but instead of getting into bed, she laid on the small sofa, which she angled so she had a direct view of the door.

*I wonder how Malcolm is doing?*

# CHAPTER NINE

Malcolm felt he had only been asleep for a second when the door of his cell opened, and the light from the hallway flooded his dark cell, startling him awake. An orderly entered, bringing in a gramophone.

"Isn't it a little late to be listening to music?" Malcolm asked. The orderly either didn't speak English or was ignoring Malcolm, or both. He set up the gramophone in the corner and wound the crank on the side. When he finished, he placed a record on the turntable and placed the arm with the needle on the record.

Immediately, Malcolm heard a high, shrill female voice singing in German over an orchestra accompaniment. He gathered he was listening to an opera, not his choice in music at all. To his surprise, the orderly pulled a chair into the room, followed by a small kerosene lamp. Before sitting in the chair, the orderly went to Malcolm's bed and pulled the blanket off of him. The orderly sat in the chair and pulled out a book and read.

Malcolm shouted to be heard over the music, "Is the book any good?" The orderly did not show that he had heard Malcolm at all. When the record finished, the orderly got up, cranked the gramophone and started the record again. *They are going to add sleep depriva-*

*tion to their tactics to get me to talk.* Malcolm used the number of times the song had restarted to estimate the passage of time. The song probably played for two to three minutes, and the act of restarting the album took another three or four minutes. That meant each replay of the song took roughly five minutes. After he reached fifty repetitions, he gave up trying to count.

Every time Malcolm would nod off, the orderly would slap him in the face to wake him up. The orderly was doing an excellent job of keeping Malcolm awake. The night stretched on interminably. At some indeterminately long amount of time, a second orderly came in and they dragged Malcolm back to the cold water room, as he had referred to it. Toth was there again, waiting patiently while the orderlies stripped Malcolm and secured him to the chair. At first, the cold water brought Malcolm to his senses, and he felt much more awake. *At least it's preferable to that damn German opera!* he thought.

After the orderlies poured several buckets of cold water over Malcolm, Toth took his place next to Malcolm. "How are you, Malcolm?"

"How many times do I have to tell you to address me as Commodore?" Malcolm said through his chattering teeth.

"My apologies, Commodore," Toth sneered. "Now, again, what happened to the Martian spaceship you and your crew brought back from Russia?"

"My answer is the same as it was the last time. I don't know. The last time I saw it was when I left the ship."

"And what can you tell me about the mysterious ship over Schloss Heiligenberg?"

"I do not know what you're talking about," Malcolm said.

Toth shook his head. "I don't think that you're telling me the truth."

"No?"

"That's alright. We'll find the truth. It's actually more fun this way."

"Fun? Fun for whom?" Malcolm said.

"For me, of course," Toth said with a smile. "I love watching people resist, so sure that they will not tell me anything. I relish the moment when they have no more strength left and tell me everything I want. Some people are harder to break than others. You are a particularly tough nut to crack, although you've only been our guest for a week. I think I will particularly enjoy watching you break."

If Malcolm hadn't already been freezing, he would have felt a chill up his spine. Toth nodded to the orderlies, who once again doused Malcolm with ice cold water. As before, his head got fuzzy. And still Toth prompted him for information: Where is the Martian spaceship? What was the ship observed over Schloss Heiligenberg? What had he been doing since he returned to the Air Service? What prompted his promotion to commodore? Malcolm struggled to keep his wits about him and give the same glib answers that he had been repeating. Between the cold water and his lack of sleep, the desire to just get this over with grew. *What if I told them what I know? They would put me out of my misery.* He flashed back to Joan visiting him in his hospital room in St. Petersburg and she threatened to kill him when he realised she was a spy. He remembered watching Frietag shoot Joan at point blank range and the anger and despair he felt when he thought she had died from her wounds. *No, I can't break. I have to get out of here. We're supposed to be on our honeymoon now, and I will not let these bastards win.* Once again, he focused on Joan and used his anger to focus.

Toth repeated the questions again and again, but Malcolm continued to give him the same answers. Malcolm noticed Toth's bemused smile, even though Toth seemed frustrated. Malcolm tried a new tact. "As a kid, I imagined you liked to pull the wings off of butterflies," he said.

"Oh, no," Toth said. "I never hurt animals. I am not an uncivilised brute. No, I learned my trade by studying people. What they desire, what they fear. I find I get my most satisfactory answers by playing on their fears and desires. This," he said, indicating the room, "strips away the facade everyone puts up for society. Tell me, what do you desire, Malcolm?"

"I desire to wipe that smug look off your face!"

"Tut, tut," Toth said as he took off his spectacles and cleaned them with his handkerchief. "There is no need for violence. We are civilised men."

"You might be surprised at how uncivilised I can become," Malcolm said.

Toth regarded him for a moment before putting on his spectacles. "You have quite a talent for provoking people. However, your tactics will not work on me."

"Don't be so sure. I'm very good at making people angry. Just ask Frietag."

"Ah, Mattias is young and undisciplined. He lets his emotions get the better of him. I, however, will not fall for your sophomoric insults."

"That remains to be seen," Malcolm said.

"Yes, it does."

"Are we done here? Because if not, I'd like to return to my cell so I can listen to more opera."

Toth chuckled. "Yes, I suppose we've finished for now," he said. Malcolm tried to lunge towards Toth, but the orderlies grabbed him before he took one step. For a brief second, Malcolm thought he saw a look of fear on Toth's face before his impassive mask returned. *There's something I can use to turn the tables.* The orderlies dragged Malcolm forcefully out of the room and to his cell. He didn't put up any resistance as they strapped him to his bed, but he held his breath to prevent the straps from preventing any movement. To Malcolm's surprise, the orderlies left without turning on the gramophone. He found the shard of glass under his mattress and rubbed it against the strap. It would take a long time before he made any actual progress, but there was no time like the present to start. He worked as long as he could, but the desire for sleep became too great, so he carefully replaced the sliver under his mattress before drifting off to sleep.

# CHAPTER TEN

Joan replayed the events of the evening in her mind as she tried to figure out how she could leave her room undetected. She would rather not have to climb out the window and down the building, since her room overlooked the Thames, and any passerby would see her descent. And then there was her luggage. *That's it!* she thought. Rising from the sofa, she went to her steamer trunk, dragging it to the floor, opened it and removed the false bottom. She climbed inside and pulled her knees together and pulled the trunk nearly close, not wanting to risk getting locked in prematurely. She was pleased to find that she could still fit inside the trunk, even with her clothes and other equipment. Rising from the trunk, she formulated her plan to escape.

The hours until dawn were interminable. She forced herself awake by walking around her suite and by opening a window to let the chilly night air keep her awake. She looked out the window to the Thames and tried to occupy herself as she looked for ships making their way to or from London. The fog made it difficult to see much, but she looked for the telltale glow of the ship's lanterns. She went through the facts of Malcolm's disappearance, looking for additional insight. Finding none, she eventually resorted to the callisthenics she endured during her military training; star jumps, situps, and press ups. She couldn't help but recall the gruelling training she endured to become an officer. The thought made her miss Malcolm even more, so she shook it from her head.

When dawn eventually filtered in, Joan rubbed her face with both hands, to help wake her up and collect her thoughts. She was eager to get away from the agents she knew would watch her room even now. For a moment, she listened at the door, but heard nothing. Sighing, he dressed in her tight fitting suit and trousers she favoured when on a mission. She put a dressing robe over her outfit and pulled the cord to call a butler. After several minutes, there was a knock on her door. She removed the chair, and keeping her gun behind her back, opened the door. She was relieved to see Ashton, the butler, who frequently attended her. "Good morning, Ashton. I'm leaving shortly. Could you have my luggage taken to the lobby? You may need additional help, as I'm afraid I have over-packed once again."

"Very good, madam. What time should I retrieve your luggage?"

Joan turned to look at the clock on the desk, mentally cursing that it was only 5:30 AM. "Shall we say 6:30? You can come in as I am about to go out for breakfast."

"Very good madam," Ashton said. "I'll return at 6:30. Your trunk will be at the baggage check. The front desk will be happy to retrieve it for you when you leave."

"Thank you, Ashton. You are most helpful."

"Thank you, madam," he said. After giving her a bow, he turned and left. Joan closed the door and turned her attention back to the trunk. She made sure that she could open the trunk from the inside. Although dead tired, she paced the room, trying to keep herself occupied for the next hour. She felt anxious, more than before any other mission. The stakes for this mission were high; if she failed, she might lose Malcolm forever. She took several deep breaths to clear her head. She remembered trying to get Malcolm to use deep breaths to calm himself and his many failed attempts, and she couldn't help but chuckle. But the thought of Malcolm was little comfort; it only reminded her what was at stake. She was tired, both from the lack of sleep and her nighttime callisthenics. She kept pacing around the room to keep herself awake. At 6:20, she finally removed the dressing robe and climbed into the trunk, leaving the lid ajar. Lying in the nearly closed trunk, she felt like she was laying in a coffin. She tried to brush that thought aside. She had nearly died when Frietag shot her four years ago. For a while, Joan had died, assuming another identity. But when Frietag saw through her disguise in Austria, she became Joan again. But this Joan differed from the one who nearly died on an airship. She had someone to live for; someone whose life meant as much to her as her own. After an interminable wait, a key unlocked the door, and she pulled the trunk close. She heard footsteps and felt the trunk raise before falling back to the floor with a thud. "Blimey, she wasn't kidding," a voice said. Although muffled, she recognised the voice as Ashton's and felt relief. "What does she have packed in here? A body?" Ashton said. Joan caught herself before she could laugh. The trunk rose again. Ashton and the other butler, grunting, moved the trunk onto a cart for the trip to the lobby after a short while; Joan felt the trunk rumble. She felt the lurch of the service lift in her stomach as it started its descent. Her legs cramped, and it was stifling in the trunk. She kept her breathing shallow, conserving what air was in the trunk. The descent seemed to take forever until she felt the trunk bump off the service lift. Her head bumped the bottom of the trunk and she did her best to stifle a cry of pain. The trunk rumbled down the hall before she felt it come to a stop. She listened intently for the butlers to leave. When she was certain that enough time had passed, she opened the trunk from the hidden latch inside and emerged. She took a deep breath of fresh air before pulling a blouse and skirt from the trunk. She hastily donned her clothes, wrinkled from her trip in the trunk. Surveying the room, she noted a few trunks and bags in the room. She crept to the door and opened it a crack. From experiences of needing to vanish, she knew the hallway to her right was the service hallway that led to the lobby. Silently, she moved down the hallway until she came to the door. She cracked the door slightly to check the lobby. Although she could not see much from her current vantage point, she heard the lobby clock chime quarter to the hour.

She waited impatiently by the door until she heard the clock chime the hour. Knowing Saxon's penchant for punctuality, she carefully opened the door. She saw Charles waiting impatiently, checking his pocket watch. Scanning the lobby, she also saw one of the German agents sitting to the side, pretending to read a newspaper. She strode briskly through the lobby to Charles.

"Where have you been? You know we have an airship to catch. Good Lord, Joan. It looks like you slept in your clothes," he said.

"It's a long story," she said. "One that I will tell you later when we are away from foreign ears," she whispered as she jerked her head slightly to indicate the German agent.

"Ah, yes. Are you ready?"

"I just need to get my luggage and settle my bill. Will you kindly escort me?"

They made their way to the front desk and the desk clerks dispatched a butler to retrieve her trunk while she settled her bill. When the butler returned with her trunk, he said, "Check that you have everything, madam. When I brought your trunk down, it was much heavier than it is now. I hope nothing has gone missing."

Charles arched an eyebrow. Joan turned to Charles and said, "Is the car waiting?" He nodded. Joan turned to the butler. "If you would be so kind as to load this in the car, I would be most appreciative." Charles and Joan turned and left the hotel as the butler brought the trunk outside and loaded it into a waiting cab. Joan reached into her purse and pulled out two one-pound notes, which she gave to the butler. "If you would be so kind as to share this with Ashton, I would be very appreciative."

"Thank you, madam," the butler said. "Are you sure you don't want to check that anything is missing?"

"I'm sure everything is fine. Thank you again for your help," she said before turning quickly to the cab. Charles hurried ahead and opened the door for Joan before moving to the other side to join her. The cab turned onto The Strand and began the trip to Hendon Aerodrome. Charles turned to ask her what was happening, but she shook her head before he could say anything, so he remained quiet as the cab made its way out of London to the Aerodrome. After another thirty minutes, the cab arrived at the offices of the Cunard Airship line. After engaging a porter to retrieve their luggage, Charles paid the cab driver, and they went inside to retrieve their tickets. As they made their way to the lounge, Joan surveyed the room, looking for any indications of additional agents. Joan steered Charles towards a couch in the corner where she could monitor the whole room.

"Are you going to tell me why you look like a wrung dishrag, or will this be a mystery for the ages?" Charles quipped.

Keeping her voice low, Joan recounted the events of the previous evening and her trip in her trunk to the lobby. Charles listened intently before asking, "Do you think we were followed?"

"I find it unlikely; we left rather quickly," she said, before noticing two men enter the lounge. She instantly recognised them as the men who watched her last night. "Perhaps I spoke too soon," she said as she nodded toward the two agents.

"Yes," Charles said. "How do you want to handle this?"

"Give me a moment," Joan said. She watched the two men, who were conspicuously avoiding her gaze. She watched as both men placed their tickets in the breast pocket of their suit coats. Joan smiled. "How are your pickpocket skills?"

"I'm a little rusty, but yes, I think they are sufficient. When do I get to practice them?"

"Let's wait until we board. I'll take the one on the left, you take the one on the right."

Joan and Charles were silent as they waited for the boarding announcement. When the steward came out to announce boarding, Joan and Charles jumped up immediately and made their way to the steward. As they approached, the two men were rising. Charles and Joan bumped into the men, knocking them back slightly.

"Oh, I beg your pardons," Charles said. "We're so eager to start our honeymoon, we were not paying attention to where we were going. A thousand pardons. Are you alright?"

"Yes, we're fine," one man said.

"Again, my apologies," Charles said as he led Joan to the steward.

After the steward punched their tickets, they made their way onto the airship and picked a seat that allowed them to watch the rest of the passengers board the airship.

"Did you get it?" Joan asked.

Charles pulled a ticket from his breast pocket. "Yes, and you?"

Joan pulled the other ticket from her purse. "What is this about our honeymoon?" she said.

"It was my first thought. Don't worry, I will not be taking Malcolm's place." Joan winced. "I'm sorry," he said. "I shouldn't have said that."

"It's alright; I understand."

"So now what?"

"We wait and hope that we have shaken the two agents. And if we have, I'm going to get some much needed sleep," Joan said.

# CHAPTER ELEVEN

Joan and Saxon watched intently as the rest of the passengers settled into the lounge for the flight to Ireland. Both were relieved to see that the agents weren't among the other passengers as the airship rose away from the Aerodrome. Joan settled into her couch and allowed herself to relax for the first time since the previous day and promptly fell asleep.

When she awoke, she found her head leaning on Saxon's shoulder. She sat up and said, "I'm sorry, Charles. How long have I been asleep?"

"Several hours. If memory serves, I believe we're over the Irish Sea. I think we only have a few hours more before we arrive."

"Can I get some food? I'm famished. I haven't eaten since lunch yesterday."

Charles called over a waiter and in a few minutes, a pot of tea, two cups, and a plate loaded with crumpets, scones, and biscuits arrived. Joan poured a cup of tea and, in a decidedly unladylike manner, devoured two scones.

"I guess you were hungry," Saxon said.

"Have you eaten?" she said, offering him the remaining scone.

"Yes, I ate a sandwich without disturbing you, but I will take some tea." Joan poured another cup of tea for Charles.

"Thank you," Saxon said after taking a sip of tea. "That was much needed."

"So what's the plan?" Joan said between bites of the last scone.

"When we arrive in Dublin, we hire a car and make our way to Wicklow Head. I only hope that we get there before the Germans."

"Me too. I fear Peter might not be as impervious to interrogation as Malcolm."

"I'm not sure about that," Saxon said. "He can be nearly as stubborn as Malcolm."

"True," Joan said. "But if they flatter him and tell him how brilliant he is, he may fall for the ruse and give up details that are better left unsaid."

"True," Saxon said. "We'll have to wait and see."

The remaining flight seemed interminable. The view from the lounge was nothing but water for hours until they finally reached the east coast of Ireland. It wasn't long before Dublin came into view. It had been many years since Joan had visited Ireland, but she instantly recognised the rectangular spire of Christ Church Cathedral, contrasting with the thin spire of St. Patrick's Cathedral. As the airship drew nearer, she could make out Trinity College and Dublin Castle. The airship gradually descended, turning to the south for the aerodrome.

When the airship made its gentle landing, Joan and Saxon hurried towards the exit so that they could find transport as quick as possible. Saxon agreed to gather their luggage while Joan went to book a car. After asking a porter, she made her way to the car hire kiosk.

"Good day," she said. "I'd like to book a car to take my husband and I to Wicklow Head."

"I'm sorry, ma'am. Someone else has already hired our only car available for the trip."

"Really? When did that happen?"

"Just this morning. A couple of gentlemen from that airship there," the clerk said, pointing to a small airship moored some distance from the Cunard airship. "The car should return in the next couple of hours. You can have it then."

"Thank you. I think we'll make other plans." She found Saxon struggling with the luggage. "I fear we're too late. Someone already hired the only available car to take two gentlemen to Wicklow Head. The clerk said that they came from that airship there. What should we do?"

"I think that you and I should pay a visit to the airship," Saxon said. "It stands to reason the airship is waiting to take our friend Peter to wherever they are holding Malcolm. Perhaps we could arrange a little surprise for them when they return with Peter. But, if there's anyone onboard, we have to be very careful. Germans use hydrogen in their airships, which means no guns. Otherwise, there will be nothing of us left to find Malcolm."

"Very well." Joan thought for a moment. "Come on, follow my lead." She made her way to the airship. The Cunard airship dwarfed the airship, but it reminded her of the *Uhuru*, the airship Malcolm, Saxon, and she had taken to their mission in the Pacific. But this airship did not have the charm of the *Uhuru*; it was very utilitarian and nondescript. It looked like any of a hundred cargo airships; much like the description of the airship that abducted Malcolm. As she approached, she started yelling, "Come on, Charles, we're going to be late! Hurry with that luggage. We're going to miss our airship!"

A man stepped out of the airship. "What are you doing?" he cried with the slightest trace of accent. Westphalia, if Joan was not mistaken.

"We're here. Come on, Charles, hurry. They are ready to lift off."

"Madam, I believe you are mistaken. This is a private airship. We are not for hire," the man said.

"What do you mean? We have tickets for this airship. See?" Joan pulled her Cunard tickets from her purse with one hand. As she flourished the tickets, her other hand pulled a sap from the purse. She pushed the tickets into the man's face. As he tried to look at them, he didn't notice the sap until it crashed against his head. Joan watch with great satisfaction as the man's eyes rolled back into his head and he crumpled to the ground. She turned to Charles and put her fingers to her lips. She snuck towards the ship and entered.

With her single shot derringer in one hand and the sap in the other, she crept forward. She heard someone humming in the airship's front. Silently, she crept forward and found a door ahead, slightly ajar. She peeked through and saw another man reviewing a map. Moving silently, she hit him with the butt of the derringer and, for good measure, followed up with the sap. Now that she had neutralised the immediate threat, she searched the rest of the ship, finding it empty. She let out a sigh of relief and return to the entry and beckoned Saxon to enter. "There was one more in the cockpit. Let's get our luggage aboard and then we can deal with him," she said, pointing to the unconscious man next to Saxon. Once he loaded the luggage, Charles dragged the man onboard, and they miraculously avoided any notice. They took a few minutes to explore the airship. It was a cargo ship; most of the area was a large cargo bay. There were two sleeping quarters near the cockpit and the engine room in the rear. They found spare rope and bound and gagged the two men.

"Alright, now what?" Saxon asked.

"We wait for the others to arrive with O'Hallarhan, and then we deal with them."

"But then what?"

"We look for a sign of their destination. For now, we wait by the entry."

Together they waited silently by the entry, listening for any telltale signs of activity. After nearly an hour of waiting, they heard O'Hallarhan say, "Is this it? It doesn't look like an Air Service airship."

"It isn't. As we said, this is a very delicate matter, and it's important that we maintain anonymity," a voice said. Again, Joan's trained ears again detected the barest hint of a German accent. She leaned against the inside of the entryway and pulled out her sap. Charles readied a spanner he found in the engine room and likewise readied to spring into action. O'Hallarhan entered first, and didn't notice them. Two men dressed in British Air Service uniforms followed him. When they entered, Joan and Charles sprang into action, hitting both men quickly and dropping them instantly. O'Hallarhan turned around,

"Commander Saxon! Lieutenant de St. Leger! What are you'd doing here? Why did you knock them out?"

"Commander O'Hallarhan, help me secure the entryway," Saxon said, instantly taking command of the situation. Together, they shut the entry way and locked it.

"What's going on?" O'Hallarhan asked.

"If I'm correct, we just saved you from being abducted by German agents," Joan said as she tied up an agent with rope. "What did they tell you?"

"They arrived at my parents' house with orders that I was to return to the Admiralty immediately. Wait, they aren't from the Admiralty?"

"No," Joan said as she searched the man. "Charles, tie up the other one."

"I don't understand," O'Hallarhan said. "Why would they want to abduct me?"

"For the same reason they abducted Malcolm. They want information about our last mission."

"Malcolm was abducted? I thought the wedding was called off because he had second thoughts."

"That was merely a cover," Saxon said. "We are certain that a German agent we know abducted Malcolm and is even now trying to extract information from him."

"Shite," O'Hallarhan said. "Sorry, Lieutenant."

"Never mind that. Now that we have them secured, let's see if we can figure out where they planned to take you." They went to the cockpit and found several maps detailing a flight to Germany. "There," Saxon said. "If I understand this correctly, they planned to take you to Colditz."

Joan thought for a moment. "If memory serves, the castle in Colditz is an asylum. That would be the perfect place to hide Malcolm." She let out a small yelp of satisfaction. For the first time since the wedding, she had a clue about Malcolm's whereabouts. "I say we take this airship and fly to Colditz," she exclaimed.

"Who is going to fly this airship?" Saxon said.

"I might get us back to London, but we're going to need a proper pilot to get to Germany," Saxon said.

Joan was crestfallen. How could two commanders of the Royal Air Service not pilot an airship? She had seen Malcolm do it many times.

"We're going to need a plan if we're going to rescue Malcolm," Charles offered. "The two of us can't just storm in with guns blazing."

"Don't you mean the three of us?" O'Hallarhan said.

"You don't have to be part of this, Peter," Joan said. She didn't want to have to worry about an untrained person if they needed to infiltrate the castle to rescue Malcolm. He was too much of a liability.

"If not for the two of you, I would be on my way to Germany right now. If we don't get him back, they'll be after me next. Besides, Malcolm risked his life to make sure I was alright when I lost my arm on Mars. I owe him a debt." Joan looked at O'Hallarhan and recognised the same set of the jaw that Malcolm had when he would not be dissuaded. She sighed. "Very well," Joan said. "Let's get this airship flying."

# CHAPTER TWELVE

Malcolm awoke at the sound of the door to his cell opening. He looked through bleary eyes. *Where the bloody hell am I? What day is it?* As he blinked his eyes, he saw Frietag and Toth enter the room. *Bloody hell, I'm still here.* He shook his head, forcing himself awake. "To what unfortunate chain of events do I owe this visit?"

"Ever the one for the so-called 'witty quips'," Frietag said.

"I certainly wouldn't expect any witty quips from you," Malcolm said. Frietag glared at Malcolm, refusing to be goaded into action. "So what will it be this time? More cold water? Or more of your so-called music?"

"Neither. I thought we'd have a civilised discussion," Toth said. The two men hovered over Malcolm. "My associate is here to make sure you do nothing...rash." Frietag grabbed Malcolm's throat with his mechanical hand and applied just enough pressure to cause Malcolm discomfort. "I'm going to release your bonds. If you try anything, Mattieu will crush your windpipe."

"Won't that make it hard for me to tell you what you want to know?" Malcolm choked out.

"That's a chance I'm willing to take," Toth said as he undid the strap.

"Please, Malcolm, give me an excuse to show you just how much damage I can do," Frietag said with an evil grin.

Malcolm remained silent as Toth finished. "You may sit up. Slowly," Toth said.

Malcolm struggled to pull himself up to a sitting position. He was weak from the trials of his captivity. He felt a little dizzy at first, but it subsided after a moment.

"Now, let's have a civilised discussion. You can make this easy on yourself by just telling you what we want to know."

"And why would I want to do that?" Malcolm said.

"Because, if you don't, I will enjoy making sure you die a slow, agonizing death," Frietag said.

"Matthias, you are not helping," Toth said. "I understand we interrupted your nuptials. You were to be married to Joan de St. Leger?"

"You obviously know that because your cycloptic friend here kidnapped me from my stag party," Malcolm said.

"Yes. Do you know where Miss de St. Leger is now?"

"I imagine that she's home worried sick about me."

"What is it you like to say? 'Pull the other ones, it's got bells on it'? You know we both know that Joan is a very capable agent," Frietag said.

"What if I told you we have information she left on an airship with your best man, Charles Saxon, for their honeymoon?"

Malcolm struggled not to laugh. He knew Charles was a homosexual and most definitely would not be on a honeymoon with Joan. Instead, he feigned outrage. "What do you mean?"

"Our agents have been keeping a close watch on your fiancé. She left this morning on an airship with Saxon for Ireland and told our agents that they were hurrying to their honeymoon."

"No!!" Malcolm cried. He did his best to look dismayed and overwhelmed by the fictional revelation. "It can't be true!" He hoped that he hadn't overplayed his hand.

"It's true. So you see, Malcolm, your fiancé and best man have deserted you. You are alone. The only people who know you are gone and no longer care about your fate."

"That's not true," Malcolm yelled in false anger.

"But, it is," Frietag said. "How does it feel to be duped yet again? When we were on the *Daedalus*, you did not know I was a spy. You aren't nearly as bright as you think you are," Frietag said with a leer.

Malcolm hung his head. "I don't believe you."

"Don't worry, you'll have proof soon enough. Even now, we have agents waiting in Ireland to catch them in the act when they arrive," Frietag said.

*Agents in Ireland?* Malcolm thought. *Why would Joan and Charles go to Ireland, and why would the Germans have agents there?* He came to the horrible realisation that the Germans were also going to abduct Peter O'Hallarhan. "Why do you have agents in Ireland?" He asked, hoping they might divulge more information.

"We are looking for one of your officers from your last command, a Peter O'Hallarhan," Frietag said.

"What would you want with him?"

"We understand he was the chief engineer under your last command. We hope he might be more…cooperative than you," Toth said.

"That arrogant bastard?" Malcolm lied. "He's got an overdeveloped sense of his abilities. He couldn't tell the difference between a spanner and a screwdriver."

"And yet, he was the chief engineer under your tutelage?" Frietag said.

"You know, we don't always get to choose our crew. O'Hallarhan had powerful friends in the Admiralty; I had to make do."

"Make do for what?" Toth said.

Malcolm was silent. He knew he had to tread carefully. He couldn't tell the Germans what they desperately wanted to know, but he knew he had to give them something. Malcolm sighed, pretending to hang his head in defeat. "The Admiralty put me in charge of a top secret engine design and they assigned O'Hallarhan to me."

"That is the most helpful thing you've said since you got here. What can you tell us about this new engine?" Toth said.

"It ran on electricity. It was a thousand times more efficient than our diesel engines."

"Interesting," Toth said. "Can you tell us more?"

"I might," Malcolm said. "If you give me some proper food, stop feeding me drugs, and let me get some sleep. It's difficult to remember details when you are in a perpetual fog."

Frietag and Toth looked at each other. "And in exchange, you'll give us the technical details of this new engine?"

Malcolm hung his head in false defeat. "Yes," he whispered. "What reason do I have to continue to hold out? As you said, my best friend has run off with my fiancé. I may as well give you what you want."

"I see," Toth said. "I'm disappointed. I thought it would take more to break you than this. We found your deepest fear; your fear of being alone."

Malcolm hung his head in false shame.

"Very well. Let us discuss your offer."

"If you have someplace I can work, I could build a prototype," Malcolm offered.

"That is most surprising," Toth said. "Very well. For now, we will not restrain you while we consider your offer. But any attempt at violence or escape will result in the most severe punishments."

"I understand," Malcolm whispered.

"You're just going to let him off the hook?" Frietag sputtered. "He's plotting something, I know it."

"What can he do?" Toth said. "If he escaped this cell, where could he go where we couldn't find him?" Frietag was silent. "Come, Matthias, we have much to consider." Malcolm sat dejectedly as he watched Frietag and Toth knock on the cell door and leave once the orderly opened the door.

When he was sure that they were long gone, Malcolm smiled. If he could get his head clear, he might just be able to come up with a plan to escape.

# CHAPTER THIRTEEN

Malcolm used his newfound freedom to walk around the tiny cell. There was barely any room around the bed, but he knew he needed to build up his strength if he had any chance of escaping. He hoped his act had convinced Toth and Freitag. If he had convinced them, he might create a means for his escape under the guise of building a prototype.

A few hours later when Toth and Frietag opened the door to his cell, flanked by two burly orderlies. "There's been a change in plans," Toth said. "You're coming with us."

"Where are we going?" Malcolm said.

"That is not important. Put on these clothes and come with us." Toth tossed clothes on the bed, the same clothes Malcolm wore when they abducted him. When Malcolm finished dressing, Frietag grabbed Malcolm's arms and put them behind his back, securing his wrists with handcuffs. Frietag marched Malcolm out of the room, and for the first time, Malcolm saw his prison. Flanked by the two orderlies, they led Malcolm through several twisty and claustrophobic hallways lined with doors barred from the outside. As Malcolm passed, he heard moaning from behind several of the doors; the smell of excrement and urine hung in the air, making Malcolm nauseous. He felt his shoulders beginning to burn from his restraints. The white plaster walls reflected so much light, Malcolm had to squint after being held in his dark cell. He quickly lost all sense of direction. They emerged on a landing with a large staircase leading to the grand entry and the doors. Malcolm considered trying to make a run for it, but disregarded the idea because he wouldn't get five yards away before they recaptured him. The oak doors opened, and they led Malcolm to a waiting car, a block like vehicle with three rows of seats. Malcolm recognised the smell of diesel exhaust. The orderlies thrust Malcolm in back and when Frietag slid in on the other side, he covered Malcolm's eyes with a blindfold.

"I don't get to enjoy the view?" Malcolm said.

"No. Now, keep quiet. If I hear so much as a peep from you, you will regret it," Frietag snarled.

The car started moving, leaving the castle. Given the bumpiness of the ride, Malcolm deduced they must be driving on cobblestone streets. The constant bumps caused Malcolm to bounce around the back of the vehicle. Every time he bumped into Frietag, Frietag shoved him into the window. Eventually, he realised they had left Colditz as the jostling ceased. After a while, Malcolm's shoulders ached from the strain of being held behind his back. But the trip was far from smooth. When they encountered a large bump, Malcolm's shoulders felt on fire, each bump hurting more than the last. Malcolm almost wished for the cold water treatment; at least then, he would be numb.

Malcolm tried to find clues about the trip. The car slowed down and the constant jostling told him when they travelled through a village or city. He heard the car labour as it climbed hills and pick up speed when the road was flat. Try as he might, he couldn't figure out where he was going; not without a map. The car eventually came to a halt and Frietag dragged him out of the car. Malcolm could smell the odours of coal smoke and realised they must be in an industrial city. He still did not know where he was, but given the duration of the trip, that would narrow down the possible destinations. Frietag yanked him up a set of steps and he could barely keep his feet under him.

They walked for some distance before they reached a set of narrow stairs. Frietag pushed Malcolm, and he fell down the stairs, each bump sending a flaming hot pain through his shoulders. He lay there in a heap until Frietag pulled him up by the collar and dragged him some distance before pushing him again. Malcolm fell once more. This time, Frietag undid the blindfold.

"Welcome to your new home, Malcolm," he said. As Malcolm eye's adjusted to the light, he found himself in a small laboratory. In front of him was a lab bench, complete with a voltage generator, an oscilloscope, and a signal generator. To the right of the equipment was a cabinet with a series of shelves marked in German. He noticed a cot in the room's corner.

"What's all this?" Malcolm said.

Toth now arrived, wiping his face from perspiration. "You said that you could build a prototype of this new engine. You now should have the equipment necessary to do so. May I introduce Walter Schottky?" A man, roughly Malcolm's age, with black hair and a toothbrush moustache, entered the room. "He will oversee your work. He's an expert in physics and will ensure that your work is on the up and up."

"How do you do?" Schottky said in heavily accented English as he held out his hand.

"I've been better, but I unfortunately can't shake your hand," Malcolm said, indicating his handcuffed arms. He turned to Toth and said, "It's going to be deucedly difficult to do any kind of engineering work with my hands tied behind my back."

Toth nodded, and Frietag unlocked the handcuffs. Malcolm shook his arms, trying to restore feeling after being pinned behind him for the trip. Malcolm reached out to shake Schottky's hand, and Frietag pulled a revolver and aimed it at Malcolm. "Come now, I'm trying to be civilised," he said, looking at Frietag. Toth nodded again and Frietag lowered the revolver. Malcolm shook Schottky's hand. "It's a pleasure to meet you."

"Before you get any ideas of escape, a guard will supervise your work, with another guard outside. You will receive meals regularly and you can sleep on the cot."

"Where is the loo?" Malcolm asked

The question puzzled Toth for a moment, before saying, "There is a chamber pot under the cot. You can use that."

"Nothing but luxury accommodations," Malcolm muttered.

"Now, I will leave you to familiarise yourself with the laboratory and begin work." Toth turned to leave, and after glaring at Malcolm, Frietag followed him out the door. The guard shut the door behind him and took a seat next to the door.

Malcolm turned to Schottky. "You are a physicist?"

"Jawohl, I work at Siemens."

"What do you do there?"

"I most recently developed what you call a screen grid vacuum tube. Prior to Siemens, I developed an equation for determining the interaction energy between a point and a flat surface." Malcolm groaned inwardly. Here was an expert in the physics of electricity and whom obviously had some practical experience if he had built a specialised vacuum tube. It was going to be very difficult to fool him. "What is your background?" Schottky asked.

"I'm an engineer by training," Malcolm said. Schottky sighed; Malcolm was used to this reaction from scientists who typically looked down on the practical application of their vaunted theories. "I have some familiarity with current theories of electromagnetic radiation. I've worked with Ernest Rutherford." Malcolm figured there would be no problem as Frietag knew Rutherford was aboard the *Daedalus* on their mission to Russia. "Have you ever met him?"

"Nein, I have not had the opportunity. But you say you know something about his work?"

"I can't say that I follow it completely, but I have a basic under-standing."

"That is good. Perhaps we will work together."

"If I may ask, where are we?"

"You do not know? We are at the University of Leipzig."

"Thank you. Now, should we look around this laboratory and see what we have?"

# CHAPTER FOURTEEN

$S$axon sat at the controls of the airship, wondering how he had got himself in such a mess. He had supervised the flights aboard the *Daedalus*, but he usually wasn't both piloting and navigating at the same time. It was already late afternoon when their stolen airship lifted off and he hoped he could at least reach the coast of England before night fall. He reasoned he might navigate by matching the city lights to his map, but he was afraid he might get hopelessly lost flying over the Irish Sea at night. It didn't help that the damn gauges were in German. Although he spoke German, he was rusty, and it took him a while to become comfortable with the readings.

Joan entered the cockpit and handed Saxon a mug. "I scoured the galley, but there was no tea, just coffee."

"That's fine. I don't detest coffee like Malcolm," he said before taking a sip. He had a mouthful of coffee grounds, which he spit back into the cup. "Although this is vile," he said, setting the mug down.

"I'm not known for my domestic skills. It was all I could do to manage that," she said.

"Obviously," Saxon quipped. They were silent for a moment before he said, "How are you holding up?"

"I'm fine," Joan said. "This is the first solid piece of information we have about Malcolm's whereabouts. I only hope we can reach him in time. How much longer until we get to London?"

"This ship is not as powerful as the Cunard airship. I don't think we'll arrive until tomorrow morning. As awful as that coffee is, I'm going to need it if we are to reach London."

"Can't O'Hallarhan take over for a while?"

"I don't think so. From what I remember from his file, he has had very little flight experience. He knows how an airship works, but I fear he doesn't have the foggiest idea of how to pilot one."

"Is there anything I can do?"

"Help keep me awake. You could monitor the radio for any communication. I hope that the previous occupants of our airship have not secured another ship to pursue us."

"That's unlikely, isn't it?" Joan asked. "How could they obtain an airship in such a short time?"

"That's probably true, but I've learned not to underestimate the ability of agents. What would you do in such a circumstance?"

"I would move heaven and earth to pursue." She thought for a moment. "Chartering an airship might be out of the question, but what about an aeroplane?"

"They are rare. I don't remember if I saw any at the Aerodrome. That could present a problem."

"How so?"

"Aeroplanes can fly nearly two to three times as fast as our little ship. And they are much more manoeuvrable. They could fly circles around us. And worse, they could fire on us from the aeroplane and we wouldn't be able to stop them. And given the flammable nature of hydrogen, one bullet might be enough to blow us out of the sky."

"Let's hope the Germans aren't as capable as you and I," Joan said. Charles watched as she picked up the headset and scanned for any transmissions. "I should check in with Mycroft and apprise him of our situation," she said.

As Charles concentrated on keeping the airship on course, he listened as Joan spent several minutes before she reached the Secret

Service and connected with Mycroft Holmes. Before she started to speak, she flicked on of the switches. "I just wanted to let you know we picked up our friend before he could leave with our other friends. We borrowed their conveyance and are returning to London even now. When we'd arrive, we like to plan our new honeymoon destination."

There was silence for a moment before Saxon heard Mycroft respond. "Excellent. When will you arrive?"

"We should arrive at our usual location around 7:00 AM."

"Excellent. I'll arrange for a car to pick you up and we can discuss your plans."

They reached the coast of Wales just as darkness fell. Saxon had done a reasonable job of navigating over the open sea, but they were further north than Saxon had intended, arriving over Holyhead as opposed to his intended target of Aberrfraw. Saxon readjusted their course, and he gave a sigh of relief that they would have the cover of darkness for most of the trip. It would be hard for any aeroplane to find them, especially since they hadn't taken the most direct route.

Eventually, Joan fell asleep in the copilot's chair as Saxon struggled to remain awake, despite drinking several mugs of the awful swill that Joan had called coffee. His eyes were bleary from checking the compass, the map, and whatever he could see from the viewscreen of the cockpit. If he ever served aboard an airship again, he would definitely have a newfound respect for the work of the navigators and helmsmen.

As the darkness lifted in the anticipation of a new day, Saxon could make out the skyline of London in the distance. Although he had watched his crew perform landings regularly, it was quite another thing to do it himself. He struggled to get the airship down; on his first approach, he was still several hundred feet above the landing field. He steered the airship in a tight circle and made another approach. This time, he was closer, about forty feet above the airfield. Circling one more time, he brought the airship down quicker when he realised he might crash the airship into the ground. He pulled back on the controls. The airship levelled out and hit the ground with a slight bump. Saxon thought back to words from his time at the Air Service Academy; any landing you can walk away from is a good landing. Maybe that was true, but it was too close for his taste. Once the ground crew secured the airship, they left the ship and found Mycroft himself waiting by a large car.

"I see you were successful," he said, as O'Hallarhan exited the airship. "Come, you can tell me about your trip on our way back." They piled into the car and made the trip back to London. Joan related her escape from the German agents at the Savoy, their escape from the agents in London, the capture of the German airship and rescue of O'Hallarhan. During this, Saxon fell asleep, exhaustion overcoming him from the overnight flight.

Saxon woke up when they arrived at the Charing Cross station. The quartet made their way down to the secret platform that housed the train that went directly to Secret Service headquarters.

"I did not know this even existed," O'Hallarhan said.

"It does not," Mycroft warned. "The only reason I allowed you to join us is that it's too dangerous for you to travel alone. Any slip about the existence of this train would be…unfortunate."

O'Hallarhan took his meaning and remained silent throughout the trip. When they arrived at the Secret Service, Mycroft showed them to a conference room with a large pot of tea and plates of scones. After they ate their breakfast, they were led to individual quarters where they could shower and refresh themselves. Two hours later, they returned to the conference room where Mycroft brought Saxon and Malcolm after he blackmailed them out of the Air Service.

Mycroft took his place at the head of the table. "Alright, let's begin. Based on your findings, we believe Malcolm is being held in Colditz Castle." He laid out a map on the table. "We are here," he said, pointing to London, "and Malcolm is here," pointing to Colditz.

"Can't we just take the airship we have?" O'Hallarhan said.

"No," Charles said. "The Germans know by now that we have their airship. They will expect us. In fact, they might have already moved Malcolm to another location."

"I concur," Mycroft said. "Given your brush with German agents, I fear we can't risk more conventional means of transport into Germany. Given the level of interest in your activities to date, they would apprehend you as soon as you arrived in Germany. We need to sneak the two of you in…"

"Don't you mean the three of us?" O'Hallarhan said.

"No, this will be a Secret Service mission. I will not risk you in this endeavour," Mycroft said.

"Meaning no disrespect, but you'll have to clap me in irons to prevent me from going," O'Hallarhan said. "While it's no secret that I didn't get along with the commodore, he protected me when I was grievously injured on Mars. I owe the commodore, and unless you do clap me in irons, I'll follow on my own!"

Mycroft regarded O'Hallarhan for a moment before acquiescing. "Very well, you are part of the mission…for now."

After debating several approaches, Mycroft decided special crates would smuggle the trio into Germany. Upon arrival, they would find and retrieve Malcolm. They would then use the same crates to smuggle themselves to Geneva. Mycroft noticed Joan wince when he said Geneva. "Is there a problem, Miss de St Leger?"

"No, sir. None at all," she said without enthusiasm.

"Besides the actual rescue of Malcolm, you will need to travel from Colditz to Leipzig. I know that Joan and Charles cannot drive. What about you, Mr O'Hallarhan?"

"Aye, I can drive," O'Hallarhan said. "I often drove into town for supplies for the lighthouse."

"Excellent, that settles that problem. Why don't the three of you get some rest and we'll reconvene tomorrow? I have several details to iron out before we begin our mission." Mycroft rose and swept out of the room.

Charles turned to Joan. "Why did you make that face when Mycroft mentioned Geneva?"

"There's nothing wrong with Geneva. It's just that my mother lives in Geneva."

"Are you glad you might get the chance to see her?"

"No. You obviously have never met my mother."

# CHAPTER FIFTEEN

Malcolm sketched out the design for his prototype electric motor. Instead of the usual rotor and armature containing windings and magnets, the design called for the use of ceramic covered aluminum on the rotors connected to the electric current. The circuit that controlled the power stopped the voltage on each pole of the rotor, allowing the technology he had learned from the Martian ship to turn the rotor before the next pole of rotor received power. Hidden within the control circuitry, Malcolm had placed an ultrasonic transducer connected to a triode and several amplifiers, matching the construction of one of the Martian weapons. When the engine was powered, Malcolm could flip a switch and the engine would emit a powerful ultrasonic wave that would kill any organic life.

Schottky stared at Malcolm's design. "I don't understand how this will work. How can the capacitance make the rotors move? I am considered an expert in the field and I know of no reason that this will work. Also, what is this transducer doing? It seems to require a great deal of power."

*Damn,* Malcolm thought, *he's on to me.* "The secret is in the ceramic used to cover the aluminum. This allows the capacitance to provide limited force, pushing the motor. While it might take more energy to charge the motor, it is more lightweight than using heavy magnets and iron rotors."

"True, but that does not explain the transducer."

"The transducer is there to regulate the oscillations of the motor."

Schottky thought for a minute. "That is possible." Malcolm mentally gave a sigh of relief. "This is farfetched. Are you sure this will work?"

"I'm absolutely sure this will work the way I designed it," Malcolm said.

"Very well. I will see about the fabrication of the rotors. It may take a week or more to build them."

"I'm in no hurry," Malcolm said.

"Why?"

"If you hadn't guessed, I am a prisoner here," Malcolm said, nodding towards the guard. "Once I deliver this motor, my usefulness ends."

"Oh," Schottky said. "Why are you a prisoner, and why are you helping us?"

"As for why I'm a prisoner, you'll have to take that up with Herren Toth and Frietag. Why am I helping? Let's say that I've lost too much and leave it at that."

"It is a shame, Malcolm. Your grasp of science is very strong for an engineer. You could do great things."

"You don't know the half of it," Malcolm muttered.

"What was that?"

"Nothing. Thank you for the compliment."

Before Schottky left for the day, they tore down the components of a small electric motor, removing the rotors and magnets. When Schottky left, Malcolm's concern was making sure that the Germans couldn't apply this basic technology to build a gravitational emitter. There was nothing he could do about the knowledge Schottky had about the design, but he had to make sure that when he escaped, the device would not survive and any notes destroyed in the process. After dinner, Malcolm laid on his cot, turning the problem over in his mind. Schottky took detailed notes in a laboratory notebook. He would need to make sure he had those notes when the engine fired up.

During the week it took for the fabrication of the rotors, Malcolm built the rest of the circuitry for the motor. Schottky watched, but said little as Malcolm worked. Every day, he inspected Malcolm's work to make sure that it matched Malcolm's design.

When the rotors arrived, Malcolm installed them in the motor. After double checking his work and the design, he called Schottky over to the bench. "Are you ready?" he asked as he donned his safety glasses. Although he was certain nothing bad would happen, one could never be too careful.

Schottky donned his safety glasses and nodded. Malcolm plugged the electric motor into the power source and applied power. Nothing happened.

"It isn't working," Schottky said.

"Hold on, let me increase the voltage." Malcolm slowly applied more voltage. At first, there was a little rocking as the rotors tried to turn. As he increased the voltage, Malcolm heard a faint whirring as the rotors spun. To Malcolm's surprise, he had actually invented this previously fictitious motor. As Malcolm increased the voltage, it turned faster and faster.

"Do you need to turn on the oscillator dampener?" Schottky asked, reaching for the switch to the ultrasonic transducer assembly.

"No," Malcolm said, abruptly. "The need for the dampener is directly related to the size of the rotor. At this size, the oscillation is minimal. But as the size of the rotors increases, so does the need for the oscillation dampener."

"That makes sense," Schottky said. Malcolm breathed a silent sigh of relief. Malcolm turned off the power to the motor, and it gradually came to a stop. "Now that we've proven it works, do you think we can talk Toth and Frietag into building a more suitably sized prototype?"

"Yes, I would very much like to see this work on a larger, more practical scale. The voltage needed is much higher than a normal motor, but as you said, the motor is much lighter. There may be advantages worth exploring. I will talk to Toth and arrange for a large motor and new rotors."

"When you talk to them, please ask that we conduct the demonstration in an area with protective glass. In some of our first tests, the rotors had a tendency to fly off the motor. I would hate for there to be any casualties as the result of our test."

"I will make sure of it," Schottky said. "This is remarkable, Malcolm. I would not have believed it if I hadn't seen it with my own eyes. This development has the potential to usher in a new age of progress by using capacitance instead of magnetism to propel objects."

*You have no idea*, Malcolm thought to himself.

# CHAPTER SIXTEEN

Joan's hope of leaving vanished when she was told it would take a week to construct the special containers that would carry the three of them to Colditz. After consultation with a physician in the employ of the Secret Service, Joan, Saxon, and O'Hallarhan would be sedated when placed inside the containers to prevent them from making noise that might draw unwanted attention. The biggest concern was making sure they would have enough air. While supplying small oxygen tanks was not an issue, the accumulation of carbon dioxide in the container could suffocate them. O'Hallarhan volunteered to work on this problem with Percy Griffiths, the Service's chemistry expert, and Quentin Boothroyd, the resident fabrication expert. Putting their heads together, they thought that a layer of activated carbon could absorb the carbon dioxide for the duration of their trips.

While they waited, Joan and Saxon plotted what would happen when they arrived in Colditz. Leafing through the intelligence, Saxon said, "The report states that the castle is currently used as a mental asylum. I guess that's fitting, because we have to be crazy to go there."

Joan chuckled. "Charles, please focus."

"I am. It's just this is a daunting task. First, we have to get inside.

Then we have to find Malcolm and somehow spirit him out without alerting the guards. Then we have to travel to Leipzig and hope that we evade pursuit."

"I agree. Let's break this down into stages, just like Malcolm would. What's the easiest way to get into an asylum?"

"I supposed bringing someone to be committed wouldn't be out of the question."

"Good. Since we both speak German, we could use Peter as the potential inmate."

"There is something to that," he said. "Do you think he'll go for that?"

"I fear he has no choice," Joan said. "He won't be of any use to us until we leave."

"Point taken," Saxon said. "How do we arrange for Peter's committal?"

"Looking through these reports, I think we will need a referral from a doctor. I believe there might be a candidate in Colditz; one Doctor Helmet Schmidt."

"Alright, so we're in. How do we find Malcolm?"

"We can try to get a tour of the facility out of concern for our dear brother Peter."

"Brother? Aren't you pushing our luck?"

Joan glared at Saxon, who put his hands up in surrender. "Fine. We commit our dear brother Peter. How will we find Malcolm?"

"My guess is there is a guard stationed outside of his cell while the regular inmates would just be locked away."

"Seems reasonable. How do we free him? We can't very well just pull guns and start firing. There are too many innocent bystanders."

"True," Joan said. "That's where I'm having problems."

"Is there anyway that O'Hallarhan could work from the inside?"

"That's an idea. He could rig that mechanical arm of his with any number of devices. We would need to create a diversion that would give Peter a chance to get Malcolm. Ideally, something that might cause the inmates to be evacuated."

"Perhaps a fire in the kitchen?" Saxon said. He laid out the map of the castle. "The kitchen is here," he pointed. "It's well away from the cells containing the inmates. We need someone to infiltrate the kitchen and start the fire." He looked pointedly at Joan. "Given your aptitude for cooking, do you think you can pull that off?"

"Malcolm was right," Joan said. "You're not half as funny as you think you are."

"Point taken," Saxon said. "I could try to infiltrate as a new orderly. That way, I could spirit O'Hallarhan and Malcolm away in the confusion."

"That might just work. Is there any way we can prepare for this?"

"Can you learn to cook in a week?" Joan's glare caused Saxon to throw his hands up. "Truthfully, I don't know. I think we're going to have to make this up as we go."

"That doesn't instil much confidence in our success."

"I know. But truthfully, how many times do our missions go according to plan? Remember Vienna?"

"I do," Joan said. "I wish Malcolm were here; he's so much better at thinking on his feet than I am."

"We'll find him, Joan. Before you know it, we'll be back in England and have that long promised wedding." He reached over and squeezed Joan's hand.

"Thank you, Charles," she whispered. She took a deep breath to regain her composure and said, "Shall we break the news to Peter that he's our poor demented brother?"

Joan and Saxon were both surprised when O'Hallarhan embraced the idea readily. "The English already think most of us Irishmen are mad; now, I'm simply playing the part."

"I honestly thought the idea might offend you," Joan said.

"Not at all. It's kind of exciting being the 'man on the inside'."

"Do you have any special abilities in your mechanical arm?" Saxon said.

"Funny you should ask," O'Hallarhan said. "I've been working with Quentin in fabrication and we've added a few new capabilities. We've added a one shot revolver, a lock pick, a small flamethrower, and a flat steel bar useful for opening doors barred from the outside. He's also developed this sleeve and glove that I can wear over the arm, so it looks at first glance like a real arm. He's been teaching me how to pick locks. It's fascinating, and I seem to have a real knack for it."

"What is it with engineers and their fascination with locks?" Joan said. "It was the one thing that Malcolm was good at on our mission."

"It's just another mechanical puzzle," O'Hallarhan said. "I don't know about the commodore, but I enjoy solving mechanical puzzles."

The trio continued to collect gadgets and equipment, including a small amount of magnesium for Joan to start the kitchen fire. When dropped into heated water, it produced hydrogen gas which was very flammable. Before Saxon could make another joke about Joan's lack of cooking skills, she shot him a withering glance that killed the joke immediately. They reviewed the few details of their plan. If everything went according to plan, within two days of arriving, they would free Malcolm and be on their way to Leipzig and eventually home.

The night before the mission, Joan lay in bed, but her mind couldn't stop turning over the problems with their plan. Would they be able to get Peter into the asylum? Would Charles be able to find Malcolm? What if Malcolm wasn't even there? No matter how she tried to get to sleep, her mind returned to the mission; a mission with highly personal stakes. After an hour of frustration, she hastily dressed and went to the conference room to review the intelligence one last time. A knock on the door startled her. "You still awake? Shouldn't you be sleeping?" Charles said, entering the conference room.

"I tried, but to no avail. Besides, we're going to get plenty of sleep tomorrow."

"It's not the same, and you know it. What's bothering you?"

"I...don't know. It's a mix of apprehension, anticipation, and fear. What if the Germans got the information from him and he's already dead? I don't know if I can bear losing him again." She remembered the anguish of seeing Malcolm's lifeless body on the floor of the airship. She wasn't sure if she could bear that pain again. Tears welled in her eyes.

"Malcolm is a resourceful man. I'm sure he's already concocted some sort of harebrained scheme to escape." Joan nodded. "Besides, Frietag would love nothing more to boast to the world that he had killed Malcolm. He knows that would devastate you as well. Two birds with one stone, as they stay. I think that if Malcolm was dead, we would know." Joan realised the truth in Saxon's words and felt her heart lighten a tiny bit.

"You have nothing to worry about. Besides, two of the Secret Service's best agents are on the case; how can we not succeed?"

Joan laughed. "Yes, but what about Peter? He's done nothing like this before. He might seize up in panic at the most inopportune time."

"I think our young engineer is more resourceful than you think. Remember when the rift in space nearly pulled us in? He kept a cool head and saved us all from a nasty demise."

"True," Joan said. Saxon's description of O'Hallarhan made Joan instantly think of Malcolm. "God, I miss Malcolm," she blurted. Images of Malcolm flooded into her mind; the times they spent together when their schedules allowed, the fights they had, and when she proposed to him. Her heart ached, and she couldn't stop the flood of tears from escaping before she found herself sobbing.

Charles moved to Joan and hugged her tight. While she appreciated the gesture, it only made her wish that it was Malcolm holding her. She struggled to regain her composure, but the tears kept coming. When she had no more tears, she pulled away. "Damn him! I always kept tight control over my emotions. Now I'm just a teary-eyed emotional woman, all because of him. I didn't want to love him, but somehow I find myself at a place that I can't live without him."

"I know," Saxon said.

She wiped her eyes with the sleeve of her blouse. "I don't know about you, but I could use a very stiff drink."

"Is that wise, considering we're going to be sedated tomorrow?"

"To hell about tomorrow. I need something to calm my nerves tonight."

"Very well. I've been told there's a secret liquor cabinet in one of the storerooms."

"What are we waiting for?" she said.

# CHAPTER SEVENTEEN

Malcolm was both surprised and relieved when Schottky told him that Toth and Frietag had agreed to allow Malcolm to construct a larger prototype. "They didn't like the idea, but I was most insistent. We need to see how this new motor could work on a practical scale. The motor will arrive later today and they have already ordered the new rotors. They should arrive within the week."

"Thank you, Walter," Malcolm said. "I look forward to the demonstration, but once it's done, my usefulness ends."

"Do you mean they will let you go?"

"No, it means they will kill me."

"That's outrageous! Why would they kill you?"

"Let's just say that Herr Frietag and I have been on opposite sides over the years. Did you ever wonder why he wears an eye patch? I cost him the use of his eye and his hand. And I've humiliated him on more than one occasion. I only hope that Toth intervenes and my demise won't be long and painful."

"I...don't know what to say."

"That's alright. There isn't much that to say."

Malcolm became lost in his thoughts. He hoped that by using the ultrasonic weapons he had embedded in the design that he could escape. But he faced the realisation that it might not work or he would fail in his attempt. The grim thought of that made Malcolm break the uncomfortable silence between the two men. "If we are successful and Freitag kills me, would you send a telegram to Joan St. Leger at The Savoy Hotel in London? Tell her I'm sorry and that I love her."

"Who is she?"

"My fiancé. My 'friend' Frietag abducted me on the eve of our wedding."

"That is horrible!" After a pause, he said, "It would be my honour."

Malcolm looked at Schottky. Over the weeks they had worked together, he felt a kinship with the man. It reminded him of his work with Ernest Rutherford on the *Icarus*. He knew in that moment he couldn't jeopardise this man in his escape attempt. "Walter, promise me one thing; do not attend the demonstration.

"Why? I want to be there to see the fruits of our labour!"

"No, if something were to go wrong, I don't want you risking your life. Develop a sudden sickness, a dead relative. Anything to keep you away from the demonstration."

The two men sat in silence as a squad of soldiers wheeled the motor in on a dolly. It was nearly ten feet long and four feet high. They spent the rest of the day carefully removing the outer casing. They spent the next two days removing the rotors, the armature, and a large part of the internal components. Malcolm got to work on first designing a much larger and powerful motor. Over the next three days, they built and installed the components of Malcolm's design in the motor's frame. However, in the darkness of night, Malcolm added another component hidden away deep inside the guts of the motor; a feedback loop that would redirect the ultrasonic transducer output back into the engine itself. In the pitch black darkness of his cell, he placed a button hidden under the switch for the 'oscillation damper'. Once the ultrasonic transducer did its damage, he would trigger the feedback loop. If his mental calculations were correct, he would have thirty seconds to make his escape. He just prayed to God that it would work.

Having completed all the work they could until the rotors arrived, both men set sullenly until Malcolm persuaded Schottky to explain his equation for calculating the interaction energy between a point and a flat surface. "Why would you want to know that now, given your circumstance?" Schottky asked.

"The transfer of knowledge is valuable. Besides, I can't sit here waiting in gloom. I need to do something useful." Malcolm's familiarity with Rutherford's research and his limited knowledge of quantum mechanics helped, but it was still a struggle. Fortunately, Schottky was an able and patient teacher and their discussions did much to dismiss the feeling of gloom that had settled over the two men.

However, the next day, the rotors arrived. Given their size, it took both men to lift them. They needed the guards' assistance to hold the rotors in place so Malcolm could attach them to the motor. It was late in the day before they completed the work. That night, Malcolm took an empty laboratory notebook and, in the oscilloscope's light, wrote a letter to Schottky on the first page of the notebook:

*Walter,*

*Please forgive me for what I've done. I mean no ill to you and would be pleased to call you my friend. I've replaced your laboratory notebook with this, but I can't let this technology fall into the hands of the likes of Toth and Frietag where I feel they would use it for ill. Truthfully, I never thought that it would work in the first place. If you have any other notes, please destroy them and try to forget anything you've seen. I can't explain more, but know that I hold you in highest regard.*

*Yours,*

*Malcolm Robertson*

Malcolm only hoped that the letter would be legible in the light of day.

The next morning, Schottky arrived, and they got to work to assemble the casing back on the motor. They finished mid afternoon.

"I have to report that we've completed work. They will schedule the demonstration for tomorrow," Schottky announced glumly.

"I know."

"I should gather my things and make my report," Schottky rose.

"Let me get your notebook." Malcolm moved to the laboratory bench, pulled out the notebook he had written last night, and quietly pushed Schottky's actual notebook under a pile of schematics. "Here you are."

"It's been an honour to work with you. I am sad that it must come to an end."

"Me too." Schottky shook his hand and left the room. Malcolm looked down and saw that Schottky had left his valise tucked under the laboratory bench. He was about to call out to Schottky when he realised that Schottky always left his valise on the laboratory table. Once the guard left for the day, Malcolm went to the laboratory bench and retrieved the valise. Opening it, he was surprised to find a bottle of apple schnapps and a letter.:

*Malcolm,*

*I wish you the best of luck tomorrow, but I believe you intend to make your own luck. I've suspected for some time that your so-called 'oscillation dampener' is something much more dangerous; I wasn't certain until this week when you begged me not to attend the demonstration. After reviewing my notes that night, I still don't know exactly what it will do, but I am certain that it will be destructive. I have taken your warning to heart and even now, I feel myself coming down with a contagious fever. I have not told Toth or Frietag about this component because I think they do you a grave injustice.*

*Please accept this bottle of apple schnapps hoping it can provide some comfort and courage for your trials ahead. I hope that some day, we will meet again.*

*Yours,*

*Walter Schottky*

Malcolm folded the letter and put it in the breast pocket of his coat. He looked at the bottle of schnapps and said, "It isn't whiskey, but I guess it will have to do." He took a long pull from the bottle and could barely taste the apple as the burning sensation of the strong liquor made him sputter. "Damn," he said to himself. "The Germans sure know how to make strong liquor. Cheers, Walter," he said, taking a much smaller sip from the bottle.

# CHAPTER EIGHTEEN

When Joan awoke, she found herself in pitch black darkness with a mask over her face. *Where am I?* she thought. *Am I in a coffin?* Reaching out, her arms only travelled a short distance before she felt wood. She must be in a crate. Then she remembered she was in the packing crate after the Secret Service physician sedated her. Instantly, she relaxed and lay still, listening for any signs of activity. After a minute, she opened the latch inside the crate and slowly and carefully raised the lid. She couldn't see much in the darkens. Holding her breath, she silently lifted the lid the rest of the way and slowly sat up. At first, she felt the room spinning. Taking deep, slow breaths, the dizziness faded. In the dim light, she saw several crates near her. *Looks like we've made it to the warehouse,* she thought. She removed her mask and gathered her backpack with her gear and clothes. As she did so, she heard movement behind her. Fearing someone had caught her already, she whirled around with her derringer in hand to find Charles struggling to get out of his crate. Joan helped Saxon up and together, they gathered his equipment. Joan kept watch for anyone coming while Saxon found O'Hallarhan's crate. A few minutes later, O'Hallarhan emerged from his crate. Silently, they gathered their things and looked around the warehouse. It was mostly empty, with a few crates of various sizes breaking the emptiness of the room. There was a door to at the far end of the warehouse and at the opposite end was a large garage door to let the delivery trucks in. Joan pointed to the door at the far end and crept silently towards the door. They needed to get out of here unseen. She held her breath until she got to the door; listening carefully, she heard nothing. She motioned to Saxon and O'Hallarhan to join her. Silently, they crept to the door. When Saxon and O'Hallarhan joined her, Joan slowly cracked the door open. Opposite the door was an office with a bored-looking clerk writing in a ledger. To her left, there was a hallway that ended in another door, probably leading to the front of the warehouse, given the location of the garage door. *I could take out the guard or we could try to sneak past.* She watched him for a minute and he seemed to be engrossed in his work, not looking up. She indicated to Saxon and O'Hallarhan to stay low and, with catlike grace, crawled silently to the door to her left. The clerk heard nothing as Joan slowly turned the knob on the door. If she could get Saxon and O'Hallarhan out undetected, they would be safe. With her hand still on the knob, she motioned for Saxon and O'Hallarhan to join her.

They got halfway when a loud horn from a motor vehicle sounded, jolting the clerk from his work. He stood up and turned to see Joan, Saxon, and O'Hallarhan crouched in the hallway. "Was ist das? Wer bist du? Was machst du hier?"

"Shite," Joan muttered. "Run," she yelled to Saxon and O'Hallarhan. The door opened into an alley. On instinct, she turned to the right and started running. Saxon and O'Hallarhan were soon on her tail. The alley opened into a street with rows of warehouse as far as she could see. On her right, she saw the truck that had awoken the clerk. She heard shouting and knew that the clerk was in hot pursuit. Knowing she needed to lose their pursuit, she shouted in German, "Help! There's a madman chasing us!". The trio ran around the truck and the driver exited and turned to look at the red-faced clerk, who was yelling for them to stop. The truck driver intercepted the clerk, giving the trio time to distance themselves. A few buildings down, they found an alleyway and ducked into catch their breath. Although relieved they had escaped for now, she had to consider how to get out of here.

"Of all the rotten luck," Charles said, as he caught his breath. "We were so close to making it out without drawing attention."

Joan pulled out a small map of Colditz from her backpack. "If we continue a few blocks further, we can double back and make our way into town. Come on, follow me," she said.

She looked down the alley. She couldn't see the clerk, but there was considerable yelling coming from the other side of the truck. "This way, walk normally and try not to draw attention to yourselves." They followed the street to the end and took a left. A little further down, the street turned back the way they came, and they followed that until they reached the bridge over the Zwickau Mulde river. They crossed the bridge and found themselves in Colditz proper. Half-timbered houses lined the street.

"I forgot how quaint this region was. It's been a long time since I've been to Saxony." O'Hallarhan looked at him quizzically. "My family is originally from Saxony; we're distantly related to the King. My family left Saxony when I was very young to live in England. Hence, my surname."

"Hush," Joan hissed. "No more English. From now on, Charles and I can only speak in German. Peter, I'm afraid you'll have to remain quiet until we can find a safe place. Understood?" O'Hallarhan and Saxon nodded. Joan consulted her map one more time, and they made their way into Colditz. The centre of town was busy; butcher shops, grocers, and various other shops lined the town centre, offering vegetables, chores, and smoked sausage. The smell of fresh bread made Joan's stomach rumble. She looked up and saw Colditz Castle, looming on a hill overlooking the city. She thought, *Hang on Malcolm. We're here to rescue you.* They continued on silently, avoiding the gazes of the townspeople going about their business, turning down several streets until they found the offices of Dr Helmut Schmidt.

Saxon opened the door, ringing a bell that startled the trio for a moment. An elderly gentleman came from the back. "What can I do for you?" he asked.

Responding German, Saxon replied, "Are you Herr Docktor Schmidt?"

"Jawohl."

"We come about our brother, Peter, who we fear is mad and a danger to himself and to others. We were told that you can refer him to the asylum here, where he might find some peace."

"I can examine him, but I'm not sure how much peace he will find there."

"What do you mean?"

"Most people who enter never leave the gates again. But come, let me examine him." The doctor led them past a small living room and down a hallway to his examination room. "Please sit here," the doctor said.

Joan guided O'Hallarhan to the table and had him sit. As the doctor watched, Joan turned and said, "He's become mute and doesn't respond to verbal instruction. We have to lead him through everything."

"I see," the doctor said.

"Do you think there's any hope for him? Could they treat him at the asylum?"

The doctor considered for a moment. "Possibly. There was one patient removed from the asylum last week. I was at the asylum to consult with their physician when I saw them take someone away. He was blindfolded and restrained, but it was unusual to see someone leave. He must have been there a while because his hair was white as snow. I thought it unusual, so I asked the physician at the asylum. He told me he was a special patient and was being taken to Leipzig for further treatment."

"Leipzig, you say?" Joan kept her face steady, but she was sure that the man the doctor described was Malcolm.

"Yes. The university there is first rate and they may have taken him to be examined by the doctors there. Perhaps they have discovered some new treatment. Now, let me examine your brother."

"On second thought, perhaps we should go to Leipzig if there's a chance for some cure for our brother's illness. Thank you. I'm sorry if we have wasted your time."

"I wish you luck with your brother. It breaks my heart to see the patients at the asylum. I wouldn't wish that on my worst enemy."

"Thank you, Herr Docktor. Come along, Peter, we're leaving the nice doctor," Saxon said, steering Peter out the door.

They walked in silence for several blocks before they found a desert alley way. Once safely out of view and out of earshot, Joan explained their exchange with the doctor to O'Hallarhan. When she was finished, she said, "I'm certain he was talking about Malcolm. Everything fits. We need to get to Leipzig."

"Finding him in Leipzig is going to be like finding a needle in a haystack," Saxon said.

"That's why we need to get there as soon as possible. The car we were going to use is in a barn in a deserted farmhouse just outside of the city."

"Then we better get stepping," Saxon said.

As the trio hiked towards the farmhouse, Joan still felt sluggish and her leg muscles were on the verge of cramping, her body still feeling the aftereffects of lying motionless for the trip to Colditz. They hiked for three miles before arriving at the farmhouse as the sun kissed the horizon. Joan had never been so glad as when they found the car with the keys inside.

"Well, at least that much has gone according to plan," Saxon said.

"If it's all the same to you, I'd like to wait until tomorrow to drive to Leipzig," O'Hallarhan said. "From what I've been told, there are several twisty roads through the mountains and I'd rather not attempt that at night."

"That's true," Saxon added. "The drive will not be easy, even in the daylight."

"Very well," Joan said. She didn't want to wait another night to find Malcolm, but her body was telling her she needed to rest.

Saxon saw the frustration on her face. "I know you want to find Malcolm, but we need to get there in one piece," Saxon said. "We won't do him any good if we drive off a mountain."

"You're right. It's just so exasperating to be so close, but have to wait."

"I know. Let's bed down here for the night. I'll look around. With any luck, someone had the foresight to leave dome food," Saxon said. After a brief search, they found a crate hidden beneath a pile of hay containing sausage, cheese, and a bottle of apple schnapps. They devoured the cheese and sausage quickly, after their stomachs realised it had been many hours since they ate. Saxon opened the bottle of schnapps, handing it first to Joan. She took a large drink and passed it back to Saxon. He took a much smaller sip before handing it to O'Hallarhan. "Careful, schnapps is a potent drink. I would start slowly if I were you," he said as he handed over the bottle.

"I drink Irish whisky. It can't be any stronger than that," O'Hallarhan said before taking a large pull. Instantly, he was coughing and sputtering. It took a few moments to catch his breath before he said, "The Germans sure know how to make strong liquor."

# CHAPTER NINETEEN

Malcolm awoke the next morning with a splitting headache. He looked regretfully at the empty bottle of schnapps and thought *I definitely should not have drank the entire bottle.* He dressed and paced the laboratory. When the guard arrived, he looked at the plate; a hard-boiled egg, sliced weisswurst, a hard seeded roll, sliced Gouda and a large mug of black coffee and he felt nauseous. Fighting back the nausea, he finished the meal slowly. He stared at the mug of coffee. He detested coffee, but since tea was not an option, drank it as quickly as he could, trying to throw it back past his tongue so he could taste as little as possible. His stomach did not appreciate the coffee, but eventually, the nausea passed.

Now that breakfast was over, he had nothing to do until the demonstration later in the afternoon. *I guess they aren't early risers,* he thought. He kept himself occupied by checking and rechecking the motor. He couldn't believe that it actually worked. *I guess some of Rutherford's lessons sunk into my thick skull.* He reviewed his plan in his head and while it was clear what he was going to do doing the demonstration; he did not know what would happen afterwards. If he was lucky, the 'oscillation damper' would incapacitate any observers. He needed to get out of the room before the motor exploded. But then

"

what? He barely knew where he was. If he was going to escape, he would need some kind of weapon; he considered a screwdriver or wrench laying on the lab table, but was not enthusiastic about either option. He picked up one of the sharper screwdrivers, which wasn't very sharp at all. It reminded of one of his Granda's expressions: "You could ride to town bare bummed on that blade." The thought made him chuckle. He smiled, thinking of home, but his thoughts instantly turned to Joan. There was a very good chance that he might not escape and he would never get the chance to live his life with her. He winced. He had been so busy trying to first build the motor, then plan his escape. The work to build the motor and plan an escape had driven Joan from his thoughts.

He saw the small motor prototype pushed aside amongst a pile of papers. The ultrasonic transducer might be useful at close range, but he would need a voltage source. Rummaging through the cabinets, he found a battery roughly the size of his fist. He connected the battery to the motor and bound the battery to the motor with gaffer's tape, turning the transducer away from the battery; it wouldn't do to kill himself while trying to escape an inevitable death. He looked at his handiwork; it wouldn't be useful for more than a couple of shots, but that might be enough to help him escape.

He tidied up the lab to keep busy, gathering any stray papers. His pockets were full between the motor, screwdriver and collection of papers. The door opened and Toth entered. "There's been a change in schedule. We will do the demonstration tonight at 20:00. Apparently, some class is working in the room until 18:00. We will collect you and the motor at 18:30 and go to the demonstration area. That will give you plenty of time to connect the motor and make any checks you need before the demonstration." He paused for a minute before saying, "I'm disappointed in you, Malcolm."

"How so? I've done everything you've asked."

"Yes, that's why I'm disappointed. You were such a challenge to break, but when confronted by your fiancé's infidelity, you collapsed like a house of cards."

"Are you married? Then you would understand."

"Yes, I married and have a son."

"How would you feel if your wife left you and took your son? Wouldn't you feel defeated?"

"No, I would be angry and those responsible would pay."

"Even your wife?"

"Yes."

"That's the difference between you and me; you're a sadistic bastard and I'm not. Besides, what good would anger do me? You will kill me after the demonstration - if it fails, I've outlived my usefulness to you, likewise if I succeed. I'm a realist."

"There's that fire that I've been missing," Toth smiled. "Sadly, you are correct. I would love to keep you to see what other secrets I could wring out of you, but I've put off Frietag for too long and he isn't a patient man."

"On that, we agree,"

Toth chuckled. "I will miss our conversations. I will make you a promise. If the demonstration goes well, I will ensure that your end will be swift and painless. I don't think you'll receive the same from Frietag."

"I guess it better go well. If that's all, I'd like to recheck everything before tonight."

"Good bye, Malcolm Robertson," Toth said as he headed for the door.

The day dragged on as Malcolm waited for the summons for the demonstration. He did anything he could to keep himself busy and avoid thinking about the fate that might await him. He checked, rechecked, and triple checked the motor to ensure that it would function, always keeping one eye on the clock. All the while, torn between wanting to getting it over with and dreading the demonstration.

At 18:30 exactly, the door to the laboratory opened, and two guards came in to wheel the motor out. Another two guards, armed with machine guns, directed Malcolm to follow. He put a hand in his pocket and felt some relief that the transducer and screwdriver were still there. Knowing he could be marching to his death, he put on a brave face and left the laboratory. Malcolm kept careful track of their trip when the entourage came to a stop before a set of large, steel blast doors, controlled by a heavy duty wheel. The doors opened into a large, two story room. As Malcolm entered the room, he took a moment to observe the layout. A large generator was located to the right and to the left was the control panel for the generator and the outlet for connecting the motor. Above the control panel was a glass panel where he saw Toth and Frietag. Toth gave no hint of his emotions, but Frietag was a different story. He was pacing; Malcolm couldn't decide if it was nervousness about the demonstration or excitement that he would finally finish Malcolm. The guards wheeled the motor into the centre of the room, and Malcolm directed them to turn the motor so that the transducer faced the glass. Malcolm soon realised, to his horror, that as he applied voltage, he would stand directly in front of the motor. And worse, the transducer would hit the control panel first, which might cut the power. *The best laid plans*, he thought.

Once the guards positioned the motor, they left, and he heard the thunk as they locked the blast doors from the outside. Malcolm plugged the motor into the panel, assessing his options. Assuming the transducer would melt the glass, he might jump from the top of the motor to the window. However, he would be in the direct path of the transducer's ray. He suddenly remembered his makeshift weapon in his pocket. Although far less powerful than the transducer on the motor, if he aimed it back at the motor, it might interfere with the ultrasonic waves enough to allow him to survive. He prayed his engineering intuition was right.

Malcolm busied himself making sure everything was in place for the demonstration and checked the panels. Although the labels were all in German, his lab experience helped him understand the dials and levers. He found the large knife switch that would turn on the generator and the lever to increase the voltage. He went back to the cabinet and picked up a pair of stiff, large rubber gloves. *No need electrocuting myself before I potentially fry myself with the transducer.*

Toth's voice came over a hidden speaker. "It is time we begin your demonstration." Malcolm nodded, unsure if they could hear him.

With both hands, he flipped the knife switch to power the generator. The generator whirled to life and Malcolm watched the voltage climb until it remained steady for several minutes. "What are you waiting for? Get on with it!" Frietag said over the speaker.

"I'm waiting for the generator voltage to stabilise. You were an engineer. You should know better!" Malcolm yelled, not sure if they could hear him.

"Gentleman, please act like civilised men," Toth said. Malcolm had his answer; there was some kind of microphone in this room.

"I'm going to apply voltage to the motor slowly. Nothing will happen at first, so please be patient," directing the remark to Frietag. Malcolm looked up as he watched Frietag turn in disgust and continue his pacing. Malcolm went to the voltage lever and, as he reached for it, his hand was shaking. He gripped the lever to disguise his nervousness and slowly raised the lever. The gauge above the level saw the corresponding rise in voltage, but the motor was still silent. Malcolm continued to raise the voltage until he heard the engine whirl to life. "It's working," Malcolm said. He continued to raise the voltage until he could push the lever no farther. The whirl of the engine was now audible, even above the hum of the generator. Malcolm walked around the other side of the motor and said, "At this voltage, I'll need to engage the oscillation dampener." He flipped the switch and nothing appeared to happen. *Damn it all to hell. What did I miss?* Several seconds went by before he noticed the glass of the window ripple. He looked over at the door's wheel lock and saw that it, too, was rippling. *Because of the power it's drawing, the beam must have been wider than I thought,* Malcolm thought. He saw sparks flying from the control panel. He looked up and a large hole had opened in the window and saw with horror Toth's face melting away in rivulets of liquid flesh and blood. The sounds of the generator and the small explosions coming from the control panel muffled his screams. Malcolm didn't see Frietag, but if he was going to escape, he needed to do it now.

He reached under the motor and flipped the feedback switch and clambered to the top of the motor and prepared to make the jump.

Nearly losing his balance as the motor wobbled, he took one last look at the control panel and the feedback voltage was growing exponentially. At this rate, it might flow into the power grid itself before the panel exploded. Taking a deep breath, he turned on his small transducer and jumped for all his worth. His hand landed on the outside frame of the window, mercifully missing the molten glass of the observation window. He instantly felt pain everywhere, no doubt an aftereffect from the transducer; his interference field sparing him the same death as Toth. His feet touched the top of the control panel. He could feel his shoes beginning to heat as the panel grew red hot. Pushing off with his legs, he swung himself up and through the hole in the window. He found two more guards in the same state as Toth. He grabbed one of their machine guns and ran for the door. A short flight of stairs descended into the hallway. Two more guards were frantically trying to open the blast door, but couldn't turn it because the mechanism was melted. He fired on them, killing them quickly. Scanning the area, he found Frietag unconscious at the bottom of the stairs; he apparently made it out before feeling the worst effects of the ultrasonic waves. Malcolm slid down the railing of the stairs and ran back down the hallway towards the laboratory. Before he got to the laboratory, there was a tremendous explosion behind Malcolm and it threw him to the ground. Before he could gather himself, he found himself in pitch black darkness.

# CHAPTER TWENTY

oan, Saxon, and O'Hallarhan awoke. O'Hallarhan, suffering from a splitting headache, walked gingerly to avoid jostling his head. "I warned you about the schnapps," Saxon chided.

"I should have listened. What I wouldn't give for an aspirin right now."

They ate the remains of the sausage and cheese from the previous night and loaded the car.

They hid any trace of their visit and got into the vehicle. Saxon sat in front next to O'Hallarhan to act as navigator, as he was the only one who had even been to Saxony. "I'll do my best. There isn't much to go from this map."

The trio set out and the road, not much better than a horse path, was bumpy. On more than one occasion, the car bumped so severally that O'Hallarhan lost control of the wheel. Their speed was agonizing slow as O'Hallarhan did his best to avoid the deeper ruts in the road to avoid getting the car stuck. They passed through several small villages, stopping for a quick lunch before continuing the arduous trek over dirt roads, cow paths, and cobblestone streets. The travel was agonizing slow because of the conditions of the so-called roads.

"This is taking forever," Joan exclaimed in frustration.

"It could be much worse," Saxon offered. "If it had rained recently, it would have taken twice as long as we would fight mud."

"You're right. Let's change the subject. What do we do when we get to Leipzig?"

"I say we start at the medical school at the University for lack of any better place to start. I doubt they will know anything, but perhaps our questioning will attract the attention that we can use to find Malcolm. It worked in Ireland."

"I daresay we probably won't be as lucky this time." Joan said.

They fell silent as they continue to travel over through the German countryside. Joan looked out of the window, thinking that the fields and small villages might be beautiful if her thoughts weren't on trying to find Malcolm. *Wish I knew where he was...if he's even alive.* She swiftly banished that thought from her head and focused on how to find Malcolm. She agreed with Saxon's assessment. They would either find him or their inquiries would certainly draw notice. *If he's even in Leipzig. I pray to God we're not on a wild goose chase and he still isn't stuck in Colditz. I don't know if I could stand another trip like this!*

Gradually, the rural nature of the countryside transitioned to more villages as they drew closer to Leipzig. The city gradually came into view; the spires of Gothic cathedrals reaching to the sky, competing with the smokestacks of the many factories, belching smoke that sometimes obscured the view. Gradually, Joan could make out more distinct details; the distinctive red-tiled roofs of houses, and the domes of churches. As they approached the outskirts of the city, the road was increasingly busy, filled with horse-drawn wagons and the occasional automobile, slowing their transit to a crawl. It was nearly 4:00 in the afternoon before they reached the city proper. Saxon stopped a passerby to get directions to the university. They made their way through the cobblestone streets to the university. As they approached, Joan said, "I think we should find a place to stay and try the university in the morning. We might have better luck."

"Agreed," Saxon said. They drove around the university before finding a gasthaus two blocks away.

"At some point, we are going to need petrol, especially if we intend to travel anywhere else," Peter said.

"Alright. Once we settle in at the gasthaus, you and Charles can find petrol for the car. We'll meet back for dinner at 7:00." Saxon and O'Hallarhan dropped off their backpacks and went out in search of petrol for the car. Joan surveyed her room. It was clean, if not modest. Besides the bed, there was a small secretary's desk and chair and a more comfortable stuffed leather chair. She was dismayed to find that she would have to rely on the communal toilet at the end of the hall. She sank in the chair and dropped asleep, tired from the long day of riding the car.

When she awoke, she was aghast to find it was nearly 7:00. She hurried to change out of her riding clothes and into a simple blouse and skirt. She hurried to the restaurant and made it just in time. About ten minutes later, Saxon and O'Hallarhan entered and joined her. "What took you so long?" she asked in German

"It was no easy feat finding petrol. We drove all around the city before we found it. But the car is fuelled and ready to go," Charles said in German. "Have you ordered?"

"No, I was waiting for you." A waitress came over and took their orders. The only option for dinner was the traditional Abendessen; a selection of breads, sausages, ham, cheese, and pickles. It wasn't Joan's choice, but it would have to do. Joan ordered a lager for O'Hallarhan and a dry Riesling for herself, while Charles ordered a Gewurztraminer. Several parties occupied tables of the restaurant, but the restaurant was not full. She heard a smattering of different languages; the predominant language was German, but she also heard French and English as well. "We can talk here," she said in English. "There's an international clientele here; we shouldn't stick out too much."

The waitress returned with their drinks and platters of meats, cheese, and pickles and a loaf of bread. Although they had a rather heavy lunch on their way to Leipzig, they were grateful for food. Darkness fell outside as they lingered over their food and drinks.

"So, what do we do now?" Joan said.

"I fear we just have to wait. Something is bound to turn up," Saxon said.

There was a loud boom, rattling the windows of the gasthaus. Moments later, the electric lights went out, and the gasthaus fell into darkness.

Simultaneously, the three of them said, "Malcolm!"

The trio lept from their chairs, Saxon threw down money on the table and they rushed out of the restaurant. People were already coming out on the street, trying to find the source of the explosion. Joan could make out the faintest hint of smoke rising back toward the university. They pushed their way through the crowd and jumped into the car. "I think it came from the university! Let's head that way and see if we can find Malcolm!" O'Hallarhan started the car and completed a u-turn to head back towards the university. "Charles, you and I will look for Malcolm."

They made their way to the university, but Joan still couldn't see the source of the smoke, partially because dark was falling and the buildings that lined the streets obscured her view. As they drove down the street, ahead they saw several police cars fly by ahead of them. "Peter, go to the end of the street and take a right. I think the explosion came from there!"

O'Hallarhan sped up as much as he dared without trying to draw attention to them and reached the end of the street and turned right. Three blocks ahead, Joan could see several police cars stopped, blocking off the area. It was mass pandemonium as people streamed away from the university building and into the street. The police attempted to create some semblance of order, but could barely contain the crowd. Joan searched the crowd for any sign of Malcolm, but didn't see him. *I pray the explosion didn't hurt him. How will we get him if he's still in the building?* She pushed those thoughts aside. *Where would Malcolm go if he escaped?* She looked around and saw the spire of a gothic cathedral. *He might go there to hide until things quiet down.* Looking at the scene in front of her, she realised it might not calm down for some time. The first ambulances arrived, and the police began clearing the area.

She leaned forward. "We better get out of here before they notice us."

"Where to?" O'Hallarhan asked.

"Head for that cathedral." Joan pointed to the spire visible over the buildings. "I have a hunch Malcolm might try to hide there."

"Let's hope your hunch is correct," Saxon said.

"I hope so too!"

# CHAPTER TWENTY ONE

Malcolm took a moment to assess his situation. His ears rang, and he felt something wet flowing out of his ears. He touched his fingers to the wetness and then put them to his mouth, tasting blood. His ears hurt and all he could hear was a ringing in his ears. Every muscle in his body hurt, but he could still move. Given the blackness of the hallway, his demonstration had also affected the electrical system of the building. He realised that his feedback device had not only shorted the generator, but had killed the power in the building as well. At least, no one would see him; however, he wouldn't see anyone else. He groped around in the darkness and found the machine gun. With some effort, he pulled himself up and groped around until he found the wall. Slowly, he made his way down the hallway, feeling his way. He almost fell when he reached the opening to the stairs. *These must be the stairs that Frietag pushed me down.* Crouching on all fours, he crept up the stairs and, as he reached the top, he heard a commotion as voices called out in German. Remembering his trip to the lab, he turned left and felt his way down the hall. Ahead of him, he saw a window. It must be near dusk, as there was enough light to act as a beacon.

As he made his way down the hall, he bumped into several people also making their way to the exit. "Verzeihung," he repeated, remembering the cursory bit of German he had picked up. There was a crowd fighting to exit the door; Malcolm pushed his way into the middle of the crowd. Realising he was conspicuously carrying a machine gun, he engaged the safety before sticking it down the leg of his trousers and covering the top with this suit jacket. Malcolm emerged from the building to a chaotic scene. People were yelling in German. He heard sirens in the distance while people checked each other for injuries. He looked around, trying to get his bearings. The building had opened in to a quad surrounded by several buildings. As he was about to decide which way to go, a young man came up to him and said something in German which Malcolm couldn't understand. "Mir geht's gut," he said, telling the man that he was fine and pushed his way past. The man yelled something at Malcolm that he didn't understand, but Malcolm kept walking. He found an alleyway three buildings past the laboratory building and, after taking a quick glance to see if he had escaped notice, he ducked into the alley. The dusky sky provide some illumination, enough that Malcolm could see. Although his ears were still ringing, he realised that his hearing was still intact and breathed a sigh of relief.

After leaving the scene of the explosion, he realised he did not know which way to go. The alley opened to a street and as Malcolm carefully poked his head out. He looked around, trying to determine his next steps. Ahead of him, he made out the spire of a gothic cathedral. *Cathedral*, he thought. *It's probably Catholic. I wonder if they still provide sanctuary.* Worse case, he might appeal to the priest for a place to stay or money to get out of the city. But where could he go if he left? He was a long way from Britain or anywhere else where he could appeal to an embassy. With no better options, he went to the church. Before he could step out, several police vehicles with sirens blaring were coming down the street towards him. He stepped back in the shadows of the alley and waited until they passed. Looking out again, he saw no other vehicles and made his way across the street toward the church.

He took the street that he thought went past the church. Night was truly beginning to fall, and it was getting dark and hard to see. The street, lined with rows of shops and apartments, gave Malcolm the feeling he was walking in a canyon. He followed the street when he heard squealing car brakes behind him. He turned to see the car back up to turn on to the street he was on. *Damn, that was too fast*, he thought. He quickened his pace, and soon found the cathedral, but couldn't find a door. He turned down a side street into a small plaza. Hearing the car getting closer, he broke into a run. Every muscle in his body protested, but he hadn't got this far, only to be caught. Ahead, he saw the large oak door of the cathedral and pushed his body as hard as he could. He tried the handle on the door and was relieved to find it open. He pushed the heavy door open and entered the cathedral, shouting, "Help! Sprechen sie Englisch? Sanctuary!" His voice echoed through the cathedral. There was some light in the church from candles on the altar and votive candles to the side, giving the cathedral a warm glow. As he entered the sanctuary proper, he realised he had passed under a tremendous pipe organ. A black-and-white marble checkerboard path lead directly to the altar. Massive columns supported the vaunted ceiling of the pink and pale green bedecked cathedral. He hurried toward the altar, repeating "Sprechen sie Englisch? Sanctuary?" Before he reached the altar, an elderly priest emerged from a door to the side.

"What is it, my son?"

"Sanctuary! I require sanctuary!"

The priest looked at Malcolm, covered in dust, a trail of dried blood from both ears down each side of his face. "I grant you sanctuary! Come, let me get you cleaned up. You are injured."

Just then the door burst opened and Malcolm pulled the machine gun from out of his trousers, and clicking off the safety as he turned towards the door, aiming the machine gun.

# CHAPTER TWENTY TWO

They crept slowly ahead and as they passed a street, Joan saw a figure with white hair walking down the street, doing his best to stay in the shadows. "Peter!" She yelled. "Stop the car!" O'Hallarhan stomped on the brakes. The brakes squealed in protest, but the car came to an abrupt halt, causing Joan to hit her head on the seat in front of her. "Backup and turn down that street!"

O'Hallarhan slammed the car in reverse and backed up to make the turn on to the street. As they turned, she saw the man turn to glance at them. Her heart lept to her throat. It was Malcolm; she was sure of it. When the man caught sight of the car, he broke into a run. "Peter, follow that man! It's Malcolm!" O'Hallarhan sped up, but when the man abruptly turned on a side street, he had to slam on the brakes to slow down to make the turn. He turned the car into a plaza and as they rounded the corner; they caught sight of the church door swinging shut.

O'Hallarhan stopped the car, but left it running. Joan and Saxon jumped out of the car and ran to the door, Joan in the lead. She pushed the heavy doors open and could see the man talking excitedly to a priest. They rushed into the sanctuary and the white-haired man turned around, aiming a machine gun at them. She was right; it was Malcolm!

Joan yelled, "Malcolm! Don't shoot, it's us! We're here to rescue!"

He stood a moment, dumbfounded, before the machine gun slid out of his hands. The two of them ran towards each other. She flung her arms around Malcolm and held him as tight as she could. Tears streamed down her face. "Malcolm! I've found you! You're alive!" She grabbed his face and kissed him as hard as she could; a kiss most decidedly inappropriate for a cathedral.

"My God! It's really you! How did you find me?" Malcolm asked after pulling away from the kiss.

"You provided us a rather obvious clue with the explosion," Saxon said as he clapped Malcolm on the shoulder, causing Malcolm to wince.

"But how did you find me? How are you here?"

"There will be time for that later." Saxon went to the door of the cathedral and peeked out. "We need to leave. Now. Joan, could you release Malcolm from your embrace long enough for us to leave?"

"I'm never letting him go again, but you are right. We need to leave now."

Malcolm ran to the dumfounded priest. He picked up the machine gun and said, "Sorry to bother you, Father. Everything is fine now… more than fine." He turned and joined the trio as they ran down the nave to the car. They jumped into the car and O'Hallarhan drove ahead for a few blocks. "Now, what?" he said.

"Peter, what are you doing here?" Malcolm asked, finally realising that O'Hallarhan had been part of his rescue.

"It's a long story, but we need to decide where to go now."

"Let's go to the warehouse where we planned to make our departure. Good Lord, I believe that it's scheduled to fly out first thing in the morning. The timing couldn't be more perfect!" Saxon said. Saxon found the map to the warehouse and directed O'Hallarhan.

"Warehouse? What's happening?" Malcolm asked.

Joan, still gripping his hand tightly, said "Our plan was to rescue you from Colditz, drive to Leipzig and we would return home as cargo aboard an airship."

"How did you ever find me?"

Joan briefly recounted the capture of the German airship that led them to Colditz, only to find that the Germans had taken Malcolm to Leipzig. "We did not know where to look for you until the explosion. We knew it had to be you; you never do things by halves." She pulled him close and kissed him again, once more tears of joy running down her face.

"Ahem, you two. There are others in the car," Saxon said.

Shortly, they pulled up to the warehouse, happy to see the office was still open. "Wait here," Saxon said as he got out of the car. He entered the building, and after several minutes, he returned, shaking his head. "We have a problem."

"What is it?" Joan and Malcolm said simultaneously.

"Because of the explosion and losing power, all airship flights in and out of Leipzig are halted."

"Why?" Malcolm asked.

"The clerk knew little, but they are on the lookout for the white-haired terrorist who caused the explosion."

Saxon, Joan, and O'Hallarhan turned to look at Malcolm. "Shite!" he said.

# CHAPTER TWENTY THREE

"Now what?" Malcolm said.

"I don't know," Joan said. "We left our equipment at the gasthaus, and anything we need to escape is locked up in the warehouse." Malcolm watched Joan think; he loved the way her nose crinkled when she concentrated.

"We can't risk going back to the gasthaus; it was only blocks from the university. Our only option is to get our remaining equipment in the warehouse. The problem is, my lock picks are back at the gasthaus."

"Not a problem," O'Hallarhan said. He raised his mechanical arm and with a flick, a set of lock picks appeared at the end of his fingers.

"One problem solved," Malcolm said. "What next?"

"I think we need to abandon the car," Saxon said. "There is a chance, albeit small, someone saw us and might put two and two together." He studied the map and found a location several blocks east of the warehouse. "I say we look for an alley, leave the car there, and sneak back here."

"We at least have a machine gun, worse come to worse," Malcolm said, holding up the gun.

"How in the world did you acquire a machine gun?" Joan asked.

"I'll tell you on the way," Malcolm said. "We should get going."

With Saxon's aid, they found an alley off of a side street in an industrial area of town. During the trip, Malcolm quickly recounted his time in Leipzig, building the motor, adding both the ultrasonic weapon and feedback device, and his escape from the laboratory building. "I'm afraid the feedback device had the unintended effect of causing the power outage."

"Why did they think you would actually help them?" Saxon said. "Frietag, of all people, should have expected you to do something like that."

"I think Toth was in charge and I let him believe he broke me when he said that you and Joan had run off on your honeymoon. I knew it was a bald face lie, but he bought it. That's how I ended up here."

"What about Frietag? Did you kill him?" Joan asked.

"I don't know; I left him lying in the hall near the demonstration room. If we're lucky, the explosion killed him."

"I wouldn't count on that," Saxon said. "That man has more lives than a cat!"

As they neared the warehouse, the quartet became quiet. They circled around to come to the warehouse from the rear entrance. The power was still out, so they used the darkness to their advantage to move to the door. O'Hallarhan flicked his arm and the two lock picks appeared. Although it wasn't a terribly complicated lock, it took O'Hallarhan several attempts before he unlocked the door. Joan motioned to O'Hallarhan to move away from the door. She took his place and opened the door a crack. "Shite," she whispered. "There's no light; I can't see a thing!"

"Hold on a minute," O'Hallarhan whispered. He turned a dial on his mechanical hand and pushed a button. Out of his thumb, a small jet of flame appeared, providing the same amount of light as a candle.

"I guess you're in the lead, Peter," Joan whispered, stepping away from the door. O'Hallarhan cracked the door and stuck his thumb inside. He indicated for them to follow, and the quartet slipped into the warehouse. The warehouse was full of crates, expecting to be shipped out the next morning. They threaded their way through the aisles, banging their shins on crates many times. After nearly ten minutes, they located their crates in the middle of the warehouse. They quickly grabbed their equipment and clothes, replaced the lids on the crates, and turned to make their way back. On a whim, Malcolm grabbed one of the oxygen tanks. They made it back to the door just as the flame went out on O'Hallarhan's thumb. They found the doorknob by flailing around in the dark and snuck out the back. Saxon led them north and, after travelling several blocks, they huddled in an alley to determine their next course of action.

"Where do we go from here?" Saxon asked. He pulled out a map. "We're here," pointing to Leipzig. "We could try to go to Berlin, hope we can find the safe house or the Embassy and see if they can get us home."

"That sounds very much like out of the frying pan and into the fire," Malcolm said.

"The other options are to head northwest to Denmark, which is about three hundred and fifty miles away. Or we head west to the Netherlands, which is also three hundred and fifty miles."

"They all sound equally impossible," Joan said.

"What was our original destination?" Malcolm asked.

"Geneva," Joan said. Malcolm raised an eyebrow, to which Joan said, "I know. It was not my choice."

"There's a chance that they might eventually find our crates set to ship to Geneva," Malcolm continued. "We have to think like Frietag. What would he think we would do? I think it is unlikely he would think we would go to Berlin; he would assume we'd take the most direct route back to England. As much as I hate to say it, Berlin is our best bet."

Saxon looked at Malcolm. "We have one problem. We need to do something about your hair. They are looking for a white-haired terrorist, and you are far too conspicuous."

"Damn." O'Hallarhan said. "We could have used the activated carbon back in the crates. I wish I had thought of it sooner."

"There may be another option," Malcolm said. "We could use oil from the car to darken it enough that if I wear a cap, I won't be instantly recognisable."

"I think I have one in my clothes," O'Hallarhan offered. He dug through his pack and puled out a small grey cap. Malcolm tried it on, but it was a little too tight.

"It will have to do for now, but I'll need a new cap before long. This thing is going to give me a headache."

The quartet retraced their steps and O'Hallarhan crawled under the car and opened the oil pan. Saxon, Joan, and O'Hallarhan took turns smearing into Malcolm's hair. For good measure, Joan picked up a couple of handfuls of dirt and sprinkled it on Malcolm's head. At least in the darkness, it had the desired effect; Malcolm looked less like the white-haired terrorist and more like an unwashed vagrant.

They made their way north, careful to avoid the major streets. It was nearly an hour before the buildings gradually became further apart. As they approached the outer edge of Leipzig, they could see a checkpoint on the road leading north. Saxon guided them east for a while before turning north for another two hours. As they travelled, they became chilled from the night air. Malcolm found it harder to keep up with the rest. His muscles still ached from the effects of the ultrasonic transducer and his weakness from his captivity. When they came upon a wooded copse some distance from the road, Malcolm suggested they rest for the night. They made their way into the copse and made camp. The ground was rocky and roots stuck into his back, but Malcolm was thankful to lie down and rest. He was also grateful for the excuse to take off the tight-fitting cap, which gave him a headache. Joan curled up next to him and, with her warmth, he fell into a deep sleep.

Malcolm awoke to bright sunlight streaming down of his face. He went to check his Granda's pocket watch out of habit and realised it was long gone. He looked around and Joan, Saxon, and O'Hallarhan were nowhere to be seen. He started to call out to them and thought better of it. Stiffly, he pulled himself to his feet and looked around. Their packs were still lying around, so he figured they couldn't be far.

A few minutes later, Saxon, Joan, and O'Hallarhan arrived carrying a loaf of bread, a hunk of cheese, and a jug of water.

"Where have you been?" Malcolm asked.

"Foraging, in a civilised way," Saxon said. "We found a farmhouse up the road about half a mile. We bought some food and water from them."

"Was that wise? Aren't we supposed to keep a low profile?"

"That's why we let you sleep. It's only been half a day since you tried to blow up Leipzig. I doubt that they have put together that Joan and I are even here in Germany."

They carefully rationed out the food and the water.

"What time is it?" Malcolm asked.

Joan pulled out Malcolm's Granda's pocket watch. "8:30, we thought we would let you rest."

"You found it?" Malcolm said, pointing to the watch.

"Yes, that's how we knew you were in trouble. It hasn't left my possession since. And now I return it to its rightful owner." She unclipped the watch chain and handed the watch to Malcolm. He took it, leaned in, and kissed Joan.

"I knew there was a reason I loved you," he said, pulling away from the kiss.

"Please, some of us are trying to eat. I'd rather not be sick and lose this valuable food," Saxon said.

"Charles, ever the romantic," Joan said, and they laughed.

"What's the plan?" Malcolm said between bites of bread.

"We walk. For a long time," Saxon said.

"Do you know where we are going?" Malcolm asked.

Saxon consulted his map. "I think we should try to get close to Bitterfeld-Wolfen. The town is on a lake. If we keep our distance from the town itself, we should have access to water and possibly food. It means probably eight or more hours. Are you up to it, Malcolm?"

"I don't really have much of a choice unless I want to return to the tender mercies of Frietag."

"Can we at least get rid of that oxygen tank? Why in the world did you take it?" Saxon asked.

"You never know when it might come in handy," Malcolm said.

"I can take it, Commodore," O'Hallarhan said. "My mechanical arm can carry it with no problem."

"Peter, you don't have to call me Commodore. Malcolm will do."

"Sorry, sir, old habits die hard," O'Hallarhan said.

"Speaking of your arm, I see that you have made more than a few upgrades," Malcolm remarked.

"Courtesy of the Secret Service. Quentin Boothroyd was great help in working out the details."

"No more engineering talk," Saxon said. "Here, give me the machine gun, Malcolm. That certainly can't help. Are you alright to walk?"

"I think so. My body hurts everywhere from my brief encounter with the ultrasonic field. At least the ringing in my ears has stopped, although they still ache."

"I'm not a doctor, but you probably have a ruptured eardrum. If we ever get to civilization again, we need you checked out by a doctor."

"I'm fine," Malcolm scoffed.

"You are not," Joan corrected. "But since we can't do anything about it now, I suggest we get moving. Do you need a hand up old man?"

"I resent that. I may feel like an old man, but I am most assuredly not old," Malcolm said, grunting as he stood up.

"Could have fooled me," Saxon said.

Malcolm picked up the cap and grimaced. "I really don't want to put this on. My head still hurts from last night."

"You don't have to," Joan said. "I nearly forgot. The farmer had a head nearly as big as yours. This should fit better." She handed him a dirty brown cap. Malcom tried it on and it was a good fit.

"Thank you, Peter. I'll have no need of this," Malcolm said, tossing the old cap back to O'Hallarhan. He strapped on his backpack. "Shall we get going?"

The overcast morning threatened rain. As they left the farmhouse, they returned to the road, using that to keep their bearings. Malcolm struggled in the morning to keep up as they moved through the low hills around Leipzig. The hills were not steep, but the added strain affected Malcolm. They passed the occasional farmhouse and did their best to keep their distance. They detoured around a few small villages, however their challenge came as they approached Delitzsch. The road ran right through the centre of the town. They worked their way to the east, using any wooded patches for cover. They found a denser patch of woods and stopped for a quick lunch from their stores of cheese and water. Malcolm didn't sit down to eat, for fear he wouldn't be able to get up and continue walking. They ate in silence, listening to a light breeze rustling the newly sprouted leaves. When they finished, they continued through the woods, doing their best to keep the town in sight. Eventually, they caught up with the road outside of the town and continued their trek.

The gentle hills had given way to flat farmland, making the trip easier for Malcolm, but leaving them with no cover. The sun poked out of the clouds, making Malcolm sweat. In the midafternoon, they saw a wagon drawn by two enormous draft horses. Malcolm pulled his cap down and lowered his head. When the wagon drew near, the driver stopped the horses and looked at the quartet before saying something in German. Saxon replied, and the driver was silent before laughing. Saxon said something else and waved to the driver, and they continued on their way. Some time later, Malcolm asked, "What was that about?"

"He asked what where we were going and why we looked so dishevelled. I told him we were on our way to visit our family and we were doing what we could to avoid it for as long as possible."

As they continued, more and more trees dotted the farmland until woods lined each side of the road. Malcolm was glad for the relative coolness of the woods. In the quiet of the woods, the only things they encountered were the occasional rabbit that scampered away as they approached. By now, Malcolm laboured to keep up; the only thing keeping him going was the thought of Frietag catching him again.

As the sun dipped to the horizon, they neared a lake. They scouted around the lake and found a hidden area in the woods close to the lake shore. Malcolm all but collapsed when they selected their camp.

The air near the lake had a chill, and they struggled to keep warm; at first Malcolm found it a welcome relief, but quickly felt cold. "Dare we light a fire?" Malcolm asked.

"Let me look around first. In the meantime, why don't you look for wood and kindling?" Saxon offered. He slipped off towards the lake and vanished from their sight in a few seconds. With great effort, Malcolm pulled himself up from his resting place and joined O'Hallarhan and Joan to forage in the immediate area around their campsite. When O'Hallarhan moved out of sight, Joan grabbed Malcolm and kissed him, long and hard.

When she pulled away, she said, "I've been wanting to do that all day! I can't believe that I have you back! I never intend to let you go."

"I missed you, too." Malcolm smiled. "The thought of losing you and never getting our chance to be together was the only thing that got me through their interrogation."

"Was it awful?"

"It was, but I'd rather not talk about it. Let me just enjoy this moment," he said as he leaned in to kiss her.

"Ahem," O'Hallarhan cleared his throat. "I thought we were gathering wood for the fire?"

"We are. Just give us a moment, Peter," Joan said.

"I'll meet you at the camp," O'Hallarhan said as he walked back towards the camp.

"Now, where were we?" Malcolm asked.

"I believe you were about to kiss me," Joan said, as Malcolm pulled her closer.

# CHAPTER TWENTY FOUR

Malcolm held Joan tight for several minutes before reluctantly pulling away. "I suppose we better actually bring some wood back to camp."

"I'd rather stay here," she said.

"Me too, but duty calls," Malcolm said.

With a sigh, they looked for long fallen wood that had dried in the air. After finding a few small pieces that would not require chopping as they had no axe, they returned to the camp. In a few minutes, Saxon returned from his reconnaissance mission. "I think we'll be fine; you can't see our site from the lake and as long as the fire isn't too smoky, we should be fine. As for food, I'm not sure what is in the lake. I scared a few frogs when I walked along the lake shore."

"Frogs' legs are good," Malcolm said. O'Hallarhan, Joan, and Saxon looked at him quizzically. "We used to catch them down by the river at my home. My ma would cut the legs off and fry them up. If we have a fire, we won't have to eat them raw." Saxon, Joan, and O'Hallarhan looked at him with a mixture of disgust and apprehension. "Now, we just have to start a fire. I don't suppose we have any matches?"

"No, I didn't think we be going on a cross-country hike," Joan said.

Malcolm thought for a moment. "Peter, what is your arm made of?"

"The frame is steel, but the mechanical comments are brass. Why?"

"I was hoping you would say that," Malcolm said. He looked around and found a rock that he thought might be flint. "Show me where the steel is on your arm." O'Hallarhan rolled down the sleeve on his arm and pointed to a support rod that ran along his forearm. "Bring it closer," Malcolm said. He took the rock and, after a dozen attempts, he generated sparks. "Excellent. Now we just need some dried leaves for fuel." They looked around and gathered the driest leaves they could find. Malcolm struck the rock against O'Hallarhan's arm. The sparks reached the leaves, but failed to catch them alight. Malcolm scowled, deep in thought. After a minute, he said, "Peter, bring the oxygen tank over." When O'Hallarhan brought the tank over, Malcolm borrowed a knife from Joan and cut off the mask, so there was just a hose. "Don't the tanks contain a higher concentration of oxygen than the air?"

"Yes, I think they were emergency tanks for diving," Saxon said.

Malcolm carefully laid the hose, so that it pointed at the pile of leaves. He turned the oxygen tank on so that it was barely open. On the first try, the leaves caught alight. Quickly, they added twigs to keep the fire burning. Gradually, they added small sticks and finally a few pieces of wood. Soon, they had a proper fire.

"See, I told you the oxygen tank would come in handy," Malcolm said.

Now that they had a proper fire, Malcolm and O'Hallarhan, who volunteered, made their way to the shore. As they made their way to the shore, Malcolm said, "Peter, I'm surprised to see you here. Why did you risk your life for me?"

"I know we've had our differences, sir. But I've realised a few hard truths about myself since we came back from Mars. I realised that I have a lot to learn about being an engineer and an officer. You taught me that. Also, you came for me when I lost my arm and made sure I got aboard the ship safely. I felt it was my duty to return the favour."

"Thank you, Peter. While I appreciate it, I'm sorry that you were dragged into this mess."

"That was my doing. Mycroft didn't want me to come, but I insisted."

"You stood up to Mycroft Holmes? Good for you! Come on, Peter, we need to hunt some frogs." They stopped for some sturdy looking sticks. They used a knife to sharpen them into points and after a half hour of stalking around the lake shore, they speared a dozen frogs.

"Behold, the mighty hunters have returned," Malcolm said, showing the frogs impaled on the spear.

"Ugh, that's disgusting," Joan said. "If you'll excuse me, I'd rather not watch as you dress them." Joan got up and turned her back to Malcolm.

Malcolm took the knife and cut off the hind legs. The hardest part was removing the skin. He butchered three or four of the legs before he could figure how to skin the frog efficiently. Using a couple of sticks, they built a makeshift spit and put the frog legs over the fire. When Malcolm assured Joan they were done with the frogs, she turned back around. After a few minutes, the flesh of the legs turned white. Malcolm removed the skewer from the fire and pulled off a leg. Without hesitation, he pulled the meat from the bones. "Needs salt, but otherwise tastes alright. Dinner, such as it is, is served."

Malcolm took his remaining three legs and handed the skewer to O'Hallarhan, who looked at with disgust. By the time Malcolm had finished his legs, O'Hallarhan took this serving and handed the skewer to Saxon. He took a tentative bite and when he finished, he said, "They aren't bad."

"Says you," Saxon said as pulled his serving from the skewer. He handed it to Joan, who held it at arm's length away.

"I don't know if I can eat this," she said, staring at the frog's leg.

"You eat caviar and eel, right? This isn't any worse than that," Malcolm offered.

Joan reluctantly pulled a set of legs from the skewer. She looked at it with disgust, closed her eyes, and popped it into her mouth. She pulled the leg bones out of her mouth and said, "You're right, it isn't bad. With the right seasoning, this might actually be good."

When they finished, they banked the fire so that the coals would continue to throw heat, but wouldn't be visible to a passerby. They laid out near the fire, using extra clothes as coverings, and drifted off to sleep.

Malcolm awoke with a start. The morning light had just begun to filter through the trees. He heard the sounds of dogs and movement in the woods. He struggled to get up, still stiff from the previous day's exertion. Creeping towards the edge of the campsite, he heard conversation in German and hurried back to the camp as quietly as he could. Shaking Joan awake, he put his hand over her mouth. "We have company," he whispered. Together, they roused O'Hallarhan and Saxon. Suddenly, three German Shepherds burst into the campsite, followed shortly by four policemen.

"You. Vagrants. Move along! We don't want your type hanging around here!" one of the policemen shouted in German.

# CHAPTER TWENTY FIVE

*S*axon replied in German, "Our apologies. We will move along. Come along, Johanna, Peter, and Michael. We have to move along." They hurriedly gathered their things and left towards the road, followed by the men and their dogs.

After they travelled some fifty feet down the road, Malcolm whispered to Saxon, "What was that about?"

"They thought we were vagrants. They didn't want us in their community."

"Do you think they recognised me?" Malcolm asked.

"I don't think so," Saxon said. "Truthfully, Malcolm, you look like a vagrant. If I didn't know better, I wouldn't think it was you."

"Why do I feel like I've been subtly insulted?" Malcolm asked.

"Not very subtle, if you ask me," O'Hallarhan muttered.

"Enough," Joan hissed. "Let's put some distance between us and them."

They trudged on for another hour before they stopped to eat. They finished their meager stores of bread and cheese and drank the rest of the water, cursing themselves for not refilling at the lake when they had the opportunity. While they ate, Saxon looked at the map and realised that they were quite a ways west of the shortest route to

Berlin. When they packed up, Saxon led them east until they found the road heading northeast to Berlin. When they stopped for the night, they found a deserted farmhouse. Although there was no food to be found, they had shelter for the night.

"How much longer before we get to Berlin?" Malcolm asked.

"I think maybe we should be there in another three days," Saxon said.

"What is our plan when we get there?"

"I believe my friend Geoffrey Pembroke is stationed in Berlin. His last letters to me were from Berlin. If I remember correctly, he has a flat on the corner of Leipziger Straße and Charlottenstraße. I suggest we start there." Joan and Malcom shared a glance, each remembering that Saxon and Geoffrey had grown close when Malcolm and Saxon were blackmailed into joining the Secret Service.

"Do we know where that is?" Malcolm asked.

"Let me think; I've been to Berlin several times," Joan said. She closed her eyes, imagining the geography of the city. "I believe it's relatively close to the British Embassy. That should be our goal, so I think that's going to work." She turned to Malcolm and looked at him appraisingly. "We're going to have to do something about your appearance, though. As Charles said, you look like a vagrant and you will stand out in that part of town."

"Agreed," Malcolm said. He sniffed. "And I certainly don't smell good either. How are we going to accomplish that?"

"Excellent question," Saxon said. "We also need food and water." Looking at the map, he pointed to a small village. "We are very close to Kempberg; it's a small village. I think we could risk Joan and I going into the village. Besides food and water, we'll get soap and some new clothes for Malcolm. I suggest we turn in for the night. We have another long day of walking ahead."

Malcolm agreed. He felt like he was over most of the effects of the ultrasonic wave, but he was tired; his arms and legs felt like lead. The walking of the last few days had taken a great deal out of him, but he knew he had to keep pushing if there was any chance of escaping. He laid down next to Joan and before he could even roll over to kiss her goodnight; he fell asleep.

When he awoke, the morning light had just poured into the farmhouse. When Malcolm tried to rise, his body protested. He was stiff all over and his legs throbbed from the exertion of the past two days. Grunting, he pulled himself up and looked around. Saxon and Joan had already left, but O'Hallarhan was also up. "How long have they been gone?" Malcolm asked.

"They left just as the sun came up; maybe thirty minutes ago," O'Hallarhan said.

"Do you hear something?" Malcolm asked.

"Like what?" O'Hallarhan said.

"Like an airship engine!" Malcolm ran to the window, scanning the skies. When he reached the southern window, he could see a German zeppelin heading in their direction. "Shite," he exclaimed. "There's a German zeppelin heading our way from the south."

"Do you think they know we're here?" O'Hallarhan said.

"I doubt it. But I would dearly like to know if it's a harmless zeppelin carrying freight or passengers or if it's on a reconnaissance mission to find us." They kept quiet and tracked the zeppelin as it approached while remaining out of sight. Malcolm was convinced that the zeppelin was actively looking for them because it flew much lower than an airship typically flew. As it continued north, Malcolm got a better look at it. It was definitely a military zeppelin; he could see the cannons mounted on the gondola under the balloon. It appeared the Germans would stop at nothing to apprehend him. He had killed a major in German Naval Intelligence, so it stood to reason that they would pull in any available zeppelin to aid in the search.

After the zeppelin flew out of sight, Malcolm dared speak for the first time since they saw the zeppelin's arrival. "This complicates matters greatly."

"I think that's an understatement," O'Hallarhan said.

# CHAPTER TWENTY SIX

*S*axon and Joan rose at dawn. Joan looked at Malcolm, sound asleep. While she dearly wished to kiss him goodbye, she didn't want to wake him. *His captivity and this forced march must have exhausted him.* O'Hallarhan woke up just as they were leaving.

"Let Malcolm sleep as long as he can," Joan whispered.

They left the farmhouse and made their way from the farmhouse to the village of Kempberg. Small whitewashed houses with steeply pitched red-tile roofs lined the narrow streets. Ahead, Joan saw the church steeple rising above the rooftops and could smell the scent of bread, making her stomach rumble. They walked to the town centre and Joan found the bakery. Joan looked at the array of baked goods; dark rye bread, a simple country-style loaf, rolls, and streuselkuchen, a sweet yeast cake topped with a buttery crumble. She looked longingly at the pastries before deciding on the country-style loaf. She favoured the dark rye, similar to the bread that her grandmother served, but picked a similar choice that might appeal to the rest of her company.

They walked the streets and found a shop where they could buy soap and purchase a bottle of schnapps from a stall on the street. They went to the public pump and refilled their jugs, not before helping themselves to a much needed drink. As Joan was finishing filling her jug, she heard a motor. She looked up and saw a German Zeppelin descending to the east. She tugged on Saxon's sleeve and nodded toward the airship. Soon it dipped below the tops of the houses and was out of sight. "We need to find some place to hide, she whispered in German. She looked around and saw a small tailor's shop just off the square. When Saxon finished filling his jug, she pulled him by the sleeve and led him to the tailor's shop.

The smell of wool hit Joan's nose as she entered. Jackets and waistcoats hung on the wall next to the shirts and a few pairs of trousers. Piles of linen and heavy wool fabric lay on a table in the centre of the shop. She heard movement and, stepping from behind a curtain at the back of the shop, a man appeared. "How may I help you?"

"We're looking for some clothes for my brother," Joan said. "A few shirts and a couple of pairs of trousers."

"Very good." The tailor appraised them. "I don't recognise you. Are you new to the area?"

"Yes. We just arrived."

"Welcome to our village. Come, let's see what we can do for you."

The tailor rummaged through his inventory and found three linen collarless shirts, two pairs of black wool trousers, and a dark wool waistcoat. As they were paying, they heard the roar of motorcycles racing through the town square. Saxon looked at Joan and she nodded. Much to her dismay, the tailor took some time to add up their purchases; clearly he was much better at tailoring than mathematics.

A motorcycle with a sidecar pulled down the street and parked in front of the shop. A soldier in uniform got out and, after removing his helmet, goggles, and gloves, entered the shop. "Good day, Herr Schmidt."

"What brings you here, Captain Mathy?" Joan saw Saxon's eyes widen at the name.

"We are on a wild goose chase, it appears. Looking for some madman who blew up a university building in Leipzig. Since I was in the area, I thought you might repair my uniform." He noticed Joan "Guter Tag, Fraulien."

"Guter tag."

"Herr Schmidt is the best tailor in Germany. He's the only one I trust to repair my uniforms."

"That's good to know."

He turned to Saxon, "Guter Tag." He stared at Saxon. "You look familiar to me. Have we met before?"

"No, I don't believe I've had the pleasure," Saxon said. Joan could see beads of sweat forming on Saxon's forehead. She realised Saxon was lying.

Joan turned to the captain. "Is there any danger? With a madman running around?" She made her eyes wide with fear and put a shake in her voice.

"I doubt it. But my superiors dispatched me with a small squad of motorcycles to look for him. Perhaps you've seen a white-haired man around here?"

"No, Captain."

"I thought not." He turned back to Saxon. "Are you sure we haven't met? You seem very familiar to me. I'm sure we've met before."

"I think I would remember if I met you," Saxon said.

At that moment, the tailor finished adding up their purchases. Joan quickly payed and gathered the clothes.

"If your brother needs alterations, please send him back."

"Thank you. You've been most kind. Guter Tag, Captain." She nodded to Saxon, and they left the shop. They went back to the town centre where they saw another motorcycle and side car roar down the street. Joan found a side street a few blocks down and guided Saxon down the street. When they were out of sight of the Main Street, she whispered, "Who was that?"

"Captain Mathy was the captain of the zeppelin that Malcolm captured during our first mission. He probably didn't recognise you because he only glimpsed you before Frietag shot you. Of all the rotten luck. It's a good thing Malcolm wasn't here; Mathy might have recognised him immediately."

"We have a bigger problem. How are we going to get out of here and avoid the patrols?" Saxon pulled out his map. After a few moments, they found a street that ended near a wood. They used the cover of the woods as far as they could, but it opened into a pasture. They tried to keep low as they made their way across the pasture, but there was little cover, as the spring grass had just started growing. Where possible, they took refuge in hedgerows or small copses of trees. Joan watched the road, looking for any sign of German patrols.

Joan saw the farmhouse ahead and breathed a sigh of relief, which was cut short when she heard the roar of a motorcycle. She turned and saw a motorcycle and sidecar approaching, still a good distance away. She considered their options; they could just let them pass or they could run to warn Malcolm. The four of them should be able to despatch the two soldiers. She yanked on Saxon's sleeve. "Let's make a run for the farmhouse."

"Are you mad? They'll know we're involved and chase after us."

"I'm counting on it. Now, run!"

# CHAPTER TWENTY SEVEN

Malcolm heard someone approaching. He and O'Hallarhan hurried to hide in what had been the kitchen; observing the door. To their relief, it was Saxon and Joan.

When Malcolm and O'Hallarhan revealed themselves, Joan said, "Grab your things. We need to get out of here. Now!" she emphasised. "Did you see the zeppelin?" Malcolm said, as he gathered his pack.

"Yes, we saw it," Saxon said. "And there are two soldiers on motorcycles coming this way."

"What do we do?" Malcolm said.

"Let's deal with the Germans first and then worry about the next steps," Joan said.

They spilt up to cover the entrances; Joan and O'Hallarhan were in the back and Malcolm and Saxon in the front, hiding either side of the door. Barely a minute later, they heard the rumble of the motorcycle approach and come to a stop at the front of the house. Malcolm heard the soldiers dismount from the motorcycle and heard one set of footsteps approaching the front. He looked over to Saxon, who was holding the machine gun; Malcolm wasn't sure how much ammunition remained, but it would at least make an excellent weapon to bludgeon the soldier. He heard the footsteps slowly approaching the door. Malcolm watched as the doorknob slowly turned and the door cracked open a bit.

Suddenly, the door flew open, kicked by the German soldier; it slammed hard into Saxon, who involuntarily reacted to the door when it hit him in the face. The soldier turned towards Saxon and aimed his machine gun. Malcolm jumped on the soldier, knocking his gun towards the ground just as the soldier pulled the trigger. Saxon yelped in pain, but Malcolm couldn't take time to notice. As they crashed to the ground, Malcolm landed on top of the soldier and delivered a couple of punches to the head, knocking out the soldier.

At the sound of the scuffle in front, the soldier at the rear burst in, but Joan was ready and had dropped him and disarmed him with no issue. Malcolm heard Saxon slump to the ground and turned to look at his friend. Saxon had blood running down his right leg and multiple shots from the machine gun tore his trousers up. Malcolm went to his friend and immediately examined the leg. The shots from the machine gun tore up the area around his knee, but the bullets appeared to miss Saxon's femoral artery. If the bullets had struck a little higher, Saxon would have bled out and there would be almost nothing Malcolm could do for his friend.

Malcolm took his shirt off and ripped it into large pieces. He did his best to use the bandages to stop the bleeding. "How are you doing?" Malcolm asked.

"How do you think I'm bloody well doing?" Saxon yelled. He took a deep breath and said, "My leg looks like it went through a meat grinder. I'm bleeding copiously, and I've ruined a perfectly good pair of tailored trousers." Malcolm smiled, realising if Saxon had regained his usual sarcastic wit, he must not be in mortal danger.

"Joan! Peter! The soldier shot Charles. Does anyone remember their medical training?" Malcolm yelled. Moments later, Joan and O'Hallarhan raced into the room and joined Malcolm by Saxon.

"What about the other soldier? Peter, make sure he doesn't escape. Joan, help me clean this mess up so we can assess the damage."

"I'm not one of your bloody airships, Malcolm. This is my leg you're talking about!" Saxon said through clenched teeth, feeling the pain as Malcolm tried to clean the wounds.

"Same principle applies, I think. Assess the damage, patch it up as best as you can until you can get proper repairs," Malcolm said.

"Your bedside manner could use some work," Saxon said.

"Damn it, I'm an engineer, not a doctor. I'm not used to the thing I'm working on talking back to me."

Joan poured water over the area, causing Saxon to hiss in pain. Worse was when she used some soap on a rag and cleaned the wounds. "Hold on," Joan said and ran back to the supplies they had purchased. "It's not much. We bought a bottle of schnapps. We can use it to clean the wound or use it to help with the pain."

"I think I'd rather drink it," Saxon said, his body rigid from trying not to thrash in pain. "Anything to dull the pain." Joan handed him a bottle, and he took a long pull. After waiting a minute to catch his breath, he took another long pull before handing the bottle back to Joan. "I don't know what's worse, the pain or the taste of the schnapps. I've never liked peppermint," Saxon said. His body relaxed a bit as he felt the alcohol take effect.

Malcolm looked at the wounds. He could see some bullets, but he couldn't account for all the wounds. He looked at Saxon. "I'm afraid I'm going to have to dig around in there to remove the bullets. I don't think I can get them all, but I'm going to get the visible ones." Saxon nodded and grabbed the bottle from Joan and took another long, hard pull. "Alright, I'm ready as I'm going to be."

As carefully as he could manage, Malcolm probed the wounds with his fingers, trying to find the bullets as Saxon winced and let out a hissing breath. Malcolm pulled out five bullets, but he feared there were more. After Malcolm's probing, the wounds started bleeding again. Malcolm knew he had to have some way to close the wounds. "Anyone have needle and thread?" he asked. Joan shook her head and Saxon muttered a weak "no".

O'Hallarhan hollered from the other room, "I have some gaffer's tape; I brought it in case I needed to make repairs on my arm."

"That will have to do," Malcolm said. He nodded to Joan, who got up and ran to get the tape.

"You're seriously not going to tape me up with gaffer's tape, like I'm one of your hurried patch jobs," Saxon asked.

"I'm afraid so, old friend. We need to get you to a doctor as soon as possible. You've lost a good amount of blood, but this should stop you from losing more."

"I never thought I'd end up as one of your maintenance miracles," Saxon said.

"Neither did I," Malcolm replied.

Joan returned with the gaffer's tape. After Saxon took another large swig of the schnapps, Malcolm pulled the skin of the wounds together as tight as he could while directing Joan to put pieces of gaffer's tape to hold the wounds together. When they finished, Malcolm took the remaining pieces of his shirt as makeshift bandages to cover the wounds, secured again by gaffer's tape. To Malcolm's relief, the makeshift bandages stayed dry. Between the alcohol and the shock from his wounds, Saxon slipped into sleep.

"What do we do now?" Malcolm asked. "We need to get out of here now before more soldiers arrive and Charles needs a proper doctor to treat those wounds."

"Let me think a moment," Joan said. "We have a motorcycle and two German soldier uniforms. I think we should keep to the original plan and get to Berlin. One of us could drive Saxon to Berlin while the others make their way on foot." She paused for a moment. "As much as I don't want to be separated from you again, I think you're the best choice."

"But…" Malcolm began.

"But nothing," Joan said, cutting him off. "The Germans are after you. We need to get you into hiding as fast as possible. While the zeppelin captain may have recognised Saxon, he didn't seem to recognise me and there's no way he would know Peter."

"I don't want to leave you again now that we're together."

"I know. I feel the same way. But I fear there's no other choice."

Malcolm pulled Joan close. "It's not fair; I finally have you back and now I have to go."

"I know."

They held each other silently for a few moments before Malcolm said, "What will you do?"

"Peter and I will continue on foot. I might use one of my former identities to get us to Berlin much quicker. Arranging that for four people would arouse suspicion, but with Peter and I, I think we won't be too conspicuous."

"What do we do about them?" Malcolm asked, pointing to the German soldier.

"Not much we can do, but to tie them up and leave them here."

"Someone will come looking for them," Malcolm said.

"I know, but hopefully by then, you'll be well on your way and Peter and I can get some distance."

The trio set about their work. After stripping the guards of their uniforms, they tied them up and used the rest of Malcolm's shirt as gags. Malcolm assessed the uniforms. Luckily, the two soldiers were similar in size to Malcolm and Saxon, so the uniforms fit, but the boots were another matter entirely. Malcolm could squeeze his feet into them, but his feet hurt almost immediately. They roused Saxon and got him into the other uniform; fortunately, the boots fit him better.

Malcolm went out to the motorcycle and familiarised himself with the controls. He started the motorcycle and took a few tentative circles around to understand how it worked. He found it less complicated than he feared. Malcolm drove the motorcycle towards the doorway, positioning the sidecar as close to the door as possible. With O'Hallarhan's aid, Malcolm got Saxon in the sidecar, although the sharp intakes of breath from Saxon told him it wasn't a painless process.

Malcolm turned to Peter and Joan. "Be careful, you two; I don't want to rescue you, too."

"Don't worry, sir," O'Hallarhan said. "I'll make sure nothing happens to Joan." Malcolm barely restrained a laugh, knowing that if there was any trouble, Joan would be more than capable of handling it.

"Thank you, Peter," Malcolm said. "Do you mind if we have a moment alone?"

"Of course," O'Hallarhan said as he went back into the house.

Malcolm pulled Joan tight and gave her a long kiss. They just held each other for several moments before Malcolm pulled back. "Be careful."

"I will," Joan said.

"If the two of you are done, can we get moving?" Saxon said from the motorcycle. "If my injuries weren't enough to make me sick, this sugary display certainly will."

Malcolm and Joan laughed. Joan went to Saxon and said, "I see that being wounded hasn't affected your cheery disposition." She kissed him on the head before turning back to Malcolm. She pulled him close and gave him one last kiss. "Please be careful and don't take any unnecessary risks."

"I won't," he said. Joan arched an eyebrow. "I promise!"

"I don't want to say goodbye, but see you shortly."

"It can't come fast enough," Malcolm said.

"Can we get going before I get sick?" Saxon said.

# CHAPTER TWENTY EIGHT

Malcolm started the motorcycle, pulling away from the farmhouse. They drove for a few minutes before Malcolm stopped.

"Why did you stop?" Saxon said.

"I don't know where I'm going. We can't very well drive into the village with the zeppelin sitting there, can we?"

"Good point," Saxon said. He shuffled through his pack until he found a map. He studied it for a moment and shook his head. "There isn't another way to go north without going through Kemberg. Unless we backtrack to Ateritz and head northwest to Rotta and Bergwitz, we can turn north and head to Berlin. That's probably going to add at least another two hours to our trip."

Malcolm pulled out his pocket watch. It was a comfort to have it back again. "It's just half past ten. I think it will take us another six hours, maybe? I'm not sure how fast I'm can drive this contraption."

"We should chance it. Ideally, it would be better if we could arrive under the cover of darkness, although it makes the navigation more difficult," Saxon said.

"I'm going to need you to stay awake as much as you can to help me navigate and to keep an eye out for the zeppelin."

"I'll do my best."

After several attempts, Malcolm turned the motorcycle around and they headed back the way they had just come. They saw no sight of Peter or Joan, which Malcolm hoped meant they would avoid other patrols.

The ride was tiring; the bumpy road jarred every bone in Malcolm's body. He could only imagine how it must feel to Saxon. Malcolm could only hear the loud roar of the engine. Given the condition of the so-called roads, it was sometimes all Malcolm could do to keep the motorcycle on the road. As they neared Rotta, they saw another German motorcycle patrol approaching. The patrol stopped and signalled for Malcolm to stop.

As they neared the waiting patrol, Malcolm leaned over to Saxon. "You'll have to do the talking. I'll just smile and nod." Saxon nodded, and they slowed up to meet the waiting patrol, but Malcolm misjudged the distance and didn't come to a stop until they were ten feet past the patrol.

As the Germans approached their motorcycle, Saxon said, in German, "Idiot! I told you to check the brakes before we left!" and slapped Malcolm on the arm. Malcolm attempted to push the motor-cycle backwards with his feet, but the additional weight of Saxon and the sidecar made it nearly impossible. Malcolm did his best to look sheepish, to hide his fear of being caught.

"What are you doing here?" one of the Germans asked.

"That's an excellent question," Saxon said. "We finished our patrol to the east and were told to swing back this way. I don't know what Mathy was thinking. But it's not for me to question the orders of the captain, even if they make no sense." Saxon laughed, eliciting laughter from the Germans. Malcolm quickly joined in and was careful to not overplay it, although he did not know what was being said.

"Have you seen anything?" the German asked.

"Nothing but cows and the occasional ox cart," Saxon said. "You?"

"Nothing. I fear this is just a mad chase."

"Agreed. We best get going or the captain will have our hide if we don't report back," Saxon said. "Good luck!"

"Same to you!" the German said before turning back to his motorcycle

Malcolm started the motorcycle, praying he could do it on the first attempt. The motorcycle roared to life as if in answer to his prayer, and Malcolm and Saxon continued on their way. When they arrived in Rotta, Saxon guided Malcolm to the road that would take them to Bergwitz and made their way north. They drove several miles before pulling off to the side of the road. They drank a little of the water left in the canteen's the German soldiers had, to wash the dust of the road out of their mouth. Malcolm thought Saxon looked pale, but it was difficult to tell with the road dust plastering his face. When Saxon moved his goggles, he looked like a reverse raccoon; white around his eyes with the rest of his face nearly grey from the road dust. Feeling slightly refreshed, Malcolm mounted the motorcycle, and they resumed their trip.

After another forty minutes, they reached Bergwitz and, after travelling another forty minutes, they were on the road to Berlin. After they passed through Wittenberg, the countryside changed from fields and farmhouses to forests that once again gave way to small villages. Malcolm needed to stop after a couple of hours; the relentless rumbling and jolts from the motorcycle were taking their toll. Malcolm was now sure that Saxon looked paler, so he forced himself to get back on the motorcycle and continue. They drove for another hour, stopping to eat a meagre meal from their half of the supplies Joan and Saxon had got that morning. So much had happened, it seemed like almost a day ago. After the stop, Malcolm reluctantly mounted the motorcycle again to make the last few hours push to Berlin.

Gradually, the villages became more frequent and then the villages transitioned to small cities. As they continued, they came into the industrial part of Berlin; factories belching black smoke in the air, putting a layer of haze in the air and a layer of soot over everything. Malcolm could taste the acrid smoke, but he continued to push forward. Gradually, the factories and warehouses gave way to row houses, and there was more traffic working its way into Berlin. An array of lorries, cars, and horse-drawn wagons all fought their way into the heart of Berlin. The sun descended as they continually picked their way through traffic. On their journey, Malcolm saw many zeppelins moored in an enormous field. He kept that in mind, just in case they needed a means of escape. He nudged Saxon and pointed to them. Saxon nodded and made an annotation on his map.

They continued into the heart of Berlin; the sky was now difficult to see as they navigated the canyons of shops and flats that lined the streets. As the gas streetlights were lit, one by one, it became harder for the duo to figure out where they were going. They kept moving north until they hit Leipziger Straße and turned right. By now, there was little traffic as most people had returned to their homes by now. Saxon tapped Malcolm on the shoulder and pointed to a building on the corner. As Malcolm brought the motorcycle to a stop, he looked at the building. The main entrance to the building was on the corner, with three large arches containing ornately carved oak doors. Above the arches, decorative sculpture making the building look more like an ancient temple. Looking up, Malcolm saw the steeply pitched, green copper roof, dispelling the illusion.

Malcolm helped Saxon out of the sidecar and saw that the pant leg of Saxon's trousers was wet with blood. Malcolm whispered, "How long has that been bleeding?"

"Only a couple of hours," Saxon said, gritting his teeth when he tried to place any weight on the leg.

"Why didn't you tell me?" Malcolm hissed.

"Because there was nothing you could do that wouldn't put us both at risk. If we stopped to see a doctor, I would have to leave you alone and you would need to respond in German."

"You're right," Malcolm said. "What can I do to help you?"

"Right now, I may need your help to get me to the door. Once in, I'm going to have to walk by myself if we're going to pull this off." Malcolm glanced around the street, and mercifully, there was no one around. Malcolm put Saxon's arm around his neck and helped him limp to the door. Saxon took a deep breath and strode in with all the confidence of a German soldier. He looked around and saw someone working at the reception desk.

"You," Saxon said in German. "I need directions to the apartment of one Geoffrey Pembroke. I understand he keeps an apartment here. It is a matter of national security," Saxon said.

The clerk, a young man with a thin moustache, nodded apologetically. "Yes, sir, let me check. Ah, Geoffrey Pembroke. His apartment is on the third floor, number 25."

"Thank you. You've been most helpful. Do I just follow the stairs?" Saxon said, pointing to the grand staircase in the middle of the lobby.

"Yes. The only other way up is a freight lift we use when moving new occupants," the clerk said.

"A freight lift?" Saxon asked. "We will use that, as he most certainly will not be expecting us."

"But sir, only the staff may use that," the clerk began.

"Do you mean you wish to hinder a matter of national security, Herr...Weber?" Saxon said, reading the clerk's name from his name tag.

"No, sir," the clerk said. "Come, follow me," the clerk said. He led the duo across the lobby to a small side hallway where the freight lift was located. He yanked on a large cord to pull the doors open. After moving the gate, Saxon and Charles entered. "Push the button for 3 and you should be there momentarily. When you're done, please make sure you close the gate and the doors. Otherwise, the lift will be stuck here, and I'll get in trouble."

"Rest assured, we will make sure we close the gate," Saxon said.

"I hope you are successful," the clerk said.

"Me too," Saxon said. When the clerk turned and disappeared out of sight, Saxon slumped back against the wall of the lift. "Push the button, Malcolm; I'm not sure how long I can keep it together."

"We're almost there, Charles," Malcolm said. He pushed the button and the lift slowly creaked into motion. Malcolm watched as it went past the next three floors, and when the lift came to a stop, he unlocked the gate and used another long cord to pull the doors open.

"We here, Charles", he said as he turned around to find Saxon lying on a heap on the floor.

# CHAPTER TWENTY NINE

*J*oan and O'Hallarhan gathered the supplies they would need and hid the rest in a closet in the house. Joan looked at the map, trying to determine the best route for them to escape the Germans and be able to get to Berlin. After a few minutes, Joan decided they should head back to Kempberg, hoping they could catch a train to Berlin. This had the added advantage of following the route that the tied up German soldiers would have taken.

They left the house and followed the road, keeping out of sight when possible, and soon arrived at Kempberg. They found the train depot and Joan purchased tickets to Berlin, although the train wouldn't arrive for a couple of hours. Joan led O'Hallarhan out of the train station and down a side street. Peter whispered, "Is it alright if I talk?"

Joan listened for a moment; the street was quiet and no one else was in sight. "Yes, it should be fine here."

"What are we going to do until the train gets here?"

"We hide. Maybe we can find a cafe away from the town centre."

"Aren't we an easy target, just sitting there?" O'Hallarhan said.

"Yes…and no. If they recognise us, we are in trouble. But I think it will be some time before they realise the patrol hasn't returned. By that time, we will be on the train."

"Oh," O'Hallarhan said.

They went back to the town centre and eventually found a small cafe. Joan ordered two coffees and cinnamon rolls. They sat in silence as they waited for their meal. After the waiter delivered their food, O'Hallarhan had picked it up in his hands, ignoring the fork laid by the plate. Joan smiled, remembering Malcolm's discomfort at learning the highly rigid standards of society dining. She couldn't help but wonder where he was right now. She hated to leave him, now that she found him again. But it couldn't be helped. She went to look at Malcolm's pocket watch and realised that she had already given it back to him. "Do you know what time it is?"

O'Hallarhan pushed up the sleeve of his shirt and pressed down on his mechanical arm, revealing a pocket watch embedded in the mechanical works. "Just after noon," he said.

"That's rather ingenious," Joan said, nodding towards his arm as he rolled the sleeve back down.

"It just made sense to allow it to have as many functions as possible," he said.

"You and Malcolm are definitely cut from the same cloth."

He drew up, as if to propose a vigorous denial, but let his breath go. "I suppose you're right." He sipped his coffee. "Six months ago, I would have been insulted if you compared me to Malcolm. Much has changed since then. I consider that a compliment now."

"As you should," Joan said. "I know that you and Malcolm haven't always seen eye to eye," she started.

"That's putting it mildly," O'Hallarhan interrupted.

Joan laughed. "Be that as it may, Malcolm thinks highly of you. He's said to me he sees a lot of himself when he was young. He's tried to spare you some lessons he learned the hard way."

"I realise that now. On our trip home and since I've been on leave, I realised that I still have much to learn. I may know a great deal about engineering, but I have much to learn about people."

"The same could be said about Malcolm when we first met," Joan said.

"If I'm allowed to return to the Service, I hope Malcolm will allow me to serve with him again. This time, I hope I won't be as hot headed."

Joan thought about replying, but finished her coffee instead. "Come, we should get going." They left the cafe and returned to the train station. Fortunately, the train bound for Berlin would leave in thirty minutes. They went and waited on the platform for the train to arrive. Twenty minutes later, the train pulled in the station. As Joan looked for the most deserted car, she caught sight of Frietag on the train, glancing out of the window. She wasn't sure if he saw her, but she didn't want to take any chances. She lowered her head and hurried her pace and led them to a mostly deserted car as far from Frietag as she could manage. "Scheisse," she hissed.

"What is it?" O'Hallarhan asked.

"Frietag is on the train." She pulled O'Hallarhan to a pair of empty seats.

"Did he see you?"

"I don't think so. This certainly complicates matters."

"What do we do? Should we get off and take another train?"

"Let me think," she said. Joan wished she had paid more attention to the train schedule to know when the next train would be bound for Berlin. If Frietag knew they were there, it wouldn't be hard to find them. She thought the best chance would be to get to Berlin, where they would have a much better chance of escaping detection.

"No, we might risk the chance of being discovered." She handed O'Hallarhan a ticket. "We should split up; Frietag knows me, but there's an excellent chance he does not know who you are. I'll sit a few rows back. But Peter, promise me, if Frietag discovers me, do not intervene. It's vital that he doesn't discover your identity, or you may face the same fate as Malcolm did at Colditz."

"But," O'Hallarhan protested.

"But, nothing. Please do nothing to draw attention to yourself. You'll need to get to the British Embassy in Berlin as soon as possible."

She pulled some money from her wallet and stuffed it into O'Hallarhan's hand. "When you leave the train station, follow Anhalter Street to Wilhelmstraße until you get to the embassy at number 70."

"I can't very well leave you to Frietag," O'Hallarhan said.

"You must. If Frietag captures you and discovers your identity, he will go to great lengths to find out everything you know about our last mission. I can't allow that to happen."

"But what about you?"

"I can handle myself," she said. "Besides, I have a score to settle with Herr Frietag," she said as she rubbed the scar on her abdomen.

# CHAPTER THIRTY

Malcolm rushed back to Saxon and was relieved to find he had simply passed out. He pulled Saxon up and put Saxon's arm around his neck. Dragging Saxon out of the lift and down the hall, he breathed a sigh of relief when he found number 25. He banged on the door repeatedly; the sounds echoing down the hallway. After a few moments, he heard a voice say something in German. Malcolm responded in English. "It's Charles Saxon. Let me in."

The door opened and Geoffrey Pembroke looked at Malcolm and said, "You're not Charles."

"But he is," Malcolm said, nodding his head toward Saxon. "I'm Malcolm Robertson. We've met before, but right now, we need your help."

Pembroke stared at Malcolm for a moment before he recognised him and Saxon. "Quickly, come inside," he said. He helped Malcolm pull Saxon into the apartment and together, they moved Saxon to a small couch. Malcolm turned to leave and Pembroke said, "Where are you going? What's happening?"

"I'll explain in just a minute, but I need to close the service lift before the staff investigates."

Malcolm ran back to the lift, closed the gate and the doors before hurrying back to Pembroke's apartment. The apartment looked like what Malcolm imagined the apartment of a diplomat would look like; a plush couch, two matching armchairs, with a mahogany coffee table between them. Bookshelves lined the walls, and a writing desk sat on one wall with a typewriter and telephone. Three large windows dominated one wall of the room; Malcolm could see the gaslights of Berlin twinkling.

"What's happening? What's wrong with Charles? I heard the Germans had kidnapped you. How did you get here?"

"One thing at a time," Malcolm said. "Charles was shot this morning in the leg as we tried to make our way here. I tried patching it up, but I'm afraid he lost a good deal of blood and needs to see a doctor immediately. Is there someone you could call to handle the matter…discretely?" Malcolm asked.

Pembroke was silent for a moment before he said, "Yes, let me call our embassy doctor." Malcolm looked at him quizzically. "Don't worry," Pembroke said. "He is one of us." Pembroke went to the phone and in a few moments, contacted the Embassy doctor. "He should be here in twenty minutes. What can we do?"

"Let's remove his trousers and see what's happening," Malcolm said. Pembroke blushed before helping Malcolm remove Saxon's trousers. Blood soaked the makeshift bandages Malcolm had applied that morning. Carefully, he removed the bandages to find that the tape he had used to hold the wound together had come unstuck, and the wound was bleeding freely. "We need something to stop the bleeding. Do you have any bandages or anything we can use?"

"Yes," Pembroke said. He went to a room off of the living room and returned with a sheet that he started ripping up. "This will have to do," he muttered. Together, they put the makeshift bandages on Charles' wounds and applied pressure to slow the bleeding.

"What happened? How did you get here?" Pembroke asked.

Malcolm relayed how Joan, Saxon, and O'Hallarhan had found him in Leipzig, their plan to escape to Berlin, Saxon's encounter with the German soldier, and their trip to Berlin. "I'm sorry to impose on you, but Charles thought you would be the right person for us to contact the British Embassy."

"Yes, of course," Pembroke said. He looked at Charles and said, "I don't think there's anything more we can do until the doctor arrives. Can I get you anything? Coffee? Tea? Water?"

"I'd kill for a cup of tea," Malcolm said. "It's been a very long time since I've had one."

"Tea it is," Pembroke said as he left the living to the small kitchen where he put the kettle on the stove. He returned a few moments later and sat down in one of the armchairs. "Your escape from Leipzig has certainly drawn a great deal of attention from the Germans. Their Foreign Minister visited the Ambassador, demanding that if you turned up, we should turn you over to German authorities immediately to pay for your crimes."

"I see. How did the ambassador reply?"

"He said that considering the Germans illegally kidnapped from British soil and imprisoned you, the Ambassador explained how it would be in the German's best interest to let you leave Germany. I'm not sure how convinced the Foreign Minster was."

"What has been the impact of my escape? We've been trying to keep a low cover since Leipzig and I do not know what's happening."

"Your escape killed several people, including Major Arnold Toth of German Naval Intelligence. The only casualties were German military personnel; thankfully, no civilians died. Leipzig's electricity was out for the better part of two days. What exactly did you do?"

"I created an overload in the motor they had me build. My goal was to destroy both the motor and provide an opportunity for escape. It seems I overshoot my goal."

"I would say so," Pembroke said. "But because of the amount of damage, the government has branded you as a 'terrorist' and is pulling out all stops to find you."

"I figured as much when we found a zeppelin patrolling this morning, followed by motorcycle scouts."

"It's a miracle you've made it here," Pembroke said. He started to say something else, but the shrill whistle of the tea kettle interrupted him. Pembroke went to the kitchen and five minutes later, returned with a pot of tea, two cups, a small pitcher of cream, and a sugar bowl. "I didn't know how you took your tea," Pembroke said, pointing to the cream and sugar.

"Usually, black and as strong as possible. But since it's been weeks, I may not wait that long," Malcolm said.

"I would give it a few more minutes; it's barely coloured water at this point. How did you end up in Leipzig in the first place?"

Malcolm explained how Frietag had abducted him and held him at Colditz Castle. He explained how he let Toth think Joan's 'abandonment' crushed him and convinced Toth he could create a new motor. To Malcolm's surprise, it worked, and they moved him to the laboratory in Leipzig. "You know the rest," Malcolm finished.

"I understand, but how did Charles and company find you in Leipzig?"

"It was sheer luck. They had captured two German agents in Ireland and found that they were headed for Colditz. Upon arrival, they discovered my transfer to Leipzig the previous week. They arrived in Leipzig the day of my escape. From what I understand, they were eating dinner at a restaurant close to the university when they heard the explosion. They figured it was my doing, and they came in search of me."

A knock on the door interrupted their conversation. Pembroke answered the door and showed the embassy doctor to the sleeping Saxon. As the doctor began his examination, Pembroke picked up the tea tray and motioned that Malcolm should follow him to the kitchen.

Once in the kitchen, Pembroke poured the tea, and Malcolm took a careful sip. After weeks without it, it tasted like heaven. Malcolm nearly burned his mouth in his desire for more tea. Malcolm poured himself another cup, which he drank more slowly. The two men waited in silence, sipping their tea, waiting for the Doctor's report.

The doctor called for Pembroke, who returned to the living room, with Malcolm close on his heels. "I think the patient will be fine, eventually. Whoever treated him did a good job of removing the bullets and cleaning the wound. But why was there tape on his leg?"

"I had no way to close the wound other than some gaffer's tape. I figured it would at least be better than letting it openly bleed."

"Hmm, a clever solution. I'm happy to report there was no major arterial or bone damage and I've sown up the wound properly. I'd like to see him go to a hospital for his care, but I understand that might pose…difficulties."

"Yes," Pembroke said. "What other alternatives do we have?"

The doctor thought for a minute before pulling out a small notebook. He scribbled notes down on a notebook before tearing out a page and handing it to Pembroke. "I'll leave something for the pain. You'll need to keep the wound clean and if it bleeds again, or he runs a fever, call me immediately. He should drink plenty of fluids and rest as much as possible."

"How soon can he leave here?" Malcolm asked.

"It could take a couple of weeks for the leg to heal enough that he could put weight on it."

Before Malcolm could speak, Pembroke took the doctor by the arm and said, "Thank you for your help. We'll be in touch if his situation changes." After he showed the doctor out, he returned to Malcolm and his tea. After taking a sip, he said, "That certainly complicates matters," Pembroke said. "We're going to have to get you to the Embassy so you can get out of here, but I don't want to leave Charles alone."

"With any luck, Joan and Peter have either already arrived in Berlin or are about to arrive. Once they make it, we can figure out our next steps," Malcolm said as he wondered to himself what Joan was doing at this moment.

# CHAPTER THIRTY ONE

*J*oan left O'Hallarhan and took a seat in the row even with the vestibule door, allowing her to be less visible from anyone coming from the car behind her, while giving her a view of anyone coming from the car in front of her. Every time the door opened, she was ready to spring out of her chair. Likewise, when the door beside her opened, she likewise turned away while using the reflection from the window to see who was passing by. There were still people coming and going, but no sign of Frietag. She wondered how long their luck would hold.

She pulled her map from her bag. The next city on the route would be Wittenberg. She knew there was a safe house there; as the starting point of the Protestant Reformation, many tourists came to see the door of All Saint's Church where Martin Luther nailed his famous *Ninety-five Theses*. It made it much easier for agents to blend in with the tourists. She herself had been to Wittenberg early in her career with the Secret Service. She looked at the map to confirm what she already knew; Wittenberg was the only city on the route to Berlin where they could slip away and find alternate routes to Berlin. It also wouldn't hurt to have additional support.

She had to decide soon; Wittenberg would be the next stop and they would arrive there in minutes. Getting off the train might mean Frietag would see them, but staying on the train made them easy targets. If detected in Berlin, their chances of escape were much lower. *Of all the lousy luck. We get on the train that Frietag is taking back to Berlin.* She wondered if Frietag had other men with him or if he was on his own. *It still might be easier to escape in Wittenberg, as they wouldn't have as much support.* The train slowed as it approached Wittenberg, and she decided.

She got up from her seat and went to O'Hallarhan. She whispered, "We're getting off here. You go first; I'll follow some distance behind. If anything goes wrong, just walk calmly to the exit."

"Then what? I don't speak German."

"Find Wintershall Export Limited on Dessauer Straße. When you arrive, tell them you urgently need to meet with Mr Cromwell."

"What will that do?"

"That will let them know the Secret Service sent you. Now, stay quiet, pretend you don't know me and we will meet up outside of the station."

When the train came to a stop, she pushed O'Hallarhan towards the door. She waited thirty seconds before exiting the train. She took a quick look around. O'Hallarhan had nearly left the platform and was entering the station lobby. Satisfied that he was following directions, she made her way to the station lobby. She quickly scanned the crowd behind. *Schiesse.* She caught sight of Frietag, pushing his way through the crowd, making his way towards her. Looking around, she saw a gendarme in the recognisable grey-blue uniform and spiked helmet just ahead. She ran to the gendarme, pretending to be scared and fleeing for her life.

"Herr Wachtmeister, please help me! That man is following me and I believe he intends to do bad things!" She pointed to Frietag, twenty feet away. "He followed me onto the train. He said the most vile things to me I dare not repeat!"

"I will take care of it, Fraulein," the gendarme said. "Excuse me, Herr" The gendarme approached Frietag and stopped in front of him, preventing him from moving towards Joan. Frietag tried to push the officer aside, but the officer grabbed Frietag and called for more help. Joan turned and ran for the exit. As she left, she heard Frietag shouting over the commotion. She had nearly reached the door to the street when a whistle blew and she heard voices yell, "Stoppen!" Her ploy had given her a brief chance to escape. She only hoped it was enough.

She ran on and pushed open the door. O'Hallarhan was standing on outside. He turned to say something when Joan yelled, "Run! This way!" Across the street, she saw more rail lines and past it, a row of warehouses. She crossed the street when she heard the rumble of a locomotive. Turning, saw a locomotive pulling several freight cars travelling toward her. It was gradually picking up speed. She turned toward the station and saw Frietag, the gendarme, and a few railroad workers emerge from the station. The engineer on the locomotive must have seen her as he started laying on the whistle. The train grew larger and Joan knew they only had moments to cross.

"Now what?" O'Hallarhan said, puffing for breath when he caught up with Joan.

"We cross. Now!" She pushed O'Hallarhan over the tracks. As she cleared the last set of tracks, the wind from the passing train buffeted her. It was a bit too close for her comfort, but this would give them time. "This way." She pointed ahead to a warehouse just ahead. For now, she wanted to get out of sight before the cover the train provided was gone. She ran towards the warehouse and continued on until they were amongst a block of warehouses. She stopped to catch her breath.

"Now what?" O'Hallarhan said. She sensed his fear; he wasn't used to the world of espionage.

"Let me get my bearings." She closed her eyes, trying to see the map of Wittenberg in her mind. The safe house was on the other side of Wittenberg. She needed to throw Frietag off their trail. She wandered along the side of the warehouse when she found a locked door. "Peter, come here."

O'Hallarhan joined her. "What is it?"

"Can you smash this door open with you mechanical arm?"

"Wouldn't it be easier to use the lock pick?"

"Yes, but I want Frietag to think we broke in here to hide. At the very least, it will slow him down or split up his group."

O'Hallarhan nodded. Pulling back his mechanical arm, he smashed the door just above the handle. The crash echoed down the alley. Joan was happy to see that the locking mechanism had broken, and the door opened easily. She left the door ajar and started toward the other end of the warehouse.

"Alright, now we get out of here and make our way to the safe house."

# CHAPTER THIRTY TWO

As they walked, Joan mulled over her options. They might
have twenty minutes before the gendarme descended on key
points around the city, like the market square. Given their luck so far,
she wasn't counting on it. While going through the market square was
the quickest route, it was also the riskiest. She opted for a much
longer route that would keep them out of the locked down areas, but
their presence in less busy areas could attract unwanted attention.
Neither option was appealing, but she felt like getting through the city
as quickly as possible was their best bet.

Using the spire of the Schlosskirche as a guide, Joan lead them
northwest until they reached Friedrichstraße, using alleys to hide.
They crossed the street and ducked into another alley, before she
found herself in an overgrown area behind the buildings that lined the
streets. She breathed a sigh of relief as they now had cover. She
strained to hear any sign of pursuit or further mobilisation of the
gendarme, but all she heard was bird song. When they neared the
Sternstraße, she caught sight of laundry hung out to dry in the back
garden of a building. Rough linen shirts and a couple of pairs of
trousers hung on a line close to the tree line. She stopped O'Hallarhan
and put her fingers to her lips. Creeping silently to the edge of the

trees, she scanned the area and saw no one. She crept forward and pulled the clothes from the line. She turned back toward the cover when she heard someone yell, "Stop! Thief!"

"Damn," she hissed. When she reached O'Hallarhan, she pulled him back the way they had come until they were deep in overgrowth. She squatted, using the overgrown shrubs as cover, and looked back the way she had come. She could just make out a woman at the edge of the overgrowth, looking in, but she showed no interest in pursuing them. Throwing a shirt and pair of trousers at O'Hallarhan, she pulled off her blouse and skirt. When she turned to see if O'Hallarhan had changed, he immediately focused on changing. Joan saw his cheeks redden. The wet shirt and trousers stuck to her skin. Worse, both the shirt and the trousers were too big for her. She pulled the long hairpin out of her hair and used it to secure the pants. Her hair, no longer held secure, tumbled down. She went to O'Hallarhan and snatched his cap and shoved her hair under the cap. She whispered to O'Hallarhan, "How do I look?"

"Fine," O'Hallarhan stammered, again, his cheeks reddened.

Joan sighed. "I mean, can I pass for a man?"

O'Hallarhan gave her an appraising look. "I think so?"

She sighed and hoped that she wouldn't be easily recognisable. "Put your clothes in your bag and let's get out of here before the gendarmes arrive to investigate the theft." When O'Hallarhan finished, she lead them north. She found a side street, and sneaking towards Sternstraße, she peered out. Across from her vantage point, she saw another side street that ran along residential gardens. There was little cover from shrubs, but it would keep them off of the street. She motioned O'Hallarhan to join her. When the street appeared to be relatively empty, she confidently strode across the street and down the side street. O'Hallarhan hurried to follow her. They crept through the gardens and lawns, staying low, trying to stay out of sight. They eventually found an opening out of the houses; Joan wasn't sure if it was an alley or a street. She carefully crept down to the edge and caught sight of the Melanchthon Gymnasium across the street. From there, they could cross the street to a park that would keep them off the streets. She motioned for Peter to join her and she led them out next to the building before crossing the street to the park. Once they were under the trees, she breathed a little easier. The park was not busy. As they walked, they encountered a few mothers pushing perambulators, enjoying the spring day.

Joan kept careful watch for gendarmes as they made continued their way through the park. If she weren't worried about capture, she would enjoy the quietness of the park, a sharp contrast to the last several days. They continued on, walking beside a pond that ran through the centre of the park. Several swans glided over the still waters of the pond. They passed a small group of children throwing bread to ducks, who eagerly devoured the bread, quacking for more. For a moment, Joan allowed herself to enjoy the sights and sounds of normal life. As they neared the end of the park, she was on alert again. She remembered another park to the west, but couldn't remember how close they were. Just across the street, she saw another alley. After making sure no one noticed them, they crossed the street and into the alley. They continued west through a series of alleys and walkways until they came to the end of the alley. Joan peered out carefully and saw the park just across the street. As she turned to look to see if the street was busy, she realised they had come out next to the police station and a gendarme was looking directly at her. "You there! What are you doing?" The gendarme barked.

Joan's stomach fell. She spun around to O'Hallarhan. "We need to run. Now! Follow me!" She sprinted across the street into the park and kept running. She briefly turned her head to make sure O'Hallarhan was behind her. Whistles blew and even as Joan moved deeper within the park, she could hear the gendarme beginning pursuit; the sound of their boots clattering on the path. Joan raced ahead, trying to keep the spire of the Schlosskirche in sight. When she came to an intersection of the paths, she picked the one she thought would take them closer to the church.

As they travelled further into the park, she heard whistles coming from her left; she turned her head and saw another gendarme entering the park, attempting to cut them off. When she came to an intersection, she veered right, away from their goal of the south end of the park. She hoped it might prevent the gendarme from cutting them off. As she ran, the trees became denser, and she soon lost sight of the spire. They continued further into the trees and just when Joan felt they might have lost their pursuers, a shot rang out and a bullet struck a tree just to her right. She slowed down long enough to glance behind her. Peter was labouring to keep up and further back, she saw a gendarme aim his revolver at her. She ducked down as the gun fired again; the bullet whizzing over her head. *We need to get out of here now,* she thought. She scanned ahead and could see through the bushes that a street was ahead. *We at least have a better chance of losing them down a side street.* She pushed herself ahead and as she pushed through the bushes found herself on a street, nearly running over a woman with her kids. She waited for Peter to crash through the bush.

"Now, what?" O'Hallarhan was huffing hard and barely got the words out.

Another shot rang out, and they heard the bullet strike a tree behind them.

"This way!" Joan pulled O'Hallarhan across the street over to an alley. They continued to zigzag from alley to alley until, after a while, Joan did not know where they were. They stopped to catch their breath and Joan listened intently for sounds of pursuit. "It looks like we've lost them for now. But they won't give up looking for us. It looks like it's back streets and alleys."

"Do you know where we are?"

"Not exactly. When we get to a street, I hope we can figure out where we are."

They continued slinking through alleys, backyards, and side streets until they reached an intersection. The buildings were sparse here. *We must be near the outskirts of the city,* she thought. She led O'Hallarhan across the intersection and ducked into space between the few houses that were available. She caught sight of the spire, some distance away. As she looked in the opposite direction, she saw open fields. Using whatever cover they could find, they continued west. As the buildings became fewer and fewer, she steered them south, through more backyards and side streets. The going was slow and after nearly an hour of darting through backyards, gardens and alleys, she saw a train track ahead; the same tracks that had brought them into Wittenberg. When they neared the tracks, they hid behind bushes. Joan scanned the tracks and there were no trains in sight. They quickly crossed and ducked down a side street. To Joan's surprise, the street came out on Desssauer Street. In fact, from her vantage point, she saw the safe house: Wintershall Export Limited.

*What was it Malcolm says? Even a stopped clock is right twice a day,* she thought.

# CHAPTER THIRTY THREE

*P*embroke threw together an impromptu meal of sausages, cheese, and bread. It had been some time since Malcolm had eaten and it tasted heavenly. After eating, Malcolm's eyes were heavy, and he had to fight nodding off. Pembroke said, "Malcolm, you should get some sleep. You can barely stay awake. Here, you take the couch; I'll sleep on the floor since Charles has the bed."

"Absolutely not. I will not let you sleep on the floor in your own home. After the last few days, the carpeted floor would be a vast improvement." They bickered for several more minutes before Pembroke gave up in the face of Malcolm's obstinance. Malcolm went to the bedroom and, after receiving a sheet and blanket, made a nest on the floor and dropped fast asleep.

When he awoke the next morning, Malcolm struggled to pull himself from the floor; his back protesting at the effort. He still felt the lingering aftereffects of his own encounter with his weapon, the long motorcycle trip, and sleeping on the floor had made it worse. Once on his feet, he took his time to put on the only clothes he had, a German army uniform. He checked his pocket watch; it was nearly 9:00. He hadn't slept that long in a very long time, but he must have needed it. Making his way to the living room, he found a teapot covered with a cosy and a tray with some rolls, hard-boiled eggs, and cheese and a note from Pembroke.

*Malcolm,*

*Please excuse the meagreness of the breakfast, but I wasn't planning on houseguests!*

*I have left for the Embassy and will relay the situation to my superiors. I will return at noon so we can discuss the next steps.*

*Please make sure that Charles also eats.*

*Yours,*

*Geoffrey Pembroke*

Malcolm poured a cup of tea, now very strong from sitting in the pot for a long time. Most people would have hated the bitterness or attempted to cover it with sugar, but not Malcolm. After putting a roll, an egg, and some cheese on a plate for himself, he made another plate for Charles. He poured a cup of tea for Charles and filled it with milk and sugar, the way he knew Charles liked his tea. He took the tray with their food and made his way to the bedroom. Using his foot to knock on the door, he said, "Charles? I have breakfast for you."

"About bloody time," Saxon said behind the closed door. "I'm starving,"

Malcolm smiled and opened the door to the bedroom. At first, Saxon started seeing Malcolm in the German uniform, but relaxed when he realised it was Malcolm. "I'm afraid it's not much," Malcolm said as he placed the tray on Saxon's lap, careful not to touch his wounded leg.

"I think I would eat anything," Saxon said, digging into the roll immediately.

"How are you feeling?"

"Other than famished," Saxon said with a mouthful of roll. "Better, I suppose. The leg is still very painful, but I'm loath to take any more pain medicine than I need; it knocks me right out." He continued to attack the plate with gusto. "By the way, where are we exactly?" Saxon said after eating nearly everything on the plate. "I remember arriving at Geoffrey's apartment building and going into the service lift, but after that, it all gets muddled."

"You are safely ensconced in Geoffrey's bedroom. He called the embassy doctor who cleaned and sewed up your wound. It's going to be a couple of weeks before you will heal."

"Where's Geoffrey?"

"He left for the Embassy; he will return around noon to help us figure out the next steps."

Saxon took a sip of his tea. "Now that I've eaten, I might rest until Geoffrey arrives."

"Not before you drink at least two cups of tea; the doctor said you need lots of fluids."

"You know, you aren't my commanding officer anymore, right?"

"That may be so, but that doesn't make it any less important. The doctor said you needed lots of fluids and I'm going to make sure you get them."

"I see," Saxon said. "I know better than to argue with you when you've made up your mind."

"Thank you."

Saxon sipped his tea. "Have you heard any news about Joan or O'Hallarhan?"

"No. I'm hoping Geoffrey will have some news when he returns. If they took the train to Berlin, they should have arrived at the Embassy last night; probably before us."

They sat in silence, drinking their tea. After Saxon finished his second cup, Malcolm picked up the tray. "I'll leave you to rest," Malcolm said as he left the room. After unloading the dishes in the kitchen, Malcolm returned to the living room. He looked around for something to occupy himself; there were several newspapers, all written in German. He had a rudimentary knowledge of written German from attempting to read technical papers. Looking to see if there was any news about his escapades in Leipzig, he found one article and struggled to read it, but he just didn't have the vocabulary for the task. The one thing he got from the article was outrage and anger at the crime. That would make getting out of Germany that much harder.

After giving up on the paper, Malcolm sat on the couch and he jolted awake when Pembroke returned. "Hello, Malcolm. I'm sorry if I woke you."

"No, I'm slightly embarrassed I fell asleep," Malcolm said.

"Don't be; you have been through much in the past few weeks." He looked towards the bedroom. "How's Charles?"

"As good as expected. Cranky as ever. He ate breakfast, and I made him drink two cups of tea. And before I forget, thank you for breakfast."

"I'm just sorry it was so meagre. Shall we check in on Charles? That way, I can share the news one time only."

"Yes. He's probably resting, but I know he wanted to be awakened when you came back."

They went to the bedroom, knocked on the door, and received no answer. They entered and Pembroke went over to Saxon and gently shook his shoulder. "Charles, it's Geoffrey. Are you awake?"

"I am now," Saxon muttered, his eyes still closed. As he opened them, he said, "Geoffrey! It's good to see you again. Sorry to be such an imposition!"

Geoffrey grabbed Saxon's hand, "Nonsense! I want to do anything I can to help." Pembroke squeezed Saxon's hand, before self consciously pulling away when he remembered Malcolm was in the room.

"Speaking of helping," Malcolm said, trying to change the subject, "what news do you have?"

"Yes. Everyone is quite relieved to know that you have escaped German custody and even now, arrangements are being made to get you out of Germany discreetly."

"What about Joan and O'Hallarhan?" Malcolm asked. "They should have got here by now."

"No one I talked to at the Embassy has seen them. Is there anyplace else they might have gone?"

"I don't think so," Malcolm said. "The plan was to meet at the Embassy so we could figure out how to get out of here. But given Joan's knowledge of Germany, if something happened, they could be anywhere."

"When I return to the Embassy, I'll relay that information to my superiors and we'll begin a search. Where do you think they embarked on the train? That will help narrow the search area."

"We were near Kemberg before the zeppelin arrive. The next closest train station would be Bitterfeld-Wolfen," Saxon offered. "She probably booked their tickets there."

"Thank you, Charles," Pembroke said. "How are you feeling?"

"As well as I can, considering the circumstances," Saxon said. "Although this one," he said, gesturing to Malcolm, "has the bedside manner of Attila the Hun."

"Be nice, Charles. You should know that the doctor was impressed with how Malcolm treated your wounds."

"I suppose I'll never hear the end of it," Saxon said.

"Speaking of which, we should probably change the dressing on your leg," Malcolm said. "Would you rather 'Attila the Hun' change it, or Geoffrey?"

"Goodness gracious," Pembroke said. "I don't know the first thing about dressing a wound. And to be honest, I get nauseous at the sight of blood."

"Attila the Hun, it is," Malcolm said as he went to the bed and uncovered Saxon's leg.

# CHAPTER THIRTY FOUR

oan and O'Hallarhan made their way into Coswig in the dark. Even with the moonless night, they saw a baroque castle on a gentle rise overlooking the village. They passed by several half-timbered houses with tile roofs. The cobblestone streets were uneven from years of traffic, making the journey difficult. They reached the town centre; shops lined the square. Past the square, they saw a church spire with a clock telling them it was 11:18. "Damn," Joan muttered. It was much too late to secure a bed at a hotel, gasthof, or pension and too late to catch a train. If Frietag realised they had jumped ship, Joan reasoned he would expect them to take the train, and she had no desire to repeat the trip from Kempberg. For now, they needed to find a place to stay to dry off and make plans for their departure. Just then, it sprinkled.

"Damn," Joan said. "We need to get to shelter before this gets worse."

"Do you have any suggestions?" O'Hallarhan asked. The sprinkles became more frequent, turning into drizzle.

"Maybe we can try the church." Joan pointed to the church with the clock tower. "At this hour, it might be our best bet." As they made their way to the church, Joan cursed. She did not have her umbrella with her; despite being a formidable weapon, she wished she had it for its primary function of keeping the rain away. By the time they made it to the church, it was a full-blown rain and between their swim in the river and the rain, they looked like drowned rats. Their luck changed for the better when they found the door unlocked. They opened the door slowly and peered inside. The interior was lit by several candles around the altar; their light cast flickering shadows everywhere. Cautiously, they made their way inside. When they reached the first row of pews at the back of the church, Joan slid in, but O'Hallarhan stopped. He bowed towards the altar and crossed himself before sliding into the pew.

"You know this is a Protestant church," Joan said.

"I know; old habits die hard," O'Hallarhan said. "Besides, I figure we could use all the help we can get."

"True." They sat in silence for several moments before Joan asked, "Are you religious?"

"Aye. I attend Mass every week. You?"

"I would have said no, but I have seen things that have caused me to reconsider my position." Images of Malcolm being impaled by the Spear of Destiny flashed back and his sudden revival after they fled the lost city of R'lyeh. Joan shook her head to clear the memories. "We should take turns sleeping. You go first."

"Are you sure?"

"Yes. I don't think I could sleep if even if I wanted. I'll wake you in a couple of hours." O'Hallarhan stretched out on the pew and, to Joan's frustration, was asleep within minutes. She looked around the church. She stood up and walked around the back of the church. Joan turned to look at the altar. She thought about her own relationship to faith; her mother's rather tenuous connection to her Russian Orthodox upbringing contrasted with the Anglican faith of her father. She thought of St. Peter's Church, the small stone parish church near her father's home where she was to marry Malcolm. Tears fell unbidden as she thought of Malcolm and gave a silent prayer that he had made it safely to Berlin. She flashed back to the first time they met in St. Petersburg; how she felt a spark of connection. She played through their relationship in her mind; their times together, their fights, and their reconciliations.

Lost in thought, she heard a voice say, "Fraulein, what are you doing here? The Church is closed." She turned to the voice and saw a middle-aged man, dressed in a black cassock over black trousers and shoes with a simple cross hanging from a chain.

"I beg your leave, Pfarrer," Joan replied in German. "Our motor carriage broke down outside of town. By the time we walked into town, it was late and the weather had turned. All the places to stay were closed; we came here seeking a place of warmth and comfort to escape the rain."

"We?"

"My brother. He's sleeping on one of the pews." Joan pointed to the pew.

"Not unlike many of my parishioners," the man said, eliciting a polite laugh from Joan. "Still, they intentionally make the pews uncomfortable. Your brother must have fallen asleep from exhaustion.

"He did."

"Come, bring your brother and I at least can put you up in the rectory. The couches are much more comfortable than the pews."

"We don't want to be an imposition."

"You won't be an imposition. I rarely have company and it will be a welcome change. Wake your brother and you can follow me. I am Pfarrer Hoffman, caretaker of this church."

"I'm Margarete Weber; my brother is Peter." Joan went to the sleeping O'Hallarhan and put her hand over his mouth as she shook him. She whispered, "We're going to the pastor's and I need you to be absolutely quiet. Nod if you understand."

O'Hallarhan nodded, and Joan removed her hand. He rose and gathered his things. He nodded to the pastor.

"You must excuse my brother; he's mute."

"Very well. Follow me," the man said.

He led them out a side door by the altar, to a vestibule, and then back outside. The rain was coming down hard again, and they dashed over the stone path that led to a modest house near the church. The pastor waved them inside as he held the door open for them. Once they were inside, he lit a candle and led them to his living room. "I'm afraid I can only offer the use of the couches." He pointed to two worn, overstuffed couches. "But is better than the pews and will keep you out of the rain."

"Thank you," Joan said, as she gestured to O'Hallarhan to sit on the couch.

"Can I get you anything to eat?"

"No, we're fine. However, we are most eager to continue on our trip. Are there any cars for hire here?"

"There are very few cars here; most are owned by Duke Frederick II. There are some trade vehicles that travel between cities making deliveries. Where do you need to go?"

"We were trying to get to Potsdam." While Potsdam was in the general direction she wished to travel, she didn't want to give away their actual destination.

"Why don't you use the train? We have a station in town."

"My brother is deathly afraid of trains; it is the reason we took a hired car."

"It is very late. You should rest, and we can figure out how to get you on your way in the morning."

When Hoffman left, O'Hallarhan whispered to Joan, "What's the plan?"

Joan thought through the options. "I'm loath to go by train, although it's probably the fastest means of transport. Liberating the Duke's car for our use means that we draw attention that we certainly don't need. I hate not having a plan, but I think we should see what opportunities await us in the morning. For now, we should get some sleep."

Joan lay on the couch, and although not as uncomfortable as sleeping on a pew, it was lumpy and hard. Despite that, the events of the day caught up with her and she fell asleep quickly.

She awoke early the next morning by the morning sun streaming through the windows and directly into her eyes. She sat up; O'Hallarhan was still sleeping. Quietly rising, she went through her bags;

everything was still wet from their swim in the river. Sighing, she shut her bags, preferring to wear dry clothes. Now that it was light, she could see the room. It was sparsely furnished; other than the two couches, there was an armchair, side tables next to each end of the couches. A few paintings of religious scenes decorated the walls. A mirror hung above the lone fireplace in the room. She went to the mirror and did her best to make herself look presentable; she doused herself with perfume to rid herself of the smell of river water that clung to her.

O'Hallarhan woke shortly afterwards. After making the same assessments of his clothing options, he whispered, "What now?"

"We should head into town and see what options are available."

Before she could continue, she heard movement in the hall outside. Putting her finger to her lips to indicate that O'Hallarhan should remain quiet, she went to the hall where she met Pfarrer Hoffman. "Ah, you're awake. I've prepared a simple breakfast of rolls and smoked fish and I also made a pot of coffee if you would care to partake before you leave."

"That is most kind and most unnecessary," Joan said.

"Nonsense. It's been ages since I've had anyone here to share my morning repast. And as the Scriptures say in Luke 3:10, 'Anyone who has two shirts should share with the one who has none, and anyone who has food should do the same'. What kind of Pfarrer would I be if I failed to help strangers in need?"

"We would feel honoured to have a meal with you, but we also wish to show our hospitality in return," Joan said she opened her purse.

"I require no repayment, but a donation to our church would be most welcome. Come, I'm sure that you both must be hungry." He showed Joan and O'Hallarhan to the dining room, where rolls, a plate of smoked fish, and a large pot of coffee were waiting. As she smelt the food, she realised she was starving, not having eaten since the previous morning in Wittenberg. *Had it really only been one day?* she thought. She fought her desire to help herself to several rolls and settled for two with a few slices of the smoked fish. The coffee was a welcome treat; she smiled to herself, thinking how Malcolm would absolutely hate being forced to drink coffee.

"How do you plan to continue you trip?" Hoffman asked.

Joan passed for a moment to finish eating a bite of her roll. "I'm not sure. It thought we'd go into town and see what options are available."

"What makes your trip to Potsdam so urgent?"

"We're going to meet with a doctor who says he might cure my brother's muteness." It seemed a plausible excuse.

"I understand. I hope that God, through the doctor, can ease your brother's burden."

"Thank you. Again, thank you for your hospitality." As she finished her breakfast, she rose and pulled O'Hallarhan away from his food. "My brother does like to eat, but we should be going." She reached into her purse and pulled out a 10-mark coin, pressing it into the Pfarrer's hands.

"You are most generous," Hoffman said. "May God bless you and keep you on your journey."

"Thank you. Come Peter, we should be going." Joan grabbed O'Hallarhan by the elbow and led him away from the dining table. They gathered their things and left the rectory.

As they made their way into town, they kept their eyes open for transport to Berlin. Coswig was a small town and their presence as outsiders drew stares from people going about their business, housewives shopping at the market stall, the wagon drivers delivering goods. As they made their way around the town centre, Joan noticed a few policemen questioning vendors and she quickly led O'Hallarhan outside the town centre and found a quiet area where they turned down an alley to talk. After making sure they had escaped detection, she whispered to O'Hallarhan, "I think they are onto us. Did you see the policemen talking to the vendors? We need to leave, and quickly."

"How? If they are on our trail, how can we leave without detection? I'm new to this whole spy business."

"Let me think." Joan considered her options. The sound of an approaching motorcycle jolted her from her thoughts. She slipped down the alley to peer into the street. A motorcycle driven by a German soldier with another sitting in the sidecar slowly made its way down the street towards them. If they could ambush the soldiers, they might take the motorcycle. But that would draw attention once the Germans realised the motorcycle had failed to return. But disguised as German soldiers, they could at least slip out of town unnoticed. She hurried back to O'Hallarhan.

"There's a German Army motorcycle coming up the street. We're going to ambush them and take their motorcycle."

"Are you crazy?" O'Hallarhan hissed. "Isn't that going to put them on our trail even quicker?"

"It's likely, but we can get at least an hour's head start before they realise anything is amiss." She rummaged through her bag and let out a thankful sigh when she found two ether grenades. "Quick, find a place to hide. I'll draw them down here and we can knock them out with these," holding out the ether grenades.

"Then what?"

"We take their uniforms and get out of here as quickly as possible."

O'Hallarhan crouched behind a rubbish pile as Joan made her way to the street. She pretended to peer out cautiously, but made sure the two soldiers saw her. She shrieked and hustled back down the alley, joining O'Hallarhan. Waiting until she heard the motorcycle come to a stop at the top of the alley, she watched as the two soldiers dismounted from the motorcycle and pulled their revolvers. Joan pulled her handkerchief out and tied it around her face, gesturing to O'Hallarhan that he should do the same. The soldiers crept carefully down the alley. Joan waited until they were within 10 feet and threw the grenades, striking both soldiers in the chest, the force of the impact breaking the membrane on the grenades. The cloud of gas engulfed the two soldiers. Within seconds, the two soldiers stopped and lost their balance. Joan held her breath as she jumped from her hiding place and quickly knocked out the two soldiers with well-prac-ticed ease. She indicated to O'Hallarhan to join her and they removed the soldiers' uniform coats. The sickly smell of ether clung to the jackets; she hoped it wouldn't make them light-headed. They donned the jackets; even the biggest jacket was too small for O'Hallarhan and Joan was virtually swimming in the smallest. They searched the soldiers for anything they could use, but other than the revolvers, there was nothing of use. Joan pulled out a length of rope from her bag and they tied and gagged the two soldiers. Donning the uniform jackets, helmets, and goggles, Joan slid into the sidecar and O'Hallarhan climbed onto the motorcycle seat. He stopped to familiarise himself with the controls.

"Have you ever driven one of these before?" Joan asked.

"No, but I think I have the gist of it. Which way do we go?"

Joan pulled out her waterlogged map. "We need to go north." She thought for a moment and said, "Drive back the way we came and before we get to the town centre, take a right. We should be able to find the road to Berlin from there."

"Here goes nothing," O'Hallarhan said as he put the motorcycle into gear. They lurched forward, but after a few seconds, O'Hallarhan had the motorcycle under control, and they made their way back to the town centre.

# CHAPTER THIRTY FIVE

Malcolm did his best to clean Saxon's wound and apply a clean bandage, despite the constant barrage of complaints from Saxon. When he finished, he left Saxon and returned to the living room. As he did, the phone rang, making Malcolm jump. Pembroke answered the phone. After a quick conversation where Pembroke simply replied, "Yes, I understand." He hung up the phone and turned to Malcolm. "We have some news about Joan and O'Hallarhan, and it doesn't appear to be good. My superiors instructed me to bring you to the Embassy to discuss this further."

"Do you have something I can wear? I can't very well go dressed as a German soldier." Malcolm pointing to the uniform.

Pembroke regarded Malcolm for a moment. "We seem to be close in build. Let's see if I have a suit you can wear." They returned to the bedroom, where Saxon said, "Now, what do you want? Aren't you done with the torture?"

"No, Charles. We're simply looking for something for Malcolm to wear. We're going to the Embassy."

"I'll go with you," Saxon said as he swung his legs out of bed. As he moved the wounded leg, he winced in pain.

"You'll do no such thing," Pembroke said. "You are in no condition to walk and we can't have you drawing attention as you try to limp your way down the street. Stay here and rest."

"Bloody easy for you to say," Saxon muttered. "Very well."

Pembroke opened his closet and pulled out a non descriptive grey suit, trousers, a clean white shirt, and a simple black tie. Malcolm went to the lavatory and stripped out of the uniform, and changed into the suit. He lost weight during his captivity and he was thankful at this point because it was all he could to button the trousers. The shirt and suit hung loosely over him. He looked in the mirror as he struggled with the tie before giving up.

"I gave up on the tie," he said as he returned to the bedroom.

"For crying out loud, give it to me," Saxon said. Malcolm gave him the tie and, with practiced ease, Saxon tied the tie loosely around his throat before slipping it off and handing it back to Malcolm, who donned the tie and adjusted it. "Don't pull it so tight or you're going to undo all my work! How have you got so far in your life without learning how to do this? You wear a tie with your duty uniform every day!"

"I had someone tie them for me and left them, so all I had to do was slip them on," Malcolm said sheepishly.

Saxon shook his head. "The suit certainly doesn't fit you well, but I suppose it would have to do."

"We should be back in time for dinner," Pembroke said. "Get some rest."

"All I do is rest," Saxon groused. "But I suppose there's nothing else I can do."

Malcolm and Pembroke left the room, shutting the door behind them. Pembroke gathered his briefcase and gave Malcolm a black derby hat. It was too small and Malcolm struggled to pull it on his head. Once out on the street, Malcolm took a second to see Berlin in daylight. The streets were bustling with pedestrians. As they made their way down Leipziger Straße, they passed many shops as the building continued several floors above, decorated with wrought-iron balconies and stucco ornaments. As they turned onto Wilhelmstraße, Malcolm could not help but feel conspicuous as they walked past government buildings; he truly was in the heart of Germany. Malcolm already felt a headache coming on from wearing the too tight derby, but he struggled to pull it further down to shade his face. They continued several minutes up the street when Malcolm saw the Union Jack flying from what he could only describe as a palace and he had never been so happy to see that flag; an oasis of home in a hostile land. As they approached, Malcolm could see the Embassy in more detail. A two-story portico graced the centre of the building, an ornate feature starkly different from the surrounding buildings. As they approached the gate, Malcolm was relieved to see the guard. Pembroke spoke to the guard for a moment and soon they were inside the British Embassy.

Although Malcolm had seen his fair share of impressive architecture in his travels, the ornate foyer of the embassy momentarily took him aback. Immediately ahead were two carpeted staircases on either side of the room, leading to a landing and a single staircase leading to the second floor. Underneath the landing was an ornate fountain and several doors leading further into the embassy. Pembroke led Malcolm up the right-hand staircase and they continued to the second floor. Pembroke led Malcolm down a hall, past several doors, before stopping and knocking at a door. After a moment, he ushered Malcolm into an ornate conference room. The large room had high ceilings; white plaster mouldings decorate the ceiling edges, contrasting with the green damask wallpaper. There were several tall windows on one side, covered with heavy burgundy curtains. A brass chandelier lit with electricity provided light. A large mahogany table sat in the centre, lined with leather-upholstered chairs and a large map of Germany laid out on the table. Already seated at the table were two men; a man Malcolm did not recognise with dark hair and a grey, bushy beard and moustache. The other was Mycroft Holmes.

"Sir Edward Goschen, allow me to introduce Commodore Malcolm Robertson," Pembroke said. "Sir Edward is His Majesty's Ambassador to Germany."

Malcolm went to the ambassador and shook his hand. "I'm very glad to meet you, Ambassador. I can't tell you how relieved I am to be here." He turned to Mycroft and offered his hand. "I'm even glad to see you again, Mycroft," who harrumphed at Malcolm's remark, but shook his hand anyway. "Do you have news of Joan and O'Hallarhan?"

"Please sit, Malcolm," Mycroft said. "Can we offer you anything before we get down to business?"

"I wouldn't mind a cup of tea," Malcolm said. Pembroke went to a sideboard near the table and poured a cup of tea for Malcolm. and sat after setting it down before Malcolm, who immediately took a sip.

"I must say, you have made my job much more difficult, Commodore Robertson," Goschen said. "Your escape from Leipzig was rather much like swatting a hornet's nest with a cricket bat."

"That was not my intent, Ambassador," Malcolm began.

Goschen raised his hand. "Have no fear. It's nothing I can't handle. I am thankful that you have made it here."

"Have you heard anything about Joan and O'Hallarhan? Have they made it to Berlin?"

"Alas, no," Mycroft said. "We received a message from an agent stationed in Wittenberg. Miss de St. Leger and Mr O'Hallarhan left by train from Kempberg, but Miss de St Leger and Mr O'Hallarhan disembarked the train at Wittenberg after seeing Frietag on the train."

"We have to rescue her," Malcolm interrupted.

"Malcolm, please let me continue," Mycroft said. "They were able to elude Frietag and the gendarme and made it to a safe house. They attempted to make their escape by barge, but Frietag and his men caught up to them near Coswig." He pointed to the town on the map. "Mr O'Hallarhan and Miss de St Leger slipped off of the barge at Coswig. At present, their whereabouts are unknown."

Malcolm gave a sigh of frustration. "So what do we do? How do we find them?"

"I have a plan. Knowing they are being pursued, Miss de St. Leger will not hazard to take the train to Berlin and will try to reach Berlin by any other means. I have arranged for an airship piloted by a mutual acquaintance to leave as soon as possible to fly to Coswig. When we find them, he has been instructed to fly directly to Geneva as originally intended. From there, we will arrange passage for all of you to return to England."

Malcolm guessed the airship pilot was none other than Colfax Mingo, the airship pilot who had flown them on several missions. Although it wasn't much of a plan, he felt relieved knowing Colfax would be their pilot. "When do we leave?"

"As soon as possible." Mycroft assessed Malcolm. "I took the liberty of having some clothes made for you based on you measurements when were an agent. It appears they might be too big for you."

"Beggars can't be choosers," Malcolm said. "What about Charles?"

"We've arranged for a car to take you back to Mr Pembroke's apartment that will take the two of you to the airship with travelling clothes. When you arrive in Geneva, one of our doctors will wait to check on Charles." Mycroft stood. "I am relieved to see that you are none the worse for wear after your time with Frietag. I must insist on a thorough interview with you about your time with Frietag when you return to England."

"After Joan and I are married," Malcolm said in a tone that brooked no dissent.

"As you say," Mycroft relented.

Malcolm turned to the ambassador. "Again, my apologies for making your job more difficult."

"Nonsense. The Germans are clearly in the wrong for abducting you from our shores. They deserve to reap what they have sown. God speed, Commodore."

"Thank you, Ambassador." Malcolm turned to Mycroft. "Thank you, Mycroft. We'll find Joan."

"I know you will." Mycroft offered his hand, which Malcolm shook.

Pembroke led Malcolm out of the room and, as Mycroft promised, a car was waiting just outside the Embassy gates. The trip back to Pembroke's apartment was barely faster than walking, as wagons and other cars filled the streets. When they returned to the apartment, they roused Saxon, who had been sleeping and helped him change into new clothes. Saxon put his arms around the shoulders of Malcolm and Pembroke and they helped him to the freight lift. Malcolm couldn't help but think back to last night when he dragged Charles up here. They gingerly helped Saxon through the foyer and into the car. Saxon hissed in pain as he pulled his wounded leg into the car, but after a moment, he seemed to relax. Pembroke stood silently next to Saxon, and after a moment, Malcolm realised he needed to check on their luggage to give them a moment alone. Malcolm rechecked his suitcase and found, besides his clothing, Mycroft had provided new identification papers, a wallet with an assortment of currencies, and a revolver with a shoulder holster. Malcolm looked around and, when no one was watching, removed his jacket and put on the shoulder holster and placed the gun safely inside. He looked up and saw Pembroke shutting the door to the car. Malcolm offered him his hand. "I'm sorry. I hope we weren't too much of an imposition."

"Nonsense." Pembroke shook Malcolm's hand. "I'm glad that I could be of assistance." He hesitated for a moment before adding, "Please take care of Charles. He means a great deal to me."

"I understand," Malcolm said. "I will do everything I can to keep him safe."

"I'm holding you to that," Pembroke said.

Malcolm got in the car and after thirty minute drive, they arrived at the airfield that Malcolm noted on their way into Berlin. Eventually, the car stopped in front of a small, nondescript airship and Malcolm saw Colfax Mingo approached the car. "I bet you didn't think you'd see me again so soon, Commodore?" He said as he offered his hand to Malcolm.

Malcolm shook his hand, his own can nearly crushed by the strength of Colfax's grip. "I could say the same." Together, they helped Saxon out of the car and, to Malcolm's surprise, Colfax lifted Saxon in his arms and carried him into the airship. Malcolm grabbed the suitcases from the back of the car and followed them in. The airship was a basic cargo airship. The interior was one empty bay, with a few chairs and a couch. As Malcolm entered, Colfax put Saxon on the couch. As

Malcolm stowed the luggage, Colfax raised the gangplank and secured the cargo bay doors.

"I'll have us in the air momentarily, Commodore. We'll find Miss de St Leger and Mr O'Hallarhan."

"I know we will," Malcolm replied.

# CHAPTER THIRTY SIX

As O'Hallarhan manoeuvred through Coswig, Joan watched to ensure no one followed them. Although the sight of a German Army motorcycle was a rarity, no one seemed suspicious. They eventually made their way out of Coswig and onto the road to Berlin, the town giving way to forests, providing cover if a patrolling zeppelin was looking for them. The roads were bumpy and the ride jarring as they slowly picked their way past horse-drawn wagons, often having to come to a complete stop to wait for the wagons to pass one another. The fellow travellers on the road seemed to give little deference to the military motorcycle, frustrating Joan at their lack of progress. She was constantly on watch for any sight of pursuit, but thankfully, she saw no one.

After about an hour, the forest thinned and after they passed through the village of Boßdorf, they travelled through farmland, no longer enjoying the cover of the woods. They travelled past farmland and several small villages. After they passed through the village of Beelitz, there was a loud pop. O'Hallarhan struggled to control the motorcycle long enough to pull it off the road. He dismounted to inspect the motorcycle and shook his head in despair.

"What is it?" Joan said, pulling her goggles up onto the helmet.

"It's the front tire. It's blown."

"Can you fix it?"

"I could if I had a spare tire, which I don't." He bent down to inspect the wheel. "I don't think I can even patch it."

Joan pulled herself out of the sidecar, her muscles protesting after hours of confinement in the sidecar. She went over to O'Hallarhan and, even without his mechanical knowledge, she realised the futility of trying to repair the tire. "Shite," she said, kicking the tire.

"What now?"

Joan went back to the motorcycle and unloaded their bags. "We walk."

"What about our pursuit?"

"We'll have to deal with them when it happens," she said. "We should at least try to hide this motorcycle; it might throw them off our trail." Ahead, Joan spied a small copse of trees just off the road. "Do you think we can push this to the trees and hide it there?"

"We can try." Even with the additional strength provided by O'Hallarhan's mechanical arm, it took all they had to push the crippled motorcycle; the task made more difficult because of the flat tire. They collapsed on the ground for a few minutes to catch their breath before they broke off some low, leafy branches and covered the motorcycle. Joan went back to the road to assess their work. Someone driving by wasn't likely to notice, but anyone diligently searching would likely see it. "It's going to have to do." She picked up her bags and said, "We better get started. We've got a long way to go."

"I was afraid you were going to say that." O'Hallarhan picked up his bag and together, they started the long walk to Berlin. They walked for an hour before reaching the town of Seddiner See. They contemplated going into town, but pushed ahead, until they stopped by the lake and washed off the road dirt from their motorcycle trip; both looking like raccoons when they removed their goggles. They pressed on, but their pace slowed as they grew more tired. After stopping at a farmhouse to buy some cheese and some water, they sat in the shade of some trees by the side of the road and quietly ate their food. When they finished, they looked at one another, stood up, hefted their bags, and trudged down the road.

The day was cloudy, so it was difficult to tell the time from the sun. They continued on, walking through villages that became more frequent the closer they got to Berlin. Late in the afternoon, roughly an hour after passing Nuthetal, Joan thought she heard the sounds of engines. She looked around but saw nothing. "Peter, we should hurry."

"Why?"

"I thought I heard engines. We need to get to the next village; if there is someone coming, it will be much more difficult to find us." They hurried their pace, but the road ahead was uphill, making the effort even harder. As they reached the top of the hill, Joan looked back towards Nuthetal and thought she could make out a squad of motorcycles heading their way. "Run," she yelled, looking for any place to hide. But all she could see around her was farmland with no place to hide.

Joan was panting from the effort of running, but the sound of engines seemed even closer before she realised that the sound was coming from in front of her. She looked up and saw a German airship descending and approaching them. Joan was about to yell to O'Hallarhan to change direction when she saw a white-haired man dangling from a harness on the side of the airship. She didn't know how, but she was certain it had to be Malcolm. Only he was daft enough to hang from the side of an airship. He saw the two of them and waved to get their attention. Joan stopped and waved back. He pointed to the rope and Joan instantly understood what to do. "Peter," she yelled. "Run for that airship and grab the rope. It's Malcolm; he's come to rescue us!"

"Are you certain?" O'Hallarhan was gasping for breath.

"Yes! It's either that or get chased down by the motorcycles!" She turned her head and she could see the motorcycles gaining on them. She pushed herself as hard as she could as she ran towards the dangling rope. O'Hallarhan made to the rope first and waited for Joan. "Start climbing!" she yelled. "I'm only going to slow you down!" O'Hallarhan hesitated for a second and then began climbing. By the time she made it to the rope, she could hear the motorcycles nearing her. As she grabbed the rope and climbed, shots rang out before she heard a tremendous crash. She dared to look behind her and saw the motorcycles had crashed together in a heap. She looked up and saw Malcolm holstering a gun. Her arms burned as she struggled to pull herself up. Some ten feet away from the cargo door, arms wrapped around her and pulled her close.

"Do you need some assistance?" Malcolm said.

"Ordinarily, I would say no, but who am I to prevent my white knight from rescuing me?"

"Let's get you aboard." Together, they made their way up the last 10 feet until they were both safely inside and shut the cargo bay door. As they did, they heard shots hitting the door.

"Colfax, get us up as fast as you can! They're taking potshots at us!" Malcolm yelled.

"Aye, aye, sir. Hold on, I'm dropping the ballast!" After a moment, the airship nosed upwards and Joan fell towards the back of the airship, but Malcolm caught her in his arms.

"Fancy meeting you here," he said with a smile before pulling her close for a kiss.

# CHAPTER THIRTY SEVEN

$\mathcal{M}$alcolm pulled away from Joan after a moment. "Hold that thought. I want to check on your pursuers." He released Joan, who momentarily lost her balance from the speeding airship. He went to a small window and peered down at the rapidly shrinking group of German soldiers, drenched from the release of ballast water. They were still firing, but Malcolm could tell that they were already out of range and thought they would have minimum impact on the airship. He watched for a few more seconds as they slowly shrank out of view. He came back to Joan and pulled her back into his arms, and kissed her again.

"Enough with the maudlin displays of affection. Some of us are trying to recuperate," Saxon said.

Joan pulled away from Malcolm and turned to see Saxon lying a couch. She turned to Malcolm and said, "How did you find us?"

"It was a stroke of luck, to be honest. I can't believe I actually found you." He pulled her close into a tight embrace. "I was so worried that Frietag had captured you. I don't know what I would have done."

"You still haven't said how you found me."

"After we made it to Berlin, Geoffrey took me to the Embassy where Mycroft had already secured this airship for our departure. The agent from the warehouse told us you were in Coswig, so we flew there as soon as we could. We would have been here sooner, but someone was complaining about his leg. Something about being shot." He looked over at Saxon, who harrumphed at the jab. "To be honest, I wasn't sure it was you until we saw you break into a run with a squad of German motorcycles heading for you." He pulled her close and held for several moments before he said, "What happened to you?" Malcolm lead her to a chair and moved one next to her. He sat down and held her hands.

Joan told them about the train trip from Kemberg, their trip through Wittenberg, escape from the gendarme, and their attempted escape down the river, only to end up going ashore at Coswig. She told them about their night at the church and their trip this morning. "We might have made it to Berlin already if the tire hadn't failed."

Malcolm turned to O'Hallarhan. "Thank you, Peter, for your part in this."

Joan turned to Saxon. "Charles, how are you doing?"

"Except for the pain in my leg, I'm fine," Saxon said. He nodded towards Malcolm. "This one fancies himself a doctor after the proper doctor praised him for patching up my log."

"I never said I was a doctor. I'm a mechanic; I just patched you up like would any machine."

Before Saxon could respond, Joan interjected. "Is there any water? I'm parched from all this exertion."

"That we do. Although are accommodations are bit spartan," Malcolm said as he gestured around the cargo hold, "Mycroft ensured we have ample provisions for our trip." Malcolm opened a crate and after rummaging around for a few moments, took out a bottle of water and handed it to Joan.

She took a long drink from the bottle. "And where are we going on this trip?"

"Geneva," Malcolm whispered.

Joan groaned before taking another drink. "Mycroft's idea?"

"Unfortunately," Malcolm said. "Stay here and rest. I'm going to see if I can give Colfax a hand with the piloting." Malcolm squeezed her hand before he turned and make his way to the cockpit.

Malcolm knocked on the cabin door before opening it. "How is everything up here?"

"All good," said Colfax. "Please, have a seat," he said, pointing to the empty copilot's seat. "I don't know how you drag me into all of your adventures," he said.

"Lucky I guess?"

Colfax deep laugh rumbled in cockpit. "That's one word for it."

"How long until we make it to Geneva?"

Colfax looked at the map next to him and did some mental calculations. "Another eighteen hours, give or take."

Malcolm pulled out his pocket watch. It was already after 5:00 PM. "So tomorrow night around 11:00 PM?"

"Give or take. Depending on weather and if any of your friends try to pursue us."

"How are we going to get back to England?"

"We leave the next evening, after I refuel and take on more supplies. Mycroft arranged everything."

They sat in silence for several moments before Malcolm broke the silence. "Do you need any help in piloting?"

"Not right now, but I will need a break in a few hours. I'll come and get you and you can take a turn at the helm. I've plotted the course here," he said, pointing to the map. "It's a fairly simple route, provided we're not pursued. Between you and me, we can't get out of Germany fast enough."

"Agreed." Malcolm rose and turned to leave. "Let me know when I can relieve you." He left the cockpit and went back to Joan, who had settled in the chair, her eyes closed. "Are you alright?"

"Yes." Joan opened her eyes and sat up in her chair. "It's been a tiring two days. Seems much longer."

"I know. We both have had plenty of excitement the last two days. You should rest. I think I'll do the same before Colfax lets me take over."

"You can't help yourself, can you?" Joan smiled at Malcolm. "Am I ever going to drag you away from flying?"

"I can think of ways you might convince me," Malcolm said as he leaned in close.

"Ahem." Saxon cleared his throat. "I'm already in pain. Please don't add to it by making me nauseous. Besides, you're making poor Mr O'Hallarhan blush."

"Killjoys," Malcolm muttered under his breath, eliciting a chuckle from Joan.

"When do we arrive in Geneva?" Saxon said.

"If all goes well, late tomorrow evening. We leave early the next evening."

"Hopefully, we'll have civilised lodging for a change. If I have to spend more than one night on this couch, I will be rather grumpy," Saxon said.

"And how would that be different?" Malcolm couldn't resist the chance to take a jab at Saxon.

"I'll have you know I am not grumpy. I'm convalescing," Saxon said with an indignant tone in his voice.

"Are they always like this?" O'Hallarhan asked.

"Yes," Joan said. "You get used to it after a while."

"Not bloody likely," muttered O'Hallarhan.

# CHAPTER THIRTY EIGHT

After a few minutes, the quartet fell asleep. Malcolm woke up an hour later and realised that he was hungry. He rummaged around and found a hamper filled with sausages, cheeses, pickles, and four loaves of bread. He also found two bottles of wine, a bottle of his favourite whisky, a bottle of gin, two limes, and a bottle of vodka. Although Malcolm eyed the whisky, he knew if he was going to fly, he should avoid the whisky for now. He took the food out and put them onto plates. After cutting a few slices of cheese, a few pieces of sausage, and a hunk of bread, he sat and ate in silence until, one by one, everyone woke up and joined Malcolm in the meal, all save Saxon. Under his direction, Joan made a plate for him and brought it to him.

While the others broke into the alcohol, Malcolm opted for water instead, but admonished O'Hallarhan, "Don't drink all the whisky! I'm going to want some later."

"Not much chance of that," O'Hallarhan said. "I'll have to lower my standards to drink that instead of proper Irish whiskey, which is far superior."

"You know, those are fighting words," Malcolm said, and the quartet laughed.

They chatted for another hour before Colfax called for Malcolm to relieve him. Malcolm took his place in the pilot's seat and familiarised himself with the gauges and equipment. Colfax pointed out their location on the map; they were approaching Erfurt. Malcolm nodded to Colfax, who left to get some food and some rest. Malcolm relaxed as he settled in; he really enjoyed flying. Joan was right, it was very hard for him to give up the opportunity to pilot a ship, be it an airship or a spaceship. In his wildest dreams, he never thought he'd enjoy piloting as much as he did. All he had ever wanted when he joined the Air Service was to be an engineer; now he felt as at home in the cockpit as he did the Engine Room. He chuckled, thinking that he had been on the ship for nearly four hours and he hadn't visited the Engine Room once.

As night fell, Malcolm no longer had any landmarks to guide his navigation. He kept a careful eye on his heading with the compass and hoped he wouldn't fly them too far off course. He checked the map and realised the flight path wouldn't take them near any cities until they passed near Frankfurt, nearly four hours from now.

Malcolm's time in the pilot chair passed quickly and just when the lights of Frankfurt were in sight, Colfax returned to the cockpit. It was nearly 11:00 PM and the cargo hold was dark as Malcolm made his way back. In the dim light from the cockpit, it looked like everyone had found a place to sleep; Saxon remained on his couch. O'Hallarhan had made a nest away from Saxon, while Joan slept on the other couch. Malcolm smiled as he watched her sleep; he never tired of seeing her. Sure to his word, O'Hallarhan had barely touched the whisky. Malcolm took a swig directly from the bottle, not wanting to rummage around for a glass. He relished the taste and enjoyed the warmth. He took one more swig before going to the couch where Joan slept. Gently kissing her on the head before laying down on the floor next to the couch, he fell asleep in a few minutes.

What felt like a moment later, a loud pop awoke him. He sat straight up and Joan roused as well. "What was that?" she asked.

"I don't know," Malcolm said. He started towards the cockpit when Colfax came out. "We have a problem. We've lost our engine."

"Do you want me to look?" Malcolm asked.

"If you could," Colfax said. "I'll do my best to keep us on course, but it will be tough without an engine." Before Malcolm could ask, Colfax pointed to the far end of the cargo hold. "The Engine Room is behind the door." Malcolm fumbled in the dark until he reached the door. When he opened it, he immediately smelled the acrid smell of overheated oil. He fumbled around the wall inside until he found a switch. The light barely made a difference, as a cloud of black smoke nearly obscured the room. He made his way to the engine and before he could touch the housing, he could feel the heat. He hurried back to their provisions and grabbed two bottles of water., which he poured over the engine housing. The water turned to steam almost immediately. He searched the room until he found a pair of heavy gloves. Hoping they were tough enough to protect his hands, he carefully laid a hand on the engine housing. Although he could still feel the heat through the gloves, he didn't think he would burn himself. He opened the housing and his worse fears were realised; the pistons had melted in place and the engine was no longer turning. He tried to move the piston, but it had fused solid. There was nothing he could do. He rummaged in a store cabinet until he found an electric torch and examined the engine in more detail. He checked the oil pan and unsurprisingly found it bone dry. As he shone the light into the pan, he found the reason; a hole about the size of a bullet was visible. They had been leaking oil since they rescued Joan and O'Hallarhan.

Malcolm closed up the engine housing and went to Colfax in the cockpit. "The engine is dead; it's fused tight. Seems our German friends got off a lucky shot and put a hole in the oil pan. It's bone dry."

"That's odd; the oil pressure gauge says everything is fine." Colfax banged the gauge with his fist, and the needle fell back to the empty reading. "Damn ship," Colfax muttered. "This never would have happened on my ship."

"So what do we do?" Malcolm said.

"There's not much we can do. We'll have to put down somewhere and get the engine repaired."

"That's going to take days."

"I know." Colfax looked at his map. "I think we're close to Karls-ruhe. I know there is an airstrip there. If I can keep her on course and land her there, that's the best chance to get the ship repaired. You wake the others; it's probably going to be a rough landing."

# CHAPTER THIRTY NINE

**M**alcolm went back to the cargo hold and turned on the light, immediately eliciting complaints from every.

"What the bloody hell did you do that for?" Saxon said, shielding his eyes from the sudden illumination.

"We have a problem. One of the Germans got off a lucky shot and we've lost all the oil from the engine. The oil pressure gauge wasn't working, so we didn't know until the engine fused itself solid. Colfax is going to land at an airstrip near Karlsruhe. Hopefully, we can get it repaired and be on our way."

O'Hallarhan was silent for a moment, lost in thought. "Depending on the extent of damage, that could take days."

"Aye, it's going to take days."

"What do we do?" O'Hallarhan asked.

"Right now, prepare for what's likely to be a very bumpy landing, since Colfax can't use the engine to set us down gently."

While the descent was smooth, Malcolm's assessment of the landing was spot on target. The airship hit the ground, throwing everyone to the floor. Before they could regain their balance, another bump followed by two more before the airship came to a stop. Saxon cussed as he tried to pull himself back to his couch. Colfax came out of the cockpit. "Sorry for the bumpy landing. It was the only way to get us to stop without overshooting the airstrip."

Malcolm pulled himself up. "We should go inspect the gondola for damage."

Colfax shook his head. "No point in doing that tonight; even with electric torches, we can't address the damage. I think at this point, there's nothing to do but drown our sorrows and get some sleep. We'll do an inspection in the morning."

"I feel like I'm never going to get out of Germany," Malcolm muttered as he took a swig of the whisky. He handed the bottle to Colfax, who wiped the mouth of the bottle and took a large swig.

Colfax was lost in thought. He took another swig of whisky. "I was just thinking; perhaps it would be better if we blew up the airship."

"What?" Malcolm sputtered.

"Hear me out. The Germans know this airship rescued Miss de St. Leger and Mr O'Hallarhan. Since we crashed, if we make it look like it exploded after the crash, that might buy us some time before they realise we weren't actually in the airship when it exploded."

"That's an excellent idea," Joan said. "We still don't know how we're going to get out of Germany, but it buys us some time. You would make an excellent agent, Mr Mingo."

"Lord, I think I've been hanging around you lot too much; I'm thinking like you." Colfax's comment elicited laughter from the group.

"How do we do it?" Joan asked.

"We still have quite a bit of fuel; it wouldn't take much to ignite it."

"The only problem is, that will draw a great deal of attention," Malcolm offered.

"I don't see why we can't set it up on a time delay," O'Hallarhan offered. "I think we could use the airship's clock to give us time to put some distance between us and the ship."

"Sorry to rain on everyone's parade, but what about me? I can't exactly walk all the way out of Germany," Saxon said.

"Let me reconnoitre around the hangar; there might be a lorry we can borrow to make our escape. Peter, why don't you come with me and we'll leave Malcolm and Colfax to rig up the bomb?"

"I'd feel better if I was with you," Malcolm said.

"Can you start a truck without keys? And can you drive it?" Joan looked at Malcolm, who shook his head. "It's settled. You and Colfax will rig up the explosion, and Peter and I will see about our transportation."

"I'll just sit here, waiting for the explosion," Saxon quipped.

Before Joan and Peter left the ship, the group carried Saxon and his couch out of the airship.

"Be careful," Malcolm said as he pulled Joan in for a kiss. "I'd hate to rescue you again."

"I will. I don't want to be rescued again." She kissed him one more time. "Come, Peter. Hopefully, we have a truck we can borrow."

Malcolm watched them hurry off until he lost sight of them in the evening darkness. "Right, Colfax. Let's build a bomb!" The two men entered the airship and went to work. Colfax removed the clock from the cockpit, while Malcolm found the main batteries that supplied the internal lights. He dragged the battery near the fuel tank and yanked some out some of the ship's wiring to use with the bomb. Colfax brought the clock into the engine room and they examined it to see how they could make it work as a switch. Malcolm decided the best way would be to bend the hour hand up so that at the right time, the minute hand would make contact completing the circuit. To test his theory, Malcolm connected wires to the hands of the clock and wired a light bulb between the clock and battery. When everything was set, he completed the connection to the battery and waited. Two minutes later, the lightbulb went off. Malcolm detached the clock from the battery and removed the lightbulb. He took two long strands of wire and looked at the fuel tank and frowned.

Colfax stood next to Malcolm, looking at the fuel tank. "What is it?"

"This runs on diesel, correct?"

"Yes."

"A spark won't be strong enough to ignite the fuel. We need to generate a great deal of heat if I'm remembering my material science correctly."

"How much?"

"At least 200 degrees Fahrenheit."

Colfax thought for a moment. "On my ship, I have an electric toaster. It uses very thin wires to produce the heat to make toast. Do you think we can do something like that?"

"It's worth a try. Help me lug this battery out of the ship. We'll see if we can ignite a small amount of diesel outside." Together, they lugged the heavy battery outside. While Colfax fetched a small can of diesel, Malcolm stripped a section of wire and pulled out individual strands until he had one very thin strand left. When Colfax returned, Malcolm put the wire in the diesel and connected one side to the battery. After making sure they were well away from the diesel, Malcolm attached the other side. A few short seconds later, the diesel ignited. Malcolm quickly disconnected the wire and threw dirt into the can to extinguish the fire. He turned to Colfax. "I think this is going to work."

Malcolm heard the approach of a vehicle and quickly ducked into the shadows of the airship. A lorry pulled into view and once it was close enough, Malcolm saw Joan and O'Hallarhan. He stepped out of the shadows and waited for them to stop. Joan jumped out of the lorry. "We need to hurry. Thankfully, nobody was around, but I heard inquiries about the crash on the radio. I think the police will be here shortly."

Malcolm frowned. "Let's get Saxon in the back of the lorry. After that, Colfax and I will take the battery inside and connect the bomb. While Colfax and I do that, you can load the luggage."

With their combined efforts, they lifted Saxon into the back of the lorry. Malcolm and Colfax brought the battery back to the Engine Room and connected the clock to the setup. Malcolm stripped a long length of the wire and pulled the strands until there were only two or three individual strands. He put it into the fuel tank and connected the end to the battery. He turned to Colfax. "How much time do we need?"

"Five minutes?"

"Five it is," Malcom said, setting the clock to five minutes before midnight. He pulled out his pocket watch and noted the time, so he could tell if they had succeeded. They hurried out of the airship where Joan, with O'Hallarhan's help, had loaded their luggage in back and even brought a bottle of vodka and a bottle of gin. Malcolm went to Joan's side of the lorry. "We have less than five minutes to get out of here."

"We may have a problem," Joan said.

"What now?"

"Look!" She pointed and Malcolm could see vehicle lights approaching the hangar.

"Do you think we can get on the road undetected?"

"We might. For now, let's put some distance between us and the airship."

"Agreed." Malcolm ran to the back and jumped into the lorry. Once inside, he banged the wall to let O'Hallarhan know he was aboard. The lorry lurched into motion, throwing Malcolm off balance. He sat down and pulled out his pocket watch and an electric torch. After illuminating the watch, he watched as the seconds ticked by slowly. As it approached five minutes from when he set up the bomb, he held his breath. He tensed when the pocket watch reached the time. Nothing happened. Malcolm waited for another thirty seconds before saying to Colfax, "I don't think it worked."

The moments the words were out of his mouth, there was a loud boom and the lorry rocked a little from the force.

"I think it did," Colfax said.

# CHAPTER FORTY

O'Hallarhan put the lorry into gear and it lurched forward. "Sorry, I'm not used to the clutch." He slowly drove towards the road, not daring to turn on the headlights. It was a dark, moonless night, so he could barely see five feet ahead of him.

"Shouldn't we go a little faster?" Joan said.

"I can barely see where I'm going. It won't do us any good if we get stuck, or I hit something."

"I understand, but I don't want to be near that thing when it goes up!"

"Point taken." O'Hallarhan applied as much gas as he dared. They were nearly at the road that ran parallel to the airstrip when the lorry rocked from the impact of the explosion of the airship. Joan turned and looked back to see the aftereffects of the explosion. "We're certainly cutting a path of destruction through Germany."

"What?"

"Nothing. Let's get moving."

O'Hallarhan manoeuvred the lorry onto the road and once he had put some distance between themselves and the airstrip, he turned on the headlights and increased his speed. After a moment, he said, "Now what?"

Joan had had the foresight to bring her map up front. It was still damp from their swim in the Elbe and threatened to tear at the slightest mishandling. She pulled out an electric torch and studied it for a moment. "We need to go southwest; let's continue on this road a bit; hopefully we'll see a sign."

They drove until Joan saw a sign pointing to Vimbuch to the left. They turned onto the road. When Joan saw they were, in fact, travelling in the right direction, she turned to O'Hallarhan. "How are you doing?"

"I'm a little tired. As you said, it's been a long day."

"How long can you drive?"

"I don't know. I'll try to drive until daylight and then we can figure out a plan. I imagine that our passengers in back will be eager to get out."

Joan flashed back to a similar trip; when she, Malcolm, and Saxon fled Austria in the back of a similar lorry. She remembered arguing with Malcolm about getting married. Then, she was vehemently afraid of attaching herself to Malcolm for the rest of her life. She barely recognised the woman she was then. After nearly losing Malcolm forever on that same mission, she realised she couldn't live without him and they couldn't get married soon enough. *If we ever get out of Germany,* she thought.

She sat in thought, considering what to do next. She looked at the map to see if there were any other routes that would take them out of Germany faster. There was no guarantee that Frietag wouldn't continue to pursue them, but he wouldn't have the support of the local authorities. France wasn't any closer than Switzerland, so she kept to the plan. If they could make it to the border with Switzerland, they could leave the truck and travel by train, as it would be harder for Frietag to track their movements.

She looked over at O'Hallarhan, who was blinking and look like he was about to fall asleep. "Now that you've been on your first secret mission, what do you think?"

"I think I will be much happier working in the Engine Room than running around avoiding capture. I'm not cut out for this level of excitement and don't have the temperament or talent for all this subterfuge."

"It's definitely an acquired skill. To be honest, I'll be quite content to leave this world behind. God help me, but I found serving in the Royal Navy Auxiliary much more rewarding than this constant game of cat and mouse. Except for the food; the food is atrocious."

O'Hallarhan laughed. "That it is. I know when we got back from our last mission, I was happy to eat anything that wasn't fish or root vegetables." They laughed and were silent for a minute before he spoke. "You really intend to return to duty after you're married?"

"God willing, yes. A few years ago, I would never consider giving up the freedom that I thought I had as an agent. But I'm not the same person I was then." She paused. "What about you?"

"Definitely. On our last mission, I learned I still have a great deal to learn about being an officer. I thought it was just ordering people to do what I wanted, but Malcolm taught me it's much more than that. He had every reason to make sure I was no longer part of the Royal Space Service, but from what I understand, he was quite adamant about supporting me. I guess, like you, I'm not the same person I was even a year ago."

"Life has a way of doing that," she said.

They continued to chat as they drove; she asked about his family and his childhood in Ireland. She told him about her life in Geneva, leaving out the more salacious details, and how she came to work in the Secret Service. As the sun rose, they reached the border of Switzerland. When they neared the checkpoint, a lone guard walked out of the guardhouse carrying a rifle. He put his hand up. Joan said, "Let me do the talking."

As they stopped at the checkpoint, a guard approached the driver's side of the lorry. "What is your business and what goods are you carrying?" he asked in German.

"Good morning!" Joan said brightly. "We're delivering a couch to my aunt in Geneva and bringing back some of her furniture that she no longer wants."

"What's in back?"

"Just the couch and friends that offered to help load the truck for a trip to Switzerland."

The guard stared at Joan for a moment. "Open the back, please."

"Certainly." Joan exited the cab and walked to the back of the truck. As she walked in front of the guard, she slipped a sap out of her bag. She hoped it wouldn't come to blows, but the guard's behaviour put her on edge. She struggled to lift the back door, but its weight was too much.

"Why didn't the driver help?" the guard asked.

"He doesn't speak German. He's a cousin from England. I can get him."

"Never mind," the guard huffed and put his rifle down and helped Joan left the hatch.

Joan eyed the rifle leaning against the truck. For a moment, she thought about taking it, but the guard picked it up before she could act.

As the door of the lorry opened, Malcolm, Saxon, and Colfax shielded their eyes from the sudden onslaught of light. It had been pitch black in the lorry and even in the early morning light was too much for them.

"Who are they?"

"Friends. I promised them a trip to Geneva in exchange for helping me haul the furniture."

"Geneva? Where in Geneva?"

"Rue des Pâquis 50" It was the address of her mother's apartment in Geneva and the first address that came to mind.

The guard regarded Malcolm, Saxon, and Colfax. His gun was at waist level. Joan watched intently for any movement. Her hand tightened around the sap.

The guard pointed with his rifle at the trio in the truck. "I assume they all have papers?"

"Yes, sir. I can get them if you wish," Joan said.

The guard stared at them for a moment. Joan silently took a step, so she was behind the guard. She raised her sap.

"No need. Everything seems in order. Have a safe trip," the guard said as he returned to the checkpoint. Joan motioned for Malcolm to close the door and she returned to the cab. She nodded to O'Hallarhan, and the lorry pulled through the checkpoint and they were now safely in Switzerland.

She let out a long breath. *At least I hope we're safe*, she thought.

# CHAPTER FORTY ONE

Joan directed O'Hallarhan to an alley in an industrial area where they could park the lorry and make their plans. O'Hallarhan opened the back, and the trio shielded their eyes from the early morning light. Malcolm jumped out of the back of the lorry, eager to stretch his legs. "We're made it to Switzerland; now what?"

Joan thought for a moment. "We have a few options. We could try to secure passage from here directly home, but I doubt that there is a direct flight from here to England."

"Where exactly is here?" Malcolm said.

"Basel." Joan lied out her map and pointed to the city. "We have a few options; we could travel to Bern and try to contact the British Embassy there. Or we could continue to our original destination of Geneva, where we might still escape. How are we set for currency?"

Malcolm rummaged through his wallet, handing over what currency he had. Saxon likewise tossed his wallet to Malcolm, and he added its contents to the currency. After adding the currency she had left, she assessed their options. "I don't think we have enough to get to Geneva, let alone out of Switzerland. I think Bern might be the best destination."

"How do we get there?"

"Train would be the fastest."

Malcolm looked at Saxon. "How are we going to get Charles to the train station and on the train? While we're at it, how are we all going to get to the train station? Can we take the lorry to the train station?"

Joan thought for a moment. "We could, but I would feel better if we left the lorry here. We don't need to give Frietag any other clues as to our destination."

"My question remains; how do we get Charles to the train station?"

"I can get around. I'm not an invalid." He tried to rise from the couch, but the second he put weight on his leg, he hissed in pain and sat down immediately. "Well, maybe I am."

"Let me reconnoitre the area and see what are options are," Joan said. She looked around and started back to the main road.

"I can go with you," Malcolm offered.

"No, it will be better if I go alone. We're barely out of Germany and you're still a wanted man."

"Too close, as far as I'm concerned. Be careful." Malcolm pulled Joan in close and gave her a kiss.

"I'll be back in a few minutes." Joan slipped down the alley and was soon out of sight. Ten minutes later, she returned. "We're in luck. There is a trolley stop near this alley. We can take it train station."

"That's good, but how are we going to get Charles on?"

"I think the two of you," she said, nodding to Malcolm and O'Hallarhan, "will have to be Charles' crutch for the time being. When we get closer to the city centre, we might find a wheelchair or at least some crutches. Charles, it might help if you appear to be drunk. Given our appearance at the moment, it will be an apt cover."

"Let me help," Saxon said. He took the bottle of gin and took a large swig. "That will help with the pain. This will help with the cover." He poured a small amount into his hand and splashed it on his face. "Seems like a waste of perfectly good gin."

"Alright, let's get Saxon out of the lorry. Colfax, can you help me with the luggage?" Joan said.

"Aren't I the ranking officer here?" Malcolm said.

"You are, but this is my area of expertise," she offered. "Can't take orders from a woman?"

Malcolm bit his tongue; he knew better than stepping into that verbal trap. "You heard the lady. Let's get a move on." He, Colfax, and O'Hallarhan lifted Saxon and his couch out of the lorry. Saxon took one more swig of gin before packing it away. With O'Hallarhan's and Malcolm's help, he could rise without putting weight on the leg. Colfax and Joan managed the luggage. They made their way down the alley and true to her word, there was a trolley stopped just down the street. They hurried as best as they could while half carrying Saxon. Joan ran ahead to make sure the tram driver would wait. Malcolm and O'Hallarhan got Saxon to the doorway and held him as he made the step into the tram, but there wasn't enough room for them to assist, so he had to take the next two steps by himself. Saxon hissed in pain when forced to put weight on his injured leg when he took the next step. He grabbed the panel to his left, holding tight until his knuckles were white as he lifted his injured leg to the next step. He repeated the process until he was in the tram. To their great fortune, there was a bench near the front of the tram. As Malcolm entered, the driver said something in German. Joan replied, and the driver nodded. When they were all aboard, the driver put the tram in gear and it pulled away from the stop.

Malcolm leaned over to Joan and whispered, "What did he say?"

"He asked what was wrong with Charles. I told him he had been injured at work and we were taking him to see a doctor."

As the tram made its way out of the industrial area, leaving behind the factories with their large chimneys belching smoke and gradually made its way into a more residential area. The tram driver expertly navigated the tram through the narrow cobblestone streets past rows of neat houses, packed closely together. Malcolm could feel the morning chill blowing in through the open windows. He looked over at Saxon, who was wincing from the constant jostle of the tram over the tracks; Malcolm had to admit, even he found it annoying. Eventually, the tram reached a stone bridge crossing the Rhine as the tram made its way into the centre of Basel. The neighbourhoods had given way to shops, cafes, and restaurants. It gradually made its way through the city centre, just beginning to awake. The tram continued until it reached the train station.

The train station had two towers with domed roofs of verdigris standing on either side of an arched roof, with large windows all along the face. A low roof ran the length of the station, providing covering the entrances of the two towers. The building looked relatively new; the smoke of the industrial area did not yet tarnish the light colour of its sandstone. When the tram came to a stop, Joan disembarked first, followed by O'Hallarhan and Malcolm. Saxon made his way, hissing in pain as he repeated the process to get off the tram. Once off, Malcolm and O'Hallarhan put Saxon's arms around their shoulders and helped him into the station.

The main hall was bustling with activity as passengers hurried to catch their trains. They found a bench and sat Saxon down. Joan said, "Let me get us tickets. Stay right here." She hurried off to the ticket office. Malcolm watched the people coming and going. His stomach rumbled, and he realised he hadn't had a proper meal in a while. After looking longingly at the kiosks selling pretzels and sausages, he looked in vain for a kiosk that sold tea. To his dismay, coffee or water seemed to be the only choices for beverages. He hated coffee, but he might have to drink it.

As he was bemoaning to himself the lack of a civilised beverage, some activity caught his eye. At the far end of the station, he saw two men dressed in suits talking with anyone moving to the platforms. They stopped everyone for a brief conversation before letting them proceed. Malcolm watched as they slowly made their way through the station.

Joan returned to the group. "Five tickets to Bern. The train leaves in twenty minutes." When she handed the ticket to Malcolm, she noticed his scowl. "What is it?"

"There are two men, wearing grey suits, stopping and talking to everyone heading to the train platform. It could be nothing, but I'd rather not take any chances."

Joan looked up and soon spotted the two men. She watched for a few moments before she leaned over to Malcolm. "I think you're right. Frietag must have radioed any agents in Switzerland to be on the lookout for us. Being so close to the border, this would be an obvious place to look for us."

"Now what? It's going to be nearly impossible to get Charles on the train without notice."

Joan sat in thought. "Maybe not. So far, Frietag only knows that you and I were in Germany. With any luck, he doesn't realise that Charles is with us and, to the best of my knowledge, he doesn't know Peter or Colfax. Perhaps we can be a distraction to allow the others a chance to board without notice."

"How do you intend to do that?" Malcolm looked at Joan.

"You and I are going to lead them to a train platform away from our train. I'm hoping we can either get the jump on them or at least lose them. I wish I knew this train station, but I rarely travelled here and if I did, it was usually as a stop on my way to somewhere else. Come, let's tell the others."

Joan returned to O'Hallarhan, Colfax, and Saxon and informed them of the plan. "Under no circumstance are any of you to follow us. Your sole concern is getting on the train to Bern."

"But," O'Hallarhan began.

"No, I mean it. We can take care of ourselves. You three must make it to Bern. On the odd chance that we get caught, I need you three to notify our...employer that we are missing." She stopped to look at the massive clock in the centre of the station. "You have fifteen minutes before the train leaves. Unfortunately, the platform is the furthest away, so I suggest as soon as you see us get the attention of the two agents, you make your way to the train." She glared at the trio. "Under no circumstances are you to get involved. Do I make myself clear?"

"Yes, ma'am," Saxon said.

"We'll meet you on the train." Joan moved over to Malcolm. "Come on."

Malcolm rose and Joan slipped her hand through his arm. "Follow my lead," she whispered.

"Always."

They walked towards the centre of the train station, putting some distance between themselves and their compatriots. Joan guided them towards the train platforms away from their train. "Come on, Malcolm. We're going to be late," she said in English and loud enough to get some attention from a few of the other patrons.

Catching on, Malcolm said, "Can't we stop to get something to eat, Joan? We have had nothing for the last two days!"

"Is your stomach all you think about? I sometimes wonder why I agreed to marry you."

"It's not too late to change your mind!" Malcolm said. He pretended to pull his arm away from Joan and turn so he could survey the station. The two men stared at him and they hurried from the other side of the station, fighting their way through the crowd.

He lightly grabbed Joan by the elbow and leaned in to whisper in her ear. "It worked; we have their attention. Now what?"

"Your guess is as good as mine," she said.

# CHAPTER FORTY TWO

Malcolm noticed a hallway ahead, running parallel to the station. He steered Joan toward the hallway and, to his relief, it was a long hallway with several doors that continued on before turning to the left. They broke into a run, checking each of the doors. To their dismay, the doors were all locked, and neither wanted to take the time to unlock them. As they were three quarters down the hall, they heard someone shout, "Halt!" They turned and saw the two men reach into their suits and pull out Luger pistols. Malcolm and Joan ran, hoping that they wouldn't dare fire the pistols inside the train station.

That hope was cruelly dashed as they rounded the corner at the end of the hall and shots hit the moulding right next to them, a little too close for his comfort. This hall only ran a short distance before opening onto a covered train platform. Ahead of them were six different platforms; only two had trains. Malcolm debated which way to go when Joan said, "There, the second one on the left. Let's head there."

They ran towards the platform and were surrounded by the passengers disembarking the train, heading back towards the terminal. For half a second, Malcolm considered slipping into the crowd, but they would quickly be back in the open. They needed to slip out of sight. Malcolm hazarded a look behind. The two agents had just come onto the platform and trying to find Malcolm and Joan in the crowd.

"Quick, we have some cover. Let's get on the train!" he said. They found an open carriage and boarded it. A conductor looked surprised and said something in German. Joan responded and pushed past him. As they exited the car, they stopped in the vestibule between cars to catch their breath. "Now what?"

"We need to continue to lead them away before we lose them," Joan said.

"I'm not keen on getting shot at," Malcolm said.

"Neither am I, but we have little choice. Let's continue down the train. I'm hoping they catch sight of us."

"You want them to see us? Do you want to get shot?"

"I'm sure that Frietag wants us alive so they won't shoot to kill."

"That's not very reassuring," Malcolm said.

"It's all I have right now. Come on, we need to get moving." She opened the vestibule door and made her way through the car.

Malcolm wasn't in favour of this plan, but since he had nothing more to offer, he deferred to Joan. Malcolm followed her and just as they reached the vestibule on the other side, he heard shouting in German. He glanced behind and saw out the windows that the two agents had spotted them. One of them was entering their car, while the other ran ahead to the next car. "They found us, like you wanted. One is coming on, the other is going ahead to cut us off. Now what?"

"Quick, this way," she said, opening the door away from the platform. Joan disappeared through the door and Malcolm followed. He found a five-foot drop to the tracks below. Cursing, he jumped. As he landed, he felt his ankle turn and shouted in pain.

"What is it?" Joan said, turning towards him. She was already making her way across the tracks and she was about to pull herself onto the platform.

"I twisted my ankle."

"Can you walk?"

"Yes, but it hurts."

"You'll have to deal with it until we get away. Come on!" Joan pulled herself onto the train platform.

"You would make a lousy nurse. You have no bedside manner," Malcolm said as he limped his way towards the platform. He nearly jumped out of his skin when he heard a train whistle. He turned and looked to see an engine coming towards him. Although it was slowing, he wasn't sure if he could make it. Each step made him wince with pain. He reached the platform and spared a glance. The locomotive was bearing down on him. He grabbed the edge of the platform, jumped and swung his legs up. He rolled away from the edge just as the train pulled past him. Joan offered him her hand and helped pull him to his feet. He put weight on his ankle, but it was too painful. He could limp, but there was no way he could run.

"I can't run. I can probably limp, but that's the best I can do," he said.

Joan looked around. She spotted stairs leading up to the footbridge. "Let's blend in with passengers getting off this train. By now, our pursuers have figured out we aren't on the train and they don't know we're here. Come on."

Malcolm hobbled towards the centre of the station. As they made their way toward the footbridge, the passengers disembarked from the train. Soon, a sea of people surrounded them. They moved with the crowd towards the stairs. Malcolm looked at the clock hanging from the ceiling of the platform; they only had seven minutes to make their train. "We're running out of time to catch our train. How far do we have to go?"

Joan said, "Our train is platform five. I think once we get to the footbridge, it should be too far."

They walked with the crowd, keeping themselves in the centre until they got to the stairs leading to the footbridge. As they made their way up, Malcolm turned his head to check on his pursuers. They were still some distance away, trying to fight their way through the crowd. Malcolm nudged Joan, who looked. Joan hurried her pace up the stairs. Malcolm tried to follow suit, but every time his hurt ankle had to bear weight, he hissed in pain. By the time he made it to the top of the stairs, he had to stop for a moment, the pain in his ankle almost too much to bear.

"Come on," Joan hissed.

"I'm not sure I can."

"I'm not leaving you here. Come on, we have little time to catch our train." Without a care for decorum, Joan slipped Malcolm's arm around her shoulders so he could keep his weight off the injured ankle.

"You don't have to do this," he said.

"Nonsense. You can hardly stand to put weight on it. This way, we can at least make it to the platform. We have little time. Come on!" With Joan's help, Malcolm limped down the footbridge toward their platform. But as Malcolm watched the clock, they were running out of time to catch the train. As they neared the stairs to their train, they heard the whistle, indicating the train would pull out shortly. Malcolm looked at the stairs leading down to the platform. He could never navigate them in time. An idea came to him. He limped over to the bannister and sat on it. "Follow my lead," Malcolm said. He sat on the railing and slid down the railing. Fortunately, there was no one else on the stairs as he descended. When he reached the bottom, he tried to land, but ended up landing on his injured ankle, which couldn't take the weight. He sprawled face first on the floor of the platform.

He turned to look back and saw Joan sliding down the railing. As she reached the bottom, she executed a perfect landing. She helped Malcolm to his feet just as the train moved. She pulled Malcolm towards the train and pushed him into an open car door. As the train picked up speed, Joan turned to run after it when a bullet whizzed by her ear. She turned to see the two agents at the foot of the stairs firing at her.

Joan put her head down and ran as fast as she could. The train was picking up speed, making it harder for her to keep up. She reach the door when Malcolm reached out and grabbed her hand and pulled her in. She fell into Malcolm and they landed on the floor of the car.

Although Malcolm welcomed Joan lying on top of him, he realised there was a train car full of people and he had to keep some manner of decorum. He gently rolled away from Joan and pulled himself up with some difficulty. He reached down and helped Joan up. They made their way through the car until they found an empty seat. Malcolm looked out the window as the train pulled out of the station, and he thought he saw the two agents.

Malcolm leaned over to Joan. "I think we lost them."

# CHAPTER FORTY THREE

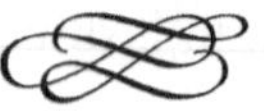

"I should hope so," Joan said. "We should try to find the others. Can you walk?"

"As long as I don't have to run, I should be fine." They left their seats and made their way back through the train. After passing through several cars, they eventually found Saxon, O'Hallarhan, and Mingo.

"Where have you two been? I was worried that you didn't catch the train," Saxon said. He claimed enough space on the bench to put his injured leg up.

Malcolm described their encounter with the agents when Joan interrupted him. "Let's look at that ankle. If it's broken, we don't want to you putting more weight on it and hurting it further." Malcolm removed his socks and shoes while Joan assessed the ankle. The cool touch of her hands felt good. To his untrained eye, he thought it looked swollen, but waited for Joan's pronouncement. "I think you just twisted it; I didn't feel any broken bones." She looked around until she said, "Malcolm, give me your tie."

"What for?" he said as he untied it.

Joan snatched the tie from Malcolm's hand. "To give your ankle some support so you can walk. We do not know what will happen when we get to Bern. I imagine we might have a welcoming committee when we arrive." She wound the tie tight around his ankle, lamenting that it wasn't as long as she would have liked. "Try standing and put some weight on it."

Malcolm did as instructed. "It's better. It doesn't hurt nearly as much when I put my weight on it." He sat down again and leaned close to the group. "What do we do now? I'm sure that our friends in Basel have already figured out we're bound for Bern and will have a party waiting for us." A sudden thought came to Malcolm. "Is this a direct train or will there be stops?"

"It's not direct," Joan said, looking at her ticket. "We have stops in Liestal, Olten, Zofingen, Langenthal, Burgdorf, before we arrive in Bern."

"Then they have several opportunities to board," Malcolm said.

"Not necessarily," Joan said. She pulled out a map from her purse. "Olten is a major junction for the Swiss railroads. We should arrive there in about another hour. I doubt Frietag could get anyone there before we arrive." She sat in thought for a moment. "I think we should disembark at Olten."

"Are you sure?" Malcolm asked.

"Yes. We can purchase new tickets for any major city in Switzerland; Bern, Zurich, Lucerne..." She paused for a moment before adding ", or Geneva."

"What's our best route?" Malcolm asked.

"Probably Zurich or Lucerne. Lucerne is further away from Germany; it's very unlikely that there will be agents there."

"What about the original plan of getting to Geneva?"

Joan gave Malcolm a hard glare before relenting. "To get to Geneva, we still need to go through Bern. The Germans know we are on this train, so they will wait for us there. Yes, the more I think about it, the better I like the idea of Lucerne. If I remember correctly, we have agents stationed there; the trick will be to find them. Lucerne has several options for travel. We could even get an airship back to London with any luck."

"Then, Olten it is," Malcolm said. They sat quietly for the next hour watching the scenery pass by them; fields and forests, all the while, in the distance, were the Alps. When the train reached Olten, Malcolm and O'Hallarhan helped Saxon off the train while Colfax grabbed the bags and Joan went to get tickets for Lucerne. They gathered in the main hall of the train station. When Joan returned, she handed everyone tickets for a train two hours later. Malcolm looked around the train station and saw a station cafe. "Would it be possible to get something to eat? I don't know about the rest of you, but I'm starving!"

"Although it pains me to say so, I agree with Malcolm," Saxon quipped.

They made their way to the cafe and took a seat at a table. A relatively simple buffet was available containing rye bread, cheese, sausages, smoked pork, boiled eggs, and pastries. To Malcolm's great delight and utter surprise, tea was also available. Although not as good as the tea at home, Malcolm savoured the tea. The quintet ate in silence, everyone glad to have a proper meal. When they finished, Joan stopped to pick up a paper from a newsboy as they returned to the main hall to wait for their train.

Joan read the paper in silence for several minutes before Malcolm asked, "Any news we should know?"

"It doesn't appear so. It seems we successfully kept our destruction of Germany out of the news.

"What is it?" Malcolm knew she read something that bothered her.

"The situation in the Balkans is deteriorating quickly. There's talk that the Kaiser will visit Archduke Franz Ferdinand to discuss solutions. That is not a promising development."

"Perhaps it will help us. If the Germans are more worried about the Balkans, can they afford to send agents after us?"

"Perhaps not. But this is personal for Frietag. He'll stop at nothing to get at you, Malcolm."

"He's bloody single-minded about it," Malcolm muttered.

"Whether you intended it or not, because of you, he's lost an eye, a hand, and any standing he had in German intelligence. Capturing you is the only way he feels he can regain his stature. Remember, he had been deep undercover for years before you foiled his plans. If he had succeeded, he'd have been a hero. His only redemption is capturing you... or us." Joan looked at Malcolm. "Do remember how you felt when Mycroft forced you out of the Air Service?"

Malcolm considered the question. The rage he felt then came back in an instant. Even now, he had a difficult time forgiving Mycroft. He could easily have given into that rage and might have had it if not for the support of Joan and Saxon. He was sure Frietag had no one on his side. Malcolm was forced to admit that he might follow the same path as Frietag if their roles were reversed.

"I think I understand now. So what do we do now? Since he knows you are here, he'll look for you to get to me."

"That's why I think Lucerne is our best bet." Joan sat in silence, reading the paper.

Malcolm took the hint that she didn't want to talk about it any more and watched the other travellers, keeping an eye open for any agents that might look for them. He kept checking his pocket watch, checking to see how much longer before they could board the train. He shifted on his bench, trying to find a comfortable position.

After twenty minutes of this, Joan looked up from the paper. "What is it?"

"I just want to get on the train so we can get out of here," Malcolm said. "I've had my fill of looking over my shoulder for Frietag and his agents."

Joan put down the paper and reached over to grab his hand. "I know."

"How do you keep so calm?"

"A lifetime of practice." She smiled at him and once again, he remembered why he would do anything to spend the rest of his life with her. "Let's pretend for a moment that we are just on a trip."

"You're saying we should let down our guard?"

"Absolutely not. I'm just saying that we shouldn't let Frietag control us. We're nearly there, Malcolm. Shortly, we'll be home and we can finally get married and begin our life together."

"I hope it will be as simple as that." He squeezed her hand.

"It won't be, but let's just hold on to that thought." She snuggled close to him and he felt some of the anxiety melt away. "Try to enjoy the trip as much as you. Lucerne is exquisite."

"Have you been there?"

"Many times. My parents had a villa on an island in Lake Maggiore. We often took the train to Lucerne on our way there." Joan sat up bolt straight. "Oh, no."

"What is it?"

"I just remembered what you said about Frietag looking for me. My mother loves to spend the spring and summer at the villa. What if he goes after her to get to me? My mother is, shall I say, flamboyant, and the villa is an artist's colony. It's common knowledge that she spends spring and summer there."

"Why were you so concerned about going to Geneva, then?"

"That's her other home; I hadn't stopped to think that she might have returned to the villa."

"What do we do?"

Joan frowned. "There's nothing we can do right now. When we contact the Service, maybe they can send someone to check on her."

"Should we go?"

"No" Joan startled herself with the vehemence of her answer. "Sorry. I hated that place."

"Let's not worry about that until we have more information."

"You're right." Joan looked at the clock. "God, I wish we could get on the train to Lucerne now!"

"Didn't you just say that we shouldn't let Frietag control us?"

"You're right." Joan snuggled closer to Malcolm. He put an arm around her and hugged her tight, but he could sense her anxiety. He looked at his pocket watch again. "Are we ever going to leave this station?"

# CHAPTER FORTY FOUR

After a very long thirty minutes, the quintet made their way to the platform for the train to Lucerne. They found seats near each other; Joan upgraded their seats to second class, so they wouldn't have to sit on wooden benches. O'Hallarhan and Malcolm helped Saxon onto the train, and soon they took their seats. As the train blew its whistle and left the station, Saxon leaned over to Malcolm and said, "What's going on? You and Joan both look anxious."

Malcolm relayed Joan's concern about Frietag going after her mother, and Saxon nodded. "That would be exactly what he would do to draw you and Joan out. Do you think it is likely?"

"I don't know. But I have this sinking feeling that we are not out of the woods yet."

"I concur. Nothing about this whole escapade has gone to plan." Saxon looked at his wounded leg.

"How are you doing, Charles?" Malcolm realising that in the middle of all this action, he hadn't checked on his friend.

"It's fine," brushing off Malcolm's concern. "It isn't really, but except for having to hurry here, there and everywhere, I think I'm slowly on the mend. I feel like so much dead weight."

"I, for one, will be glad when I don't have to carry you around anymore." Malcolm's remark elicited a smile from Saxon.

They sat in silence as they watched the train leave the city and travel past fields, farms, and several picturesque small towns. After an hour, they began their approach to Lucerne proper. The Alps, visible even when they were in Olten, were now more prominent, looming over the scene. The fields gave way to hills and soon, they could see the turquoise waters of Lake Lucerne. In some ways, it reminded Malcolm of Scotland, although the Alps were much more rugged than Scotland. Snow still capped many of the mountains. The train followed a river for some distance before turning towards the centre of Lucerne with its colourful medieval buildings, towers, and looming cathedrals. Malcolm enjoyed the views, despite himself.

When the train stopped at the station, Joan hurried everyone off the train, snapping at Malcolm and O'Hallarhan to get Charles off as quickly as they could manage. Colfax, carrying their luggage, leaned over to Malcolm and asked, "What's got into her?"

"She just wants to get us to safety as soon as possible." Malcolm felt awful for telling Colfax a half truth, but this wasn't the time or place to get into it.

When they reached the main hall of the train station, Joan said, "You should stay here. I'm going to make contact and arrange transport for us."

"Shouldn't someone go with you?" Malcolm asked.

"No," Joan said emphatically. Malcolm knew better than to disagree. As Joan hurried out of the station, the quartet looked around and found a cafe serving beer and wine. With nothing better to do, they found a table and ordered drinks; Malcolm, Colfax, and O'Hallarhan opted for beer, while Saxon chose a Riesling.

After the drinks arrived, O'Hallarhan leaned over towards Malcolm. "Is something wrong? Miss de St Leger seems out of sorts."

Malcolm relayed Joan's concern that Frietag might be after her mother to draw them out. "She's worried. I think she wants to get in touch with the Service as soon as possible so she can know for sure if her mother's safe."

O'Hallarhan looked panicked. "Do you think my parents are safe?"

"Yes," Saxon said. "Before we left, we made sure that your parents and Malcolm's parents received protection. Damn, I didn't think about Joan's mother."

"She has had little contact with her mother, so I think it's an understandable oversight."

"What are we going to do if Frietag has her mother?"

"I don't know." Malcolm took a drink of his beer. It was some kind of lager; not his favourite style, but it tasted good at this point.

The quartet made small talk for the next hour when Malcolm noticed Joan stalking over to them. He took one last drink of his beer and rose to meet her.

"Here I've been running around Lucerne, making arrangements and the four of you are just lazing around drinking!"

"You wanted to go by yourself. We thought this was a way to be less conspicuous," Malcolm whispered. "We're ready to go, aren't we?" The others nodded, and even Saxon rose quickly. "What's the plan?"

"Follow me." Without further discussion, Joan strode back to towards the exit. The quartet hurried after Joan, and as they exited the train station, found two cars waiting. Malcolm and O'Hallarhan helped Saxon into one car while Colfax stored their luggage. Malcolm joined Joan in the smaller of the two cars. He reached his hand to hers. "Is everything alright?"

She pulled her hand away. "I don't know. They are sending an agent from Milan. He should be there first thing in the morning."

"Frietag won't do anything to her until he lures us out. If he kills her, his leverage over us is gone. And, in fact, puts him in a much more dangerous position, as you will be out for revenge." He reached his hand to hers and this time, she let him hold it. "We'll figure this out."

"Thank you, Malcolm," she whispered. With her other hand, she quickly wiped away a tear; Malcolm pretended not to notice.

The car turned towards the river, travelling past docks and warehouses before stopping in front of a nondescript warehouse. They were escorted to a secret stairway and into a conference room with a mahogany table and several overstuffed leather upholstered chairs. Past the conference room. An agent ushered them to the table where tea, coffee, and an assortment of pastries awaited. Malcolm immediately helped himself to a cup of tea.

A balding man with grey at his temples and wire-rimmed glasses joined them. "Welcome! I'm Archibald Clark, head of our office. When Miss de St. Leger arrived, we were relieved to know that you had not perished in the airship crash in Karlsruhe."

"You know about that?" Malcolm asked.

"Let's say that your escape from Germany has not been very secretive." Clark pushed his glasses up on his nose. "We didn't have time to learn all the details since Sir Malcolm and Mr Saxon left Berlin. Perhaps you will share them with me?"

Joan recounted O'Hallarhan's and her from Frietag in Wittenberg, their pursuit in Coswig and Malcolm's rescue of the two by airship. She continued on to describe the crash and their decision to destroy the airship. She detailed Malcolm's and her encounter with the agents in Basel and their decision to make it to Lucerne.

Clark absorbed the information and sat in thought for a moment before saying, "I can't fault your decisions, although it would have been nice if they had been less…flamboyant."

"When can we get out of here?" Malcolm asked.

"Straight to the point. I'm afraid that it will be at least four days. Our 'firm' owns an airship. However, it's actually delivering cargo to Geneva and won't return until then." Before Malcolm could say anything, Clark raised his hand. "That will give us time to ascertain the safety of Miss de St. Leger's mother. In the meantime, we have suitable lodging available and showers. I'm sure after your recent exploits, a hot shower and a proper bed would be most welcome." Another agent came in and escorted them to their rooms; Malcolm was thankful that Joan's room was next to his.

Malcolm's room was perfectly suitable, if modest. A bed with an electric lamp on a nightstand and an upholstered chair. Off of the bedroom was a small bathroom, complete with a shower. Malcolm availed himself of the opportunity for a hot shower. He rummaged through his luggage for some clean clothes and sat in his chair. He must have dozed off because he jumped at the sound of a knock on his door.

Malcolm opened the door. Before he could say a word, Joan burst in and nearly knocked him over as she passed him. "What is it?"

"I can't get the thought of Frietag holding my mother out of my head." Joan paced, her eyes red rimmed, and she dabbed at her nose frequently with her handkerchief. "I have had no desire to see my mother for quite some time, and now all I want to do is make sure she's safe."

Malcolm pulled Joan into a hug. She resisted at first before relaxing into it. Malcolm held her by the waist. He reached up and brushed a curl away from her face. "We'll make sure nothing happens to her. I promise."

"I don't know why I'm so worried. My mother and I have barely been on speaking terms for years."

"And the fact she thinks you're dead."

Joan glared at Malcolm before letting out a sigh. "I've been so worried about losing you, that now that we're safe, the thought that Frietag can ruin that and hurt my mother just guts me."

Malcolm pulled her close and kissed the top of her head. "It's going to take a great deal more than Frietag to lose me." He hugged her tightly. "Why don't we try to find some dinner? I don't know about you, but it seems like forever since I've had a proper meal."

"One thing never changes," Joan said.

"What's that?"

"Your desire to eat."

# CHAPTER FORTY FIVE

*M*alcolm took Joan's arm, and they returned to the conference room. To their surprise, they found O'Hallarhan, Saxon, and Colfax already seated and food laid out on the table. Malcolm noticed that Saxon's leg had a proper bandage and Malcolm noticed Saxon seated in a wheelchair.

"What took you two so long? I'm sure the food is cold by now," Saxon put up his hand. "Wait! I don't want to know. I don't want to ruin my appetite."

"If you must know, I fell asleep," Malcolm said as he pulled the chair out for Joan.

"A likely story," Saxon said. "Let's eat! I'm famished!"

It was a relatively simple meal; barley soup; grated, fried potatoes with bratwurst and onion gravy, and stewed red cabbage. But all of them were glad to eat a proper meal. They drank several bottles of a Swiss wine called Chasselas. Although Malcolm was not an expert in wines, he enjoyed its light, floral taste. Everyone seemed to relax in the relative safety of the British Secret Service offices. For the first time in many weeks, Malcolm felt like he could breathe and he wasn't waiting for the other shoe to drop. He looked over at Joan; although she attempted to be part of the conversation and giving off a carefree attitude, he could tell she was still worried about her mother.

Eventually, the wine caught up with them, and they all made their way to their respective bedrooms. Malcolm walked Joan to her door and kissed her good night. "Are you sure you don't want to come in?" she said, raising one eyebrow provocatively.

"I think for now, we could all do with a good night's sleep. And I think you just want to use me so you don't have to think about your mother."

"Am I that transparent?"

"Not to many others; possibly Charles because he has a keen sense of people. Instead of worrying about it, why don't you do what you do best? Channel that anxiety into developing a plan to rescue your mother from Frietag. If he doesn't show up, you've diverted yourself for a few days; if he does, we'll be ready to deal with him."

"To be honest, I've already been running through things in my mind."

"Tomorrow, let's get everyone together and come up with a mission plan if we need to rescue your mother from Frietag. It will give us something to do. I imagine everyone will get a little bored if they have to sit around more than another day."

"Thank you, Malcolm." She kissed him. "How did I ever get so lucky as to find you?"

"No, I'm the lucky one. I can't believe such an intelligent and lovely woman would want to marry me." He returned her kiss and held her tightly for several moments.

"Are you sure you don't want to come in?" she said in her husky voice that drove him wild.

"As much as I want to, I'm sure that if I lay on a bed, I'll be asleep in mere seconds. Then what good would I be?"

"Oh, you'd be surprised." Joan winked at him.

"Good night, dear. I'll see you in the morning." Malcolm kissed her head and went to his room. After stripping out of his clothes, he lay on the bed. He was right; he fell asleep in seconds.

When Malcolm awoke, he momentarily panicked, not realising

where he was. As he got his bearings, he reached over and turned on the electric lamp, and checked his pocket watch. 7:30. He stretched and had another shower, not knowing what the future would bring. As he looked in the bathroom mirror, he couldn't help but think back to nearly two years ago, when he was a civilian working for the Peninsular and Oriental Steam Navigation Company. He hadn't missed that job; it was spectacularly boring. Although, given the last several weeks, boring would be nice.

He made his way to the conference where breakfast has already been laid out. Malcolm opted for a couple of slices of bread and butter with marmalade and a few pieces of meat and cheese. After pouring a cup of black tea, he sat at the table and ate. He was joined first by Saxon, now manoeuvering in a wheelchair, then O'Hallarhan and Mingo. Malcolm told them that Joan was still worried about her mother and they would spend the day planning a mission to rescue Joan's mother.

"I'm not sure how much I can help in the actual execution of the mission, but I'm happy to assist in its planning."

O'Hallarhan turned to Colfax. "Mr Mingo, do I understand that you built a mechanical leg for yourself?" When Colfax nodded, O'Hallarhan said, "Let's put our heads together and see if we can figure a way to make Mr Saxon more mobile."

"I'd be very appreciative. It's very embarrassing to have to be carried everywhere. And if there's anything I can do to help Joan, I would be happy to do it."

"What do you mean?" Joan entered the conference room. Malcolm could tell that she had showered and dressed in clean clothes. She wore a forest green jacket over a long mahogany skirt; Malcolm caught sight of her petticoat under the skirt. With her oxblood boots, she stood much taller. Malcolm thought she had never looked lovelier.

"It seems that Mr O'Hallarhan and Mr Mingo intend to subject me to some kind of engineering experiment in order to allow me to move without the use of this," Saxon said, pointing to the wheelchair.

"Why would they do that?" Joan picked at the food on the table, settling for a slice of bread, butter, and marmalade.

"Because your fiancé wants me to take part in the potential rescue of your mother." Saxon said.

"Malcolm…" Joan began.

"The horse is out of the barn now, so to speak. We should pool our knowledge and figure out how we can rescue your mother, should the need arise," Malcolm was quick to add. "After you finish your breakfast, we can start."

"Nonsense. I can eat and plan at the same time." Joan said.

"Alright. Let's start. What do we know about the geography?"

Joan gave a quick history of the villa. There had been the remains of a convent on the island of San Pancrazio. Her father had bought the island for her mother and set about to renovate the convent as a villa and create botanical gardens from plants all over the world; bamboo, camellias, palm trees, azaleas, rhododendrons, eucalyptus, and magnolias. The villa itself lay on the north end of the island on top of a small knoll. The villa had two floors; two sets of windows on the one corner of the house led onto a wrought-iron balcony. There was a main entrance with a grand lobby; vaulted arches, and a large crystal chandelier with the grand staircase leading up to the second floor. Off the lobby was the salon; a library where her mother often entertained writers and artists, which had French doors that led out on a terrace. The dining hall was also off the lobby, with the kitchen connected at the back of the dining hall. There was also a door off the kitchen for the servants and deliveries.

"Getting there is going to be an issue. If we dare take the train, it's a five-hour trip to Locarno. From there, we would need to rent a boat to get to the island. By automobile, it's even longer. If we could get an airship, it might be faster, but we would fly over the mountains."

"That shouldn't be an issue," Colfax offered. "The bigger issue is where we get an airship?"

"Mr Clark said that their airship wouldn't be back for a few more days," Saxon offered.

"It appears the train might be the best way," Malcolm said. "I think with the aid of Mr Clark, we might come up with better disguises, especially if Charles can walk unaided. Assuming we get to Locarno and can find a boat, what's our plan?"

Joan sat in thought for several moments. She sketched out a rough map of the island and drew a rectangle to indicate the house. She sketched the location of the dock, the ruins of the old convent near the water's edge, and drew circles to represent the more dense areas of foliage. "It's been some time since I've been back, but this is what I remember. Frietag will probably have guards stationed at the dock, on the remains of the tower of the convent and in a perimeter here," pointing at a circle around the house above the dense foliage. "There are a few garden paths that lead from the terrace off the salon. He'll probably have guards stationed there, as well as at the service entrance." She marked x's on the map to show where she thought he might station guards.

"That seems like a lot of resources for him to acquire. Do you think he can get that many?" Malcolm asked.

"You blew up a portion of a major university and put the city of Leipzig in darkness for days. The Germans are highly motivated to find you," Saxon stated.

"True," Malcolm said. He counted the x's on the map. "How are we going to deal with as many as ten men just to get inside the villa? We know that's where Frietag will be, but how many more? I would imagine he'll have guards at your mother's room, possibly guards watching the servants. Another four or five? That's a lot for you and I to deal with," he said to Joan.

"You're not going alone," Saxon said. "If Mr O'Hallarhan and Mr Mingo can rig up some kind of contraption so I can get around, count me in."

"Count me in," O'Hallarhan said.

Colfax sighed. "Someone has to keep an eye on you. I'm in."

"This isn't your fight," Joan said.

"Yes, it is," Saxon said. "If you remember, Frietag would have killed me if not for Malcolm's quick thinking. I have plenty of reasons to stop him. Permanently."

"And he tried to abduct me. I, too, want him dealt with, if only to make sure he doesn't go after my parents," O'Hallarhan said.

Everyone looked at Colfax. "I'm just here for the ride. And someone has to keep an eye on you lot."

Joan looked at everyone. "Thank you. It means so much to me you're willing to risk your lives to rescue my mother." A tear rolled down her face; she quickly wiped it away before turning back to the map. "Now, let's get to work!"

# CHAPTER FORTY SIX

The group spent the rest of the morning discussing plans to eliminate the guards, rescue Joan's mother, and deal with Frietag. They stopped their planning for a simple lunch of bread, cold meats, boiled eggs, and many cheeses. After lunch, O'Hallarhan and Colfax set off to build a mechanical brace so that Saxon could walk. As they were leaving, Saxon realised he would be left alone with Malcolm and Joan. "Wait for me! If you're going to experiment on me, I should see what it is you intend to do!" He wheeled out of the conference room, following O'Hallarhan and Colfax.

"We seem to be all alone," Malcolm said. "How convenient." He reached over to hold her hand, but she resisted. "What's wrong? This can't be all about worrying about the rescue, is it?"

"No, I'm not as worried about rescuing her; I'm more concerned about facing her and telling her we're getting married." Malcolm started to speak, but Joan put her finger to his lips. "Let me finish. You know my mother insisted I marry nobility and was against me going to school, let alone university. But what I haven't told you was she literally locked me in my room at the villa. When I was sixteen, I snuck away with the help of the gardener, who hid me on his boat when he returned ashore. Looking back, it was probably the start of my career as a spy."

"Where was your father in all of this?"

"By then, he and my mother were living apart. When I escaped, I made my way to Naples, where my father was working for the British Consulate. He sent me first to a private school in Geneva and then to university. From there, Mycroft recruited me to join the Secret Service and you know much of the story from there."

"When was the last time you spoke to your mother?"

"It's been five years now, before you and I met. I visited her for Christmas; the Alps in the winter are a magical place. I thought if I showed her how successful I was, she might relent. I was barely in the door when she started on about how I wasn't married, how at my age, I'd never find someone, and how disappointed she was in me. When I tried to convince her I was successful, able to support myself, and living the life I wanted, she wouldn't listen. I tolerated it for one day before I returned to London."

She paused for several moments. "After my 'death' at the end of the Russian mission, I chose not to tell her the truth; I just couldn't face her scorn, ridicule, and disappointment. I had an easy excuse to avoid yet another confrontation. Now, I'm going to be forced to face something I've avoided for a very long time." When she finished, Malcolm noticed tears well in her beautiful green eyes.

"If it's any consolation, you can tell her you are marrying a baron when I get invested." Malcolm squeezed her hand.

"That is true, but I'm afraid she'll disparage even that, since you aren't nobility by birth. She'll be apoplectic to learn you're the son of a shipyard worker."

"Wouldn't be the first time I've heard that, and likely not the last." Joan gave a nervous laugh. Malcolm squeezed her hand. "Consider it my baptism by fire. I'll just have to use my natural charm to win her over."

"Oh, God! We're going to be in so much trouble in that case." She laughed, and Malcolm joined her. They looked at each other for a long moment.

Malcolm leaned in and kissed her softly. "When you meet your mother this time, you won't have to do it alone. I'll be there supporting in any way I can."

"Thank you, Malcolm. I fear I'm going to need all the help I can get." She kissed Malcolm on his forehead and wiped her eyes.

"It sounds like dealing with Frietag is going to be easier than dealing with your mother."

"Don't underestimate Frietag, Malcolm. He avoided detection for many years. He nearly captured the Daedalus and abducted you with ease. And he has a personal vendetta against you. That makes him extremely dangerous. He's well trained in hand to hand combat and if it comes to fight, he will be extremely difficult to defeat."

"But he had two important weaknesses; he lacks depth perception because he only has one eye and he gets sloppy when angered. And I seem to be very good at making him angry."

"I'd be careful doing that, Malcolm. While he might get sloppy, his anger will make him incredibly dangerous."

"Our only saving grace is that he wants to make me suffer as much as possible and won't just shoot me on sight."

"True, but I wouldn't count on that." Joan looked at Malcolm. "When we confront him, please be careful, Malcolm. I almost lost you once, and I don't know if I can go through that again."

"The same goes for you. When I thought you were dead, I was miserable. And the thought of losing you so close to our chance to spend our lives together is more than I can bear."

They looked at each other for several moments before Joan said, "Let's get back to planning so we can make sure that neither of us has to worry." They turned back to the map and spent the afternoon going through various scenarios and how they might rescue Joan's mother and neutralise Frietag. Despite Malcolm's previous protestations about hating espionage, he was quite adept at developing plans and counterplans.

Just before dinner, Colfax and O'Hallarhan returned to the conference room. Malcolm asked, "How did your afternoon go?"

"See for yourself," O'Hallarhan said. He stepped to the side, and Saxon was standing. A brace ran down to his ankle to help secure the mechanised knee brace in place. Around his knee were a series of interlocking plates that held the knee in place. On either side of his knees, a series of gears and springs aided in the mobility. He walked slowly into the room and took a seat at the table.

"It's not stylish, and it's a little slow, but as you can see, I can get around by myself," Saxon said.

"With a little more work, we can make it faster and more reliable. This was just our first attempt." O'Hallarhan was very pleased with himself. Malcolm noted the use of the word "our" and was happy that O'Hallarhan hadn't attempted to take all the credit.

"Excellent! Congratulations, gentleman! If either of you decide to leave the Service, you could probably make a fortune selling this," Malcolm said.

"What about you two? Did you get any work done this afternoon?" Saxon raised his eyebrow.

"For your information, Charles, we did." Malcolm shot a dirty look at Saxon, and Saxon raised his hands in defeat. "Joan, would you care to share what we did this afternoon?"

Joan went through the scenarios she and Malcolm had developed. When she finished, O'Hallarhan shook his head. "I'm not sure I'll be able to remember all of that."

"Don't worry; by the time we may have to execute them, I promise you'll remember everything," Joan said.

"That's what I was afraid of," O'Hallarhan said, eliciting a laugh from the group. As if on cue, dinner arrived at the conference room; this time, it was roast chicken seasoned with thyme and rosemary, shredded potatoes fried to a golden brown, and a medley of carrots, leeks, and green beans.

"I could get used to this food," Malcolm said. As they finished dinner, Archibald Clark entered the conference room.

"Please, join us," Joan said.

"I'm afraid I'll have to pass. I come bearing bad news. Our agent arrived in Locarno this morning. He just reported that a small German airship flew over Locarno late this afternoon, heading for your mother's villa. It appears to have landed on the south side of the island."

Joan stood up. "We have to leave immediately!"

"Leave?" Clark said.

"Yes, we need to rescue my mother!"

Clark shook his head. "I can't let you leave, not until the airship returns to take you back to England."

"You'll have to put guards on my door if you think you're going to keep me here. And if you've read my file, you know I am more than capable of dealing with them."

"Miss de St. Leger," Clark began.

"I am going and nothing you can do will persuade me otherwise."

Clark shook his head and let out an exasperated sigh. "Very well. It's a five-hour trip by train. I'll book tickets on the train for first thing in the morning and direct my agent in Locarno, Rupert Ashford, to meet you at the train station in Tegna and drive you to Locarno, in case Frietag has agents watching the train station. I trust you have a plan?"

"Yes," Joan said. "I'd rather not divulge it in case things go poorly. That way, you have plausible deniability."

"Let me say I'm against this idea." Clark looked around at the five determined faces. "But I can see there is no use fighting you. I'll make the arrangements. I suggest you retire soon because the train leaves at 8:00 tomorrow morning and it will take some time to get the five of you to the train station."

"Thank you, Mr Clark," Joan said. "I'm sorry to make this difficult for you, but it is my mother. I trust you understand."

Clark's face softened for a moment before he said, "I understand. Please excuse me. I must make the arrangements. I'll leave one of my assistants at your disposal if you need anything else." Clark left and within a few minutes, a young agent joined them in the conference room. "What can I do for you?"

"Thank you, Mister…" Joan began.

"Lockwood. Edmund Lockwood."

"We're going to need clothes, equipment, and weapons. Lots of weapons," Joan said.

# CHAPTER FORTY SEVEN

They spent the evening reviewing Joan's plans and gathering equipment they might need: a variety of weapons such as rifles, machine guns, pistol, and rather large guns that could fire a grappling hook or small rockets; ether, stun, and smoke grenades; binoculars; electric torches; a disguise kit; several sets of travelling clothes; and a set of special clothes designed to help with infiltration. Colfax and O'Hallarhan scrounged for spare parts for Saxon's mechanised knee brace. They had hoped to improve on its design, but there was no more time. By ten o'clock, they had done all that they could and made their ways to their rooms.

Malcolm walked Joan to her room. "Are you alright?"

Joan nodded. "I think so. Not knowing what was happening was worse than hearing the news. I think we can do this." She moved close to Malcolm and put her arms around him. "Do you want to join me tonight? Just in case this is our last night?"

"Nothing would make me happier," Malcolm said, pulling her close for a kiss. Without breaking the kiss, Joan opened the door, pulling Malcolm in and, when he was in, kicking the door shut.

Malcolm awoke when Joan got out of bed for her shower. He turned on the electric lamp next to his bed and looked at his watch; it was five o'clock. He slipped out of bed, gathered his clothes, and snuck back to his room to take a shower. All during his shower, he couldn't shake the feeling of anxiousness; he worried about Joan, her mother, and facing Frietag yet again. He'd been lucky so far and come out on the winning side. But what if his luck had run out? He shook his head to clear away the thoughts, but he was only partially success-ful. They lingered in the back of his mind, ready to pounce if he let his guard down for a moment.

When he dressed, he went to the conference room, where he found a simple breakfast of bread, butter, and marmalade, as well as pots of tea and coffee. Malcolm helped himself to a cup of tea and tried to force an interest in eating; his stomach too, joining in his general feeling of anxiety. Joan arrived shortly after Malcolm sat down. After getting a cup of coffee and bread, she sat down next to him. She looked at him, "Are you alright? Is something wrong?"

"No," Malcolm said. "I'm just nervous about dealing with Frietag again. What if I can't outsmart him this time?"

"You will, Malcolm. I have faith in you. I wouldn't want anyone else by my side for this mission. Although it will make things more interesting with my mother."

"I told you; there's nothing to worry about. I'll win her over with my charm." Malcolm could barely keep a straight face as he said it, and they both burst out in laughter, doing much to relieve Malcolm's anxiety.

Colfax, O'Hallarhan, and Saxon joined them in the conference room. "I would have been here sooner, but it took me twenty minutes to get my trousers on over this contraption," he grumbled as got his breakfast. Malcolm could tell, despite the protestations and complaints, Saxon was glad to be moving under his own volition.

They sat silently, eating their breakfast, sipping their beverages, while monitoring the clock. Wordlessly, they made their way to the exit where Archibald Clark was waiting. He handed each of them a packet containing their train tickets, identification papers, and a small bundle of currency for Italy and France. "Do I have your word that as soon as you secure your mother, you will return to England immediately?"

"Absolutely," Joan said. "We hope to get back to England as quickly as possible. If all goes well, we intend to take Frietag's airship and fly first to France, then straight to England. Even if he could catch us, I would doubt Frietag would dare to shoot us down over France."

"I don't suppose I can talk you out of this?" Clark asked.

"No," Joan said emphatically, clearly indicating there would be no further discussion of the matter.

"Very well. I wish you all Godspeed and good luck."

"Thank you, Mr Clark. I'm sorry if we've made your life more difficult."

"Such is the life of a station chief. Field agents rarely do what I want. Here's our radio frequency; let me know when you escape." Clark pressed a piece of paper into Joan's hand. "I wish you the best." He opened the door and two cars were waiting for them; their equipment and luggage already loaded. Joan, Charles, and Malcolm rode in the first car; O'Hallarhan and Colfax in the second. The cars whisked them back to the train station. After a brief wait, they boarded the train bound for Locarno.

Malcolm sat silently, watching the scenery as the train left station and wound its way around Lake Lucerne and Lake Zug before turning south towards the Alps. The vibrations of the train as it travelled lulled Malcolm to sleep. When he awoke, they were approaching a tunnel carved into the mountain.

"I woke you up, Malcolm," Joan said. "We're entering the Gotthard Tunnel. I knew as an engineer you would want to see it firsthand."

"What about you?"

"Oh, I hate it."

"Why?"

"You'll see in a moment." The train continued toward tunnel and, in moments, was swallowed by darkness. Their car wasn't completely dark because the electric lights had turned on as they approached, but it gave the cabin an eerie feel. "I hate this part," Joan said. "Between the semi-darkness and worrying about the tunnel collapsing, it's all I could do to get through it."

Malcolm reached over and grabbed her hand. "You don't have to worry. I'm here."

"Thank you." Joan squeezed Malcolm's hand hard for the twenty minutes it took for the train to traverse the tunnel. When the train exited, the sunlight was blinding. After a few moments, Joan relaxed her grip on Malcolm's hand, much to his relief. She looked down at his hand. "I'm sorry. I must have crushed your poor hand."

"It's fine," he lied. "What is it about the tunnel that you hate? I've seen you crawl around in tight spaces, so it can't be that."

"I think it's what it represents. I hated going to the villa; although there were plenty of books to keep me company, there was nowhere for me to play when I was young. And it was always too dark to read while we travelled through the tunnel. Coming through the tunnel meant we were on the Italian-speaking side of Switzerland and away from Geneva, which I considered home." Joan made a short laugh. "The last time I visited my mother here, I came from Italy, just so I wouldn't have to travel through that damn tunnel."

"How much longer do you think we have until we arrive?"

"Another two hours. When I was growing up, they were the longest two hours of my life."

"We'll have to do something to pass the time more quickly."

"Here? On the train? In front of everyone? Mr Robertson, you shock me!" Joan smiled as she said it.

Malcolm turned beet red. "That's not what I meant, and you know it."

Joan leaned over to Malcolm and whispered in his ear, "A girl can dream, can't she?"

Malcolm pulled away. "Keep that up, and I'll trade places with Charles and you can listen to him complain the whole way." Now it was Malcolm's turn to smile.

Joan sighed. "You are a killjoy. What should we do to pass the time?"

"Let's talk about our wedding when we get back to England."

Joan picked up Malcolm's arm and pulled it around her, cuddling into his side. They discussed the logistics of doing the wedding again as soon as possible when they returned. It would need to be a much more intimate affair; which suited Malcolm well. As they talked, they watched the train make its descent out of the mountains and through the mountain valleys before eventually reaching the town of Tegna.

When the train reached the station, Joan practically bounded off the train in excitement. She waited impatiently for Malcolm to bring their luggage off of the train. She tapped her foot, waiting for Colfax, Saxon, and O'Hallarhan. As Malcolm and Joan waited on the platform, a man in a dark suit approached. "Are you my guests from Lucerne? I'm Rupert Ashford." He reached his hand out to shake Malcolm's hand. Malcolm caught a flash of something, but wasn't sure what it was.

He noticed a sheen of sweat on Ashford's forehead, but the spring air still held a chill. As Ashford kissed Joan's hand in a gentlemanly gesture, Malcolm caught sight of a ring. He focused on the ring; a gold signet ring with a black cross. It brought back a memory; Joan and Saxon had told him the attacker who shot him in Russia was wearing a similar ring. The ring designated the person as a member of the Teutonic Knights, a secret German order. *Shite*, Malcolm thought. *Frietag is already onto us.* "Let's get this luggage to your vehicle and we can go."

"We need to get going right away," Malcolm said, as he used his eyes to indicate Ashford and looked down at his hand. Joan followed his gaze. Her eyes widened when she saw the ring and gave a silent nod. They hurried to gather their luggage when they heard O'Hallarhan yell, "Wait for us! We're coming?"

"Are they with you?" Ashford asked.

"I do not know who they are," Malcolm said. "I'm so glad that Mr Jones sent you."

"Yes, it was fortuitous that I was near Locarno," Ashford said, confirming Malcolm's suspicions. As they moved off the platform and through the train station,. Ashford led them to a lorry parked just down the street. Malcolm let Ashfold get to the back door of the lorry when Malcolm grabbed the man's head and smashed it into the back of the lorry. The man crumpled to the ground. Malcolm quickly searched the man; he found a Luger in a shoulder holster, German identification, and several sets of handcuffs.

"What have you done?" O' Hallarhan puffed. He had run with his luggage to catch up with them. Malcolm looked up and saw Colfax and Saxon leaving the station and heading their way.

"This man is a German agent," Malcolm said. "Frietag must have expected us to arrive here. I suspect that the real Mr Ashford is dead somewhere. Let's get this door open and get him off the street." Malcolm and O'Hallarhan lifted the door and found another body in the back of the lorry. "I suspect that's the real Mr Ashford." Malcolm and O'Hallarhan lifted the German agent and set him in the back of the truck. Malcolm took one set of the handcuffs and secured the agent's arms behind him. By now, Saxon and Colfax had joined them. "Quick, get your gear loaded. We need to get out of here as soon as possible. Peter, you'll have to be our driver; Joan, you need to direct Peter."

"What's going on?" Saxon asked.

"I'll explain once we're out of here," Malcolm said.

Joan pulled Malcolm aside. "Thank you, Malcolm. How did you know?"

"Something about him felt off. He was sweating when he greeted us and it's certainly not that warm. Then I noticed he was wearing a ring of the Teutonic Order, and he didn't know that Mr Clark was the one who gave him the orders. My guess is he had little time to kill Ashford and assume his identity. If he hadn't been as sloppy, I might not have put everything together."

"I should have seen that! My sloppiness nearly got us killed!"

"But it didn't. Right now, I need to you to direct Peter to Locarno. In the meantime, Saxon and I will have a little conversation with our guest when he wakes up."

# CHAPTER FORTY EIGHT

Malcolm climbed into the back of the lorry as O'Hallarhan closed the door. A battery-powered electric lamp provided some illumination so they wouldn't sit in the dark for the entire trip. Malcolm kept the Lugar pointed at the German agent. Malcolm looked at the German agent's identification. It listed his name as Friedrich Gruber, although Malcolm doubted that was his real name. After several minutes, Gruber stirred and sat up. He thrashed when he realised he was handcuffed.

"I would keep still if I were you," Malcolm said. "My finger is very twitchy on this trigger and I would hate to kill you before we get to know one another."

The agent stared back at Malcolm with hatred in his eyes. "Ich spreche kein Englisch."

Malcolm cocked the hammer of the pistol. "Don't pull that with me. Your English was good enough to lure us away. It's probably better than mine." The agent glared at Malcolm. "Now, let's start again, shall we? We know Frietag sent you and you killed the person who was to meet us. What was the plan?"

"Why should I tell you?"

"So I don't kill you?"

The agent sneered at Malcolm. "You won't kill me. Frietag told me you were weak, and he is right. You don't have the guts to kill me."

"No? Are you sure you want to try me?"

"Do it!" the agent shouted, calling Malcolm's bluff.

"You know what? You're right. I don't kill indiscriminately. I'm not a monster like your cycloptic boss." Malcolm opened the door of the truck and dragged the agent over. "I'll give you a chance. If you survive the fall, you can walk back to town." Malcolm pushed the agent out of the truck and watched as he landed with a thud. Soon, the dust from the road obscured the man from view and Malcolm shut the door.

"Do you think that was wise? Pushing him out like that? We might have got more information," Saxon said.

"I doubt it. He was more of a liability. However, it does concern me what we might find waiting for us in Locarno." Malcolm rubbed his temples. "Just once, it would be nice for something to go right."

"Can someone please tell me what's going on?" Colfax said. Malcolm explained how he figured out the agent's identity and knocked him out. Malcolm felt the lorry slow down. Concerned, he kept the Lugar pointed at the door. A few minutes after the lorry came to a stop, O'Hallarhan opened the door. "Miss de St. Leger thought we ought to decide our next move. I noticed our passenger was no longer with us."

Malcolm moved out of the lorry and waited to help Saxon. Although the mechanical brace increased his mobility, he couldn't jump from the truck easily. With O'Hallarhan's help, they assisted Saxon out of the lorry. Joan and O'Hallarhan joined the trio.

"I thought now that we were out of town, we should plan our next steps." Joan sounded uncharacteristically uncertain. "We know Frietag is expecting us and expects us to arrive at Locarno. Unfortunately, there's no way to get closer to the island without going through Locarno."

"Do you have a map?" Saxon asked. Joan produced a map and laid it against the side of the truck. "What's this?" Saxon pointed to a strip of blue going northwest from Lake Maggiore.

"It's the Maggia; it's a river."

"It looks like we're very close to it right now. What if we were to get a boat? Could we sail down the river?"

"We would need canoes; it flows through a rocky valley, and there are sections of rapids and then shallows. I've never done it; I would be loath to attempt it without knowledge."

"I agree." Saxon stared at the map. "Could we skirt Locarno and continue east to Tenero-Contra?"

Joan considered the option. "I don't know; what do you think, Malcolm?"

Malcolm looked at Joan and instead of the strong, decisive woman he usually saw, she looked uncertain and diminished. "Can I have a word with you, Joan?" She nodded. "How about the four of you study the map and come up with some options?" He led Joan to the front of the lorry, away from the rest of the group. "What's wrong? Something is definitely bothering you."

"I nearly got us all captured!" she hissed. "I let my guard down. What if you hadn't noticed his ring? We would be on our way into a trap and right into Frietag's hands!"

Malcolm tried to hug her, but Joan turned away. He took her hand and turned her toward him. "If I had made a mistake like this on any of our missions, what would you say to me?"

She lowered her eyes and murmured, "I'd tell you that you're human and you wouldn't make the same mistake again." She pouted for a minute. "But..."

Malcolm put a finger to her lips. Although they often butted heads, her strength and confidence were the thing he loved the most. Seeing her frightened and insecure broke his heart. "But nothing. You need to follow your own advice. I need my fearless, dare I say, ruthless Joan who can assess the situation and come up with a plan. You know this area better than any of us. You can do this; I've seen you do it dozens of times." She still wouldn't look at him. "Is there another reason you're so upset?"

She was silent for several moments before she whispered, "All that talk about the wedding made me wish we were already married, so when we find my mother, she wouldn't try to talk me out of it."

"Could she?"

"Hell, no!"

"Then what's the problem?"

"It's…I just wanted to show her that my life meant something and I was right."

"Your life means something. Any success I've had; my promotions, my titles, my accolades; they are all a result of you. I couldn't have done any of that without you. You have made a difference in my life, and I can't imagine what my life would be without you."

"Thank you, Malcolm." She pulled him close and gave him a kiss. She wiped a tear away from her eyes. "How do you always know what to say?"

"It's my natural charm." He smiled and Joan laughed. He waited a moment before he asked, "Are you alright?"

She straightened herself, and Malcolm saw the strong woman that he loved. "Yes, thank you. Now, let's figure out how we get to the island." They returned to the trio, who glanced down at the map, trying to appear as if they hadn't heard the conversation with little success. Joan walked with purpose to the map and looked at it for a few moments before saying, "Yes. We should skirt around Locarno and head for Tenero-Contra. There should be plenty of boats that we can hire and we can sail from there to the island come nightfall." She looked up and said, "Well, what are we waiting for? Let's get going!" She took the map and hurried to the passenger door.

Malcolm smiled. "You heard the lady, gentleman. Let's get going!"

# CHAPTER FORTY NINE

When everyone loaded in back, O'Hallarhan put the lorry in gear and they made their way south towards Locarno. The trip was challenging; O'Hallarhan often had to slow to a crawl to navigate the twisting road. Joan noted the scenery and did her best to keep track of their progress on the map. They travelled through mountain passes, sometimes the road was right next the Maggia. The rough road tossed O'Hallarhan and Joan; she could only imagine how uncomfortable the trip would be in the back.

Malcolm had made her feel better, but the fact she hadn't detected the fake agent still gnawed at her. She had got carried away with the idea of finally wedding Malcolm that she had dropped her guard. *But was that a bad thing? Isn't part of loving someone letting your guard down and letting them in?* She shook her head. *But now isn't the time.* She steeled herself and concentrated on the task at hand; getting them to Tenero-Contra.

As they neared the outskirts of Locarno, the road levelled out and they would have made more time if they hadn't encountered the local traffic of horse-drawn carts making their way into the town. She expertly directed O'Hallarhan around the town and soon they were making their way to Tenero-Contra. She looked out at Lake Maggiore and begrudgingly admitted to herself that it was a beautiful sight; the emerald green lake lay before them, with the Alps providing a rugged backdrop. Growing up, she hated this area, but she had to admit, it was beautiful. Seeing the lake again brought back the familiar feelings of dread, but it was mixed with something else; pride. On this visit to the villa, she would show her mother why her life was important. She laughed to herself, hearing her mother tell her they wouldn't be in the mess if she had married a prince.

Once they turned east, they took a more northerly route to Tenero-Contra to avoid getting closer to Locarno; it would take longer, but she wanted to stay as far away from Locarno as she could. As they approached Tenero-Contra, she felt her confidence return, and she started planning the next steps; securing a boat for the trip to the island. She looked at the sky and frowned. Although they had enjoyed sunshine for the entire trip, she could see dark storm clouds in the southwest; from her years at the villa, she recognised rain. That would be a mixed blessing; it would reduce visibility and help cover their approach to the island, but it would make their mission that much more difficult.

It was late afternoon when they pulled into the village proper. Joan had to guess as to the best route to the docks on the river. She had never really visited this village in her time here; when she left the island, it would be to Locarno. This village was quant; the buildings were much less ornate and coloured white as opposed to the bright colours of Lacuna and their terracotta roofs. More than once, O'Hallarhan had to back the lorry out of a side street that suddenly ended. They eventually made their way to the lakeside and found several boats docked. O'Hallarhan stopped the lorry and went to the back to open the door. Joan heard a great deal of groaning as the men got out of the lorry while she strode to the dockside.

After several animated conversations in Italian, no one would go out on the lake at night, preferring to spend the evening with their families. She took a different tack and offered to trade the lorry for a boat; eventually finding a taker. She knew she was being swindled, but she had no other alternative. She led the group over to the boat; a small fishing boat with a cabin that might hold two people. It would be a tight squeeze to fit all of them on the boat. Malcolm looked and shook his head. "I hope the boat is more seaworthy than she looks."

"If you can do better, you're more than welcome to try," she said. "Otherwise, this is what we have to work with." They unloaded their equipment from the truck and, as soon as it was empty, the new owner drove it away.

"Was that wise? Haven't we put a target on that man?" Malcolm asked.

"I doubt it. Frietag might be on guard, but he can't have that many men at his disposal. He's probably only just realised that his man hasn't returned. What I'm more concerned about is the weather. It looks like rain."

"Wonderful," Saxon muttered. "It would have to rain."

"Let's get the gear stowed and make our plans for tonight." After careful manoeuvring, they got the gear on the boat to keep much of it dry. After a great deal of discussion, although Malcolm had the most experience on naval ships, O'Hallarhan had more experience with small boats from growing up on the Irish coast and would pilot the boat. They still had several hours before it would be dark enough to travel across the lake. Joan volunteered to go into the village to secure food that they could eat on the boat. She made her way back to the town centre and purchased two loaves of bread, an enormous chunk of salami, and an equally enormous chunk of cheese. She brought the bounty back to the boat, and using one of the knives in their equipment, they cut the food and ate in silence. When everyone finished eating, she laid out a map and explained her plan.

"We'll stay close to the coast line until we get to Gerra, then we'll head west to the south end of the island. We'll have to travel considerably south of the island in case they are lookouts at the ruins of the convent on the south of the island. There is a small stretch of beach on the west side where we can probably land undetected."

"Shouldn't we get closer to the villa?" Saxon asked.

"Landing on the south would allow us to remain undetected as long as possible. I doubt Frietag has enough men to watch the entire island and will concentrate on the easier places to land. I won't lie. It won't be an easy trek to the villa. My mother loves bamboo and much of the trip will be through bamboo forests. I can tell you it won't be easy travelling."

"Oh, joy," muttered Saxon.

"Once we find his airship, we should capture it. Peter and Colfax will prepare the airship to lift off as soon as possible. Malcolm, Charles, and I will continue on to the villa."

"Aren't you going to need more help?" O'Hallarhan interjected.

"I doubt it. Frietag will spread his forces out to maximise the area he can watch. The three of us should have little problem dispatching the guards. Breaking into the villa might be another story. We're going to need a diversion to draw out his guards so I can slip in."

"Don't you mean we can slip in?" Malcolm said. "I'm not risking losing you to Frietag again."

Joan glared at Malcolm, who returned the glare with equal intensity. "Fine," she humphed. "We'll go together. Charles, would you be able to create a diversion?"

"Creating the diversion should be easy with the grenades we have; my problem is that I won't be able to get away easily."

"Point taken." Joan sat in thought.

"What about using the boat?" O'Hallarhan said. "Once we have the airship, we won't need the boat. We could jam the rudder, set it on its way, and build a bomb to detonate. That would get their attention."

"Excellent idea," Joan said. "I'll leave that up to you and Colfax to figure out how to make it happen. Charles could stay in the tree line, providing sniper support if needed, while Malcolm and I break into the villa and extract my mother. We'll make our way back to the airship and leave. We should fly due east to France and then turn north for home."

"That's an excellent plan," Malcolm said. "I hope it goes as well as you've planned."

"Me too," Joan said.

# CHAPTER FIFTY

*A*s Joan predicted, within the hour, the dark clouds rolled in and the rain began. It was a gentle, but steady rain. They huddled in the boat's cabin, trying to stay out of the weather with decidedly mixed results. They remained mostly quiet, except for occasionally grumbling about the rain. Joan broke away from the group and stared out at the lake, hugging herself. Malcolm came up behind her and wrapped his arms around her. She jumped for a moment, but relaxed when she realised it was Malcolm.

"How are you doing?" He hugged her close, and she relaxed into him.

"Oddly, I'm fine. Now that I have a plan, I have something to focus on."

Malcolm kissed the top of her head. "We'll rescue your mother."

"Oddly, that's what scares me the most."

"Why?"

"All I can hear is her constant berating. She's a difficult woman."

"And you can't be difficult?"

"You're not nearly as funny as you think you are," she said, digging her elbow into his ribs.

As darkness fell, they pushed off and made their way out into the lake. O'Hallarhan turned the boat south. Malcolm kept watch to make sure they remained away from the shore. The trip was slow; the rain and the dark made it difficult to see over fifty feet ahead. They didn't dare use an electric torch to provide light to see the map. With Joan's help, they spotted Gerra and O'Hallarhan turned the boat southwest. After a long time, they could finally make out the island in the distance. They continued further south until they could barely see the island before O'Hallarhan turned the ship northwest. They sailed further west towards the opposite shore of the lake before swinging around towards the island. As they neared the island, O'Hallarhan cut the engine and let the boat slowly drift towards the island.

With Joan's keen eyes and knowledge of the island, they found a small cove, and the boat floated in. As they floated in, Joan noted the location of the airship tied down near the ruins of the convent. She made out the lights of the villa. Malcolm noticed Joan and whispered, "There are lights on the villa. Is there a generator somewhere? Should we try to disable it?"

"Possibly. But the problem is that it's in the basement, so we would need to get in while the lights are on." Malcolm nodded and left her alone to figure out the next steps.

They carefully lowered the anchor into the water to not make a splash and carefully entered the frigid waters of the lake. They carefully carried their equipment to shore and wordlessly distributed it. When everyone had their equipment, Joan laid out the plan. "Just past the beach is a path to the convent. That's where the airship is. I'll take point, followed by Malcolm and Charles. Peter and Colfax, you bring up the rear. We'll use the path while we're out of sight of the convent. Once we get there, we'll figure out our next steps." She donned a black poncho, pulled up the hood, and crept off the beach to the path, staying low. It was nearly fifty feet to the path. She crouched in the foliage near the path and looked in both directions. When she saw nothing, she waved the rest of them to join her.

She crept along the side of the path so she could make a quick move into the rhododendrons if needed. Joan could hear her mother yelling at her for hurting her precious flowers. She crept slowly, stopping every twenty feet before summoning the others to move forward. Slowly, they travelled two hundred feet until she could just make out the ruins and the airship. She held her hand up to tell the group to stop as she carefully crept through the rhododendron bushes and into the thick bamboo. Navigating the bamboo was difficult because it was unyielding and would shake if pushed. She remembered hours perfecting the art of moving silently through the bamboo to hide from her mother, careful not to disturb a single stalk. *Who knew that time would train me for this?* She made her way to the edge of the tree line. There were two bored looking guards carrying machine guns at the gangplank of the airship; she made out one more at the top of the ruined convent tower. They were bored and inattentive and she smiled. This would make them easy targets. The two guards by the airship were chatting in German; she couldn't make out much of the conversation, but she gathered they were complaining about being stuck down here in the rain instead of the villa. She stayed still for a long time before one guard said something and went into the airship. The other guard turned his back to Joan to yell back to the guard in the airship.

Joan knew this was her opportunity. She drew her gun and, like a panther, she crept out of the tree line, quickly and quietly closing the twenty feet between her and the guard and leapt. She jumped on the guard, wrapping her legs around his head, muffling his cry of surprise, and used her momentum to pull him down to the ground. On the way down, she hit the guard on the head with the handle of her gun and he was unconscious as he hit the ground. As she landed, she pulled the machine gun from his hand and rolled to the side of the gangway. A few seconds later, the guard emerged at the gangway and noticed his compatriot lying on the ground. Before he could say a word, Joan had grabbed his machine gun, pulled him out of the airship, and as he flew out, she hit him on the back of the head with her gun and he too, was unconscious before he hit the ground. She took his machine gun. She pulled out a pair of handcuffs from the German agent in Tenga and secured the two men. She stuffed their hats in their mouth as a makeshift gag so they couldn't alert the guard on the tower. *Two down, one to go.*

She stayed under the bottom of the airship and made her way to locate the guard on the tower. He was looking out at the lake, his machine gun hanging unattended as he blew on his hands to warm himself. She silently crept to the ruins and made her way to the tower. Silently, she scaled the side of the tower. Again, she remembered the times she climbed this very tower, to the consternation of her mother. She pulled herself up to the top of the tower. The guard didn't notice Joan until she was already on him; another blow to his head dropped him. She took his gun, secured him with another set of handcuffs, and made her way back down the tower. She crept along the path until she reached the rest of the group.

"I neutralised the targets. We can secure the area," she said.

"I thought we were all going to neutralise the guards," Malcolm said.

"I had an opportunity, and I took advantage of the situation."

Malcolm frowned. Even in the dark, Joan could see the displeasure on his face at operating out of his sight. "Fine. Let's get to the airship," he muttered, gathering his gear.

The group made their way quickly down the path to the airship. Carefully, they entered the airship. Colfax went to the cockpit to assess the controls, while O'Hallarhan went to the engine room. After their inspection, they agreed they could get the airship under motion.

They moved the two guards into the brush and O'Hallarhan and Colfax stood guard.

"It's time for the next phase; get to the villa and rescue my mother," Joan said, with a determined look on her face.

The trio crept along the path, keeping to the side so they could disappear quickly. It was dark, and the rain reduced the visibility. While it worked to their advantage, Malcolm knew it was a double-edged sword; they might not see a threat until it was nearly on top of them. After travelling roughly three hundred feet by Malcolm's best guess, the path forked. Joan, in the lead, directed them to the left. They continued for another hundred feet when Joan put a hand up, indicating to stop. She directed the trio into the brush on the right-hand side and when they huddled, she whispered, "The boat launch is just over there. I'll scout to make sure there are no guards before we continue."

"No," Malcolm hissed. "I'm not letting you go ahead without me. If you get captured now, we're lost because none of us know the island like you."

"I won't get captured," Joan said, bristling Malcolm's remark.

"As much as it pains me to say, Malcolm is right," Saxon said. "We can't risk losing you at this point. Let Malcolm join you; I'll stay here as rear guard."

"Fine," Joan huffed. Malcolm knew she wasn't happy, but Saxon's interjection had defused their conflict.

Joan motioned to Malcolm, and they crossed the path into the brush on the other side. Malcolm watched carefully as Joan picked her way through the bamboo and palm trees, doing his best to follow her path and to not disturb the foliage. While Joan easily picked her way through, Malcolm's size made it much more of a challenge. A few times, he lost sight of Joan, but was relieved when she stopped to let him catch up.

After several long minutes, they reached the edge of the foliage. Malcolm peered into the darkness and couldn't see anything. Joan started to move out of the foliage, but Malcolm grabbed her. She turned and gave him a furious look. She came over and hissed in his ear. "What are you doing? I need to see if the dock is clear."

"I don't want you going alone."

"Malcolm, you know as well as I, one person has less chance of being seen than two. You can cover me from here in case something goes wrong."

Malcolm could see the anger and determination burning in her eyes, and knew he couldn't win this fight. "Fine. But I don't like it one bit."

"Noted." She crept out of the brush and was soon out of sight. Malcolm waited impatiently, trying to decide how long he should wait before he would go after her, when he caught sight of her creeping back towards him. When she reached him, she whispered, "No guards in sight. My mother's boat is docked in the boathouse."

"What do you think we should do?"

"Now, you're going to listen to me?" she said. Malcolm let the jab go unanswered. After a moment, she said, "I think we could dare to start the engine and set it adrift. If we have the airship, we leave Frietag with no way to get off the island. Follow me and stay low."

Joan crept out, and this time Malcolm followed her. As they moved forward, he eventually caught sight of the dock and the boathouse. When they entered, Malcolm saw a large motorboat with a cabin that ran nearly the length of the boar, stopping just short of the bow sitting in the water. Mercifully, the boat pointed out towards the lake. They made their way down the dock on the starboard side and entered the boat. As Malcolm familiarised himself with the controls, Joan found a broom hidden in a closet and, with Malcolm's help, wedged the handle in the wheel. He found the starting crank and looked at Joan. She nodded, and he cranked the handle. After several iterations, the engine sputtered to life. As the boat moved forward, they slipped out of the cabin and jumped onto the dock. Malcolm was pleased that despite the ship's size, the engine was relatively quiet; all he heard was a gentle purr; the sign of a well-maintained engine. They watched as the boat slowly pulled out of the boathouse, heading to the eastern shore of the lake. After a moment, Joan tapped Malcolm's arm and pointed to the exit. They made their way back to the main path and rejoined Saxon.

"Mission accomplished," Joan whispered. "Although my mother will be livid when she learns we set her boat adrift."

"Now what?" Saxon asked.

"We have roughly two hundred and fifty feet until we reach the clearing around the villa. Once we get there, we'll reassess the situation," Joan said. Malcolm and Saxon nodded, and they made their way towards the villa. The ground was slick with mud now, making progress difficult. Saxon, in particular, had trouble with his footing as the mechanical brace wanted to move more quickly than he wanted. A few times, he slipped and fell, letting out a mild curse. Malcolm also felt like cursing; he was soaked, cold, and miserable, but he pressed forward.

As they grew nearer to the villa, although they were still in a forest of bamboo and palm trees, the foliage near the path had changed. There was a greater variety of plants and flowers, none of which Malcolm recognised. As they advanced, Malcolm saw the lights of the villa. It was a large two-story house; ivy or some other foliage covering the much of the walls. As they approached the clearing, the bamboo thinned, leaving large gaps in the foliage. They carefully crept between the palm trees, trying to keep hidden. As they neared the edge of the woods, Malcolm got a better look at the villa. He made out two guards at the front entrance, looking wet and miserable. Watched for another minute, he caught sight of another two guards patrolling around the clearing.

He leaned close to Joan and said, "Now what? There are two guards at the door and another two near the edge of the clearing."

"You missed one; there's another stationed on the balcony at the corner. That would be directly outside my mother's room."

Malcolm looked again and saw the guard come into view. "Now what?"

"We'll have to wait for Colfax and Peter to provide us a diversion."

"I was afraid you were going to say that," Saxon said.

Suddenly, the guard on the balcony yelled something to the two guards below, pointing to the lake. The two guards went inside, leaving the door unguarded. The guard on the balcony was looking toward the lake.

"They noticed the boat leaving," Joan said. "Now's the best time to make it to the house unnoticed," Joan said as she moved towards the edge of the clearing.

Malcolm nodded. When Joan gave the signal, they made moved quietly to the house, crouching low. They had nearly made it to the house and under the balcony when four more guards came out of the house. One of them caught sight of Malcolm and Joan and shouted something in German. The group stopped and levelled their machine guns at Malcolm and Joan.

"Shite," Malcolm thought.

## CHAPTER FIFTY TWO

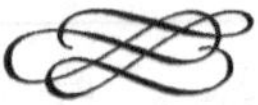

*B*efore the guards could fire, a spray of machine gun fire came from the brush. Joan squinted toward the edge of the clearing and saw Saxon with a machine gun pointed at the entrance. He gave Malcolm a thumbs up. Malcolm and Joan continued to the house, and took shelter under the balcony, around the corner from the front entrance.

"So much for getting here undetected," Malcolm whispered. "Now what?"

Another burst of machine gun fire erupted and there was a loud thud coming from the balcony above them. Joan turned to Malcolm. "Sounds like we can get in via the balcony. Come on!" She crept to the end of the balcony and pulled a rope and grappling hook from her pack. After unwinding several yards of rope, she swung it around and threw it up on the balcony. The hook easily caught in the balcony's railing, and after tugging several times to make sure it would hold, she climbed up the rope. She easily scurried up the rope, swung herself over the railing, and landed silently on the balcony.

Malcolm had a much harder time climbing; the rope was now slick from the rain. It took several attempts before he made any progress, but he eventually made it to the railing. He pulled himself up and half fell, half somersaulted over the railing, landing on his back with a loud thunk. Joan, who was working on the locks of the French doors that lead off of the balcony, turned and hissed, "Be quiet!" Before Malcolm could retort, Joan had opened the French doors and silently entered the room.

As Joan entered the room, something crashed over her head, almost knocking her down. Her vision momentarily dimmed, but when it cleared, she wheeled around with her gun pointed and saw her mother holding the shards of a vase.

The two women stared at each other for several moments. The remains of the vase slid out of her mother's hands. She whispered in Russian, "Joan, is that you or am I seeing a ghost?"

"It's me, Mama." Despite her protestations earlier, she was glad to see her mother again. Despite everything that had transpired between the two women, she felt a sense of relief and even comfort at seeing her mother again.

Her mother's eyes brightened and tears rolled down her cheeks. "How is it possible? They told me you died on one of your stupid missions."

"A necessary deception. We can go into that later. Right now, we need to get you out of here."

"What do you mean a 'necessary deception'? I demand to know why you lied about such a thing!"

"Mama, now's not the time for this discussion. We need to get out of here."

"I'm not going anywhere until you tell me why you felt it was necessary to think my only daughter had died!"

"Mama, there isn't time. We need to get you out of here now."

"Who is that strange man? In my bedroom?" Joan's mother pointed at Malcolm, who had entered the room. Joan saw the puzzled look on his face. She realised they were talking in Russian and he would not understand their conversation. In English, she said, "This is Baron Commodore Malcolm Robertson of the Royal Navy...and my future husband."

Her mother launched into a torrent of Russian. "So now you are marrying some muzhlán? I raised you to marry a prince, and you chose some...Englishman? First, you abandon me when I need you the most to go off for a...job. Then, you let me think you are dead and now I find out you're going to marry someone obviously unsuitable for you rank?" She pointed repeatedly at Malcolm during her tirade.

Joan felt her stomach tighten. It was a continuation of the years long conflict between them. Her feelings of relief and comfort vanished, replaced with a headache. In clipped tones, she said in English, "Mama, stop! We have to get you out of here before..." As the words left her mouth, she heard footsteps running up the stairs. She motioned to Malcolm, and they took positions on either side of the door.

"I demand to know what is happening," her mother yelled in Russian.

"Enough, Mama. Be quiet for once in your life!" Joan hissed. Her mother glared at her and turned away. Joan rolled her eyes, but forced herself to focus on the situation at hand. The footsteps approached the doors, followed by the sounds of keys, unlocking the door. Two guards rushed in, guns out. Malcolm and Joan hit both of the guards in the back of the head with the butt of their guns. The guards fell to the floor. They both hit the guards again to make sure they were unconscious. After taking one of the guard's machine gun, Joan ran to the door, shutting it most of the way, using the opportunity to see if there were any more guards coming. By the time Malcolm had disarmed the other guard, she had shut the door and locked it. She turned and said in English, "Mother, get dressed. We have to leave right now."

"I will not let these interlopers run me from my home! And I demand an explanation! What are you doing here and with him?" Joan's mother said, glaring at Malcolm.

"Mama, we don't have time. Please get dressed or I will haul you out of here in your nightdress," Joan said.

"I'd like to see you try!" her mother retorted.

"Don't tempt me," Joan said, taking a step towards her mother.

Malcolm quickly got between the two of them. "Ladies, there's a time and place for this and it is not here. Baroness," Malcolm turned to Joan's mother, "you must get dressed unless you wish to go out in the weather in your nightshirt. Joan, maybe you should watch the door." Malcolm tried to direct Joan's mother towards her screen, but she refused to move.

"Get your hands off me, you barbarian!" Joan's mother pulled away. "Why should I listen to you?"

"Because the men that hold you will have no compunction about killing you when your usefulness to them has ended," Malcolm said. "And, for Joan's sake, I'd very much like to avoid your death."

Before anyone could respond, they heard gunfire outside. "Please, Baroness, we have to get you out of here as quickly as possible," Malcolm pleaded.

After hearing the gunfire, Joan's mother was less resistant. She went behind her screen and changed into a white fluffy blouse and a long skirt. Malcolm turned to Joan, who was watching the hall. "Anyone out there?"

"Not yet. The coast is clear. When Mama is ready, I'll scout ahead and see if we can leave out the back. My hope is the gunfire drew more of them outside." She turned to her mother. "Are you ready yet?"

"I have to pack my trunk. I refused to leave without suitable clothes."

Joan turned toward her mother. "Mother, there isn't time for that. We can get you more clothes when we reach Paris. I know you can't resist shopping."

Joan's mother let out an exasperated sigh. "Very well, but I will hold you to that, Joan!"

Joan poked her head out of the door. She checked the hallway and took a few tentative steps into the hall. She turned and put her fingers to her lips to indicate everyone should stay quiet. Hoping her mother would comply, she motioned to Malcolm and her mother, and they crept down the hall. It continued to the left before turning out of sight. Joan had made it to the corner and was peering around the corner. As Malcolm and her mother approached, she nodded and turned the corner. Malcolm and her mother followed suit. Joan crept to the staircase and when she saw there was no one below, she hurried to the other side of the staircase and continue down the hall. Eventually, Joan took them to another set of stairs that lead down.

"What are these?" Joan's mother asked.

"These are the stairs used by the servants, if you must know," Joan whispered. "Let's go!"

"I will not take the servant's stairs!" Joan's mother hissed.

"It's either that or face the gun fire out front!" Joan hissed in return.

They glowered at each other for several seconds before Joan's mother harrumphed, which Joan took as acquiescence. Silently, the trio crept down the narrow, steep stairs. Joan listened at the door at the end of the staircase and after a moment, slipped out of the door and turned left. Her mother followed as Malcolm brought up the rear.

Joan kept down the hall at the end of the stairs and through the kitchen to the back door. She turned and waited for Malcolm and her mother; Malcolm crouching low to avoid hitting his head on the low hallway. When they reached Joan, she once again put her fingers to her lips before she slowly cracked the door. Ahead was a guard with his back to the door. Fearing her mother might say something, she opened the door slowly and before the guard knew what hit him, he was lying face down in the mud after a blow to the head from Joan's gun. She took the guard's gun and whispered, "Follow me!"

"You want me to go out there? In the rain? Without a parasol?" Joan's mother sputtered.

"How the bloody hell do you expect us to get out of here?" Joan hissed.

"There is no need to curse! I see your association with the Navy has taught you to curse like a sailor."

"Mama, we must leave. Now."

"Please, Baroness. If it helps, you may have my overcoat." Malcolm set down his guns, removed his overcoat, and handed it to her. "I'm afraid it is already wet, but it might prevent some of the rain from soaking through."

"Thank you," Joan's mother said, giving Malcolm an appraising look. When she secured the overcoat, she followed Joan outside.

Joan crouched low as she made her way down to the palm trees and bamboo, her mother and Malcolm close behind. Once under the cover of the trees, Joan's mother asked, "Now, what?"

"We make our way down to the south of the island, where an airship is waiting to take us away."

"Why can't we use the path instead of making our way through the forest? If you destroy any of my plants, I will be most cross," Joan's mother said.

"Mama, if we don't get off this island soon, the plants will be the least of your worries. Now please be quiet and follow me." Joan made her way back along the side of her mother's room and started toward the path when the trio heard.

"Malcolm? Joan? Show yourself! If not, I'll shoot Charles," a voice said in perfect English.

Malcolm and Joan clamoured to the edge of the forest and saw Frietag standing in front of the entryway of the house, holding Saxon by the throat with his mechanical hand as with the other hand, he had a revolver pointed at his head.

# CHAPTER FIFTY THREE

Once they realised the guards weren't going anywhere, Colfax and O'Hallarhan explored the airship. The airship was slightly bigger than Colfax's *Uhuru* and appeared that its primary purpose was to haul personnel. There was a small cargo hold, but other than the cockpit and the engine room, most of the space was open areas like a meeting room or the galley, or personal bedrooms. The two engineers were relieved to see that for the size of the ship, it had powerful engines, allowing them to outrun most airships.

Once they understood the ship, they looked for materials they could use to create an explosion on the boat. Using Malcolm's idea for destroying their previous airship, they searched for a clock, finding a mechanical alarm clock in one bedroom. After a thorough search of the ship for something to use to start the explosion, they didn't find a power source strong enough to ignite the diesel on the boat without removing the airship's batteries.

As they sat in thought, Colfax hit his head with the palm of his hand. "What idiots we are!"

"What do mean?" O'Hallarhan said, bristling at being called an idiot.

"This is a German zeppelin, right?"

"Yes."

"And what do the Germans use to make their airships float?"

"Hydrogen…oh, you're right. What idiots we are!"

The two searched the ship for a means to capture some of the ship's hydrogen and were delighted when they found a spare canister. One spark would be enough to ignite the hydrogen; their problem would be how to prevent the hydrogen from igniting prematurely. They raided the engine room for tools and spare wire and made their way back towards their boat. O'Hallarhan's mechanical arm came in handy as its added strength allowed him to carry the canister with ease.

As they returned to the hidden cove, Colfax pointed out to the lake. "Is that a boat leaving?"

O'Hallarhan stared out at the lake and Colfax was right; a boat was moving away from the island. "What do you suppose that means?"

"It means we better get working on this," Colfax said. "Let's get to work." They took a length of wire and connected it to the boat's battery. Using gaffer's tape, they did their best to secure the wire between the hammer and the bell of the alarm clock so that the bare wire would contact the hammer when the alarm clock activated. Like-wise, they took another piece of wire and secured it close to the first without them touching. When the hammer hit the bell, it would complete the circuit and ignite the hydrogen.

"Now, we just need something to cause a spark," Colfax said.

"If only we had a capacitor," O'Hallarhan said. He rummaged around the boat, but there were no capacitors to be found. But he smiled when he found a tin of sardines and some wax paper. "We might not have a capacitor, but we can make one!" He pulled the lid off of the sardines and tossed them overboard. After rinsing out the interior of the can, he used his mechanical hand to flatten the tin. He ripped a large piece of wax paper and covered the tin. Taking the lid, he placed it on top and, using the gaffer's tape, he held them together at the short edges.

"I'm not sure if it will work, but it's better than nothing," O'Hallarhan said.

Just then, the sound of gunfire interrupted their work.

"It sounds like they made it to the villa. We've got to get this going!" Colfax said.

"Just a minute," O'Hallarhan said, as he had another idea. He took several pieces of wax paper and taped them together to make a makeshift balloon. O'Hallarhan put his capacitor inside the wax paper contraption and took it over to the canister. He used the canister to fill the makeshift balloon and quickly used gaffer's tape to seal the end with the makeshift capacitor inside. He started the engine of their boat and turned the ship around so that it would travel northward. After finding a pole to jam the steering wheel, he set the alarm clock for five minutes, cracked the valve on the hydrogen container so that a small amount of hydrogen would leak out, and put the boat into motion. He jumped to the dock before the boat pulled away. He looked at the watch built into his arm and hoped that within five minutes, the hydrogen would detonate.

They hurried back to the airship; O'Hallarhan went to the engine room to start the engines while Colfax went to the bridge. Colfax looked at the gauges and frowned; everything was in German. After a few moments, he guessed which the purpose of each gauge. He looked around the cockpit and found a bank of switches underneath that were labelled in German. Taking no chances, he flipped them all. "O'Hallarhan, are you there? How much longer until the boat explodes?" He asked as his voice boomed throughout the entire ship.

After a few seconds, O'Hallarhan's voice came over a speaker in the cockpit. "I'm here. We have just over a minute. I'm trying to figure out how to start the engines. You don't happen to read German, do you?"

"Unfortunately no. I have the same problem up here."

"Give me a moment and I'll puzzle it out," O'Hallarhan said. The line went silent and after about thirty seconds, Colfax saw one gauge jump; it was labelled "U/min"; he assumed that meant RPMs, telling him the engine was running. "Good job; now what do we do?"

"The boat should explode in another thirty seconds," O'Hallarhan said. He counted out every five seconds until he reached ten. "Ten, nine, eight, seven, six, five, four, three, two, one." Colfax held his breath, waiting to hear the explosion. After ten seconds, he said, "Now what? Shouldn't it have gone off by now?"

O'Hallarhan said, "It should have; maybe the clock's timing is off." And then it hit him; he hadn't wound the clock. "Shite."

"What is it?" Colfax said.

"We didn't wind up the alarm clock. The extra weight of the wire might have caused the clock to run down."

"So now what do we do?" Colfax said.

"We could try to shoot the boat to cause the explosion," O'Hallarhan offered.

"Can we get close enough to shoot it without getting caught in the explosion ourselves?"

O'Hallarhan did some quick mathematics in his head. Given all they had was a single machine gun, its range probably about fifteen hundred yards, give or take. If they flew low, it would increase the distance between the zeppelin and the boat. It would be close, but O'Hallarhan didn't have a better idea. "I think so, but we'll have to come in as close to the water as you can; that will give us the most distance."

"Now the question; who's going to fire? Are you a good shot?" Colfax asked.

"Not particularly; I made it through basic training, but that's about all. You?"

Colfax sighed. "I'm probably a little better than that. Do you think you can pilot the ship? It's going to be tricky in the rain to keep the ship above the water."

O'Hallarhan gulped. "I've only done the basics; I never liked the bridge."

"Damn engineers," Colfax muttered.

"What was that?" O'Hallarhan said.

"Nothing. Alright, I'll get us in the air and headed out toward the lake. Hopefully, all you'll have to do is hold it steady. Once we're airborne, come up to the cockpit and I'll hang out of the gangway and shoot at the boat."

"Is this going to work?" O'Hallarhan said.

"It better work. Malcolm, Joan, and Saxon are counting on us."

# CHAPTER FIFTY FOUR

alcolm looked at Joan, and they nodded to one another. Joan went to her mother and whispered, "Stay here. If you get the chance, head towards the south end of the island; there's an airship waiting."

"But," Joan's mother began.

"No, you must do this. That man out there," she pointed to Frietag, "would shoot you as quick as look at you."

"I...I can't lose you again," Joan's mother muttered.

"You won't," Joan said. Her mother's concern threw her off guard for a moment. For a moment, the years of frustration and conflict evaporated, and she saw her mother as she had when she was a little girl. Joan reached down and squeezed her mother's hand and held it as they looked at one another. After a moment, her mother withdrew her hand and nodded.

"Come now, I'm getting impatient and bad things happen when I get impatient," Frietag called.

"He won't know the meaning of bad things if I get my hands on him," Malcolm muttered.

"Malcolm, keep your cool. We need you level headed if we're going to get out of this," Joan whispered. "But you may have to stand in line to get your revenge."

They looked at each other for a moment. They reached for each other's hands and after giving a squeeze, Malcolm yelled, "Alright. We're coming out."

"Throw your guns out and raise your hands where I can see them," Frietag yelled.

Malcolm and Joan tossed their machine guns out into the clearing and rose with their hands above their heads, slowly walking into the clearing. Quickly, two of Frietag's men pulled their arms behind them and pushed them towards Frietag.

"I'm sorry," Saxon said. "The damn gun jammed, and they were on me before I could get away."

"That's enough from you," Frietag said, hitting Saxon in ribs with his gun. "Malcolm, Joan. So nice you could join our little soiree. This is even better than I planned. Returning all three of you to Germany will secure my rightful place in the Abteilung III b." The guards marched them right up to Frietag. He took his gun and hit Malcolm squarely in the jaw, causing him to see stars. "That's for the little show you put on in Leipzig." Malcolm spit blood from his mouth and glared at Frietag. "What, no clever come back?"

"Oh, I have plenty to say to you, but there are ladies present," Malcolm spat.

"You can't possibly be talking about your bride to be? We both know she's no lady."

Malcolm's temper rose, but he fought it down. "Leave her out of this and I'll go willingly. I'm the one you want. Why else would you go to such lengths to get me?"

"True. When I started this, I only wanted revenge on you. But I can think of no better revenge than watching your friend and your bride to be die at my hands before I take my time in making you suffer in ways you can't imagine."

"If I have to listen to you drone on, you can just shoot me now and put me out of my misery," Malcolm said. Just then, Malcolm thought he heard an engine; it was some distance away, but he was sure it was an airship engine. *What are Colfax and O'Hallarhan playing at?* he thought. He stared at Frietag, who didn't appear to hear the engine. Malcolm spat at Frietag, who hit Malcolm again with his gun. Malcolm let himself fall to his feet, towards the sound of the engine. After his vision cleared, he thought he could make out the outline of the zeppelin barely flying over the top of the lake. As the guard yanked him to his feet, he caught sight of their boat, some two thousand yards ahead.

"I think I might start by pulling out your tongue, because I am sick of hearing you talk," Frietag said.

"Can't stand to hear the truth? You blame us for your downfall, but the truth is, you're just incompetent. You botched the mission to capture the *Daedalus*, couldn't keep us in Austria, and you couldn't even keep me captive for more than a few weeks. And to top it off, you weren't even that good of an engineer."

"Enough!" screamed Freitag, spittle flying from his mouth. He tightened his grip around Saxon's neck, who clearly was having trouble breathing now. "I will kill your friend for your insolence!"

"Because you aren't man enough to take it out on me!" Malcolm retorted. "Let him go and face me like a man, instead of the cycloptic coward you are!"

The sound of machine gun fire rang out over the lake and a few seconds later, an explosion erupted on the lake. As everyone's attention turned to the lake, Saxon used his mechanically braced leg and kicked at Frietag's kneecap with all his might. Frietag howled in pain and fell to the ground, dropping his gun and releasing Saxon. Malcolm likewise kicked back at his guard with all the force he could muster and heard the pop as his guard likewise fell to the ground. After taking the gun from the guard, he turned and Joan had already flipped her guard onto his back and knocked him out as well.

Malcolm went to Saxon, who was bent over, trying to catch his breath. "Are you alright, Charles?"

"I will be in a minute," Saxon said. He picked up Frietag's gun and gave him one more powerful kick in the groin for good measure. "How did you know what would happen?"

"I didn't, but I heard the engines of the zeppelin and figured that something was about to happen. Come on, let's get out of here!"

"Let me get my mother," Joan said as she ran back to the edge of the woods. As she suspected, her mother was too stubborn to leave and had watched the whole affair. "Come on, mother. We're leaving." She grabbed her mother by the arm and yanked her out of the clearing.

The group ran towards the edge of the clearing facing the lake. The light from the burning ship provided enough illumination so that Malcolm could see the zeppelin. He yelled as loud as he could, "Over here!!!" He fired the gun in the air. Moments later, the zeppelin slowly turned toward the island and gradually ascended.

They reached the edge of the clearing and Malcolm saw that at the edge of the clearing; the ground dropped sharply; he guessed it must be nearly a twenty-foot drop to the water. As the zeppelin approached to the island, he wished it would arrive faster. He turned back and saw Frietag and the guard that Malcolm had kicked struggle to their feet, both yowling in pain. Frietag, his face twisted in rage and pain, lumbered slowly toward them. Malcolm fired toward Frietag, who dived for cover, but after three shots, the gun was empty. When Frietag heard the click of the gun, he rose and started towards them.

The zeppelin had reached the edge of the clearing and Malcolm saw Colfax hanging from the empty cargo hold. He dropped a rope out. Joan dragged her mother towards the ship and quickly tied the rope around her and yelled to Colfax. Malcolm backed slowly, watching as Frietag slowly made his way towards the group. Saxon fired four more shots toward Frietag before his gun was empty as well. Malcolm spared a look toward the zeppelin and saw that Colfax had yanked Joan's mother into the airship. Malcolm yelled to Joan, "Give me your gun and get on board and see to your mother!"

Joan tossed her gun to Malcolm and stopped for a moment; she produced the small ray gun Malcolm had given her as a present on their trip to Mars. She tossed that to Malcolm before Colfax tossed the rope down. Not waiting to tie the rope, she shimmied up the rope and into the airship. "You next," Malcolm said to Saxon. "I'll keep them at bay." Saxon started to protest, but saw the look on Malcolm's face and nodded. He grabbed the rope and likewise climbed into the ship.

Malcolm backed towards the rope and fired the remaining shots from the gun Joan had taken from the guard. When it too was empty, he waited a few seconds longer before Frietag was in range and fired the ray gun. Frietag howled in pain and dropped to the ground, writhing in agony from the ultrasonic ray. Malcolm turned and climbed the rope; he had never been an expert climber and the last few weeks had done little to help his conditioning. His arms burned as he concentrated on pulling himself up the rope. When he got within arm's reach, Colfax and Saxon grabbed him and pulled him into the airship. Colfax yelled, "Peter, get us out of here!"

"Peter? He's piloting the ship?" Malcolm said.

"Someone had to blow up the boat," Colfax said. As Malcolm rose to his feet, he felt the airship slowly turn back towards the lake. His relief was short-lived as he looked back and saw Frietag had grabbed the dangling rope with his mechanical hand and pulled himself up the rope. Malcolm looked around for something to cut the rope when Joan handed him a large knife. Frantically, he sawed at the rope as Frietag drew closer to the ship. Just before Frietag could grab the bottom of the gangway, the knife cut through the rope and he watched as Frietag fell some twenty feet to the ground. Malcolm hoped that the fall had finally finished him, but as the zeppelin moved towards the lake, the last sight Malcolm saw was Frietag sitting up.

*I knew it was too much to wish,* Malcolm thought.

# CHAPTER FIFTY FIVE

"Would someone explain to me what is going on? Why have I been forced to leave my home and fly on this uncivilised contraption?" Joan's mother sputtered.

"Just a moment, Mama. What are our orders, Malcolm?" Joan said.

"Colfax, you take over from O'Hallarhan. Steer us west towards France. While I don't think they will catch us soon, they wouldn't dare follow us through France. Charles, see if there's anything you can do to help Colfax or O'Hallarhan. We'll stay with the Baroness."

Colfax and Saxon left for the bridge, and Malcolm and Joan escorted her mother out of the cargo hold.

"What is going on? I demand to know what's happening this instant!" Joan's mother said.

"Baroness, let's find a place where we can have a civilised talk and perhaps a strong drink?" Malcolm offered.

"That's the first sensible thing I've heard all evening," she said.

They found a meeting room containing a table and several cushioned wooden chairs. "Ladies, please have a seat while I look to see if there's any alcohol on board," Malcolm said, before setting off on his quest.

Joan's mother looked at the room and sighed before taking a seat at the table. Joan took a deep breath and took a seat opposite from her mother. The two looked at each other for several seconds before her mother said, "Well, what do you have to say for yourself?"

Joan took a deep breath to quell the anger rising in her. "What do you want to know, mother?"

"How are you alive? What are you doing here? Why was I removed under threat of violence from my home? Who is this oaf that you say you will marry?"

Before her mother could continue, Joan put up her hand and said, "Enough, Mama! One thing at a time." Her mother snorted and crossed her arms. "I went on a mission and sustained a wound. My work for the Secret Service had become common knowledge, so I faked my death so that no one would come after you to get at me."

"Does your father know you're alive?"

"Yes, I told him some time ago."

"And you didn't think I wouldn't want to know?" Joan's mother said.

"You never approved of my life and I thought you would rather enjoy your feeling that you had been right along."

"Why, I," Joan's mother began.

"You what? You told me that if I left, I should never come back. I was simply abiding by your wishes."

Joan's mother glared. "Do you know how hard it was, believing my only daughter was dead?"

Joan was about to speak when Malcom returned with a bottle and three glasses. "I'm afraid all I could find was schnapps. I hope that will do?"

Joan's mother harrumphed, but Joan said, "Thank you, Malcolm. That will be fine." Malcolm set out glasses for Joan and her mother and before he could pour, Joan snatched the bottle from his hand, filled her glass, gulped it down and poured herself another glass before handing the bottle back to Malcolm. He then poured a glass for Joan's mother; she picked up the glass, wrinkled her nose, and like-wise gulped it down. She thrust the glass back at Malcolm, who dutifully refilled it. When Malcolm poured his glass, there was only half a glass left.

The trio sat in silence; Joan and her mother glaring at one another. Malcolm broke the silence. "Baroness, I'm sorry for our hurried introduction. I'm Commodore Malcolm Roberts." He offered his hand, but Joan's mother stared at him contemptuously. Malcolm withdrew his hand and said, "Perhaps I should leave you two alone; I'm sure you have much to discuss," as he rose.

"No," both women said simultaneously.

"Very well," Malcolm said, sitting back down. "I'm happy to meet you finally. I realise that all of this is a shock; first finding that Joan is alive and then to find out she's going to marry someone like me."

"I thought Joan said you were a baron," her mother replied grumpily.

"I am, although my formal investiture hasn't happened yet, but will occur this fall."

"What holdings do you have?" Joan's mother asked, sipping her schnapps.

"I'm afraid my holdings are quite modest," Malcolm said. His mother snorted, crossed her arms, and turned away from Malcolm. He took a large swig of the schnapps before he replied. "Let me put all of my cards on the table. I'm the son of a shipbuilder and come from a very humble beginning. My rank and title have come from my hard work. It may not mean much to you, but I have worked hard for everything I have. I may not be the husband you wanted from Joan, but I love her more than anything, and I do everything in my power to make her happy."

Joan's mother turned on Joan. "How are you going to live if this… gentleman can't support the life you were born into?" Although polite, her sneering tone left no doubt that she thought Malcolm was anything but a gentleman.

"Enough, Mama. Must I remind you of your own humble beginnings?"

"I was the daughter of Tsar Alexander II!"

"The illegitimate daughter of the Tsar. As you yourself told me many times, the support ended after his death. You married my father for money and to improve your social standing. That's not something I've ever wanted. I will marry a man I love and who loves me in return."

Joan's mother sat in silence, staring at Joan. Malcolm broke the uncomfortable silence. "I intend to marry Joan when we return to England. I had planned to marry Joan before my abduction."

"What do you mean, abduction?" Joan's mother said.

Malcolm relayed the events of his abduction, their escape, and the reason that Frietag arrived at her house to re-capture him. The Baroness sat in silence for several moments before she said, "This is the reason I was against your leaving. Your wilfulness has caused this and now I'm forced to leave my beloved home because of your self-ishness!"

"Me? Selfish?" Joan said, barely keeping herself from yelling. "You care only about yourself and your 'precious' villa. What have you ever done for anyone else?"

"I'm a patron of the arts! I support artists and give them a place to work!"

"Only so you can be the centre of attention! You've done nothing else without thinking about how you can benefit!"

"Ladies, perhaps we should get some rest," Malcolm interjected. "It's been a long day for everyone, and I think we should all rest before we say things we'll regret."

The two women glared at Malcolm before Joan said, "That might be for the best." She rose and moved to the door. "Are you coming, Malcolm?"

"Just a moment. I'm going to check with Colfax and Peter to see if they need anything."

"Very well. I'll see you when you're done."

"You're not sleeping in the same room with him!" her mother interjected.

"Yes, Mother, I'm sharing a bedroom with my future husband, whether or not you approve." She stormed out of the room and found their bedroom. After undressing from her soaked clothes, she snuggled under the blankets, trying to get warm. She lay in her bed, unable to sleep, still seething from her talk with her mother. *This is the very reason I don't talk to her,* she thought. But that was little consolation as tears fell from her eyes. She was once again the teenager, forced to listen to her mother's tirades about how unladylike she was. All the times her mother displayed dismay at her academic pursuits, at her refusal to take part in her mother's social events. One memory came flashing back in vivid detail. She had received the Prix d'Excellence en Langues award from school for her excellence in language. When she showed her mother the certificate and medal for the prize, Joan's mother snatch them from her hand and tore up the certificate. "Why are you wasting your time on such drivel?" her mother scoffed. "You should find a suitable man to marry!" When her mother left, Joan picked up the pieces of the certificate, now soggy from her tears. Despite searching for it every chance she had, she never found the medal. Not long after that, she resolved she would never become the woman her mother wanted her to become. Now, she was proud of who she was now; self sufficient, capable. *Hell, I've even helped save the world. Why can't she see my life has meaning?* She wiped the tears away with her hand, her mind still replaying the conversation. *Why do I care so much about her approval?*

A few minutes later, Malcolm returned to the bedroom. He sat on the bed next to her and put his hand on her. "Are you alright?"

"Yes," she said hurriedly, before sighing. "No. My mother is so infuriating! I can't have a conversation with her without losing my temper! Nothing I do is ever good enough for that woman!"

"I know," he gently offered. "Is there anything I can do?"

"Please get in bed and hold me."

"With pleasure," he said as he undressed. He slid into the small bed and lay next to her, wrapping his arms around her. Within moments, she fell asleep.

# CHAPTER FIFTY SIX

Early the next morning, Malcolm slipped out of bed and, after dressing, went to the cockpit of the zeppelin to check on Colfax. They had just reached Lyon. "What are your orders, Commodore?" Colfax asked.

"We should head back to England," Malcolm said. "How are we fixed for fuel?"

Colfax looked at the gauge and did some quick arithmetic. "We might make it to England, but it will be close. If it were up to me, I'd suggest we refuel at some point. I think Paris might be our best bet. We definitely have enough fuel to make it there. I know the airfield there and we should have no problem resupplying."

"And Joan promised her mother a shopping trip in Paris," Malcolm said.

"I couldn't help but hear the conversation last night."

"I'm pretty sure they heard it in Germany," Malcolm muttered, causing Colfax to laugh. "Do you need to be relieved? You must be tired by now."

"I would appreciate that, sir."

"Go get some rest and I'll work on getting us to Paris." Malcolm took his place in the cockpit and, once he familiarised himself with the controls, piloted the airship towards Paris. There were still considerable clouds from the rain last night, so he ascended above the cloud cover to escape detection. A few moments later, Joan knocked on the cockpit door and settled into the seat next to him.

"How are you doing?" Malcolm offered.

"I'm alright," she said, but Malcolm knew she was lying. "Where are we? I can't see anything but clouds."

"We just reached Lyons and we're heading to resupply in Paris."

"What can I do?"

"You could use your communications training and monitor the German frequencies to see if there's any talk of pursuit. Also, we'll need to arrange our landing and resupply in Paris." Malcolm knew if he gave her a task, it would keep her mind off her mother and keep them separated.

"How long until we reach Paris?"

"Maybe another six hours.," he said.

"Very well. Do you know where the radio is located?"

"To be honest, I'm not sure. Now that you're here, do you mind taking over from me for a few moments? I should check on O'Hallarhan and Charles and I can look for the radio."

Joan's face went pale. "Me? Fly an airship? Malcolm, I don't have the foggiest notion about what to do!"

"Truthfully, it's very easy." He demonstrated the use of the control levers. "Hold this one steady; it controls our altitude. This one controls direction; up, down, left, and right." He pointed to the compass. "Keep our course pointing in this direction and adjust as needed."

"I don't know, Malcolm. I'm scared I'll crash this and kill us all."

"You scared? This is easy compared to many of the things I've seen you do."

"But,"

"But nothing. That's an order, Lieutenant," he said with a smile. "I wouldn't ask you to do this if I didn't think you could handle it."

"Thank you, Malcolm. I guess seeing my mother has me second guessing everything."

"You are an amazing woman, Joan. I just wish that your mother could see it." He leaned over and kissed her as he left the pilot's seat.

"Doesn't kissing one of your subordinate's break military protocol, Commodore?" she said playfully. He was glad to see a smile on her face.

"I won't tell if you don't," he said with a wink.

Malcolm went back to the Engine Room and found Saxon, much to his surprise. "So you're an engineer now?"

"Hardly," Saxon said. "After we were under way and Mr O'Hallarhan had no need of me, I got a few hours of sleep. I relieved him about an hour ago, so he could get some sleep; he could barely keep his eyes open. He told me to watch these gauges," he said, pointing to the engine temperature, rpm, and balloon pressure, "and to wake him if anything changed."

"I relieved Colfax just a short while ago, myself."

"If you're here, who's piloting the airship?" Saxon asked.

"Joan."

"Trying to turn her into an airship pilot?"

"About as much as O'Hallarhan has turned you into an engineer." The two men laughed. "By the way, in your travels, have you seen a radio?"

"It's a few doors towards the front on the right."

"Since you have things in hand, I'll leave you to it; unless you'd rather take over piloting?"

"Neither option is appealing. This seems easier."

"We'll make an engineer out of you, yet," Malcolm said.

Saxon harrumphed, and Malcolm left to find the radio right where Saxon directed him. He returned to the cockpit and noticed Joan's knuckles were white from gripping the control levers so tightly. "I'll take it from here," Malcolm said.

"Thank God," Joan said as she left the pilot's seat. "It was nerve-wracking. I don't know how you do this!"

"It is nerve-wracking. I can't tell you how scared I was when I piloted the *Daedalus* out of the hanger in St. Petersburg for the first time as captain. But like anything, the more you do it, the easier it becomes."

"That was more than enough for me," Joan said. "Did you find the radio?"

"It's at the end of the hall on the left. I left the door open so you could find it."

"Thank you. I'll report back once I've contacted the Secret Service."

Malcolm turned his attention to piloting the airship and keeping track of their progress. Joan's knock on the door interrupted him a while later. He looked up and saw her frown. "That doesn't look like good news."

"Mycroft informed me we won't be able to take the zeppelin any further than Paris," she said. "I tried to impress upon them the seriousness of our situation and the need to return as quickly as possible. Mycroft disagreed with my assessment."

"Figures," Malcolm muttered. "Why can't we take the airship?"

"His concern is that as a German zeppelin flying to England, it will be recognisable and easy to intercept. Mycroft also added the Germans considered our taking the airship as an act of piracy."

"Piracy?" Malcolm laughed at the thought.

"It is outrageous, given everything that has happened. But he thought it best if we left the airship in Paris and took public transportation, as it would make it that much more difficult for Frietag to attempt something."

"Is it possible that he could pursue us?" Malcolm asked. "We've only just left; it's unlikely he's even got off the island at this point since we removed all of his means of transportation."

"I agree, but we both know he has a nasty tendency of showing up when least expected."

"True," Malcolm sighed. He paused in thought. "What if we encourage him to show up?"

"Are you mad?" Joan sputtered.

"Hear me out," Malcolm said. "Suppose we get to Paris and take public transportation back to England without incident? He knows that you and I intend to get married shortly after we return. What will stop him from abducting one or both of us again?" He paused. "I don't know about you, but I'm sick of Frietag dictating the terms. I don't intend to spend the rest of my life looking over my shoulder for Frietag."

Joan stood silent for a moment. "It's dangerous, but I agree. We can't live our lives watching for Frietag. What do you have in mind?"

"Nothing specific. I think we need a plausible reason to delay our return to England that will give Frietag time to find us and act. Given the success he has had so far, do you think he'll act alone, or will he have a team?"

Joan thought for a moment before saying, "It's hard to know. Given his inability to keep you in captivity and failing to capture us at my mother's villa, his superiors might have lost faith in his abilities. And there's the factor of time. Frietag will know he will only have a small window of time in Paris to abduct either of us. It would be difficult to pull together anything other than a small team."

"If it's just Frietag, you and I should be able to deal with him, but we're going to need help if he has a team, even a small one. Does the Secret Service have the resources in Paris to assist?"

"I'm not sure, but if not, I'm sure we can approach the Deuxième Bureau for help." Malcolm looked at Joan quizzically. "That's the name of the French Secret Service." Malcolm was silent for a moment before a sly smiled crept onto his face.

"I think I have an idea to lure Frietag," Malcolm said. "But it's going to require you to reconcile with your mother."

"That would take a miracle," Joan said.

# CHAPTER FIFTY SEVEN

A few hours later, Colfax took over from Malcolm. Malcolm knocked on the door to the cabin the Baroness had taken the night before. "Baroness, there's tea in the conference room where we talked last night." He waited for a sign that she had heard and then repeated himself. "I heard you the first time," the Baroness said through the still closed door. "It would be my honour to escort you," he said. Listening, he heard an exasperated sigh, and the door flew open.

"Very well," the Baroness said. "If you feel you must." Malcolm offered his arm, but she pushed past him and stomped toward the conference room. Malcolm took a deep breath and hurried after her. When they arrived, the Baroness said, "Where's the tea?"

"If you'll take a seat, I'll return in just a few moments." He pulled out a chair for her and waited. She let out an exasperated sigh and stomped over before flouncing down in the chair. "Well? What are you waiting for? Go get the tea!"

"Yes, Baroness," Malcolm said, as sweetly as possible. He left and returned to his cabin where Joan was sitting in the lone chair in the cabin, looking out the porthole. "Would you join me in the conference room? I want to discuss the plan."

"Of course, Malcolm," she said. He offered Joan his arm, and she quickly took it as they walked to the conference room. When he opened the door and Joan saw her mother, she let out a barely audible gasp.

"I must confess that I have brought you both here under false pretences. I want you to talk." He moved to a chair opposite Joan's mother and held it for her. "Please, Joan, have a seat." She glared at Malcolm and, after letting out a heavy sigh, stomped over to the chair in much the same way as her mother had minutes before. Malcolm took a seat at the head of the table. Both women crossed their arms and glared at each other.

Malcolm took a deep breath and started. "First, Baroness, I owe you an apology. I'm very sorry that we had to remove you from your home in the middle of the night in such an undignified manner. It's my fault. The man who held you hostage in your own home was using you to get to Joan and me. He is a German spy, and he blames me for his failures. I had only just escaped his clutches when we learned of your captivity. Joan insisted we rescue immediately." The Baroness glared at him for a moment before turning towards Joan.

"Is that true?" the Baroness asked.

"Yes, mother," Joan replied.

"If you cared so much about me, why did you let me continue to believe you were dead?" the Baroness hissed.

"I was trying to prevent the very thing that just happened," Joan said, choosing her words carefully.

"You obviously weren't successful," the Baroness quipped.

"Don't you think I know that?" Joan rose from her chair and move towards the door.

Malcolm grabbed her hand. "Joan, please stay."

"Why? Nothing I say or do will ever be good enough for her!" She glared at her mother. "I should have told you, but to what end? You would have just continued to berate me because I have my own life and it doesn't measure up to what you expect. You have never valued a single thing that's important to me!"

"I only wanted the best for you!" the Baroness said.

"What you thought was best for me," Joan retorted; her eyes were filling with tears.

Malcolm put up his hands. "Baroness, I don't think you realise how much influence you've had on Joan." Joan's jaw dropped as she turned toward Malcolm. Before she could utter a word, he said, "When I first met Joan, she was a Special Envoy to the Court of Tsar Nicholas II. She is at home amongst royalty and carries herself admirably; a trait I believe she shares with you. And like you, Joan is independent, and pardon me for saying it, strong willed. You two have far more in common than you think." Joan and her mother looked at each other, not with the icy stares of moments from earlier, but with softness and recognition.

"Baroness, I know you are angry that Joan let you think she had died. For months, she let me think she had died at the hands of the man who has pursued us. When she finally revealed herself to me, I was both over-joyed and angry, but mostly overjoyed. I realise that you have been through a great deal in the last few days and you need time to come to terms with everything. But I know that despite your differences, Joan loves you. And I know you love Joan. She may not have followed the path you wished, but I would hazard to say that things have turned out for the best. Despite their wishes, parents can't control the person their children will become. They can shape, guide, and influence, but life sometimes has different plans for us. My parents' wish was for me to attend university to become an engineer. My father was injured in an accident at work and there was no longer money for me to attend. They were against me joining the Royal Navy. But I daresay, that decision has brought me all manner of success I doubt I would have achieved had I followed my parents' plan." He looked at both of the women, who avoided his gaze.

"It may be too much to ask, but it is my most sincere wish that you come to some sort of accommodation." He turned toward the Baroness. "I understand the pain you must have felt when you thought Joan was dead. Perhaps this is an opportunity for a clean start for the two of you? I know there are years of anger between you, but life is too short to hold on to anger." Malcolm's speech silenced both Joan and her mother for several minutes; both of them looking down, avoiding each other's glance.

Joan broke the silence. "Mother, I'm sorry that I let you continue to think I was dead. Please know that I did it to protect you. I'm sorry."

Joan's mother was silent, looking up at Joan. After a long moment, she whispered, "I forgive you."

Before Joan could speak, Malcolm interjected. "Thank you. I'm going to leave you two alone to talk."

Joan broke the long silence that settled over the room. "Do you think we can put everything behind us? Your disappointment? My anger?" Her mother sat silent. "I'm willing to try. Despite our differences, you are my mother. I'm tired of our constant arguments. What about you?"

Her mother sat silent for several moments. "Yes," she whispered. "I'm also tired of the fighting. I will try." After a long pause, she said, "I suppose that if that man can get us to agree, he might have some redeemable qualities."

"Mother, Malcolm is a good man. He's infuriating and stubborn, but kind and gentle. He's the smartest man I've ever met, and I love him. That's never been easy for me to say. I almost lost him two years ago, and I realised then I didn't want to live without him."

Joan's mother considered Joan. "He really means that much to you?" she whispered.

"He does."

Joan's mother was silent for several moments. "If he means that much to you, I will agree to your marriage," she whispered. "But I reserve the right to say 'I told you so' if it ends unhappily."

Joan smiled. "I'd expect nothing less."

"You were to marry him before his abduction you said?"

"Yes, we were at Father's estate in Kent when they took Malcolm. I really want you to attend my wedding."

"At the Kent estate? That awful place?" The Baroness let out an exasperated sigh. "Well, if I can endure the intrusion into my villa and being virtually kidnapped, I suppose I can endure Kent and your father for a few days."

"Thank you, Mama," Joan said. She launched from her seat and hugged her mother. At first, her mother sat rigidly before she returned the hug. After a few seconds, she extracted herself from Joan and said, "I thought I taught you better. Such displays of affection are most distasteful."

Joan barely stifled a laugh. "Yes, Mama. I'm sorry. It won't happen again."

"See that it doesn't."

# CHAPTER FIFTY EIGHT

Joan excused herself and went to look for Malcolm, who was on his way back from the bridge. "Is everything alright?" He asked when Joan pulled him close and stopped his mouth with a kiss.

"What was that for?" Malcolm asked. "Not that I'm complaining."

"For mediating with my mother. I think for the first time in my life, she might have seen things from my side. She might not agree with my choices, but I think she realised they are my choices. And she even agreed to attend our wedding. If I didn't know you better, I'd say you would make an excellent diplomat if you can sway my mother."

"Why does everyone think I can't be diplomatic?" He smiled. It had been an ongoing joke between them that Malcolm's usual approach was to make the other person angry and using that against them.

"Shut up and kiss me," she said, as she pulled him close. They kissed for several minutes before Joan pulled away. "Why were you eager to have me reconcile with my mother?"

"First, I hate seeing you estranged from your mother. I only have my parents and although I don't see them often enough, I would hate to not be able to see them."

"Are you going to elaborate on how this plays into your plan?"

"Not yet, but soon."

"Very well," Joan sighed. "I'll have to work on my interrogation techniques," she whispered into his ear before giving him a kiss.

"Maybe when we get to Paris, we can have a private interrogation session," Malcolm said.

"Most definitely," Joan purred. Malcolm reluctantly pulled himself away and returned to the cockpit to assist Colfax.

The flight through the afternoon was easy. About an hour before their estimated arrival, Malcolm had Joan contact the Secret Service to arrange cars to take them to the embassy. They kept the zeppelin above the clouds until they were within fifteen miles of their target, the Issy-les-Moulineaux Aerodrome. As the zeppelin floated down, Malcolm took a moment to orient himself. Ahead, he could make out a few landmarks of Paris; the Eiffel Tower and Notre Dame Cathedral. His eye followed the Seine as it wound past the Eiffel Tower, continuing south west. Colfax pointed out the aerodrome; at this distance, it was just a green dot next to the blue ribbon of the Seine. As the zeppelin descended, the Aerodrome grew larger. Factories and other buildings dotted the area around the aerodrome, broken up by patches of farmland, meadows, and trees.

Colfax expertly guided the zeppelin to the ground. Once the ground crews had tied down the zeppelin, everyone gathered their things and exited the zeppelin. As promised, several cars were waiting to take them to the British Embassy. Joan rode with her mother, much to Malcolm's surprise. Malcolm got in a car with Saxon, while O'Hallarhan and Colfax entered another. After crossing the Seine, they turned onto the Avenue de Versailles, running parallel to the Seine as they approached Paris. Malcolm looked out the window, watching boats travelling up and down the river. When they turned north, Malcolm's jaw dropped as they passed the Galeries Nationales du Grand Palais; the sunlight reflected off of the glass domed roof, running the entire length of the building. Its entrance was magnificent; the gigantic portico contained several massive columns, behind which Malcolm could just make out the large iron and glass doors. Many sculptures decorated the tan stone facade. Before Malcolm could discern any details, they were past the building and cross the Avenue des Champs-Élysées. Malcolm strained to look down the avenue and caught sight of the Arc de Triomphe in the distance. In a blink, they were past the famous avenue, turning by the Palais de L'Elyess before arriving a few minutes later at the British Embassy. Its tan stone facade held a multitude of long, symmetrical windows. The cars drove to the entrance where a massive wooden black door lead into the building.

Their drivers hustled the group out of their cars and lead them into the embassy where the British Ambassador, Sir Francis Bertie, greeted them. His white hair extended down into side wings on either side of his head, accentuating his receding hairline. His large moustache dominated the lower half of his face. He went first to Joan's mother. "Lady de St Leger, I am most relieved to hear you are safe. How is Lord de St Leger?"

"The devil if I know," Joan's mother said, before catching herself. "His Lordship has been away for some time, and I have not heard from him."

"Ah," Bertie said. He went next to Joan. "Miss de St Leger, it's a pleasure to receive you once again." The diplomat kissed Joan's hand, and Malcolm felt his blood boil. The diplomat turned to Malcolm next and offered his hand. "Commodore Robertson, I presume?" Malcolm nodded. "Your escapades through Germany have caused quite a stir in our circles. Serves them right!" After greeting the rest of the group, "If you would, please follow me and we will arrange for your safe return to England." Malcolm was about to object when the ambassador turned and led them through the grand foyer to a gently curving grand staircase with wrought iron balustrades. He led them inside to a large room with a mahogany table and several red leather upholstered chairs. On one side of the room, windows overlooked a courtyard garden. The white plaster walls picked up the early evening light, making the room feel bright and airy. Sitting at the table was Mycroft Holmes.

"Good day, all," Mycroft said as he rose. He went to Joan's mother first and kissed her hand. "Baroness, I haven't had the pleasure of meeting you before. I am Mycroft Holmes."

"Are you the one responsible for my daughter's current employment?" Joan's mother said sweetly, but with an edge that could cut like a knife.

Mycroft was momentarily surprised before replying, "In a manner of speaking, yes. But she is now a member of the Royal Navy and out of my jurisdiction." Mycroft's discomfort made Malcolm smile. "Please, everyone, have a seat. I've taken the opportunity to bring in sandwiches and tea. After your recent adventures, I'm sure you are hungry."

Malcolm hadn't realised just how hungry he was until he bit into the roast beef sandwich. He drained his teacup in one go before refilling it. Malcolm looked around the table and found his companions were equally attacking the fare. After everyone had finished, Mycroft began. "Let us discuss the plans to return you to England."

"Mycroft, if it's all the same, I'd like to suggest something else," Malcolm said. Mycroft raised an eyebrow before gesturing for Malcolm to continue. "If we return to England and have our wedding as planned, Frietag is still out there, free to make another attempt. I think after his failures to hold me in Leipzig and to capture us at the Baroness's villa will drive him to make more attempts to capture me. I would like to lure him here so we can deal with him once and for all."

Mycroft considered Malcolm for a moment. "Interesting. How do you intend to lure him here?"

Malcolm turned to Joan. "The same way he abducted me. Our wedding." Joan whipped her head toward Malcolm. "I know it isn't exactly what we had planned, but we can still go through the wedding at your father's estate once we deal with Frietag."

"Thank you, Malcolm," Joan whispered, trying to hold back tears of joy.

"There is merit to this idea. How do you intend to lure him here?"

"My thought was to wire Baron de St. Leger to inform him we would first be married here and want him to attend the wedding. I would bet that Frietag has someone watching the Baron. Baroness, am I correct in assuming you have many friends in Paris high society?"

"Why, of course," she said.

"Perhaps you could arrange some kind of engagement party here so that word will get out that we are staying her to wed."

"Would you consent to that?" the Baroness asked Joan.

Joan took a breath as if to say something quickly, but Malcolm caught her eye. She let out the breath and said, "Yes, mother. I would like that."

Mycroft looked at the two women and then back at Malcolm. He nodded before asking, "What if Frietag doesn't take the bait?"

"No harm, no foul. Joan and I are legally married, which is what we've wanted for over a year now," he said pointedly to Mycroft, who had derailed their first wedding attempt by drafting them into the Royal Space Service. "The thing is, I don't have the foggiest idea what's involved in getting married in Paris."

"Don't worry, I can handle the bureaucratic details," Sir Bertie offered.

"And I will take care of the wedding itself," the Baroness said.

"If I decide to grow through with this, I will need to know all the details so we can make plans accordingly."

"Absolutely," Malcolm said.

Mycroft was silent for nearly a minute; everyone stared at him, waiting for his response. He looked at Malcolm and said, "I suppose I owe you as much since I forced you to miss your first wedding. And as you said, there's no harm if he doesn't take the bait. My biggest concern is everyone's safety."

"I agree. That's why I'm asking you for your help," Malcolm said.

Mycroft was silent for another minute before saying, "It appears we are to plan a wedding."

# CHAPTER FIFTY NINE

*I*f Malcolm thought planning a military operation took a great deal of planning, it had nothing on the planning of his wedding to Joan. Joan's mother took over and immediately created the guest list for the engagement party and worked out the details of the wedding ceremony. As Sir Bertie explained, France required a civil wedding ceremony at a town hall, or mairie, of an arrondissement of the city. She immediately decided that the wedding would take place at the Hôtel de Ville, the Paris City Hall, by none other than the Mayor of Paris, Jean-Baptiste Bienaimé Bonnel. The engagement party would take place at the Ritz, where Joan's mother insisted they stay while in Paris. It was nearly ten o'clock before they could drag the Baroness away. Two British Secret Service agents escorted them for the twelve minute walk to the Ritz.

The brightness of the lobby immediately struck Malcolm; the ornate gilded mouldings complemented the creams and gold of the walls. It had much of the same wood panelling that Malcolm had seen at his many visits to Joan at the Savoy, but the wood was much lighter in colour. The hotel felt like he was walking into a palace. At Joan's mother's insistence, Malcolm and Joan had separate rooms; "If I'm introducing you to the society of Paris, I will stand for no impropriety. Do I make myself clear?"

"Crystal," Joan muttered.

"What was that?" the Baroness said.

"Yes, mother. It is clear."

To make certain that Joan and Malcolm could not see each other, the Baroness made certain theirs rooms weren't on the same floor. As they made their way to their rooms, Malcolm stopped when he reached his floor. He leaned in to kiss Joan when he heard a disapproving "Ahem" from Joan's mother. Malcolm sighed and instead took her hand and kissed it. "Good night, Joan."

"Good night, Malcolm," Joan said. Subtly, she glanced at her mother and rolled her eyes. Malcolm smiled, nodded, and left for his room. Suddenly, he realised just how tired he was and promptly went to bed and fell asleep before taking any notice of the room. Next thing he knew, knocking on his door threw him out of a sound sleep. After taking a minute to throw on trousers and a shirt, he went to the door and asked, "Who's there?", taking no chances that it might be yet another trap.

"It's me, Malcolm," Joan said. "Mother is demanding you come down for breakfast. She has a long list of tasks for you."

Malcolm fumbled to find his granda's pocket watch, surprised that it was 8:30. He opened the door. Although wearing the same clothes from the previous day, she had definitely showered; Malcolm could smell the clean scent of the lavender soap mixed with her perfume. "Give me a few minutes to make myself presentable, and I'll be down."

"Can I come in?" Joan asked.

"That might not help me get ready quickly," Malcolm said. "I'm afraid I have little to wear except for yesterday's clothes."

"That's one of your tasks. Purchase clothes suitable for a baron," Joan said. She leaned in and gave him a quick kiss. "Please hurry as quickly as you can. While I may have a truce with my mother, she is driving me crazy!"

"I'm a military man; I'm used to taking quick showers; especially on the older ships when you had to worry about running out of hot water." He leaned to kiss her before shutting the door. Once in the shower, he fought the urge to luxuriate under the hot water, but sped through his ablutions. Fifteen minutes later, he had showered, shaved, and joined Joan and her mother for a late breakfast.

"There you are," the Baroness said. "For a military man, I'm surprised that you slept so late!"

"My apologies, Baroness. I'm afraid that the strain of the last few days caught up with me. It won't happen again."

"See that it doesn't," the Baroness said. She snapped her fingers and summoned a waiter. "Il voudrait des œufs brouillés avec des saucisses et un café, s'il vous plaît."

Although he didn't speak French, he understood café meant coffee. He held his hand up to the waiter, "No café, thé, s'il vous plaît."

"Très bien, monsieur," the waiter said as he spun around and took the order to the kitchen.

"Do you speak French?" the Baroness asked.

"Very little. That exchange nearly used up most of my French vocabulary," Malcolm said. The Baroness frowned. "I understand you have a list of tasks for me?"

"Yes." The Baroness produced a foolscap and handed it to Malcolm; the page was nearly covered with her elegant handwriting. "But I insist the first thing you do is buy some new clothes and get a haircut. I will not have you seen with me in public looking like that." She wrinkled her nose in distaste.

"The haircut will be easy, but I'm afraid that I'm not very good at shopping for civilian clothes. Perhaps Joan could assist?"

"Out of the question! She will be too busy with her own list. Perhaps one of your companions could assist, although from the look of them, I doubt they would be much help."

Before Malcolm uttered a word, Joan interjected, "Perhaps you could enlist the aid of Charles?" She turned to her mother. "Charles is a member of the Sax-Coburg family; he can guide Malcolm."

"I suppose we must make do," the Baroness said. Malcolm, trying not to respond, looked at the list. He needed to acquire a new wardrobe for a dozen days, a tailcoat for the engagement party, and a morning suit for the wedding proper, all from Charvet. Even if he were back home in London, he would not have the money to afford the wardrobe.

Sensing the troubled look on Malcolm's face, Joan said, "Mother has agreed to pay for your wardrobe."

"Thank you, Baroness. Your generosity is most appreciated."

"As it should be," the Baroness said. Malcolm fidgeted, hoping his breakfast would arrive and give him an excuse to avoid further conversation with the Baroness. A moment later, the waiter set out Malcolm's breakfast; scrambled eggs, four links of sausage, a croissant, and a small pot of tea.

If he thought that eating his breakfast would keep him out of the Baroness's watchful eye, he was mistaken. She watched his every move; how he poured his tea, how he held his cutlery, how he drank his tea. Malcolm, despite his best efforts to remember all of his high society manners, felt waves of disapproval from the Baroness. He wanted to hurry to shorten the ordeal, but he knew even that would elicit a comment about eating too quickly. Trying to turn the attention away from himself, he asked Joan, "What are your plans today, if might ask?"

"Very much the same as yours," Joan said. "We will spend the day shopping for both of us. Malcolm, I might add that you may want to purchase a few prêt-à-porter suits."

"Do what?"

"Prêt-à-porter; it means ready to wear. If we are to be seen around town, you will need something to else to wear. Perhaps, do that first, before you go to Charvet. I'm afraid that given your current state of your clothes, they would kick you out immediately."

"Very well," Malcolm said. He was silent for the rest of the meal. When he finished, "If you ladies will excuse me, I'll fetch Charles and we'll start on the list." He rose and gave a small bow to the Baroness and kissed Joan's hand, and turned to leave.

"Where are you going? You'll need this," the Baroness said, pulling a letter from her purse.

"Thank you, Baroness," he said as he left as quickly as he could without running.

Malcolm returned to his room and flopped on to the bed, let out a large exhale. He now understood exactly why Joan didn't want to spend much time with her mother. He looked at the envelope that the Baroness had given him. It was a letter of credit drawn on Rothschild Bank. His anxiety about how he would fit into Joan's family jumped considerably. He waited another thirty minutes before knocking on Charles's door. A few moments later, he heard Charles say, "Who is it?"

"It's me. Malcolm. Can I come in?"

Charles carefully opened the door and relaxed when he saw it was truly Malcolm. "Come in." Malcolm strode right in and plopped into a chair. Charles shut the door and turned to Malcolm. "Is something the matter?"

"The Baroness. She's impossible! She watches everything I do, and I can feel her constant disapproval. God, I don't know how I'm going to make it to the wedding."

"Joan tried to warn you about her mother."

"I thought she must be exaggerating; if anything, she understated her case."

Saxon was quiet for a moment. "What brings you here? I'm sure you're not here just to sputter about your future mother-in-law."

Malcolm paled at that thought that the Baroness was the epitome of the caricature of the mother-in-laws found in Punch magazine. He leaned over, putting his head in his hands. "What have I got myself into?"

"I tried to warn you," Saxon said with a smile. "Now, why are you really here?"

"I need your help, Charles." Malcolm handed Saxon the list. "I need to get a new wardrobe and I don't have the foggiest idea what to do."

Saxon looked at the list. "This is quite a list. It will take some time to get these suits tailored for you."

"Joan mentioned I should get some pretty ported, or something like that."

"What?"

"It was a French phrase; it means ready to wear."

Saxon laughed. "Prêt-à-porter?"

"That sounds right."

"Yes, I know some tailors that have decent suits that you can purchase. Some of them actually make suits for our specific requirements. I am also in need of a new set of clothes. Come, let's get going; we have a busy day ahead of us."

They left the hotel and went first to a tailor that worked directly with the British Secret Service. When Saxon explained what they needed, the tailor took measurements of Saxon and Malcolm and, after several minutes, brought back six suits for them both. Saxon examined the suits, rejecting two of them that looked too common. He next worked with the tailor for to obtain shirts, ties, undergarments, socks, and two pairs of shoes. After two hours, the two men left with their arms filled with garment bags containing their haul. They return to the hotel to deposit their suits before meeting in the lobby to continue their shopping. Malcolm picked out a suit and matching shirt and tie. Saxon made sure that the combination of shirt, suit, and tie worked together.

If Malcolm thought their trip to the first tailor was taxing, it had nothing on the trip to Charvet. When they entered the shop, the tailor looked at them both and said something in French. Malcolm didn't understand the words, but he certainly understood the message; they were not welcome in this establishment. Saxon spoke French to the tailor, and after a moment, the tailor seemed to acquiesce grudgingly to serving them.

"Malcolm, let me have the letter of credit," Saxon said.

Malcolm handed it to Saxon. When the tailor opened it, his demeanour changed immediately. He snapped his fingers, and several tailors emerged from the back. After a discussion with Saxon, the tailor immediately barked orders to the other tailors.

Malcolm leaned over to Saxon. "What did you say to him?"

"I first told him I was a member of the Saxe-Coburg family. That was the proverbial foot in the door. Your letter of credit from the Baroness sealed the deal."

The tailors engulfed Malcolm and Saxon. The tailors removed their suits, not without a look of disgust at the suits, and took every conceivable measurement. They left and returned dozens of bolts of fabric of different colours and weaves. Saxon inspected them all, picking out the fabrics that would look good on Malcolm and himself. Malcolm just watched as Saxon conversed in French and, after two hours, they had placed orders for six new suits, a tailcoat, and a morning suit for each of them.

As they left, Malcolm said, "I can't thank you enough, Charles. I would probably still be at the first tailor, trying to pick out one suit."

"You're welcome," Charles said. "Truth be told, I was glad to get a new wardrobe myself. Why don't we drop these off at the hotel and get a bite to eat?"

"Sounds good."

They set off down the Place Vendôme, past the column with a statue of Napoleon on its top, back to the Ritz. As they entered the hotel and made their way through the lobby, Saxon passed for a section to inspect himself in the mirror. He whispered to Malcolm, "I think we're being followed. See those two men loitering in the lobby trying to look nonchalant? They've been following us since we left Charvet."

"How do you and Joan do that? I didn't notice at all," Malcolm hissed.

"Practice," Saxon said. "What should we do?"

"Let them follow us. If they're German, they will let Frietag know we're here."

"What if they try to abduct us first?"

"I doubt it. If I know Frietag, he will want to do it personally."

"I hope you're right," Saxon said as they continued walking.

"So do I," whispered Malcolm.

# CHAPTER SIXTY

The rest of the day was uneventful. Before dinner, Malcolm changed into one of the new suits and went to the dining room to meet Joan and her mother. As he joined them, he couldn't help but notice the Baroness's look of disapproval at his suit. "Good evening, Baroness, Joan," He said, taking a chair. "Were you successful today?"

"Yes, although I would say you were only marginally successful," the Baroness said, wrinkling her nose as she looked at Malcolm.

"It's the best I could do on short notice," Malcolm offered. "I have proper suits that will be ready in a few days."

Before her mother could speak, Joan interjected, "Yes. We had to make do with what was available. We've arranged for our engagement party for a week from tonight. Do you think that's enough time for our…special guest?"

"I think it will," Malcolm said. "Charles and I may have encountered some friends of our guest, but they were too shy to engage with us." Joan cocked her head slightly, instantly understanding Malcolm's hidden meaning.

"I wish the two of you would talk plainly instead of hiding what you say. It's most unseemly," the Baroness huffed.

Before Joan could respond, Malcolm interjected, "You're right, Baroness. This isn't the place to discuss the matter. Perhaps I could prevail upon you to let Joan join us at the British Embassy tomorrow, where we will be free to discuss matters more freely."

"We must attend to a myriad of details for this engagement party. I can't possibly let Joan go," the Baroness said.

"Mother, you don't need my help," Joan said. "If I stay, we're still going to end up doing it your way; this way we avoid more arguments."

The Baroness glared at Joan before relenting. "You are right. I am much more suited to planning the engagement party than you." Before Joan could respond, the waiter came with their meal. A glacial silence followed as they focused only on their meals. When they finished the meal, Malcolm stood. "If you'll excuse me, I'll take my leave. Joan, shall I meet you in the lobby at 9:00 tomorrow morning?"

"Yes, Malcolm. I'll be there."

Before Malcolm retired for the evening, he stopped by Saxon's room to tell them they would go to the embassy in the morning to discuss plans.

The next morning, Malcolm found Joan waiting in the lobby. She wore an emerald green jacket and matching skirt, a cream coloured blouse, and boots. He still couldn't believe that such a beautiful woman wanted to marry him. When she saw Malcolm, she hurried over and gave him a peck on the cheek. "I am so glad that you pried me away from my mother's clutches. Yesterday was almost more than I could bear."

"I could tell," he said. "And truth to be told, we really need to prepare for our trap."

"Are we ready, or are you going to continue to make eyes at one another?" Saxon said as he stepped close to them. "You two really must be more aware. I walked right up on you without either of you knowing."

"Don't be too sure," Joan said. Saxon looked down, and Joan had pressed a small dagger against his abdomen.

"Touché," Saxon said. "Shall we go?"

As they walked to the embassy, Joan took Malcolm's arm, and he put his hand on hers. Saxon rolled his eyes, but they walked quietly until they reached the embassy. They went to the same conference room where they met Mycroft. Within a few minutes, a cart of tea appeared in the room and while they drank their tea, Mycroft Holmes arrived. After fixing his tea, he joined them at the table. "What brings you here?"

"I thought it best that we give you an update. And to be blunt, to have some time away from the Baroness," Malcolm said.

Mycroft sipped his tea. "Yes, I can see the importance." Joan stifled a giggle before collecting her composure. "Please update me."

Joan began, detailing what she knew of the planned engagement party. It would take place six days from now at the Ritz. "My mother wanted to hold it in the main dining room, but I was at least able to convince her to hold it in the Salon d'Ete."

Mycroft considered this for the moment. "It limits access to the room, but the courtyard is a problem; anyone could slip in."

"But it is more easily controlled than the main dining room," Joan offered.

"True." Mycroft was silent for a few moments. "Do you think six days is enough to lure Frietag here?"

"I do," Malcolm said. "Unless you had agents following us, Charles was certain that he saw agents following us yesterday while we were out."

Mycroft turned to Saxon. "Is that true?"

"Yes. When we came back from Charvet, I noticed two men in grey suits and fedoras following at some distance. They followed us to the lobby of the Ritz. They left when they saw I noticed them. If they are German agents, it's likely that German intelligence knows we're here. I think they have taken the bait."

Mycroft sat in thought for a minute. "I think we should be prepared for an attempt at the engagement party. The venue is less public than the Hôtel de Ville. I don't think Frietag would do something as bold as abduct anyone from there in broad daylight. But the engagement party seems to present its own set of problems."

"Such as?" Malcolm asked.

"Drugging the food and drink," Saxon said. "Freitag has a penchant for using food and drink as a weapon. If you remember, he drugged both of you in Russia before trying to kill you and all three of us in Vienna. We'll have to ensure no one tampers with the food."

"Very good, Mr Saxon," Mycroft said. "We'll get some agents to pose as waiters to ensure nothing is drugged before it's served. Additionally, I will ensure that all of you have strips to test for drugs. I also think that if possible, please stay in the hotel and if you must go out, I suggest you go in pairs. That will discourage an attempt before we're prepared."

"What about Colfax and Peter?" Malcolm asked.

"Colfax has already left for another destination. Mr O'Hallarhan is a unique problem. We can't have him leave, as he would be a target for Frietag. I suggest that you all monitor him. I'll arrange for a room for him at The Ritz so you're all in one place. While I hate putting all the proverbial eggs in one basket, there's safety in numbers."

For the rest of the morning, they analysed the floor plan of the hotel, determining the best place to place agents. When Mycroft was satisfied, he discharged the trio. Although tempted to explore Paris, Malcolm took Mycroft's words to heart and returned to the hotel. After another taxing lunch with Joan's mother, Malcolm found himself with nothing to do for the first time in weeks. He went to his room. After a few hours, he grew restless and familiarised himself with the hotel. He went to the Salon d'Ete. The salon itself was as elegant as he thought it would be; ivory walls edged with gold with gold drapes to match. A large crystal chandelier hung in the centre of the room. One wall of the room was windows and entry to the Grand Jardin. He walked out onto a terrace and descended into the garden itself. Ahead was a water fountain and heard its soft trickle. As he explored the garden, he found dozens of alcoves in the huge hedges that lined both sides; the perfect place for an intimate rendezvous or an unexpected ambush. He continued to the other side, where another terrace led back into the hotel. He continued on and found himself near the Ritz Bar. It was too early for him to have a drink, so he eventually made his way back to his room. After an hour of boredom, he visited Charles and told him about his reconnaissance. Saxon decided he should see for himself and, not having anything better to do, Malcolm accompanied him. This time, when they reached the bar, Charles easily convinced Malcolm to join him for a drink. Saxon eschewed his usual gimlet for an expertly prepared dry martini while Malcolm contented himself with a glass of Chivas Regal served neat. Malcolm sipped his whisky in silence, lost in thought.

"What is it, Malcolm?"

"I think I'm having second thoughts."

Saxon nearly spit out his martini. "About your wedding?"

"Heavens, no! It's the...engagement party. What if our plans fail and I end up captured again? I don't know if I can go through that again."

"Try not to worry. Mycroft is an expert at planning these kinds of operations. If Frietag shows up, we will capture him."

"You're asking me to place my trust in Mycroft?" Malcolm asked. "Now I am worried," he said, taking a large sip of his whisky.

# CHAPTER SIXTY ONE

The days leading up to the engagement party were excruciatingly boring. Each day, Malcolm ate his meals with Joan and her mother, while Saxon wisely dined with O'Hallarhan. Each one was its own trial by fire. Malcolm never left the hotel; he had the concierge pick up his clothing. To keep Malcolm from brooding, Saxon brought O'Hallarhan and taught them the card game Napoleon. At first, Malcolm was reluctant to play, but his competitive side got the better of him, and soon the games became cutthroat. It had the desired effect. It stopped Malcolm from brooding about the upcoming event. However, it did nothing to help his mood after meals with Joan and her mother. Although he was happy to see Joan, her mother's constant disapproval of anything that Malcolm did was death by a thousand paper cuts.

On the morning of the engagement party, the Baroness ordered Malcolm and Saxon to report to the salon for a walkthrough of the engagement party. When he arrived in the salon after breakfast, he wasn't surprised to find that Mycroft Holmes was waiting. He was, however, surprised to see Joan's father. He went to him and shook his hand. "Baron St. Leger, I'm so glad you made it."

"I came here to see that you actually marry her this time," the

Baron said darkly. "I didn't know *she* would be here," indicating the Baroness.

"I understand. There are times I regret rescuing her," Malcolm said. The Baron looked at him quizzically and Malcolm recounted how they had rescued the Baroness from the clutches of Frietag, the man who had abducted him on the eve of the wedding.

"I suppose there was nothing that could be done," the Baron said.

Before Malcolm could reply, the Baroness snapped her finger to get everyone's attention. "It's very important that everyone understands their role at tonight's party. I will not have you embarrass me in front of my friends." She specifically looked at Malcolm, who nodded. "From 5:00 to 5:45, the guests will arrive. Champagne and light refreshments will be served. You," she said, pointing at Saxon, "in your role as Best Man will greet the guests." Saxon nodded. "At 6:00, the Baron and I will arrive with Joan and Malcolm for their formal presentation. Mr Saxon, you will organise the receiving line. I have written the order of the receiving line and I expect you to follow my wishes to the letter. After the receiving line, Joan's father," she said, not even looking at her husband, "will give the toast to the new couple. At 5:30, there a small chamber music group will perform before the buffet dinner at 6:00. At 7:00, the waiters will clear the food and dancing will start, ending promptly at 8:00. Joan and Malcolm will thank the guests for coming and the party will be over. Any questions?" She waited for a moment before saying, "Very good. I expect all of you to do exactly as I've planned. I will stand for no deviations. Do I make myself clear?" She looked directly at Malcolm. "You are dismissed until the party."

Malcolm waited for everyone else to leave before he approached Mycroft. "What do you think? When might Frietag strike?"

"It's hard to say. The receiving line is an excellent opportunity to get to either of you. As we mentioned earlier, dinner would be the perfect time to drug you and take you off. Likewise, the dance would be another time to get either you or Joan alone."

"That narrows it down," Malcolm muttered.

"It simply means deploying our resources carefully. I have two agents placed as waiters; I've assigned one to make sure they are the ones that bring you food and drink, while I assigned another to make sure nothing happens to the first. Four of my agents will be disguised as guests, and I've made sure that they are spaced evenly throughout the receiving line."

"How did you know where the Baroness would place people?"

"A fairly easy deduction. The Baroness would have the most prominent guests early in the line. Fortunately, the Baroness invited people based on their title and prominence. From what Joan tells me, she doesn't really know over half of the guests."

"You've spoken to Joan? I thought she hadn't left the hotel."

"She hasn't. I arranged for a courier to collect letters daily as the Baroness confirmed the party details. Why? Haven't you talked to her?"

"Let's just say that the Baroness prefers that we only meet at meals, and it's not a conducive time to talk."

Mycroft nodded. He reached into his suit pocket, removed a small revolver with a shoulder holster, and handed it to Malcolm. "Just in case it's needed. I talked to the tailor at Charvet and they factored it into the design of your tailcoat for the party. Consider it an engagement present."

"Thank you, Mycroft. What about Joan?"

"If I know your fiancé, she will have several weapons hidden on her person."

"Now what do we do?"

"We wait and hope our prey takes the bait. If you'll excuse me, I have several things to do," Mycroft said.

"Will you be joining us at the party tonight?"

"Heavens, no. Far too many people. I will be in my car outside the hotel, ready to direct the operations."

"Thank you, Mycroft. Although I know this wasn't your idea, and as much as she complains about her mother, I think this party makes Joan happy."

"You're welcome. Best of luck tonight…and happy hunting."

Mycroft left, and Malcolm sought Saxon, filling him in on his discussion with Mycroft. Saxon turned to Malcolm. "Do you think this will work?"

"I think so. Frietag must be desperate at this point and I don't see him passing up the opportunity."

"I agree." The two were silent for several moments before Saxon said, "Did you know we are disguising Peter as the son of Baron Ravensdale, who received his title a few years ago? It was Joan's idea. I think Peter found it very humorous."

"Am I the only one who hasn't really talked to Joan this week?"

"I don't doubt that under the Baroness's watchful eye, you've had no chance to really talk to her. We've met in passing for brief conversations."

"Lucky you," Malcolm muttered.

"You'll have all the time in the world to spend with Joan in shortly." Saxon put a hand on Malcolm's shoulder. "Come on, we should probably start preparing for the party."

"Now? It's only 10:30."

"And it will take you until 5:00 to figure out how to tie your bow tie."

"I was counting on you to help."

"Why am I not surprised? Come, let's see if we can find the next Baron Ravensdale and play a few hands of Napoleon."

The card game did much to keep Malcolm occupied until midafternoon when he left to get ready for the evening's festivities. After a hot shower and shave, he laid out his formal attire. As he dressed, he couldn't help but admire the fit of the tailcoat. And true to Mycroft's word, the holster for the revolver was not noticeable under his tailcoat. After fumbling for nearly half an hour with the bow tie, he went to Saxon's room and Saxon dutifully tied it for him in just a few seconds. They chatted before Saxon had to take his place to greet the guests. Malcolm hung around his room, pacing, until he couldn't stand it anymore, and went down to the Salon Louis XV where Joan and her parents were waiting for the formal presentation.

When Malcolm caught sight of Joan, his breath caught. Joan wore an elegant emerald green sheath dress; embroidered silver vines twisted up the bodice, ending in leaflike seed pearls and beads at the neckline. She wore her auburn hair in a chignon with a long silver pin holding it up. Malcolm thought she never looked lovelier. He went to her, took her hand, and kissed it. "If we weren't already engaged, I'd ask you to marry me right now."

"My fiancé might object to such forward behaviour," she said with a smile.

"I think he would understand," Malcolm said.

"Stop making eyes at each other and let me see if you look presentable," the Baroness said to Malcolm. He stood at attention as the Baroness inspected his tailcoat. After a moment, she nodded. "Acceptable," was all she said. *Talk about damning with faint praise,* Malcolm thought.

The table held an array of light refreshments; cucumber sandwiches, smoked salmon on brioche, pastries, macrons, petits fours, champagne, sherry, and even a bottle of Chivas Regal. Malcolm reached for a plate and, remembering Mycroft's warning, decided not to partake. Joan, too, reached for a glass. Malcolm caught her eye, and she instantly understood his silent warning. Her mother looked at her quizzically; Joan replied, "I'm just a little nervous. I think it would be best to wait until after the party." This did not stop Joan's mother and father from helping themselves to a plate of food and a glass of champagne.

There were a few minutes of silent as Joan's parents ate. Malcolm noticed the Baroness's eye seemed unfocused. "Is something wrong, Baroness?"

"I suddenly feel sleepy. I don't know what's come over me," she said, beginning to slur her words. She slumped over, passed out. A moment later, Joan's father also passed out. Malcolm checked the Baroness. She had a pulse, but was completely out. Malcolm checked her father and found him similarly incapacitated.

"I think they were drugged," Malcolm said. "They seem to be fine otherwise."

Joan reached into her clutch and pulled out a vial. She poured a glass of champagne. Taking the dropper off of the vial, she carefully dripped a few drops into the glass. After a couple of seconds, the champagne turned purple. "Drugged," she said. "I assume the other bottles are likewise drugged."

"Yes, they are," said a voice from the door to the Salon d'Ete. Malcolm and Joan looked up and saw Frietag point a gun at them. "Allow me to congratulate you on your engagement, although I don't expect you'll be alive before the wedding."

# CHAPTER SIXTY TWO

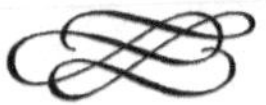

alcolm's first instinct was to reach for the revolver hidden in his tailcoat, but fought that instinct, waiting for the right time. Malcolm noted Frietag held the gun in his non mechanical hand. "I should have known you'd show up. You hang on worse than your mother's case of the clap."

Frietag's face twitched. "Using such language amongst high society? Whatever makes you think you could ever fit in amongst these people?" he said, gesturing to the Baron and Baroness.

"Whatever makes you think a one handed, cycloptic failure such as yourself could ever return to German intelligence?" Malcolm said. After the week of enduring the Baroness's disdain, Frietag's barb had hit close to home, but he was not doing to give him the satisfaction of knowing that.

Frietag's faced reddened. "If I'm such a failure, how come I'm the one with a gun pointing at you?"

"Because this entire party was a setup just to draw you here. Even now, there are many agents ready to apprehend you as I speak," Malcolm said.

"Really? The ones in the garden which my men have already

knocked out? Or the ones in the kitchen we also dispatched? Don't you think I knew this was a trap?"

"Honestly, no, I didn't take you as bright enough to work that out," Malcolm said.

"Enough!" Spittle flew from Frietag's mouth. "I've had enough of your insults. You will be quiet and come along with me now, or I might have to take drastic measures." He nodded towards Joan's parents.

"If you harm them, there will be no place on earth safe from me," Joan said, teeth clenched.

"Then come along quietly and I won't harm them."

Malcolm and Joan looked at each other. He saw the concern for her parents etched on her face. He turned to Frietag. "Very well," he said.

"Excellent. See, we can be civilised people," Frietag said. "Come." Keeping his gun fixed on them, he walked behind Joan and pressed the gun into her back. "No funny business, or your fiancé will be your late fiancé." Frietag pushed them towards the door. When Malcolm looked around, he saw all the party guests lying on the floor. Broken glass was everywhere, broken when the guests dropped their glasses before passing out. Malcolm scanned the room and couldn't see Saxon or O'Hallarhan lying on the floor. It gave him a measure of confidence that they might still apprehend Frietag.

His hope failed when he saw four men enter the salon from the garden terrace. They said something in German and Frietag answered. "This way," he said, pushing them towards the doors to the terrace. Malcolm tripped over one of the unconscious party guests and fell to the ground. Frietag hauled him up with his mechanical hand, but not before Malcolm had grabbed a large shard of broken glass. When they reached the doors to the terrace, Malcolm thought he saw movement in the shadows to his right. He reached down to hold her hand and carefully placed the piece of broken glass in her hand. She acknowledged by squeezing his hand back. Praying the movement was Saxon, Malcolm put up more resistance to walking as they neared the steps down into the garden. In his impatience, Frietag gave Malcolm a shove, and he stumbled down the steps of the terrace, landing in front of the water fountain. As he lay there, he pulled the gun from his coat. He turned to see Joan stab Frietag in his gun hand with the broken shard of glass. Frietag yelped in pain and dropped the gun. Shots rang out from the alcoves on either side of the doors, dropping two guards immediately. The other two wheeled towards the alcove and fired back.

Malcolm crawled on his hands and knees and hid behind the fountain, joined momentarily by Joan. The guards backed down the steps, firing into the alcove to cover their retreat. Malcolm turned to Joan, who nodded back. When the two retreating guards backed toward their hiding spot, Malcolm and Joan jumped out. Malcolm knocked out his guard with the butt of his revolver. Joan jumped in the air, wrapped her legs around the agent's neck and pulled him down. Malcolm heard the rip of her dress, followed by the loud thud as the agent's head hit the courtyard floor.

Frietag looked around and bolted back through the doors and into the salon. Malcolm fired a shot, but barely missed as Frietag changed direction at the last moment. Malcolm got up. "Is everyone alright?"

"Yes," Saxon and O'Hallarhan said simultaneously.

"Are you alright Joan?"

"Yes, although I believe I've torn my dress. My mother would be livid."

"I'm going after Frietag," Malcolm said. "Charles, Peter, go through the other side of the garden and we'll see if we can cut him off." They nodded and started running through the garden.

"If you think you're going without me, guess again," Joan said.

"But," Malcolm began.

"But nothing. We have to get going if we're ever going to catch him. Now is not the time to argue!" She started back towards the salon and Malcolm knew there was no point in trying to stop her. He hurried after her and they hurried across the salon, doing their best to avoid the fallen guests. When they reached the door, they had lost sight of Frietag, but saw drops of blood leading into the Hall Psyché. They rushed down the hall towards the entrance and caught sight of

Frietag as he ran out of a door, pushing aside a bellhop. As they ran through the lobby, patrons cried out in alarm. Malcolm realised he was still holding his gun. They ran out of the doors just to see a car pull away.

"Damn it all to hell, he got away," Malcolm said.

"Malcolm, Joan!" a voice called from a nearby car. Malcolm looked up and saw Mycroft. "Get in!" Malcolm and Joan ran to the car and as soon as they were in, the car pulled away and began pursuit.

"What happened?" Mycroft added.

"Frietag drugged the beverages. Everyone is unconscious except for Charles and Peter," Joan said. "Charles and Peter took care of Frietag's men, but in the fight, he escaped."

"Apparently, he had a car waiting out of sight. As soon as he stepped out of the hotel, the car appeared and he jumped into it. They sped off across the Place Vendôme, heading south past the barriers towards Rue de Rivoli. That's when I saw you."

Once they cleared the Place, they saw the car make a sharp turn to the left onto Rue de Rivoli. "Follow that car!" Mycroft ordered. The driver sped the car through the narrow streets. He barely slowed as he turned on to Rue de Rivoli, throwing Malcolm and Joan into Mycroft. He gave them a disapproving look, and they pulled themselves away. Frietag's car turned onto Place de la Concorde, continuing south. Frietag's car continued to gain distance; Malcolm banged his fist on the seat in front of him in frustration. They were so close to capturing Frietag, he didn't want to lose him now. As they drove past the Obélisque de Louxor, they say Frietag's car stop near the River Seine. Frietag got out and jumped into a boat. Once Frietag was aboard, the boat started moving west.

"Follow that boat!" Mycroft said to the driver. When they neared the river, the driver turned onto the Cours la Reine, speeding west. After a few minutes, Malcolm spotted the boat. It was some distance ahead, but they appeared to be gaining.

"We need some way to stop that boat," Malcolm said. "All I have is this revolver, with very few shots left."

"Miss de St Leger, if you reach under your seat, I believe you should find something that might be useful." Joan, after pushing the skirt of her dress away in a very unladylike fashion, fished around and pulled out an oversized pistol. Malcolm immediately recognised that it was like the guns Joan typically took on a mission. She fished around some more before finding two rounds that looked like small rockets.

An evil grin crossed Joan's face. "Yes, these will do nicely. If we can get to a bridge, I should be able to stop the ship."

"More like blow it to kingdom come," Malcolm said, remembering how she used similar rounds to blow up a German fuel supply on their first mission together.

"Yes, but I will stop it," she said.

They continued running parallel to the river, doing their best to keep tracking the boat. Traffic slowed them down as they reached any of the many bridges across the Seine, but they made up time on the streets. By the time they passed the Pont de l'Alma, they had pulled ahead of the boat. Malcolm looked up and saw the Eiffel Tower looming over Paris and saw a bridge ahead. "There," he pointed. "We should try to stop him there." The car continued to careen down the street and made the tight turn onto the Pont de l'éna. They travelled to the midpoint of the bridge and Mycroft ordered the driver to stop. Malcolm and Joan got out of the car. They could see the boat coming towards them; the small motorboat was steadily approaching, but still some distance away. Joan loaded the two rounds into the oversized gun and went to the bonnet of the car. Using the bonnet to steady her grip, she looked down the gun and got the boats in her sight.

"Malcolm, I'm going to need your help. I have the boat in my sights, but at this distance, by the time the round reaches the river, the boat will be long gone. I need that mathematical mind of yours to figure out where I should target."

"And me without my slide rule," Malcolm muttered. He took out his granda's battered watch. He timed the boat for several seconds to get an idea of its speed. Doing his best to estimate the distance and the time it would take for a round to reach the boat, he stepped behind Joan and guided her to fire some distance ahead of the boat.

"Mr Robertson, are you getting fresh with me?"

"Just fire the bloody gun," Malcolm said as he stepped back.

"Killjoy," she muttered. She took a breath, and as she exhaled, she squeezed the trigger. The report of the gun momentarily deafened Malcolm. He tried to follow the rocket as it drove towards the river. To his disappointment, it hit the water some ten yards ahead of the boat. He hit the bonnet of the car in frustration. The boat immediately turned and made for the shore. "Merde," Joan muttered. She got the boat in her sights again. It had slowed as it turned toward the shore. She took another deep breath, tracked the boat as it made its way to toward the shore. Exhaling, she squeezed the trigger, and the roar of the gun deafened Malcolm again. He held his breath as he watched. This time, he watched a fireball engulf the boat just before it reached the shore. "Got him," Joan exclaimed.

"I'll believe it when I see his corpse," Malcolm said. "Come on, let's get down there to make sure." They jumped back into the car. "Driver, head towards that explosion!" Malcolm ordered. The driver put the car in gear and sped down the bridge, turning onto the Champ de Mars and speeding towards the flaming wreckage of the boat. As they approached, they saw a figure limping across the street towards the Eiffel Tower.

"Bloody hell," Malcolm said. "Frietag has more lives than a cat."

# CHAPTER SIXTY THREE

The car roared down to the spot where they saw Frietag limp across the street and squealed to a halt. Malcolm and Joan jumped out of the car and sprinted towards the Eiffel Tower. They scanned the crowd and some fifty yards ahead; they saw a figure pushing through the crowd. "There!" Malcolm pointed. They picked up their pace, but the crowds of Parisians slowed their progress. Malcolm heard the cries of alarm and several swear words as they closed the distance. The commotion caught the attention of a policeman who approached Frietag. When the policeman drew close, Frietag backhanded the policeman, knocking him to the ground. Frietag bent down and pulled the policeman's revolver from the holster. Looking back, he saw Malcolm and Joan gaining. He turned and ran north, away from the tower.

"Where is he going?" Malcolm gasped. The effort of running had caught up with him, his lungs on fire. They followed Frietag, who stopped some fifty feet from the policeman, struggled to pull aside the sewer grate and climbed into the opening.

"He's going into the sewers. If we don't get there soon, we're going to lose him," Joan said.

Malcolm pushed himself as hard as he could, and by the time they reached the opening, he struggled to catch his breath. The odour of stagnant water and sewage caught his nostrils, and he nearly gagged.

Joan looked at him, and between heavy breaths gasped, "You take me to the most romantic places. Come on, we need to catch up with him." Malcolm looked down and saw a series of iron rungs leading down. Carefully lowering himself into the opening, he made sure he placed his foot securely on the rung and made his way down. It was slow going as the rungs were slick with moisture, but with effort, he came down on a narrow walkaway. He stepped aside, waiting for Joan to climb down and to catch his breath. He drew the revolver and checked; only five shots left.

When Joan reached the sewers, he whispered, "Now what? He could have gone anywhere." Even his whispers echoed through the tunnel. He looked around for the first time. Ceramic tiles covered the sides of the tunnel, eventually giving way to limestone blocks that arched to over the channel below. Malcolm realised that there was some amount of light in the tunnels; gas lights at regular intervals supplied enough light to allow him to see about ten feet ahead.

Joan put her fingers to her lips to quiet Malcolm and listened. After a moment, they heard the sounds of irregular footsteps echoing through the tunnels. After a few moments, she pointed to the left and took the lead as they crept down the slick walkway. They crept carefully down the tunnel, the flickering shadows from the gas lights making Malcolm jumpy, until they came to a four-way intersection. They stopped to consider which way to go when they heard a splash and "Scheiße!" coming from the left. Malcolm and Joan looked at each other, nodded and followed the tunnel to the left. They travelled another fifty feet when they arrived at a Y intersection; the tunnel curving into two tunnels going right and left. Stopping for a moment, they listened, and Joan pointed to the right-hand tunnel.

As they continued, Malcolm had the distinct feeling the tunnel was sloping down. They came upon another tunnel to the right that sloped down more. Malcolm realised they were heading back towards the river. He pointed to the tunnel, and they made their way down the tunnel. They came to another four-way intersection. Malcolm saw that the tunnel straight ahead curved to the left and out of sight. Just then, he caught a flicker of a shadow passing out of sight. He pointed and Joan nodded, acknowledging she had seen it, too. They now had two options: getting into the channel and the sewage to cross the intersection or try to jump to the other side. Neither option appealed to Malcolm, who had struggled this whole time from the combination of the slick walkway and the lack of grip of his dress shoes. Malcolm decided he would try to jump the channel. He nearly made it, but his foot landed in the water, making a large splash that echoed through the tunnel. He mentally cursed, trying to remain quiet.

"Is that you, Malcolm?" Frietag's voice echoed through the tunnel. "I think you are the one who hangs on worse than a case of your mother's clap." Malcolm took a deep breath, again cursing mentally. He crept a short distance up the walkway and waited for Joan, who made the jump easily with only a whisper of noise.

"Is that Joan with you?"

Malcolm ignored Frietag's taunts and continued to creep forward. About thirty feet ahead, the tunnel curved sharply to the left. Malcolm stopped at the start of the curve. He carefully looked around the curve and caught sight of Frietag at the moment he saw the flash of the gun. Malcolm ducked back immediately, the bullet striking the corner of the tunnel, causing shards of ceramic to fly everywhere. The sound of the gun echoed in the tunnel, masking any further sound. In Malcolm's quick glance, he saw burns on Frietag's face and it looked as if the explosion on the boat had burned the right side of his body. The arm with his mechanical hand hung limply.

"Ah, it is you," Frietag's words echoing everywhere.

"Give it up, Frietag. You're never going to make it out of here."

"Maybe not, but I'm going to make sure that you never make it out of here, either. If this is where I am to meet my end, the only consolation will be to take you and Joan with me."

Malcolm looked questioningly at Joan. She put her hand up for a moment before she pulled him close and whispered into his ear, "Cover me. I'll creep up on him and take him out."

Malcolm whispered into her ear, "With what? Do you have a

weapon?" She pulled out the pin holding her hair up and, despite its beauty, he could see that it came to a sharp point. He pulled her close. "Let me go; you're a much better shot than I am."

"No," she seethed into his ear. "We do this together. I will give us cover fire as we both go after him." She pulled back and looked into his eyes. Even in the dim light, he saw the fire in her eyes and knew she couldn't dissuade her. He looked at her for several moments before he nodded and handed her the gun and she handed him her hair pin. He leaned in and kissed her. After a moment, they pulled back, and Joan nodded. She counted down from three on her fingers, and turned into the tunnel, firing as she did.

Malcolm couldn't tell if Frietag had returned fire; all he could hear was the endless echoing of gunfire as they charged down the walkway, Joan leading with the gun, Malcolm with the hairpin. They wheeled around the corner and caught sight of Frietag limping hurriedly down the hall. He turned to fire and Joan shot first; the shot exploding a tile just to the left of his head; the sound echoing through the tunnel. They both jumped back around the corner when he saw Joan gasp. A red clutch welled up on her left leg, staining the beautiful dress.

"Are you OK?" Malcolm couldn't hear himself talk, let alone hear Joan's response, deafened by the gunfire.

"Yes," she nodded. They carefully looked around the corner and lost sight of Frietag. They moved back into the tunnel and came to another intersection. Malcolm looked down the tunnel and saw Frietag, backlit by daylight. Malcolm couldn't tell how close he was, but he knew he couldn't let him get away. He was ready to jump across the intersection when Joan put her hand on his arm.

"I don't think I can make it. I'm having trouble putting weight on the leg." The ringing in Malcolm's ears had receded slightly, and he could just make out what she said. She pushed the gun into his hands. "Take this. There's only one shot left, so make it count." She gave him a quick kiss and let him go. Malcolm looked at her. He didn't want to leave her bleeding in the sewer, but Frietag was getting away. He kissed her on the head. With the gun in his right hand and the hairpin in his left, he made the jump and continued down the tunnel.

Frietag turned and their eyes locked. Malcolm saw the flash of the gun as Frietag fired and he dropped onto the walkway. The bullet flew just over Malcolm's head. He raised his gun towards Frietag, but couldn't get a clean shot. Frietag had four bullets left to Malcolm's one. Frietag continued moving towards the end of the tunnel instead of firing again at Malcolm. Malcolm got up and ran down the tunnel, desperately trying to maintain his footing.

Frietag reached the end of the tunnel, hesitated for a moment before firing once more at Malcolm. He could not dodge and the bullet struck him in the left shoulder. Malcolm yelped in pain and nearly dropped the hairpin from the shock, his hand already growing numb. The blood was already soaking into his shirt. Malcolm went to take aim, but as he levelled the gun, Frietag vanished out of sight.

"Shite," Malcolm yelled. "He made it out!"

# CHAPTER SIXTY FOUR

Malcolm hurried to the exit and onto a small ledge over the Seine. He looked and saw Frietag struggling in the water some fifteen yards away. He pointed the revolver at Frietag. Still not a clean shot. Cursing, Malcolm took a deep breath and dived into the Seine towards Frietag. As he did, he saw Frietag point the gun at him and fire. The bullet whizzed by his head as Malcolm hit the water. The river was cold and foul smelling, a mixture of sewage and fuel oil. When he surfaced, he was only about ten yards from Frietag. Taking a deep breath, he dived under the surface and swam toward Frietag. His wounded shoulder refused to cooperate, so he had to rely on his good arm and his legs. He was thankful that Frietag's injuries made it equally difficult for him to swim. Opening his eyes, the water made his eyes burn. He couldn't see much in the murky water, but he detected movement and swam toward it.

As he got close, he saw Frietag turn, and he fired the gun at Malcolm. The bullet only travelled a few feet before it lost all of its speed and it sank harmlessly to the bottom of the river. Undeterred, Malcolm swam towards Frietag, now frantically splashing. He almost got a hand on Frietag's foot when the foot struck him in the head instead. Malcolm nearly blacked out and expelled all the air from his lungs. For a second, the world turned black before his lungs screamed for air. He surfaced and took a huge gulp of air. He shook his head, trying to clear it. When his head cleared, he saw Frietag was five feet away and had the gun pointed directly at Malcolm's head. Frietag pulled the trigger, but the bullet never appeared. Malcolm gave a silent blessing and swam towards Frietag, grabbing him.

As they wrestled, they both went under the water. Frietag got his mechanical hand on Malcolm's shoulder, using its weight to keep Malcolm from surfacing. Malcolm tried to struggle away, but Frietag wrapped his other arm around Malcolm's neck. Malcolm's lungs screamed for air and he was he knew he had little time before he blacked out. He remembered the hair pin and jammed it into the arm around his neck. Frietag released him and Malcolm shot to the surface, gasping for air. Frietag cursed as Malcolm could see the water around Frietag turning pink. It hadn't been a serious puncture, but it gave Malcolm the time he needed. Frietag had moved five feet away from Malcolm and once again fired the gun towards Malcolm.

There was a massive bang, and the gun exploded; the previous bullet had lodged in the barrel and the combined pressure of the two caused the gun to explode. Frietag screamed in pain and after the smoke cleared. Frietag passed out and slid below the surface.

Malcolm hesitated for a second. He could just let Frietag die doing nothing. He could just let him sink and he would be out of his life forever. But before he knew him as Frietag, he was Matthew Frye, his friend. He flashed back to their time on the *Daedalus* where they worked hand in hand. If Frietag dies, so would Matthew Frye. Or had Matthew Frye ever really existed? The man who even now was sinking into the Seine had nearly killed Joan and kidnapped and tortured him. Surely, the world would be better off if he wasn't in it.

He shook the thoughts out of his head and dived under the water and swam towards Frietag, who already was four feet below him. Malcolm fought his way down to Frietag and grabbed him by the coat. He got his good arm around Frietag and struggled to get them to the surface. His shoulder screamed in pain from the gunshot wound, and it was all he could do to get them to the surface. He looked around and saw some twenty feet ahead was a quay. Malcolm concentrated on keeping them both afloat and let the current take him down the river as kicked towards the quay. When the quay was within reach, he shifted Frietag to his wounded arm and grabbed the side of the stone platform. He yelled "Aide! Aide!" Two surprised dock workers came over. Malcolm handed Frietag to them, and they pulled him out like a fish. Moments later, they yanked Malcolm out of the water and he laid on his back.

Malcolm heard a great deal of shouting in French, but did not know what was happening. He turned his head to look at Frietag. He was breathing, but he was seriously injured. As Malcolm thought, the right side of his body was badly burned; his left hand looked like it had gone through a meat grinder and there was a large shard of metal embedded in his cheek. He assessed his own condition. As the adrenaline of the last few minutes passed, the pain in his shoulder grew more intense. He felt himself wishing to just take a nap, but struggled against it. Malcolm pushed himself up to his knees and looked around. He saw a car approaching him, much to the apparent consternation of the dock workers. Malcolm realised that in the struggle, he no longer had the gun, but found Joan's hairpin in his hand. He struggled to pull himself up, brandishing the hairpin. The car stopped and Mycroft came out.

"Malcolm, it's Mycroft. You're safe. You can put the hairpin down." Malcolm lowered the hairpin, and when he did, his last burst of energy failed him and he dropped to his knees.

"You're injured," Mycroft said. He turned to the dock workers and gave orders in French. The dock workers stood in shock for a moment before dispersing. "Where's Joan?" Mycroft said.

"I had to leave her in the sewers. Frietag shot her in the leg and she couldn't go on. Please, find her!" Malcolm pleaded.

"I will. Let me help you up and get you to a hospital." Mycroft reached down and helped Malcolm to his feet. They limped to the car.

Suddenly, Malcolm heard a roar. He turned and saw Frietag coming toward him, barely holding on to a knife in his mangled hand. Malcolm raised his good arm and plunged the hairpin into Frietag's neck before he could stab Malcolm. Malcolm pulled the pin from Frietag's neck. Blood sprayed from his neck, covering Malcolm. Frietag looked down and saw the blood spraying. He looked at Malcolm; his eyes were wide with fear. Frietag tried to speak, but Malcolm only heard a gurgling noise. A second later, Frietag's eyes rolled back into his head and he fell to the ground.

Without a word, Mycroft helped Malcolm into the car, and soon the car was moving again. Now that he was safe, Malcolm could no longer fight the feeling of sleep and passed out.

# CHAPTER SIXTY FIVE

Malcolm woke up and, at first, all he could see was white. As his eyes focused, he realised he was in a hospital ward. Sitting by the bed was Saxon. "Are you joining the land of the living?" Saxon said.

"Apparently," Malcolm said. He tried to move and regretted it. Getting his bearings, he realised the doctors and nurses had bandaged his shoulder and swaddled him in blankets to warm him. "Where's Joan? Is she alright?"

"Joan is fine. Mycroft sent a car for us after he got you to the hospital. Peter and I searched the sewers and found her where you left her. She had lost a good deal of blood, but the doctors have assured me she will be fine."

"I want to see her," Malcolm said as he tried to sit up. Pain shot through his shoulder and he quickly laid back down again.

"Not until the doctor clears you. You also lost a great deal of blood. You're lucky you survived."

Malcolm was silent for a moment. "Frietag is dead. I killed him."

"I know."

"There was a moment when we were struggling in the river where he had passed out and was sinking. I could have just let him go, but I couldn't. But when he came at me with the knife, I acted on instinct. I can't shake the look on his face as he died."

"I'm sure." Saxon rested a hand on Malcolm's arm. "You did what you had to do."

"But," Malcolm began.

"But what? Freitag would have killed you if you hadn't reacted." Saxon sat silently for a moment. "Malcolm, you're a good man. You rescued the man who has tried to capture and kill you. You showed compassion. It was Frietag's decision to refuse that compassion and he faced the consequences of his actions."

"I know. But it doesn't make it any easier."

"Nor should it." Saxon rose. "I will tell Joan that you're awake. You need to get some rest."

"Give her my love."

"If I must." Saxon smiled, but before turning to leave, he said, "But you owe me a new tailcoat. After trudging around in the sewers, I'm afraid I'll have to burn it."

"Put it on my account," Malcolm said before falling back to sleep.

Malcolm spent the next five days in bed before he could visit Joan, after a great deal of pleading to anyone who would listen. With the help of a nurse who chaperoned the visit, he went to Joan's bed in the female ward. She was lying in bed, her eyes closed.

"Hello, Joan," he said, his words failing him.

"Malcolm!" Joan opened her eyes and sat up. "Thank heavens you're alive!" He went to give her a kiss, but the disapproving cough of the nurse cause him to just hold her hand instead.

"How are you?"

Joan grasped his hand. "I'm reasonably well, all things considered. The gunshot went straight through my leg and missed any major arteries. I'm not able to stand and I'm still tired and weak from the blood loss, but I'm told that otherwise, I'm fine."

Malcolm sat silently for several moments, just holding her hand. "I killed Frietag," he finally said.

"I know. Mycroft told me what happened."

They sat silently for nearly a minute before the nurse coughed once more, indicating the visit was over.

Malcolm and Joan endured two more weeks of recovery before they left the hospital. During their recovery, Saxon filled in the details of everything that had transpired since they left the party. Their chase through the hotel had put the staff in a tizzy, and when they found the unconscious guests and dead agents in the garden, it had the effect of hitting an anthill with a cricket back. Fortunately, the drug that Frietag and his men had used was merely a sedative, and none of the guests, including Joan's parents, were none the worse for wear. The police arrived and immediately questioned Saxon and O'Hallarhan. Saxon tried to explain the situation, but was about to be arrested by the police when Mycroft arrived. He immediately dispatched Saxon and O'Hallarhan to find Joan. They entered the sewer near the Eiffel Tower and started calling for her. When she heard it was Saxon, she answered, and they found her rather easily. She was weak from blood loss, but they got her out of the sewers and took her to the hospital. In the meantime, Mycroft made a few calls and settled the whole matter, keeping it out of the papers for the sake of the hotel.

Joan's mother was livid that her party had been ruined, but Mycroft placated her, apparently, by having the Secret Service pay for the ruined party. The baroness blamed Malcolm for the fiasco, and it took a great deal of argument and persuasion to change her mother's mind. Her father took it all in stride, just happy that Joan was safe.

There were no ramifications for the death of Frietag as the German government was not interested in exacerbating the situation since they had effectively poisoned much of Paris high society and tried to kill a British Commodore. As far as the German government was concerned, the matter was closed with Frietag's death, who they had deemed a "rogue agent". Mycroft then arranged for Malcolm's parents to come to Paris since there was no longer any risk.

On the day after their release, Joan and Malcolm, both sporting bandages under their wedding clothes, stood before the mayor of Paris. She was a vision of loveliness — her ivory gown covered in rose patterned lace. The seed pearls decorating her gown made her look iridescent. Her auburn hair was swept up under her veil. Malcolm looked resplendent in his morning suit. Clasping hands, the mayor asked Malcolm, "Sir, do you take Mademoiselle Joan Antoinette de St. Leger, here present, as your wife?"

"Oui," Malcolm said, smiling.

"Mademoiselle, do you take Monsieur Malcolm Francis Robertson, here present, as your husband?"

"Oui," Joan said, beaming with excitement.

The mayor continued. "The spouses owe each other fidelity, support, and assistance. The husband owes protection to his wife; the wife owes obedience to her husband." Joan's face darkened, but she didn't say a word. "The spouses are obliged to live together. The father and mother have the duty of protection, maintenance, and education toward their children. I declare you legally wed."

Malcolm and Joan pulled each other close. Malcolm winced when Joan accidentally grabbed his wounded shoulder. They kissed, causing a gasp from Joan's mother from the public display of affection. As they pulled away, Malcolm whispered in Joan's ear, "I'm sorry. I'm not sure I'll be able to give you much of a honeymoon."

"Don't worry," she said. "Conserve your strength; you're going to need it."

* * *

THE END

# AUTHOR'S NOTE

In the spirit of full disclosure, the following artificial intelligence tools were used in creating this book.

CHATGPT AND CLAUDE were both used for the research used in this book. ProWritingAid was used for the editing of the book.

TO THE BEST of my recollection, the content within this book was created by the author and not generated by artificial intelligence

# ACKNOWLEDGMENTS

* * *

It takes many people for a story to make its way out of the author's head and into the book you hold in your hands. This book would not be possible without the following people:

* * *

Thank you to my editor, Lauren Humphries-Brooks, for her invaluable guidance. Her insight helped me turn the manuscript into the book you see before you.

* * *

Thank you to my wife Colleen for putting up with me, either exiling myself to my office to write or blathering on about something driving me crazy in the book. Thank you also for your love and support. It means everything.

* * *

And finally, thank you to you, the reader, for giving this book a chance.

* * *

If you're interested in keeping up with what I'm doing, go to my website at http://www.reluctantauthor.com and sign up for my email newsletter.

* * *

And one last thing, if you could leave a rating or review wherever you purchased this book or on https://www.goodreads.com, it really be helpful to me!

# ABOUT THE AUTHOR

Michael Tefft is a software developer, musician, and writer who lives in Central New York. This is the fourth novel in the Reluctant series. Previously, he has written two one-act plays *The Job Interview* and *Musical Chairs*.

Michael's other passion is music. He can often be found playing trumpet in local community bands and two Big Bands.

When he's not doing the above, Michael is a fan of hockey, role-playing games, and Star Trek. He's proud that he's been a long time fan of Captain America and The Avengers, way before the movies made them cool.

# ALSO BY MICHAEL TEFFT

<u>The Reluctant Series</u>
The Reluctant Captain
The Reluctant Agent
The Reluctant Spacefarer